Neither Here Nor There
by E.J. Gambles

I0635788

Neither Here Nor There

Feathers Series, Volume 2

E.J Gambles

Published by E.J Gambles, 2025.

NEITHER HERE NOR THERE

First edition. December 20, 2025.

Copyright © 2025 E.J Gambles.

ISBN: 979-8998852435

Written by E.J Gambles.

"And the world never seemed to run out of monsters."

— **Angela Panayotopulos, The Wake Up**[1]

1.   https://www.goodreads.com/work/quotes/ 65265021

Neither Here Nor There
By E.J Gambles
Copyright@2025. E.J Gambles
ISBN: 979-8-9988524-3-5
Written by E.J Gambles.

Prologue: Flee

Orsclick was very close. As she looked back over her shoulder, she could see his large, grey wings violently flapping in the air, trying to close the distance between them. Out of the corner of her eye, she could make out the glare of his crissum. She had to lose him, even if that meant she took cover amongst the trees. With her own bright red plumage, she was an easy target.

Sirenna was quicker and a lot younger, but there was still no way that she could escape him. Captain Orsclick was one of her father's best knights. His covey status was legendary. This was real. There were a great many of his prey he had cut down with his infamous serrated crissum. All it would take is one swift slice, and he could bring her down rather quickly. Whatever bounty he was being paid must have been considerable.

Orsclick was closing in, and she had no choice. She would have to use the Greywood to escape and to slow him down. She just hoped it would give Evelyn enough time. Orsclick called out, taunting her.

"It's futile. You know I will catch you, little sprout!"

She took a deep breath and tried to stay focused. She couldn't let him get inside her head. *You can do this!* Sirenna dive bombed very low through a clearing of branches, then veered right down into a series of pines. She hoped this would give her momentary cover.

She quickly extended her long legs out, prepared for a series of side steps. She was going too fast and was in too much of a hurry to make a more graceful landing. As soon as she established her footing with the approaching ground, she immediately started to sprint. She tucked her wings back into her shoulder blades and quickly looked back over her shoulder.

Good, there was no sign of him. He was much larger and a bit slower. She quickly flanked through the trees as she made her way to the sound of the stream. She may be able to get some coverage with her wings hidden now. Unfortunately, she was now on foot, and Captain Orsclick was much quicker on his feet than in the air.

Sirenna dashed the water. There was still no sign of him coming. As she reached the bank, she scanned the scene. She was on the verge of hyperventilating when she heard the sound of wings fluttering from above. She quickly ducked down low behind a bramble bush in anticipation.

Orsclick's hulking figure landed knee deep in the stream about ten yards from her. He still wore his helmet as he tucked in his large wingspread. He sniffed the air, trying to pick up her scent. Sirenna moved closer into the foliage. She hoped that the brambleberries would cover her scent.

"You can't hide, sprout. I will find you."

He moved closer to the brambleberry bush as he eyed the branches. Sirenna held her breath as he reached his gloved hand into the branches. Suddenly, he pulled his hand out with a fist full of brambleberries. He gently sat his crissum against the edge of the bush, as he tilted his head back and violently shoved a mouthful of berries into his throat.

Sirenna saw her opportunity as she swiftly snatched the handle of the crissum and drove the blade into Orsclick's armpit. Being the only chink in the armor, the blade cut deep into his flesh. Sirenna shoved the blade with such force that it almost went completely out the other armpit.

Orsclick's reaction was just as quick as he grabbed her throat with his feeding glove and lifted her into the air. His other hand seemed unable to function with his own blade embedded in his side. His eyes glared at Sirenna as he gasped for air. Suddenly, he dropped her back down and stumbled backward off the bank into the stream. With his good hand, he slowly slid the crissum back out of his side with a series of wheezing and coughing.

Sirenna watched in horror as he removed the bloody crissum from his armpit. The heavy blade dropped into the flowing stream at his feet. Orsclick slowly bent down to retrieve his weapon when he keeled over, face down into the water with a loud splash. He lay motionless as she approached him.

She watched intently for several moments to make sure he wasn't playing possum. When she was sure he was dead, she finally let out a sigh of relief. She reached down to retrieve his crissum, but alas, he was partially lying atop the handle. On his side, she spied a hand axe and quickly removed it from its holster.

She was almost out of breath as she staggered to the edge of the water. She squatted down and extended her neck forward. Sirenna took a few moments to steal a few sips of water before continuing across the water to search for Evelyn. She prayed that her sister was still alive.

Chapter 1:

The Turtle

Thelma and Herb Lutz were driving down West Sabine on their way to breakfast. It was their usual morning routine. They would sit at the same table, have a cup of coffee, and a bran muffin. Sometimes they would have cranberry juice. Herb was a retired real estate agent who had made a pretty penny when he was much younger.

Thelma was a 2nd grade schoolteacher who taught at a challenging inner-city school. At the age of forty-four, Herb had a massive stroke and was partly paralyzed. Because of his condition, Thelma was forced to take an extended leave of absence and take care of him while he went through a difficult year of recovery.

Soon after, they both left the city and retired to Meadowlark. Even though they were sleeven, most faigal liked the Lutzes. They were the pleasant elderly couple who were always together. They started the day like any other and would have probably ended the same, except one variable was different. Thelma spied a turtle in the middle of the road.

She was concerned because she knew it wouldn't be quick enough to make it across the road, even though traffic was light in a small town. Large supply trucks frequently sped down Sabine and Martin streets at frantic speeds. This reckless attitude led to a large number of roadkill and critter displacement. Herb, who was driving, hadn't noticed; in fact, he passed right over the turtle. It wasn't until Thelma tapped him.

"Herb, that poor turtle!"

"What?"

"We just drove over it, dear!"

Herb was already starting to pull the car over on the side of the road.

"Where is it?"

Thelma looked back and pointed to a tiny lump that had moved slightly to the right. Herb eagerly put on his brakes and unbuckled his seat. He then leaned over and kissed her gently on the cheek.

"I'll be right back."

"Thank you, dear."

"Fear not, malady, I will rescue the little guy!"

"You be careful, Herb."

"Yes, ma'am!"

Herb then proceeded to get out and trek back about 10 yards till he was standing right above the small terrapin. He bent down carefully and addressed the turtle.

"This is your lucky day, friend!"

He put his palm under the turtle's tail end and gently scooped it up. As he stood up, he looked about for the best place to transplant the creature. He eyed a clump of trees to the right side of the road's shoulder. He walked across the road to a patch of elm trees. He could hear the singing cicadas against a backdrop of sparrow chirping. He took a deep breath and inhaled the fresh morning air. He carefully stepped through the tall grass till he was about two feet from the tree line.

As he carefully placed it back on the ground, he became aware of a sudden silence. The cicadas and birds were no longer making any sound. Even the wind was ominously still as if it were waiting for something to arrive. Herb slowly scanned the clump of trees in front of him as if he himself could feel a perverse darkness closing in on him. Thelma was waiting for him to walk back across when she herself heard the deafening silence.

"What's wrong, Herb?"

Herb's head swiveled towards Thelma at the sound of her voice, but then quickly back at the tree line. There she stood. It was like she just appeared out of nowhere. A tall, languid female had emerged from the woods. She had wild golden hair that was so long it almost touched her knees. She was without clothing, but her long hair obstructed the view of her body. Her overall bizarre appearance was so shocking that he didn't seem to notice her lack of clothing.

Her skin discolored to an almost anti-hue, with blotches of grey over almost translucent skin. It appeared as though, if one looked hard enough, one could actually see her inner organs at work. She wore an unusually wide grin that almost stretched from ear to ear. Her large lips were stretched thin across her face to frame an alarming set of teeth. A thin stream of saliva dripped past her lips. Her mouth widened to allow a three-pronged tentacle-like object to slide out from the back of her throat. Herb could only surmise she possessed multiple tongues.

Herb whispered gently. "Sweet Jesus."

She tilted her head slightly, and he could see her alien eyes. They were white, with small black pools in the center that resembled tiny watery pupils. They appeared dilated with just a touch of madness. Nevertheless, they were mesmerizing. She was staring directly into his eyes when a sudden dark fear overcame him. Suddenly, he couldn't move; it was as if he could feel her thoughts whispering inside his head. Herb could hear Thelma scream as though from a great distance instead of from the other side of the road.

"Get away from that woman, something's not right with her!"

Before he had time to react, a long segmented arm reached out from her side. Long, talon-like bony fingers snaked around his neck. A second arm grabbed his right elbow, then a third arm seemed to come from nowhere, grasping the collar of his shirt. All her fingers were cold and claw-like as she pulled him toward her. He stumbled forward, falling on his knees. As soon as he hit the ground, it was as if he were awakened from a dream.

He quickly tore away from her grasp and turned away from her stare in an attempt to flee on his hands and knees. He started to crawl away, as the strange woman began to make odd, deep, inhuman clicking sounds.

Thelma stared in horror out the window at the sight of her husband on the ground. The odd woman squatted over Herb like some sort of feral beast. At that moment, she reminded Thelma of a spider toying with its prey. The long-haired specter glanced toward the car. For a brief moment, both women made eye contact.

Herb was almost to the edge of the road. However, she was quick and very strong, as she straddled him with her multiple appendages. She extended her arms, wrapped her fingers around his ankles, and started to pull him backward. Herb fell on his stomach and began to claw at the grassy dirt. His fingers dug into clumps of crab grass in an act of resistance.

Herb made a gallant effort; however, his attacker was strong and cunning. He felt two hands dig into both his shoulders as well as around his ankles. He felt himself being dragged backwards. Herb's eyes met Thelma, and he desperately called.

"Run, damn it, run!"

It happened so quickly that by the time Thelma got out of her seatbelt and opened the car door, the bizarre woman had succeeded in dragging Herb back into the overbrush of trees. Thelma called after him in futility.

"Herb? Herb?"

There was no answer. Thelma, in a panic, stumbled forward on her knees, but quickly rose. One of those big trucks was passing. She had to wait for it before she could cross. As soon as it did pass, she couldn't see anything. She staggered forward with her bad knees, as quickly as they would allow. She was about a yard away from crossing the road when she suddenly heard a single horrifying scream from the trees, and her response was instant.

"You leave him alone!

As the old woman reached the shoulder, she saw the trail of finger marks that Herb's fingers left in the dirt, and a deep pit rose in her stomach. She suddenly felt sick.

"Herb?"

Thelma was almost pleading as she blindly stuck her head through the branches of the thicket. She half expected to see him bloody and hurt. As she looked, she could see nothing. It was like it didn't even happen.

"Please don't take my Herb!"

Willet suddenly walked across the tall grass to where the turtle lay. In all the melee, it was knocked over on its back. The young girl carefully picked up the turtle and proceeded to carry it into the underbrush.

Thelma couldn't see Willet, so she passed directly by the old woman and stepped beyond the threshold of the trees. Willet looked at the ground for signs of a struggle. She looked about for the old man, but there was no sign of any life. It was as if hunter and prey had both vanished into thin air. Willet looked back at Thelma's face; she was frantically screaming now. So much so that her voice was growing hoarse.

Willet had seen them before. They were regulars at the diner. She never really sat and talked to them much. Tori knew them quite well; they were almost like family to her. She soberly closed her eyes and called out to the sky.

"Lady, please stop screaming!"

When Willet opened her eyes, she was still in class. Her head was down on the desk. Apparently, she had fallen asleep. Spittle had run down from the side of her mouth. Her lips were now stuck to her textbook. Startled, she quickly sat up, ripping the page. A tiny piece of paper remained on her upper lip as she tried to look normal.

Mrs. Armage eyed Willet crossly. She had been warned about sleeping in class before. Just by her expression, she knew Willet had fallen asleep. Mrs. Armage was new to Talomore, but she was well known in New Essex. She had transferred just in time for the new semester. She reminded Willet of one of those adults who try to show how much in control they are, but end up looking a bit incompetent. She had probably been a bit socially awkward in school, but loved books. She obviously had gotten along with her teachers growing up. She was like a mini headmistress in training.

She walked silently toward Willet without speaking. It was a classic intimidation tactic that authority figures used to try to create anxiety in the student, and it was working. Willet was a bit nervous. Finally, she stopped about 2 feet from her. With a white yardstick, she extended her arm and tapped on the edge of Willet's desk.

"Ms. Swift, what was the meaning of that?"

It wasn't the conversation she was expecting. "Mrs. Armage?"

"Don't act like you don't know what I'm talking about!"

"What did I do?"

"I see it on the floor by your feet."

At this moment, Willet really had no idea what the woman was talking about. She curiously peered down at her shoes. At first, she didn't see a thing, then she gasped in shock. Right by her book bag was the turtle crawling around. She was so startled she jerked back in her chair, almost tipping over. Willet exclaimed in frustration.

"Crap!"

"Our policy is not to bring pets to school."

There was a hushed laughter from the class. Willet didn't bother looking around at her classmates. Most of them were freshmen anyway. She quickly looked back at the teacher.

"I don't know where it came from; it doesn't belong to me!"

This wasn't exactly true. In fact, she had a pretty good idea where it came from. The teacher countered, "Perhaps it followed you to school this morning!"

There was more laughter. Mrs. Armage quickly snapped her stick on Willet's desk again and this time addressed the class. "Silence!"

There was a slight shift in the teacher's mood, as if she may have believed Willet... sort of. Her tone softened.

"Would you please remove that thing from my class so we can continue, Ms. Swift?"

"Yes, Mrs. Armage, right away!"

Willet got her book bag and carefully lifted the turtle by its shell and raced out of the classroom.

Chapter 2:

Leaving Campus

Willet was frantic as she nervously placed the turtle in her bookbag. She was careful not to jostle it as she had to figure out where to dispose of the thing. She knew where she wanted to place it, but Mother Hazel would have a conniption if she walked off campus. Not to mention, her mother would be horrified if she were to walk to an active crime scene.

However, Mr. Lutz's disappearance had just happened, so it was not common knowledge. Thelma would be on her way to the police, either she was driving, or someone had picked her up. The area where it happened wasn't that far from the school. By the time she had reached the sidewalk, she had all but decided to leave. She was passing through the parking lot to reduce the risk of looking suspicious when a car horn sounded.

Willet looked up, startled, as the black convertible stopped a few inches from striking her. Raven was behind the wheel with her signature black top hat. She reminded Willet of the Cheshire cat with her devious grin.

Her usual group of sycophants was riding with her. Cousin Phoebe was in the back seat, along with Iris Van Warren. Iris was one of those conservative-raised evangelicals who had a reputation for being wilder than most of her non-secular peers. Some would say it was because of the pressure of being the mayor's daughter. Raven's eyes almost twinkled as she addressed Willet.

"You were this close to being roadkill. You'd better watch where you step, Swift!"

She extended her black painted nails out the window and snapped them obscenely. Willet tried to act cool, but deep down her heart was still racing.

"You know this is a parking lot, not the drag strip?"

"You must have mistaken me for someone who gives a damn!"

Willet swung her bag onto her shoulder and headed back toward the entrance.

"Whatever."

"School is in the other direction?"

"Hey Raven, can you keep a secret?"

"Yeah!"

"Well, so can I."

Willet continued until she was at the corner. She glanced back at the parked convertible. Raven and her cronies were watching her leave campus. Great, what else could go wrong?

"Where are you going, Eve?"

Willet nervously spun around. She had forgotten about Jonas and his daily perch. There he was, sitting in that tree looking down at her. He wasn't making it any easier for her to be discreet.

"It's a long story."

"You're not leaving campus, are you?"

"Well, kind of."

"By yourself?"

He immediately hopped down and started walking toward her. He removed his headphones from his neck and placed them in his own bag. Willet glanced back at Raven's car and then looked at him curiously.

"What do you think you are doing?"

"I'm going with you."

Willet furrowed her brow. "Oh no, you're not!"

"Look, it's against the new ordinance, and it's not safe for you to go by yourself."

The situation was already hectic. The last thing she needed was to be seen by Raven talking to Jonas. It may cause serious social issues if word had gotten around.

"Maybe I'm waiting for a ride."

"I'll wait with you."

"Look, it's just a boring trip."

"What do you have in the bag?"

"It's my lunch."

"It's moving."

Willet impatiently unzipped her book bag and held it out for him to see.

"Are you happy?"

"That's a turtle!"

"Really, I thought it was a pencil box."

Willet turned away and quickly headed toward the road. She was irritated now.

"You're not allowed to bring pets to school."

"It's not mine, Sherlock!"

"Where did you get it?"

"I told you; it's a long story."

"Well, I'd like to hear about it."

"What makes you think I want to tell you?"

Jonas suddenly stopped walking as if he were wounded. "Fine!"

Willet turned around, frustrated. "Look, just leave me alone."

"I thought we were friends."

"Friends? Our families hate each other; they have been trying to wipe each other out for ages. Did you really think we could be friends?"

Willet stopped as she saw a glimpse of Jae pass into the quad on her way back to class. A sobering memory of a similar conversation she had with Jae echoed in her mind. Jonas almost had tears in his eyes as he turned away.

"Sorry, I won't bother you anymore!"

Willet quickly continued on her course; she didn't have much time. The streets were clear as she ran across the street. When she reached the other side, she looked back at the parking lot. Jonas was gone. Willet expressed a deep, painful sigh and started to sprint as she travelled down the edge of the overpass.

Raven watched the entire scene unfold from the parking lot. As she studied her wounded brother, a smile slowly spread across her face. She focused her attention on the young girl running down the side of the road to the intersection of West Sabine and Martin.

Chapter 3:

Crime Scene

Willet knew she had arrived at the area because she could see the car as she approached. She wouldn't have much time before the police removed her. She carefully walked about the edge of the trees, trying to sense something unusual. There was a strange scent in the air. She couldn't quite place it exactly. It felt like being deceived. She suddenly looked down and saw the clawed earth. She bent down and touched the dirt with her fingertips. She immediately had an image of the old man being dragged into the trees.

It remained unusually silent. All Willet could hear was the faintest hint of a breeze. It was eerily peaceful. She remembered the turtle in her bag. As she unzipped her bag, she started to hear police sirens. She reached into her book bag and pulled out the fat turtle, who was eager to return to its habitat after a bumpy ordeal in her book bag. She was about to place it down when a large white car with flashing lights pulled right beside her.

She heard an intercom from inside the vehicle address her. "Don't move, slowly rise to your feet with your arms extended over your head, then turn around."

She rose to her feet to confront the driver. She was slightly panicked as she held out her hands. She still had the turtle in her left hand. Its legs kicked in the air as it struggled to get down.

"What's that in your left hand?"

"A turtle, sir."

"A what?"

Willet could feel her breathing increase as the door opened. It was Constable Fletcher; he wore a harsh stare as he considered Willet.

"We have to stop meeting like this, Ms. Swift!" Willet remained silent. "Why are you not in school?"

"My teacher told me to return this turtle to the wild."

"A turtle?

"Yes, can I put it down?"

"And your teacher told you to leave during school hours? Why here, of all places?"

"I don't understand."

"This is a very indistinguishable piece of land, almost two miles from your school. There are plenty of other wooded areas to return your turtle, if that is indeed the truth."

"Well, its home is near a pond behind those trees."

"Those trees?"

"You don't believe me?"

"I didn't say that, but it's very curious."

"How do you mean?"

"How long have you been here?"

"I just got here a minute ago."

"Did you see or hear anything unusual?"

Willet tried to play ignorant. "Not really, what's happening?"

"This very spot you have chosen to release your friend is part of a possible crime scene."

Willet did her best to look surprised. "Crime scene, did someone die?"

"That is not your concern. I must ask you to step back against the car."

"What did I do?"

"I don't need you contaminating this area."

"Can I put the turtle down now?"

"Let me see it!"

"Why?"

"Just hand it to me!"

"Be careful, it's really scared."

The officer collected the creature from her hand. He then motioned to one of his deputies. The slightly younger guy was Hal Dresden. He was new to town and pretty much kept to himself. He had a habit of not really looking anyone in the eye.

Every time Willet had seen him, he was wearing shades. Today was no different. It gave him a very impersonal coldness. However, she hadn't seen him act in any negative way as of yet. As Hal approached, Fletcher turned to him.

"I need you to drive this child back to school and escort her to her classroom."

He nodded blankly. "Yes sir!"

Willet protested. "Really, is that necessary?"

"You're lucky I don't take you in for violating the town ordinance. No one is allowed to be by themselves away from their home until we get this thing under control."

Willet looked at Fletcher, concerned. "What do you need with the turtle?"

"That's not your business!"

Willet already knew. The turtle was most likely part of Mrs. Lutz's story, thus an integral part of the crime scene. The reason Willet had to return the thing to this spot. Unfortunately, she couldn't explain to anyone how she got hold of it without exposing herself.

As she got into the backseat of the police cruiser, she let out a plea in Fletcher's direction. "Well, please don't hurt it."

Chapter 4:

Showdown

Of course, by the time Willet returned to school, her class was long over. It was first lunch, and the quad was filled with kids. Willet was in a panic. That's all she needed was a cop bringing her to school so everyone could see. As they pulled into the visitor parking, she leaned to the driver. Hal was listening to a country song on the radio. He was almost lost, as he silently hummed the words.

"Officer Dresden?"

"What?"

"My class is now over. Could I possibly wait to get out of the car?"

"Heck no!"

"Please, everyone will see me."

Willet could hear the full extent of his country drawl as he answered. "You should have thought about that before you left school. What's the name of your teacher?"

"Mrs. Armage."

To make matters worse, the officer dialed a number on his phone. As the phone rang, Willet was visibly concerned. The quad was already abuzz with the arrival of the cruiser. Several teachers and kids stopped to stare at the vehicle from a distance. Luckily for Willet, the windows were tinted, and no one could make her out from the back seat.

When the phone finally picked up, she knew the voice immediately. A chill went up her spine. "Yes, this is headmistress Faulkner's office. How may I help you?"

"Yes, ma'am, this is Deputy Dresden. I need to have a word with the headmistress."

"One moment, sir."

Willet pleaded from the backseat. "Please, do we have to get her involved. Look, I was wrong, I learned my lesson."

"Quiet child!"

Within a few moments, Willet could hear Faulkner's voice through the car speaker.

"Yes, Deputy Dresden, this is Headmistress Faulkner. What is the problem?"

"Yes, Ms. Faulkner, I hate to bother you, but we just picked up one of your students wandering off campus."

"Oh, my goodness, what were they doing off campus?"

"I don't know, but they were found at a possible crime scene."

"Oh my, are they ok?"

"She is fine, but I'm very busy. I was wondering if I could escort her to your building, ma'am?"

"Please, right away."

"We'll be right there."

Willet's heart sank as the situation got more ridiculous. He clicked off the radio and promptly got out of his car. Willet reached into her book bag and pulled out a pair of sunglasses and quickly slipped them over her hazel eyes, as the officer made his way to her car door.

Willet knew that it was imperative to keep an emergency pair of shades on one's person. You never know when it will come in handy. Her current pair were Sirenna's that she borrowed after much pleading.

When Dresden opened the door, he immediately saw the shades. "Really?"

"You're wearing them!"

"Mine are issued."

"Look, I'm going to be in big trouble anyway. Can I just have a modicum of dignity? Please?"

Dresden put his hands up in disgust. "What do I care, it's almost lunch?"

While the deputy waited for her to get out of the car, she took a deep breath. She had to quickly get into character. As she stood, she allowed her mouth to make a kind of flirty pout and flipped her curly black hair with a condescending air. She had to make sure she walked with that; I don't care stroll and just a hint of coy model aloofness. How she presented herself in the next two minutes would determine her standing on the social pecking order at school.

As the officer led her down the sidewalk, she looked ahead. She made sure she didn't bother to look at anyone directly. She heard the occasional gasp, or her name whispered in several variations within the crowd noise as she was escorted down the walkway.

"Who is that girl?"

"What did she do?"

"It's that strange Adler girl."

"Isn't she the weirdo that carries a fire poker around everywhere?"

"Is she in some sort of trouble?"

For a few moments, she felt like a celebrity. She would be the talk of the campus. If she was going down, she had to appear cool at least. As Willet was led down the walkway to the entrance of the main hall, she could make out the image of the headmistress standing at the bottom of the steps. Standing beside her was her flunky secretary. Secretary Nash was a poor imitation of her boss. She wore similar dress styles and even glasses. The only difference was that Nash was actually attractive.

The headmistress's arms were folded, and she looked carefully over the rim of her glasses. Willet could see the moment of recognition from Ms. Faulkner when she saw who the deputy was escorting. She felt a sudden lump in her throat. Willet could see her mood suddenly changed from mild concern to irritation. They were about a yard away when the headmistress loudly exclaimed.

"Why am I not surprised?"

The deputy quickly reacted. "Excuse me?"

"Yes, well, Ms. Swift is gaining a bit of a reputation for her unruly behavior. I am not at all surprised she was picked up. She has a history of such infractions."

Willet bit her lip as the woman painted her, as a troubled child, to the officer.

"What do you have to say for yourself, Ms. Swift?"

"You won't believe me anyway!"

"Silence, this is what I am talking about, Officer Dresden!"

Suddenly, Faulkner changed gears and tilted her glasses down. Staring at the officer with the most coy expression. "Aren't you new to our town?"

"Yes, ma'am, I transferred from Big Surr."

"Well, I appreciate you trying to protect us all from these horrible murders. You must be so brave!"

Willet rolled her eyes at Faulkner's pathetic attempt at flirting. "You've got to be joking."

Dresden uncomfortably excused himself. "Well, I need to be getting back to work, Ms. Faulkner."

The headmistress fluttered her fingers daintily in his direction. "Please don't be a stranger, my door is always open."

Willet let her mouth run rampant. "Maybe you're just not his type."

There erupted a few giggles and sneers that Faulkner tried to ignore. As soon as he was some way down the walkway, a crowd started to gather around the scene. Sensing the pressure of showing her authority, the headmistress suddenly snatched the sunglasses from Willet's face.

"You have been told about your dress attire many times before."

"Hey."

"These are mine now!"

Faulkner dropped the shades on the ground and stepped on them with her heel. There was a low, deep crunching sound as the glasses shattered under her heel. The crowd reacted with a united gasp. She removed her foot and looked at Willet, as she held back a smirk forming in the corner of her mouth.

"You were saying?"

Faulkner was the type of authority figure who wanted to believe they were righteous and moral, so every attack she would inflict would be petty and subjectively vindictive, just enough to blur the lines, so the appearance of truth couldn't be doubted. Ironically, the problem these types of personalities ran into was themselves. Their main motivation was always personal on some level, and sooner or later, they would cross the line.

She was trying to get a rise out of Willet. Why else would she pull such a stunt? Her secretary and now the crowd were here as mere witnesses. Willet would have to play it cool. She couldn't show how pissed she was. There was only so far that woman would go. She would not bite. Willet had a passive look on her face as she politely replied.

"I believe that you just littered the school grounds, Headmistress Faulkner!"

There was a handful of chuckles from the crowd. Faulkner glared venomously at the onlookers.

"Quiet!"

It was at that moment that the older woman realized that she had overstepped her position. This young girl was making a fool of her in front of her students. Willet continued to speak.

"After all, they belong to you now, you yourself said so. Originally, they were Aunt Sienna's until you took them. You know, she really liked those glasses. What did you have against them? Were they not your color?"

There was more laughter from the crowd.

"You think you're so clever, Swift!"

"Well, I should hope so, especially since I'm supposed to be graduating next year."

"A lot can happen in the course of a year."

"Yeah, the seasons change, the flowers bloom."

There was a stream of laughter from the crowd. With her authority now in question, she snapped at the entire crowd.

"Silence, all of you, go back to class. Now!"

The group started to quickly disperse. Willet tried to join the crowd, hoping to blend. She had gotten only two feet away when the headmistress called after her.

"Ms. Swift, I'm not finished with you; there is still the matter of your leaving campus!"

"My teacher asked me to return a lab animal to its habitat immediately. You can ask her yourself."

"They might think you're cute, but I know what you really are."

"Can I go to class before I'm tardy?"

The headmistress gritted her teeth in frustration. "This isn't over, Swift."

Willet's response was quick as she quickly strolled down the sidewalk in an attempt to beat the bell. As soon as Willet was out of sight, Faulkner turned to her secretary.

"Ms. Nash, please take care of that mess."

She then directed Ms. Nash to the broken sunglasses that lay pulverized on the sidewalk.

Chapter 5:

Upon Reflection

Willet sat by the diner window, blindly staring at the empty sidewalk outside. As she sipped on her oat milkshake, she noticed shadows starting to form outside of Linnet's. She still had almost two hours before dark.

From the vibrant little town Willet had grown accustomed to, this was a mere shadow of itself. It felt like a ghost town. Constable Fletcher and his newly hired deputies patrolled the town in a futile attempt to restore public confidence in his abilities. It had been almost a week since Mayor Van Warren had enacted the mandatory curfew under much duress.

Within the last three months, the number of residents gone missing rose to eleven. There didn't seem to be any consistent pattern, as both adults and children were allegedly taken. Willet always thought that the word allegedly sounded smug. It was like saying; this is what you said happened, but I don't know if I believe you, even though I have no proof otherwise. Regardless, she knew the reason, as did everyone.

The sightings of the strange naked woman were the one constant. Witnesses had described seeing a spectral thin female with multiple arms, wild hair, and a cartoony grin, either right before or right after all the victims disappeared. At first, the perpetrator's description was treated with a kind of tongue-in-cheek cynicism. That was until the latest victim was taken. Willet had unfortunately witnessed the event in one of her transitory states.

Willet took it very seriously, as she had been seeing the strange creature for some time. Willet, unlike most of the Meadowlark residents, would sometimes randomly see strange things. She herself had seen the odd woman a few times moving about town freely like a frail specter, yet had to keep her mouth shut. On one occasion, she remembered seeing a glimpse of multiple appendages scrambling across the side of a building wall as Laraline drove them home from a school function one evening.

She sat somberly waiting for Tori to finish her shift, so she could drive her home. The plan was that twice a week, Willet would stay at Linnet's Diner till it closed. This way, Tori wouldn't be by herself. She would then give Willet a ride home and stay overnight. They would then head out to school the next day. Sometimes they would alternate with Tori's home. Since Tori stayed with her uncle on a houseboat, this was quite exciting to Willet. It reminded her of the times when she used to go sailing with her own dad.

Willet suddenly realized it had been several weeks since her mother had mentioned picking up their father's boat. She knew that was the plan, but perhaps her mother just couldn't find anyone willing to bring it back. Willet removed the straw from her drink and began to sip the remainder. She put her glass down and let out a deep burp that echoed through the cafe. Almost immediately, she heard Tori call across the room.

"There she blows!"

"Excuse me!"

Tori then began to cackle in a deep cockney English accent. "And to think, I thought you were a lady!"

An older gentleman with greying hair, who had just finished, gave them both an odd, disapproving stare as he passed by them. Tori noticed his disapproval and continued.

"Cheerio, dear chap, I will let the queen know you stopped by then!"

She then bowed and did the most proper curtsy and pageant wave that Willet had ever seen. The gentleman was unimpressed, as he looked at her crossly. He pushed his way out the door, and Tori quietly mumbled. "Well, excuse me for being polite, you old fart."

Willet brushed away tears of laughter as she commented. "You are definitely going to get fired!"

Tori then broke into some bland impression of an Asian kung fu master. "Oh, they no fire, Miss Tori. I number one hostess. In fact, I only hostess."

"Well, Miss Tori. Do you think you can get out a few minutes early?"

Tori was back to her own voice. "Well, I don't know. Ever since the curfew, business has been crazy right before close. Have you seen the kitchen?"

Willet quickly agreed. "That sucks!"

"Right, it's like the whole town decides to get their eat on, right before dark!"

"Yeah. Well, I wish something would eat Ms. Faulkner!"

"Stop worrying about the headmistress, your aunt is Sirenna Linnet Adler, one of the most powerful women in town. Faulkner wouldn't dare cross you too much."

"You sound like Jae."

"I'm just saying, your aunt is the shabazz. Heck, she even owns this dump!"

"She does?"

"Are you that clueless? Hey, it's not like I'm privy to her business, but where did you think the name Linnet comes from?"

"I didn't know she even liked this place."

"I don't think she does, it's probably some tax write-off."

"Well, it doesn't matter anyway. I'm kind of on the outs with Auntie as of late."

"What's new?"

"Nothing. Have you seen Jae lately?"

"I swear, you two need to squash this. I know you both miss each other. Life is too short to hold grudges."

Suddenly, Willet thought of the incident with Jonas. A melancholy overcame her. Reflecting on how she had acted toward him sickened her. However, she was also aware that she was a target. Ever since Mother Hazel announced her desire to train her, many in the Faigal community had started to treat her differently. On the surface, they seemed polite, but she could sense a seething contempt beneath.

Sirenna had all but withdrawn from interacting with her. Instead, she talked to Adelie. The other day, they even went shopping. She was starting to feel like a pariah. The situation with Jonas was complicated. There were not many people whom she felt relaxed around. She felt a growing desire to share her experiences with him. She knew, of all the faigal, he wouldn't judge her. However, she could not let him get too close because of the dynamics of his siblings.

Raven and Gavin were complete sociopaths in her opinion. Not only did they really dislike her, but they probably secretly desired to harm her. The last thing she wanted to do was give them an excuse.

Tori spoke from across the room in a sober tone. Her unusual frankness shook Willet from her musings on Jonas. "Are you afraid at all?"

"Sometimes."

"Well, I'm not going to lie. There are times when I am by myself, and I can just feel eyes watching me!"

"Do you believe what everyone is saying?"

"You mean about some crazy nude broad snatching people away in the night?"

Willet took a deep breath and closed her eyes before she continued. Then she blurted out what was on her mind. "I have actually seen her!"

Tori's eyes suddenly got big. "Shut up!"

"I'm serious!"

"Are you for real? When?"

"Different times."

"So you've seen her more than once? Why didn't you say anything, you brat?"

"I don't know, too scared, I suppose. Plus, I didn't want people to think I was crazy."

"Well, it's a little late for that, my dear!"

"Suck my fat toe!"

"When was the last time you saw her?"

"Actually, this morning."

"How? We were in class."

Willet quickly backpedaled. "On the way to school, by the side of the road."

"No way, you probably saw her right before she got old man Mr. Lutz!"

Willet just nodded in response. It wasn't exactly a lie; she did see her there, just not the way she explained. She couldn't tell Tori everything.

Tori continued. "You know, they were the sweetest couple. I'm going to really miss them. I don't know how anyone could want to harm either of them."

Willet's mind flashed to the image of Thelma screaming on the side of the road. A wave of nausea suddenly overcame her as she shook away the memory. Her visions were definitely beginning to increase in frequency.

Chapter 6:

Cracks

Jonas sat perched on the branch of the large oak tree in the peach grove on the side of his home. It was almost sunset, and the sky was a vibrant palette of warm hues. His thoughts meandered through memories of his mother. There were times when he really missed her. He wished he could share a sunset with her and laugh at her funny faces. Meadow Branson was an anomaly among the family. That rare breed of aristocrat that was generous and kind-hearted. Perhaps because she suffered so much with the sickness, she appreciated life a bit more. Even Aunt Aquila never really tried to ruffle her little sister's feathers.

He was so lost in thought that he almost didn't notice Raven standing below, at the base of the roots. She wore her black top hat and deep sunglasses as she peered up. She stood silently for quite a while before she spoke.

"Are you in mourning, brother?"

"Mourning?"

"About poor dead mummy, it's her anniversary today!"

"What do you know about mother? You were too young."

"You know, I heard Aunt Meena had the same sickness. They say that even after the body dies, the sickness continues to eat the flesh and bones. That's why mummy was cremated."

"We are all cremated!"

"Not Aunt Meena!"

"Really? It's been several months!"

"I heard there is a lot of mystery around how she died. I wonder if I dug up her body in a year, what would it look like?"

"You better not let Ephron hear you talking like that!"

"Ephron is too weak, even Gavin thinks so."

"He just lost his wife; I thought you liked her."

"Is that what you desire in a wife?"

"Look, I'm busy, can you leave me alone?"

"Busy daydreaming about a particular girl to wed?"

"Raven, leave!"

"Busy pining for that half breed lek that spurned you today? You're so pathetic!"

Jonas's anger ignited as he leaped from the branch and down atop Raven. Pinning her down with his knee, he allowed his wings to fully bloom. His speckled brown and blue wings beat furiously at the air around her face. Raven's own wings slid out from under her back as she looked up at him. They were black as coal with a splash of tiny orange spots. She struggled to release them as his knees were pressing on her shoulders. Jonas's hand reached out. It was a full claw as it closed about her throat.

Raven couldn't speak as his fingers tightened around her throat. Her eyes were slightly mad as she fought against him. The glare in his eye was almost alien to her. In a gravelly voice, she struggled to respond.

"Did I strike a nerve?"

At that moment, he wanted to hurt her. The idea of strangling her entertained his thoughts. Her face was turning reddish violet as the veins in her forehead started to bulge. His mind shifted, and his fingers loosened from her neck. She frantically sucked in the air as he huffed.

"I'm not in the mood for your mind games!"

Jonas suddenly rose to his feet. His wings decompressed back into his back, and he walked toward the road. As he walked off, Raven lay still, contemplating death. She gargled and hacked up a glop of spittle, before finally letting out a long, coarse stream of giggling.

"You're going to pay for that."

Chapter 7:

Face the Music

Laraline was livid as she paced on the porch, waiting for Tori's car to arrive. The police had called her earlier about Willets' excursion off campus, and she was quite upset. In recent weeks, Willet's behavior had become more withdrawn and defiant. She wasn't sure what was happening, but it was starting to put a real strain on their relationship.

In fact, except for Mother Hazel and Tori, Willet had pretty much shut down relationships with anyone. It was the first time she and Adelie seemed almost estranged from one another. As the car finally coasted down the drive, a twinge of anxiousness knotted her stomach. Tori was the first one out of the vehicle. She waved to Laraline almost immediately.

"Good evening, Mrs. Swift!"

"Hi Tori. Your family ok?"

"Yes, ma'am."

Laraline mused as Aunt Evelyn stepped out to greet the girls. She could tell that she was uncomfortable about Tori. After all, apart from Mrs. Weever and Ms. Broom, it was the first time a sleeven was allowed into the estate since Laraline first started to date Langston.

Evelyn nervously addressed the girls as soon as Willet climbed out of the car. "Are you girls hungry?"

Tori responded quickly. "I'm fine, Mrs. Adler. I pretty much eat at work, anyway, I'm pretty tired."

Laraline interjected. "Do you need to call your father and let him know you got here safely?"

"Yes, ma'am."

"You can use my phone. It's on my dresser in my room."

"Thank you, Mrs. Swift." Tori quickly bounced inside and down the hall to the stairwell.

Evelyn looked at Laraline uneasily. The idea of a sleeven walking around freely about the house was slightly unsettling. That old prejudice was rearing its ugly head. Laraline recognized it immediately, as much as Evelyn considered herself progressive, that old worldview of humans and faigal was still affecting her reactions to modern life.

Evelyn looked at Willet, who was slowly approaching. "Do you want anything?"

Willet mumbled. "Not really, I'm going to bed."

Laraline blocked her as she tried to enter. "Not just yet, young lady."

"What now?"

"We need to talk."

"About what?"

"Constable Fletcher called us today about your little adventure."

Willet's eyes were suddenly wide awake. Before she had a chance to respond, Laraline ripped into her. "What in the world were you even thinking?"

"You don't understand. It's a bit more complicated, mama."

"No, I don't understand. The only thing I do understand is that headmistress Faulkner called shortly after to inform me that you have been suspended for two days."

"Suspended? Are you serious?"

"Insubordination is a serious infraction."

"That bitch!"

"Willet, watch your tongue!"

Willet was now bothered, as she thought about how it would affect her. She tried to weigh the pros and cons of this latest obstacle.

"Willet, are you even listening to me?"

"Yes, it's just there is a lot of other stuff that's going on, that you wouldn't understand."

"Like what, Willet?"

"Never mind."

"That's what I'm talking about. You always have a mysterious excuse. I thought you had grown past this stage. I need you to understand that unless you start taking responsibility for your actions, you're going to lose more than two days of school!"

Willet was almost in tears as she covered her face. Laraline was suddenly confused. Willet was unusually upset, but not by the threat of punishment. Evelyn touched Laraline's shoulder. "You need to calm down."

Laraline noticed that her own hand was starting to claw up, and her face and back muscles were tight. She had always tried to be so careful. Being home and this close to the source had made her much more susceptible to the change. Laraline took a deep breath before she spoke again.

"Get ready for bed, we'll talk about this tomorrow."

"Where are you going?"

"I have to go to work."

Willet looked up, somewhat shocked. "I thought you were off."

"Well, I got called in. Greenbaum is short-staffed again."

"It's because of the curfew, isn't it, Mama?"

Chapter 8:

The New Weaver

The Elysium arrived that evening shortly after six and had docked for unloading. Avis had travelled to Monticello with Gavin and waited patiently at the gate for the new house weaver. It had been almost a month since Shahaf had departed back to his home country. His cousin was to take his place for roughly six months. After that time, Shahaf would return, and the cycle would start again.

It was the strange agreement that was put in place by Shahaf's benefactor. Avis agreed to the arrangement without any questions, as Nashca Ortega was unusually striking, so striking that nearly three cycles ago, Avis had started a secret cloaqa with the young woman. Not even Aquila had any knowledge of their relationship. Branson felt as if Shahaf had begun to suspect as much over the course of the last couple of years.

Of course, it was highly inappropriate for a lord to get involved with their own weaver. A similar situation almost led to the ruin of the Adler house, many eons earlier. Even with such prior knowledge, desire is a powerful vice that can entrap almost all highly evolved species in its web.

Avis suspected Gavin knew of his indiscretions, and because of this, he felt it gave him equal footing and a close commonality. Which, in some respect, was true. Gavin himself was currently rumored to be involved in just as scandalous a cloaqa. Many of the faigal royal lore were frequently littered with such compromising secrets and details.

The boat was finally releasing its passengers, and people began to pour from the gate. As Avis scanned the various folk passing, a sense of anxiousness overcame him. He felt like a schoolboy waiting for the new teacher to arrive. Gavin had his arms folded impatiently, as the scent of sleeven and faigal drifted across his path. The sleeven smell was most pungent to him, as he coughed into his sleeve. There were hints of that smell in Meadowlark, but here it was much stronger. The city of Monticello was much more integrated.

The natural scent of sleeven could be unpleasant to faigal. However, this reality was made even worse by the fact that the species tended to mask their own natural scent with artificial aromas. Strange creams, perfumes, and hair oils mixing with their natural body odor made the result an assault to the nasal passages for many faigal.

Gavin impatiently glanced at his father, who seemed to be lost. His eyes were transfixed on the influx of passengers departing. He was about to say something to him about leaving when he noticed a slight change in the old man's expression. Avis had a sudden look of recognition in his eyes. Gavin quickly followed his father's gaze down the walkway.

Walking down the center near the landing was a dark-haired woman with strong features. She wore a formal black dress, with matching leather boots and gloves. Her hair was in a tight casque. She was carrying a large brown satchel bag in her right hand, and in her left, she held an ivory carved walking stick.

She had a deliberate rhythm as she strolled through the crowd. She caught their gaze and waved her walking stick to get their attention. Just like her predecessor, she had that no-nonsense appearance that could be intimidating. This lent an aura of mystery to her energy.

"Mother Ortega."

"Lord Branson."

"Did you enjoy your trip? I know it was a long one."

"The scenery was quite beautiful; however, I have to get adjusted to the land again."

"Wow, I would go mad being stuck for three days," Gavin exclaimed loudly.

"Unfortunately, my homeland is twice as far as New Essex."

Avis interjected. "Well, the Elysium is one of the largest luxury liners constructed. It's almost like floating on a mini-city."

She gave a silent nod to this bit of useless trivia. Avis shifted his gaze from the woman to acknowledge his son's presence. "You remember my youngest, Gavin."

Her gaze turned to Gavin. "Yes, you have grown into a man!"

Gavin glanced at her neck and noticed she had a similar type of fork-looking tattoo that Shahaf had on his neck. It was almost the same spot. He was about to comment when Avis spoke.

"He is not quite a man; he has another year to finish school. If he can stay out of trouble, he will hopefully come to work for me."

Gavin rolled his eyes slightly at this comment from Avis. "I would rather be a guardsman in the Royal Covey."

"Nonsense, you are a Branson, you are above combat. You have royal blood."

Mother Ortega studied Gavin carefully as she engaged him. "Is that your sidearm?"

The boy's eyes lit up at the prospect of someone showing interest. "Yes, would you like to see?"

He quickly unsheathed his crissum and carefully held it out toward Nashca's face. She was taken aback by his aggressiveness but calmly entertained him.

"Yes, I can see it is well kept."

"I am unbeaten this year in fencing. Notice how even and untainted the edge is, mother!"

Gavin almost held it threateningly at her neck. She didn't flinch. She recognized his immediate need to let her know she was an outsider. Mother Ortega looked carefully before commenting.

"I notice it has a serrated edge."

"It's ideal for cutting through tougher surfaces like metal and wood."

"Or bone and muscle as well?"

Gavin gave her a curious glance as if she knew something. He, however, quickly dismissed it as Avis called to him. "Put your weapon up, this is a public place, Gavin!"

Gavin sank his head as he slowly sheathed his blade. Nashca probed him further.

"Doesn't your sister have a similar interest in melee weaponry?"

"She is quite capable with a crossbow!"

"Please excuse him, Mother Ortega. Since they were young, he and his sister have shared a morbid fascination with all manner of weapons and torture devices. His sister also has foolish notions of joining the swans, as some covert assassin."

"So I suppose she will also work with you?"

"Goodness no, she is of age. She is of royal breeding stock. The hope is that by the time she graduates, she will be betrothed. I have my eye on a young man from France."

"Do they get along?"

"Well, they will in time."

Nashca glanced back at Gavin, who seemed troubled by the conversation. "Where is she?"

"Raven is home with her studies, at least I hope."

Avis changed the subject as if he were tired of speaking about his children. "Are you hungry? As I understand, we are having a wonderful meal. Our houseboy will prepare forty pounds of Knookfish, seared to perfection."

"Well, it's hard to turn down Knookfish, Lord Branson!"

"We will have a feast then, in celebration of your return!"

"Shahaf wrote me about Meena's sudden passing. Sorry about your daughter-in-law; you have my deepest regrets."

"Thank you, mother. Yes, it was a shock, but it was expected. Ephron is taking it especially hard. Aquila has had to take over most of his duties as of late."

An uncomfortable tone erupted from her. "Aquila?"

"Come now, you remember Aquila. Is there something wrong?"

"Nothing, I guess Shahaf didn't brief you before he left."

"Brief me about what?"

"Could we discuss this at a more appropriate time, Lord Branson?"

Nashca discreetly glanced over at Gavin. Avis caught her look and nodded. "I guess that would be ok, I forgot that Shahaf sends you a report on his progress."

"Yes, he has impeccable notes, as I will do the same for when he returns."

"I don't quite understand the need for all this paperwork."

"All these things are required to keep our professional autonomy, yet a consistent understanding of the basic needs of each house. I assure you, everything is in proper order, Lord Branson."

Gavin glanced at her curiously. "So, where is Shahaf now?"

"It's hard to say."

"So is he with another house, while you're here?"

"It doesn't quite work that way."

Branson cut in. "They both contract with us exclusively as seasonal employees."

Nashca glanced at the young man. "I know you were quite fond of Shahaf, but he will return in the new year."

"In the meantime, you will address her as Mother."

Chapter 9:

After Hours

The curfew had slowed business down to a crawl. Kuzz was one of the few bars that stayed open after hours. It appeared to be just like any quirky seafood dive bar on the outside, but the interior was adorned with trophies and keepsakes from the ocean. Most of the seats were like large pews facing skipper wheeled tables. Medium-sized sharks dangled from the walls and ceilings, while thousands of shells and starfish were embossed into the railings and other spare surfaces.

Fishing was the common denominator that the faigal shared with the sleveen. Both species intersected at that one point. Meadowlark was, at heart, a fishing town. The curfew had unfortunately disrupted the flow of business.

Even though there was a curfew, different rules applied in Crecheland; this was probably why Ephron had ended up there. Ever since his wife's funeral, he seemed to live in a despondent, drunken haze. As of 10:50 PM, he had perched himself comfortably at the bar. Because of his family status and his loud, belligerent behavior, he had run off most of the other customers.

Greenbaum was quite upset. His busy season was weeks away, and there was a new city curfew. To complicate matters, a now drunken Branson was running off customers with his frequent appearances. It wasn't like you could just tell him to leave. It would be like expelling the king's son.

He was humored at first, then tolerated, and now he was avoided.

Since Ephron's breakdown, he had taken a leave of absence. Avis had reluctantly put in place an acting director to attend to the young man's affairs, as well as keep tabs on him. When the director arrived at the bar searching for Ephron's whereabouts, Greenbaum quickly pointed to the drunkard at the end of the bar. His head lay on the rum-stained counter as he hummed gently to himself. After a moment, he raised his head and proceeded to flirt with the female bartender who was serving his drinks.

Aquila approached the bar with complete disdain, as she recognized the bartender. "My, isn't this a small world."

Laraline was in the middle of pouring yet another mug of Irish ale for Ephron when she looked up at the older woman with the eyepatch. "Do I know you?"

"We haven't formally met yet."

"I suppose there is a reason for that."

"Excuse me?"

"I know exactly who you are now, your Lord Branson's sister!"

"Half-sister, and you are the Adler niece whose very presence in Meadowlark is causing so much disruption!"

"Disruption? Please explain."

"Your ridiculous demands on my wretched brother."

"You're referring to the sanctuary?"

"You should bow down before him and pray for the mercy he has granted you!"

"I take it you don't agree with his decision?"

"If it were my choice, you wouldn't even be breathing."

Laraline felt a chill from her words. In that moment, she realized just how fortunate they were that Avis was running things. She furrowed her brow and bucked back on unsure footing.

"Well, it's not your choice, Lady Branson."

"Things change. Kingdoms change, dear."

"What do you mean by that?"

"You should take your sleeven brood back from whence you came."

"Boy, you're not very subtle."

"I don't believe in wasting time with a lot of polite small talk."

"Well, I happen to work here, sister, so pretty please with sugar on top, remove your drunken nephew from the bar. Unless you want me to explain to the town how certain members of one of the most respected families, including yourself, frequent this side of town."

"Really, no one will believe you!"

"And why not? You are here now, Lady Branson, and everyone in this bar has been watching you the moment you entered."

Aquila was suddenly paranoid as she looked around the bar. It wasn't full, but there were at least a dozen heads glancing discreetly in their direction. The truth be told, she didn't really care if Ephron's reputation was soiled a bit. Ironically, she was the reason he was at Kuzz in the first place. She had encouraged him to take his troubles somewhere that important people couldn't see.

However, people are like recorders of facts and rumors that could be started by simple observation and perception.

If one couldn't control the narrative, it was best not to be a part of the narrative at all. She glared at Laraline like a cat wanting to pounce, but she kept her composure.

"It seems I underestimated you, Miss..."

Laraline corrected her. "Mrs. Swift."

"I shan't forget."

Aquila motioned for her driver to pay the tab. Laraline looked at Aquila, trying to lift her nephew from the bar. A kind of empathy overcame her suddenly.

"Wait, take him out the side door. It's more discreet."

As the driver pulled out a wad of money to hand to Laraline, she shook her head. "Don't worry about his tab. He was never here tonight."

Aquila's eyes blazed in Laraline's direction. "Don't try to make amends to me, now."

Laraline quickly spun round. "Please, this isn't about you, woman! I recognize his kind of pain."

Aquila looked confused at Laraline. She headed to the side door reluctantly as Ephron staggered against her shoulder for support. She periodically glanced back at Laraline suspiciously as they made it to the door.

"This had better not be a trap!"

Laraline finally responded to the older woman's timid actions. "I don't expect someone like you to ever understand compassion."

"That is a word for dreamers and fools."

"We all need compassion, Lady Branson. Even the most despicable of us."

"Your weakness will be your undoing. You won't survive this war!"

"Perhaps, but unlike you, I refuse to spend my life trying to figure out how to survive. I want to spend the rest of my life living!"

Aquila was silent. She had no point of reference. The idea that this Adler was still trying to be civil and helpful agitated Aquila to no end. Aquila was almost out the door when she stopped to address her again, this time with a troubled arrogance.

"We'll talk again. "

Laraline politely responded. "Let not and say we did."

Chapter 10:

Restless

Willet was having trouble sleeping. Though she had made this claim several times before, she was sure this was the worst day of her life. Well, it was a close second, as she considered the day her mother informed them of her father's death.

Tori was fast asleep. For a while, all Willet could do was watch her snore. With her red pigtails and freckles, she reminded Willet of a teenage Pippi Longstocking. After a while, Willet got up in disgust at her friend's loud, inconsistent breathing patterns.

She made her way across the dimly lit room to the dark bowels of the bathroom. As she entered, she was greeted with various shades of darkness. She squinted as she slowly tipped across the cold marble tile. While she passed each shadow, she could imagine phantoms and monsters reaching for her out of the corner of her eye.

She finally made it to the sink, fumbling for the faucet handle in the darkness. She had just rested her hand on the back of the handle when she heard coarse breathing from over her shoulder. She felt a chill on the back of her neck. She turned around to face the dark bathtub. Inside the tub, the shadows resembled the lump of some sort of figure lying stretched out inside the bottom, facing her. Willet was frozen with fear. Willet heard a single word erupt from the tub.

"Ready?"

It was like a cross between a slight whisper and a hiss. She could almost visualize lips speaking. Then suddenly, the shadows dematerialized until she could just see the bottom of the tub. Had she imagined it all?

As her eyes adjusted to the dark, she slowly moved closer till she was at the edge of the tub. She knelt and reached her hand out. With a tight fist, she popped the bottom of the tub. It rang with a deep thud.

Her hand rubbed around the side, across the black rings of burn that remained after her fateful bath several months earlier. She didn't really remember the incident, but she had flashes of images. They were all images of drowning.

It was the day that it rained fish. The day she almost died. Even though the tub was still functional, she felt uneasy about taking a bath here. She would just use Adelie's tub. In fact, this was the closest she had been to the thing in almost a month.

The aunties both strangely refused to replace it, something about luck and omens. Ms. Weaver had tried to clean the burns several times, but they seemed ingrained in the very surface of the porcelain. In fact, there was no tactile distinction.

She felt an urge to talk to Mother Hazel, even though she had mostly avoided her as of late. Her own social life was getting a bit more involved, and she didn't really want to deal with the strange dynamics of her supposed birthright. However, her dream episodes were becoming more frequent.

So much, in fact, that at times it was getting hard to tell the difference between fantasy and reality.

As Willet quietly made her way downstairs, she found herself scanning the dimly lit environment cautiously. She sensed a hint of a familiar presence. Her muscles tensed. She could almost feel her wings trying to bloom. After her first bloom, Aunt Evelyn had urged her to focus on her breathing. This would give her more control in flying. She had to calm down.

As she reached the bottom floor, she saw a familiar figure leaning against the wall in the hallway near the aviary. Willet was startled and clenched her muscles in shock as the figure addressed her.

"Our resident insomniac has graced the bottom floor with her presence. This is quite the eventful night!"

Willet looked at Sirenna's cold face and politely responded. "I just came down for a glass of water, Auntie!"

"What's wrong with the water in your own lavatory?"

"I do not like to be in my bathroom. It gives me the creeps."

"I smell fear, how unimaginable!"

Willet tried to ignore Sirenna's candid digs. "Where is Mother Hazel?"

"Isn't that ironic?"

Willet struck back. "Let me guess, she has sent you to fetch me. Is that why you are up late, creeping around?"

"You insolent little worm, in this house, when we make a promise, we are bound by our word. And last I checked, you are well overdue!"

Willet uneasily responded. "I made no promises."

Down the dark hallway, a voice snapped at the young girl's response. "I beg to differ Ms. Swift!"

The old woman stood erect with a walking stick. She was in the entrance of the lit study, waiting. Willet looked back at Sirenna, who stood against the wall with her arms folded.

Sirenna responded for Willet. "Let's go."

Willet silently complied as she followed Sirenna down the hallway.

The study was well-lit. It was a room that Willet wasn't privy to very often. However, with the ever-changing events and her abilities growing, the Adler clan's desire to include Willet was increasing. As she made her way into the study, Mother Hazel hobbled to her usual perch. The old woman sat in a wicker-laced, bound mahogany rocking chair. It was placed strategically at the edge of a large oak desk. Sirenna carefully situated herself in the grand leather-bound chair that sat behind the other end of the oak desk. She almost disappeared because of a large gold embossed globe that sat atop of her desk. Mother Hazel eased back in her chair and addressed Willet.

"Now we can begin."

"Begin, what is all of this about?"

"Your training, of course. We had a bargain."

"I made no such bargain. You informed me of what you expected, while I was half asleep."

Mother Hazel looked disturbed.

Sirenna interjected. "I told you, you're wasting your time."

"You do know what could happen to you, to all of us, if you do not comply."

"Look, can I just have a little more time? I haven't even been here for a full year. I can't get up at night to train when I go to school in the morning. I could do a few hours on the weekends."

"Training must not be sporadic!"

Sirenna clasped her hands together before speaking. "Since she has been suspended, perhaps her training can finally start!"

Willet glared with sudden clarity. "You had me kicked out of Talomore?"

"You had yourself kicked out!"

"Faulkner would not dare cross you, unless, when she called, you recommended this course of action."

"Guilty as charged."

"Is this that aristocratic way of doing things you spoke of before?"

"You learn quickly."

"Why? Do you despise me that much?"

Mother Hazel finally interjected. "I asked Sirenna to do so."

Willet tuned back to the old woman, confused. "Why?"

"For your own protection."

"I don't understand!"

Mother Hazel continued. "Willet, you can no longer drift along as a passive participant in this world. You are like a tiny warm candle in the cold, dark woods. The night is growing colder, but your flame is getting brighter. You draw your own conclusions."

Sirenna reached out with her long, thin fingernail and gently spun the globe. She passively interjected. "The future is always in motion!"

"Look, I just want to live an ordinary life."

Sirenna snapped at her. "What is this ordinary life you speak of? It doesn't exist, it's a sleeven construct to allow one to remain ignorant of the world beyond this world!"

Mother Hazel continued. "Sirenna is loyal to the Adler dynasty, first and foremost. Whatever else you may feel about your great aunt, she has the innate ability to adapt and change. It would do you well to learn this if you are to survive the storm that is coming."

"What storm?"

"Only by the grace of the first light are we granted spiritual sanctuary from the entities now prowling our streets."

"You know who is responsible for all the missing people?"

"I know the what, the who is a bit more complicated. All these disappearances are just the beginning."

"Willet glanced back and forth between Sirenna and Mother Hazel. "What are you talking about?"

The old woman glanced uneasily at Sirenna before she spoke again. "When I was much younger than you, I lived in a tiny village called Umbra. "

"Umbra, where is that?"

"It was far across the sea, positioned at the edge of a dark wood, much like this town. It doesn't exist anymore. Time and modern urbanization destroyed it long ago."

Mother Hazel seemed hesitant, as she looked to Sirenna before continuing. "The situation began with a young boy from my hamlet, named Fern. Young Fern was about two years older than me, with the brownest eyes.

Willet raised her eyebrow with a smirk. "Was he cute?"

Sirenna's response was quick as she popped the young girl's shoulder. "Silence!"

Mother Hazel continued without missing a beat. She spoke as if she were recalling a deep secret that she had been carrying for years.

"One afternoon, he was sent by his mum to fetch water for supper. An errand that I knew all too well. On this particular eve, he never returned. A night and a day passed before search parties were sent out. They found nothing, save for his water bucket. It appeared at the edge of the creek bank, almost three miles downstream. Over the next few weeks, this pattern of missing children continued. Several of the village children started to disappear out of thin air. A local curfew, like the one we have here, went into effect. Over time, men, women, and children started to go missing. That was when I first heard my mum utter the term griskin."

Willet leaned in, intrigued. "Is that what is happening here?"

"They are a mysterious species from within the fathom black itself. Occasionally, they slip into our world to scavenge for food and other items. They often drain their victims of life."

"It sounds like a vampire!"

"A what?"

"You know, a vampire!"

"How do you say this word? What does it mean?"

Mother Hazel looked to Sirenna, confused. Sirenna started to speak in the native tongue. Willet couldn't understand everything but was able to make out the word verillion.

The old woman finally shook her head. "Haaa!"

The image from the previous morning popped into Willet's head. "Does this griskin have legs like an insect?"

Mother Hazel's eyes darted back to Willet. She was fixed on Willet intently. "You've seen one, haven't you!"

Willet slowly nodded. "It was killing an old man this morning. It dragged him into the woods. It was like I was there, just like when I drifted into the black cabin. I was in class, then suddenly, I was by the woods, watching."

"I suspected as much when I heard the details of your expulsion. Whomever this griskin is, it has found its way amongst the townsfolk."

"What do you mean, whomever? I don't recall seeing a lot of insect people."

"You may not have recognized them. After all, they are changelings by nature, so they can take on the physical form of any of their prey, at will."

"So, they can weave!"

Mother Hazel glanced up at Sirenna with a curious expression. "I suppose they can, in a way."

Willet was almost beaming that she was aware of something that neither had considered. Mother Hazel was quick to change the focus of the conversation.

"The griskin is especially deadly when it is becoming or changing its form."

"Why is that?"

"They can absorb the very essence of their victim, even that of a weaver. This is what makes you especially vulnerable. You have so much raw ability; it can be quite alluring!"

"You think they are after me!"

"I don't know, but they are always searching for rare gifts to bring back to their queen, and you are quite rare; a half breed that drifts."

"I drifted so no one can see me, I'm practically invisible?"

"Only to those who exist in this physical plane. The griskin exist in the same psychic ether that allows you to drift in the first place."

"You mentioned that they come from the fathom black. I thought that place was like nothingness."

"As I told you before, it's more like an anti-world, a world between the worlds. It's a void where all things must eventually pass through in time, though some never do.

"You make it sound like a type of interstellar purgatory."

"Well, we know the Greywood is the only way they could have crossed over."

"You keep saying they, as if you think there is more than one griskin!"

"They are like roaches. Once they start to infest a territory, they are hard to get rid of."

"Once, we got roaches in our old house, and Mama never could get rid of them. Actually, we think Adelie brought them. She had a habit of sneaking food to bed. Mama would have Daddy check her pockets to see what she was hiding."

Willet suddenly felt an uncomfortable silence as both women stood staring at her patiently. Realizing she had gotten off subject, Willet cleared her throat.

"Well, what happened in your village, Mother Hazel?"

"A certain elderly mother who lived on the edge of the woods would make the most delicious fruit pies. One day, the local miller's dog got into her garden. After digging around her strawberries, it retrieved a bone from the loose dirt and brought the bone home to show its master. The bone in question was a tiny femur that obviously belonged to a child."

Willet gasped. "My goodness."

"The townsfolk formed a mob and came to her home that night to confront her. They tore apart her home, yard, and garden. Unfortunately, the old woman was never seen again. Quite by accident, a large burrow was discovered under the floorboards of her cabin. It stretched for miles underground. The officials searched deep into the lair. The found several cocoons containing the preserved remains of hundreds of victims, along with dozens of griskin eggs that had long since hatched, and faigal skins.

"Skins?"

"They typically digest their victims from the inside out."

"Yuck!"

Chapter 11:

The Hangover

Ephron was exhausted as he lay in bed, but was still vaguely aware of movement beside him. Meena rose from beneath the covers and gave him a gentle peck on the cheek. She had a coy smile as his eyes focused on her.

Her presence startled him. "I don't understand. I watched you die!"

She silently held up her finger to his lips before he could say another word. She then mouthed the word. "Hush!"

Ephron impulsively reached out and grabbed her around the waist. He then grabbed a handful of hair and pushed his face into her scalp. He closed his eyes and inhaled. He instantly recognized her scent. He exhaled as if he were breathing fresh air. "It's really you!"

She lifted her head till she was eye level. She then pressed her lips against his ear and whispered. "*Even better than the real thing!*"

Ephron jerked away as the woman lying in his bed began to laugh. She rose slightly. Just enough so that Ephron could see into her empty, cold black eyes. His immediate reaction was to scream in horror. His own screams woke him up from his sleep. It was morning, and he was alone in bed. Unfortunately, as he gained full consciousness, he realized he wasn't in his own bed. He looked around carefully in a paranoid haze. The image of Meena quickly dissipating in his fear and confusion.

Where am I?

The room had the aura of convenient, compact living. This was a hotel room or condo.

I must be in Celandine Springs. How did I get here?

His head was throbbing as he sat up, trying to recall exactly what happened. The last thing he remembered, he was at the bar. As he shifted his leg, it occurred to him that not only was he in a strange bed, but he was naked under the covers.

Where are my clothes?

He was gathering the blanket around him when the phone rang. He jerked back, startled. He looked about the room, as if he expected someone to enter the bedroom and answer the phone. The phone rang another four times before he finally picked up the receiver.

Ephron slowly put the phone to his ear. It was silent for a few moments before he heard the prim and properly irritated voice on the other end. "Mr. Branson?"

Ephron just listened.

"Mr. Branson, is this Mr. Branson's room?"

Ephron carefully answered. "This is Mr. Branson speaking. What do you want?"

"This is the front desk with your morning wake-up call."

"My wake-up call?"

"Yes, you requested an 8 am wake-up call, sir."

"I made no such request."

"About twenty minutes after you checked in, your wife called down."

"My wife?"

"I assumed she was your wife, sir."

"What did she look like?"

"I don't understand. She's your wife!"

"Please humor me and describe the woman I checked in with."

"Well, she had red hair, fair skin, about 5'7"."

"That's impossible. Where is she now?"

"I'm sure I wouldn't know, sir!"

"With whom am I speaking?"

"Really, if you have any complaints, I suggest you come to the front desk." With that, the phone clicked.

Ephron was taken aback by the receptionist's curt manner. He would have their job by the time he reached the desk. *Why wasn't Landry answering the phone?* He didn't recognize this new person. Something was off. As he made his way across the room, he quickly surmised he wasn't at The Celandine Suites.

In fact, the more he looked around the room, the more he realized that the accommodations were meager at best. This wasn't the subtle, lush lodgings he was accustomed to; this place was filled with retro greens and oranges. The ceilings were covered in that cheap popcorn that many hotels and flophouses in Crecheland used.

He suddenly felt dirty just touching the bedding. He instantly allowed the blanket to drop to the floor and walked about free as a bird searching for his clothes. His mind was occupied with the image of Meena. How is this possible? He dared not entertain the idea that she was now alive.

Something was strange. He got to the closet and sure enough, clothes were neatly hanging up on wire hangers.

Wire hangers, how disgusting!

He quickly snatched them down and began dressing. He stepped out of the door, and the strong scent of cleaners assaulted his nostrils. He almost felt the urge to retch at the flood of bleach and vinegar citrus scents. He looked around the hallway and realized there was no elevator. *Where is the front desk?* He scrambled down a few hallways, trying to find his bearings in this alien landscape. He saw a sign with an arrow that announced Front Lobby.

Finally!

Unfortunately, the front lobby's appearance was not making anything any better, as he nervously looked about the dwelling. Ephron approached the front desk, and a young girl reading a magazine behind it. Her hair was multicolored, and she had several piercings. Three on her ears, one on her lip, one on her nose, and one on her right eyebrow. Sensing his presence, she looked up as Ephron stood, waiting in front of her.

"I would like to speak to your manager?"

"If you need towels. It's the first door on the left."

"Towels, no, I just called down."

"Are you the guy in 130?"

"What? My name is Ephron Branson. Were you the one I talked to on the phone?"

"Guilty as charged."

"Do you even know who I am, girl?"

"You said you were Ephron Branson, so the question you just asked me was completely redundant."

Ephron was speechless at her apparent rudeness but decided that there were other pressing issues. "Where am I?"

"You're serious!"

"Why am I here?"

"Why are any of us here?"

"Look, I have no memory of last night. I woke up this morning in this... this... your hotel, all alone, and I need someone to fill in the blanks about what happened!"

"Why don't you just ask your wife?"

"My wife is dead! Please stop talking!"

His outburst was so sudden that it momentarily startled the desk clerk from her Zen-like apathy. Ephron was almost in tears as he contained himself long enough to continue speaking. This time, his voice was coldly calm and controlled.

"Where is the manager?"

The girl stared blankly at him for several moments until Ephron finally commented.

"Didn't you hear what I said?"

"Yes!"

"Why aren't you answering me?"

"You told me to stop talking. I was just trying to respect the whole pseudo client-customer vibe we got going on today!"

Ephron looked about the room, frustrated. "This is madness!"

The receptionist, now bored with the exchange, returned to her book. Ephron turned back frantically.

"Could you at least tell me the name of this hotel?"

The girl impatiently pointed down to the stationary sign-in sheet. Ephron bent down and squinted as he read out loud. "The Moonlight Inn?"

Chapter 12:

The Invitation

Kestrel Faulkner had been working at the Meadowlark Municipal Library for the last eight years, a job she had gotten because of her older sister. At the time, it seemed like a bit of good fortune; however, over the years, she became known as Kestrel the librarian. She had become a walking cliché, the unmarried, timid, bookish girl who never found a man and disappeared into her books. She was the invisible loser who spent her evenings all alone with her cats.

She really hated that image; however, whenever she tried to break or change, she was ridiculed or put back in her place. That was the problem with a small town. One could never really grow without ruffling a few feathers.

She remembered two years ago when she dyed her hair brown; it was almost a scandal. She got so much attention about her state of mind with unsolicited visits and advice about the need for her to just accept her natural blonde roots. Hell, even a local parish mum brought her a casserole. She hated casseroles.

The real joke was that none of these good neighbors actually cared. They just didn't like the minor disruption that she had created for them by not following the plan. Because of the possible scandalous threat created by her involvement with Gavin, she knew it would be only a matter of time before a representative of the Meadowlark moral majority would pay her a visit.

Still, she was not expecting both Peregrine sisters to come by that morning. She knew immediately when she saw them entering the double doors that they were on a mission. Violet fit her name to a tea, as she frequently wrapped herself in her signature purple and white designer scarf with matching purple formal dresses. Violet was tall, thin, and wiry. One of those bitter, middle-aged shrews who spent her days spying on her neighbors in hopes of finding irredeemable social shortcomings.

Her Sister, Deloris, was very different. She was squalid, short, and stocky, wearing dark brown designer boots that barely covered her pudgy calves. Most of her features were covered by a large black fedora that at first glance gave her an air of mystery. As much as the pair contrasted one another, there were certain familiarities and mannerisms that both shared that left no doubt they were sisters indeed. Violet locked eyes with Kestrel and nudged Deloris with her elbow.

There was no escaping them now. Kestrel took a deep breath as the odd couple made a beeline for her direction. As luck would have it, Alouette Heron approached the librarian just a moment before the duo reached the counter. It was the usual minor issue. She wanted to know the availability of a book that she had seen on the shelf months earlier. Deloris and Violet patiently waited behind her to finish.

While the Peregrine sisters waited, Kestrel took her sweet time. Trying to be as thorough as she could. However, the book Alouette was trying to acquire had been checked out the previous day. Kestrel tried her best to implore

Alouette to help her find other books similar, in hopes of discouraging the Peregrines from waiting. Alas, Alouette, having empathy for the women patiently waiting, relented her desire.

"You can wait on Ms. Peregrine; she's been waiting for a while."

Violet Peregrine immediately touched her bosom as if she were beyond honored. "Bless you, sweet child!"

Deloris set her pudgy fingers on the counter in front of Kestrel as Alouette left. "Isn't it a lovely day!"

"I suppose so."

Violet interjected. "Suppose, but not sure?"

Kestrel looked confused. "What?"

Deloris quickly interjected. "Violet and I were having a discussion, and your name came up."

"Why?"

Violet looked over. "Sunday potluck."

"Excuse me?"

Deloris clarified. "We both agreed, we would love to have you for dinner."

Violet echoed. "Most Definitely!"

Kestrel's reply was quick. "I don't think I can."

"No, is not an option, dear."

"Definitely not."

Suddenly, Kestrel felt as if she were being double-teamed. "Look, I'll have to let you know."

Both women stepped away from the counter with bright, condescending smiles. Violet snapped enthusiastically at her. "We will be expecting you at 6 pm sharp."

Before Kestrel could react, both women were gone and out the door. The entire situation was beyond surreal. They definitely had an agenda. This gave Kestrel a slight chill. High-minded religious folk always gave her chills. They were a certain obsessive behavior type who tended to fixate on those deemed immoral."

As she watched the door close behind the pair, it suddenly reopened. A sickening feeling overcame her. Don't tell me they are returning. She held her breath, just as Gavin suddenly burst inside. He looked crossly back in the direction he had just come.

"Hey, what do those two weirdos want? "

"Apparently, I've been invited to a Sunday dinner."

"Get ready for a religious conversion, doll."

Why are you here, anyway? Shouldn't you be in school?

"Probably."

"That's all I need, you coming around my job."

"Chill. I thought you would be glad to see me."

"I told you, it's over. Perhaps you should find some eye candy your own age."

"You can't just quit me, do you know who I am?"

"Unfortunately, I do."

"It's not over till I say it's over. I have several revealing pictures of you."

"Are you blackmailing me?"

Gavin, instead of replying, gave her a cocky smirk. "Well..."

"You're a monster!"

"Get your keys, you've got to take an early lunch break."

"Why?"

"We need to make a quick drive up to Moonlight Inn."

"You must be insane. I'm not going anywhere near that place!"

Gavin seemed oblivious to her animated objections. Instead, he was staring at his reflection in the shelf glass beside her, checking his teeth and hair.

"Give me one reason why I should leave my job to chauffeur you 20 minutes outside of town."

Gavin had a coy smile as he responded. "Ephron called me from there; he needs a ride back to town."

Kestrel's eyes lit up. She was almost speechless. The idea of actually being able to speak to Ephron after all this time. Gavin knew exactly how she would react. Her mood changed as she responded.

"What is he doing at that horrible dive?"

"Look, you can ask him yourself. We've got to be going!"

"Well, let me just get my makeup bag and lock up!"

Chapter 13:

The Enemy's Lair

Willet found herself walking down Blue Jay Way, away from the house. She wasn't in any mood to really deal with anyone, especially after the last twenty-four hours. It was a brisk morning as she strolled on the edge of the road. She found herself looking back at the silhouette of the Greywood. Even in the daylight, it appeared ghoulish. A stream of light mist permeated the entire perimeter of the forest. Willet was reminded of Mother Hazel's dire warnings concerning Greywood and how she should stay away.

After almost an hour of trying to bully her into training, Mother Hazel had to settle for a compromise of 17 minutes of breathing exercises before Willet went back to bed. Still, the old woman had a point. Willet knew she couldn't ignore what she was telling her. She was also aware of how little time she had left before she was an adult. The day you cross that threshold, you can never go back. In some ways, that scared her more than death itself.

Perhaps she was fooling herself, and her time for beach parties and acting silly was over. Her childhood was also the only connection to the memory of her father. He would never see her as an adult. He would never see her graduate from school, get a job, get married, or have kids. She would never get to share so many important things with him. Now she was in this alien landscape of Meadowlark. Pressured with the idea of becoming a type of witch in a world that her father was not even accepted. It not only enraged her, but it was terrifying.

Willet glanced back at the tree line obscured by mist and saw movement. It was only for a moment, but it was enough to freak her out. It was definitely a figure moving across the edge of the trees. She didn't know who it was, but she recognized what appeared to be a long, flowing white gown. It was the phantom woman from her dreams. She was sure of it!

One thing was for sure: she was definitely starting to see more things: a ghostly woman, insect people, and flying harpies. Willet thought to herself. *And Mother Hazel wonders why I don't want this life!*

She was almost at the fork where Sabine crossed Blue Jay Way when she saw her mother's hatchback approaching. Willet got a pit in her stomach. She stood on the edge of the road waiting for the continuation of her mother's wrath. *Now what?*

As the Dodge Impala pulled up beside Willet, the brakes screeched. Laraline just sat there with a weathered expression on her face. It was the first time Willet could see her mother's age start to show. Laraline finally rolled down her window and stuck her head out.

"So, where ya headed, stranger?"

Willet put her hands in her pockets and answered kind of matter-of-factly. "Oh, I was thinking of hitchhiking back to Florida."

"Can I join ya?"

Her response took Willet aback. "I suppose."

"Well, get in."

Laraline's behavior wasn't what she expected. Nevertheless, she climbed into the car, relieved. Willet shut the door and waited for her mother to bring up her expulsion. Laraline instead asked a most curious question.

"Do you mind if we make a little pit stop?"

"I guess so?"

Laraline backed the car up and did a sudden U-turn. As soon as she got the car back on West Sabine, Willet looked at her mother curiously. "So, where are we going?"

"You remember that favor I asked you to help me with?"

"Yeah, Daddy's sailboat."

"Well, I just found out from my boss last night that next month our sailing adventure is a go!"

"But we don't have the boat yet."

"That's the rub, darling."

"So what are we going to do?"

"Well, we are driving to meet someone who may be able to fix our little problem."

"Who are we meeting?"

Laraline considered the question before answering most cryptically. "We are going into the belly of the beast."

Willet didn't understand what her mother was referring to. In their current state, she didn't care much. She was glad to be spending a school morning with her mother. It was silent for a few minutes until Laraline finally inquired.

"Did Adelie get off to school ok?"

"Yeah, she left with Tori about an hour ago."

"You got bored, huh?"

"Kind of."

The Impala suddenly pulled into a large driveway that was flanked on either side by magnolia trees and weeping willows. About 70 yards in Willet could make out a large Victorian-style dwelling. It reminded her of one of those New Orleans-style southern mansions where everyone spoke in a slow southern drawl and drank mint juleps or something to that effect.

Willet looked in amazement. The house was just as impressive as the Greywood manor, yet it was aesthetically different. Dozens of ancient trees littered the front yard. Most of the trees appeared to be weeping willows. She noticed several tree branches were decorated with nooses as they ventured deeper down the driveway.

"Whose house is this?"

"This is the Branson manor, the ancestral home of Lord Branson and his family."

"Why are we here then? According to everyone, they are our mortal enemies!"

"Because I have business with Mr. Branson."

"What kind of business?"

It's a bit complicated!"

Suddenly, the car pulled to a stop. Laraline quickly put the car in park and got out. She looked back at Willet, who appeared to be in shock. *Of all the places to take a stroll.*

"Come on, Willet."

Willet was quick as she hurried out of her side of the car and joined her mother. She didn't know exactly what to expect. She felt nervous. *Jonas lives here*. She didn't want to see him. Especially after how she had treated him yesterday.

Before they reached the front porch, the front door slid open. A tall dark-haired woman emerged from within. Her long, flowing black hair almost covered her face. Her hand gripped a long ivory scepter. She had an exotic feel about her, as she gracefully met them at the top step.

"How may I help you, miss?"

"I need to see Lord Branson."

"Lord Branson is busy. Do you have an appointment?"

"Tell him Laraline Swift is here."

The woman considered Laraline's request and squinted her eyes as if to get a better look at the visitors. "So, you are Ms. Swift. I've heard a lot about you. Wait here." She then turned around and went back inside, leaving them on the steps of the porch.

Willet looked at her mother for a moment. "What does that mean?"

"I'm sure, I don't know!"

It remained silent, as the sound of crickets filled the morning air. Willet looked across the massive yard impatiently.

Across the field to an adjacent fence that bordered the property, she spied what appeared to be several small objects that were lying dangling along in a row. She moved a bit closer to see exactly what they were. As she advanced, she realized they were a variety of small animal pelts nailed to the top rung of the wooden railing.

"Oh, gross!"

"What is it, dear?"

"Animal skins nailed to the fence, someone left them out to dry in the morning sun."

From where she stood, she could see that flies had congregated about the pools of congealed blood on the ground underneath them. Willet was about to investigate further when the door opened. The woman emerged from the entrance.

"Lord Branson will see you. Please come this way."

Laraline and Willet quickly complied, as they were led into the bowels of the Branson abode. There was something distinctly familiar about their exotic greeter. Laraline curiously prodded the young woman.

"Have we met before?"

"Where would that have been, miss?"

Laraline quickly withdrew from any small talk. Judging from the woman's demeanor, she was a no-nonsense kind of person. The long hallway was decorated with deep bronze and black trim. The entire place had a very masculine feel to it. That wasn't necessarily a bad thing; however, there was a perverseness about the place that was unsettling.

As the woman led them to the large drawing room, Willet gasped at the centerpiece. It was a large spherical tank, positioned in the center of the room. She was drawn to the strange glass orb as she moved slowly toward the tank. She was about to place her hand on it, when she heard a gruff voice from behind them.

"It's quite something to behold."

An older, stocky gentleman stepped from the shadows. His dark, black, and grey hair seemed to be matted to his head. He was sporting a full beard and mustache. His voice was gruff, but his behavior was quite cordial and inviting to a point. However, there was a dangerous aura to his presence.

He was like a guard dog on a leash. As long as you kept your distance, he was fine.

The woman who brought them into the room stood quite still in the corner of the room. Her arms were lightly folded. It was as if she were a statue. She glanced at Laraline as if she were studying her. For the moment, the older man was entranced in showing off his unusual display item to his young guest. In hindsight, he rarely got the chance to do so.

Willet responded. "I have never seen anything like it before."

"I first saw one similar in Bangladesh, when our covey had to secure the city during the Octaxon Dury campaigns of 1876. It was where I met my wife. After her passing, I had this reconstructed in her memory. The original one was three times the size."

Willet rubbed her hand over the surface. "You had this made?"

"Yes, indeed, our family lore is a rich one."

"What is it, a cage of some sort? It almost reminds me of an egg. Is that what it's supposed to represent?"

Avis, instead of answering the question, directed another at Laraline.

"This must be one of your daughters?"

"This is my eldest, Willet."

Avis looked back at Willet. "You're very perceptive, Willet. How are you enjoying your stay in Meadowlark so far?"

"Well, I'll have to let you know."

Avis chuckled. "That's fair enough. I imagine this is a long way from Key West."

Avis turned his attention to Laraline, who stood patiently waiting but with an underlying sense of urgency. She had prepared herself for the formal polite exchange to unfold. She immediately bowed, with extended hands to her sides. Avis responded with the same customary bow. They both rose, facing each other as Laraline cleared her throat.

"You have a lovely home, Lord Branson."

"Thank you so much, it seems to suit one's needs. So, what brings you here so early this morning?"

"I wish to discuss a few things with you, if I may?"

"Should I be ready for another interrogation?"

"I apologize for my earlier behavior, Mr. Branson. After all, we have you to thank for the veil of protection provided to my family, these last few months."

Avis closed his eyes and began to speak out loud in the most elegant voice. "Sanctuary to all thyne children who are strangers, for they are known to thy eyes."

"That's from the Asclan, very good!"

"We Bransons are not all godless heathens."

"I never said anything!"

"I knew your mother, Oriole; she was a most beautiful creature beyond compare."

"I thought the Adlers and Bransons were enemies. How is that possible?"

"We all went to Talomore together as children. The world seemed a lot easier back then. Even as children, bitter enemies would sometimes have to form alliances for a common cause. It's hard to know what that would look like in these divided times."

Laraline nodded respectfully. "That sounds like something Aunt Evie would say."

Avis glanced at the woman standing quietly in the corner. "I don't believe you have met my new weaver, Lady Nashca Ortega."

"New? What happened to the other guy?"

The dark-haired woman finally spoke. "You must be referring to my cousin Shahaf. He will be back when it's spring."

Avis smiled. "So soon."

Nashca's response was quick. "That was the bargain, my sire."

"Well, you can go now, Mother Ortega.

"Yes, Lord Branson."

As Nashca headed out of the room, Laraline glanced at her daughter, who seemed entranced by the strange woman's walk. "Willet, could you excuse us? I need to speak with Lord Branson in private."

"Could I go back to the car and listen to music?"

"But it's such a nice sunny day, Willet."

"Mama, the yard is filled with so many flies because of those animal skins."

Branson interjected. "I apologize, my daughter Raven thinks she is some sort of clothing designer or something. She can be so messy. I've told her about putting her things up."

Laraline sighed as she removed her keys from her pocket and tossed them in Willet's direction. Her reflexes were on point, as she snatched them midair and quickly dashed down the hallway. There was a faint murmur near the front door that was opening.

"Thanks, Mama!"

As the door shut, the room got deathly silent. The tension of what may come out of Laraline's mouth was building. "Your eldest son, Ephron, showed up at the bar last night. He got extremely drunk, and I thought you may want to know, before you hear about it elsewhere."

Avis stood as if he were shocked but not surprised. He cupped his hand over his mouth before he spoke again. "What happened to him?"

"Your sister, Aquila, had a driver pick him up."

"She mentioned none of this to me."

"Perhaps she didn't want to alarm you."

"Thank you for informing me about Ephron. He hasn't been the same since his Meena passed. He hasn't taken her transcendence well."

"Perhaps, more time is needed to move past his grief."

"Sometimes... sometimes grief becomes a part of who we are. It fills in the empty spaces where the hollowness resides."

"What?"

Avis wiped a tear from his eye. "Nothing. Is that all you came for?"

"Well, I have a favor to ask."

"If I can accommodate, I will let you know."

"I need a place to dock Langston's boat."

"Well, that is not a problem; we have four docks along the entire Celandine port, which I would gladly let you use."

"The boat is still in Florida."

"Oh, well, that is a problem."

"I need the weekend to pick it up and drive it back here. I would come straight back."

I wish I could help you; however, I can't make any exceptions! I'm already getting a lot of blowback from the sanctuary. And it's not like I can just send someone to retrieve it. That would be just as bad."

"Couldn't you just turn a blind eye for a couple of days? I'm asking a favor."

"That's not the problem. I personally wouldn't go after you; I give you my word. However, when it comes to this situation, I am in a minority within my own house."

"You speak of the Lady Aquila?"

"There will be several eyes watching you. Waiting for a chance to snuff you and your family. I'm just being as honest as I can."

There was a slight fluttering sound from above, as a single crow dove from the ceiling rafters and fluttered down the hallway. Avis and Laraline both considered the bird, as it appeared and disappeared from out of nowhere.

Avis leaned closer to Laraline; he had a grave look on his face. "If you needed to take this trip in secrecy, I fear that will not be so easy now!"

Willet was making her way down the steps of the Branson manor when a most curious object caught her eye. She bent down and picked up a shiny metal triangle. It was a blade of some sort. Willet held up the object, finally realizing it was an arrow tip. Willet surmised it must have belonged to Raven. Supposedly, she was some all-star archer or something. She glanced back at the fence with the arrow tip in her hand. She considered the animal pelts for a moment when a ponderous voice addressed her.

"My, what strange bird has perched itself upon our steps this morning?"

Willet jerked up, startled. In the driveway stood a tall woman dressed in a black jumpsuit. The older woman wore shades and fancied herself quite dignified. Willet didn't know what to say, as it was as if the woman came out of nowhere.

"Pardon me?"

"You're Willet Swift. Your exploits at school and around town are becoming quite infamous with my niece and nephews. One would think they were discussing Oliver Twist!"

"Well, I'm not a homeless street urchin."

The older woman removed her sunglasses to reveal that she had but one eye. The other was covered by a shiny black eyepatch. "Are you sure, dear?"

"I see now. You must be Lady Aquila Branson."

"It appears that we have both heard of one another."

Willet noticed her expression change. It suddenly became cold and unflinching. She was like some tempered snake ready to strike. "So, I ask again, why are you here, on my porch?"

Willet was speechless, as she didn't know exactly how to respond. She was about to give some passive-aggressive quip back when she heard her mother from behind her.

"She is with me."

Laraline was suddenly in front of her daughter, almost blocking her. There was a level of rage under the surface of her mother's voice. Willet recognized this from the previous night.

Aquila took a step forward, closing the distance between her and the visitors. "And why are you here?"

"I was talking with your brother."

"What on earth could you have to discuss with Lord Branson?"

Laraline was glaring at Aquila intently. "None of your business, sister."

"You will address me as Lady Branson."

"Lady Branson!"

Aquila, Laraline, and Willet all looked back toward the house. Nashca was at the front steps calling again. "Lady Branson, Lord Branson requests your immediate presence!"

Aquila looked back at Laraline. She was about to speak when Laraline decided to end the conversation. "Your master calls."

Before Aquila could respond, Laraline hurried into the car. Willet was close behind. They could feel Aquila's eyes on them, even as they started to back up. Aquila stood glaring at the Impala as it made its way out of the driveway and down the road. Her breathing was labored as she struggled to contain her composure.

Nascha called her again. "Lady Branson!"

She impatiently snapped back at the new house weaver. "I heard you the first time!"

"Has someone gotten up on the wrong side of the bed this morning?"

"What does that mean?"

"Use your imagination."

As Aquila ascended the steps, her eye never left Mother Ortega. "Don't forget your place, you are hired help and can easily be replaced."

"Well, we are all replaceable, dear lady!"

Aquila stomped past Nashca in a huff. Her heels clacked across the gold and black marble floor. By the time she had reached the study, she found Avis near the window. He was watching the Impala as it drove down the road.

Aquila headed to the bar and fumbled through glasses and bottles until she had found a cold malt. Besides her rummaging, the room was silent. Finally, Aquila cleared her throat. "Do you want a drink?" Avis had his head turned but nodded in aloof defiance.

"I can't blame you; I usually wouldn't dare have a scotch this time of morning. The contribution of the sleveen existence, fermented drink." She conceded and quickly allowed the liquid to slide down her throat. As she set her glass down, she spoke frankly. "I know she's pretty, but I don't much care for Ms. Ortega!"

Avis was silent as he continued to look out the window. Aquila finally teasingly addressed Avis. "So, it seems your guests may be planning a little road trip. How interesting?"

"How dare you spy on me in my own home!"

"Were you going to let anyone know of this latest development. I mean, if any one of them steps foot out of this town, the protection that you seem so proud to offer will be void."

Avis countered. "Let's call a spade a spade. When were you going to inform me about the whereabouts of my son last night? He is the probable heir to this dynasty, and you failed to mention he was reeling drunk in public!"

"Probable heir. Listen to yourself, you know he isn't ready or worthy to take over!"

"Don't try to turn this around, sister. Tell me what happened!"

"I had the driver pick him up from that bar in Crecheland. He dropped him at his home, and that's all I know!"

"Why do I sense there is more you are not telling me?"

"Ok, I didn't want you to worry, but no one has seen him since last night. We've looked at all his usual ...exertions. He seems to have vanished."

"So, my son is missing, and you decided it wasn't important enough to inform me. In the midst of a murder spree. Aquila, you had better hope he is indeed found and he is safe. For your own safety."

Aquila could see in his eyes, if she were within reach, he would try to kill her. He once tried to strangle her for disobeying the sanctuary. This was his own son missing. She cautiously stepped a few steps away. Avis took a step toward her, his large hands clasped together.

"Please leave, and don't return until you find him."

Aquila nodded obediently. "Yes, Lord Branson!"

Chapter 14:

The In-Crowd

Since it was exam week, classes ended much earlier. Tori had just finished her school day and was heading back to her car. She sighed blankly as she stared at the green Volkswagen bug with the broken sunroof. It had received much of the damage after the infamous fish storm last summer. It was such a cute car. As she unlocked the door, she eyed Adelie walking past her in the parking lot. Tori called her name loudly.

"Addie!"

The young girl briefly turned her head with a most curious stare. She was slurping on some sort of box beverage with a straw. She impatiently called back.

"What?"

"Where are you going? I'm supposed to take you home."

"Don't worry, I have a ride home."

"You do! With who?"

A shrill voice called after Adelie. "Come on Addie, let's go!"

Phoebe was sitting in the back of a large black convertible. Iris Van Warren was sitting in the front passenger seat, and in the driver's seat, Raven, wearing her large top hat. Tori paused. She looked at the situation, and a certain feeling of uneasiness overcame her.

"Adelie, I don't know if that's a good idea."

"Why not?"

Tori eyed Raven, who sat drumming her fingers on the dashboard without looking up.

"Yeah, why not, Ingram?"

Tori had to be careful. She was fortunate enough that Raven pretty much left her alone. Some of her peers weren't as lucky. Raven and her flunkies, whom she dubbed her court, consisted of the most popular girls at Talomore. They targeted those whom their leader deemed below her. This, of course, meant half the school.

It was no mystery that, because of the Adler family lineage, Raven had started to harbor a subtle hatred toward Willet. This was exasperated by the fact that her older brother Jonas seemed to be enamored of the wildly eccentric outsider. The very idea of allowing Adelie to join them could only be seen as some subtle act of aggression.

"Stay away from them."

Phoebe snickered. "Keep out of this, Tori!"

"Why don't you make me, Phoebe?"

Raven finally looked in Tori's direction. She reminded Tori of a Cheshire cat with her mischievous smirk. "Don't worry, we're just going to have a bit of fun."

"Adelie, don't get in that car."

Adelie was finally irritated. "You're just like Willie. Stop telling me what to do!"

Raven chimed in. "Yeah, perhaps she wants to make her own decisions."

"Adelie, these girls are not your friends."

Adelie stood her ground defiantly. "And you are?"

Phoebe snapped. "Buzz off, sleeven."

"Make me buzz off!"

"Raven, do I need to teach this sleeven a lesson?"

Raven had a devilish grin as she softly responded. "Perhaps later. Adelie, get in the back seat next to Phoebe."

Adelie did as she was instructed. As soon as she had complied, Raven floored the gas. The car jerked back violently. Raven looked like a maniac as she almost did a donut in reverse. The car stopped for a brief moment as Raven got her bearings. Tori and Raven's eyes locked momentarily. Raven, in that moment, seemed completely demonic as she floored the gas.

"Don't wait up!"

The convertible spun out of the parking lot and down the road. Tori watched as all four girls waved their arms high as they screamed in delight. Tori stood with a lump in her throat.

"This is not good."

Chapter 15:

Pick-up at Moonlight Inn

Ephron was standing on the curb waiting when Kestrel drove up. Gavin pressed on the horn, so he would know it was them. Kestrel rolled down the window.

"Hi Ephron, so nice to see you."

Ephron looked curiously at the strange girl with a large bubbly smile. He uncomfortably nodded back. Gavin got out and helped him put his travel pack and clothes in the trunk. Ephron leaned into Gavin nervously.

"Who is that driving?"

Gavin smiled proudly. "That's Kestrel!"

Ephron had a blank look on his face. "Who?"

Gavin broke into uncontrollable laughter. "Classic."

Ephron looked even more puzzled. Gavin patted his older brother on the shoulder. "I think you two have some catching up to do."

Gavin quickly climbed into the back seat. He stretched out across the seat and posed Ephron the most obvious question.

"What in the world are you doing out here?"

Ephron still had the semblance of a hangover as he mumbled impatiently. "I don't want to talk about it. I just want to get back to town, away from this place."

Ephron could feel his fingers shaking. As the car pulled out of the parking lot, Kestrel looked at Ephron with a big smile.

"It's been such a long time!"

"Really?"

Ephron was trying to humor this strange girl, but he had no idea who she was. With the current situation, he wasn't in the mood for her flirting and pleasantries. *What exactly had happened? Was he with someone, or did he imagine everything?*

Kestrel began again. "Do you still like brownies? I remember you used to love brownies."

Ephron finally relented. "Excuse me, who are you, miss?"

"You don't remember me. Oh, how embarrassing."

"I'm sorry, I really don't."

"It's Kestrel Faulkner. We dated in high school."

"Oh yes, you're the headmistress's younger sister. I remember we went to dinner a couple of times."

"It was more than a couple of times. We were exclusive for almost two months!"

"Yeah, my mother was fond of you."

"I liked her too; she was so sweet and so beautiful. She said we made a great couple."

Gavin interjected from the backseat. "It was such a sweet and enchanting tale."

Ephron was visibly irritated but pretended not to hear. Instead, he tried to focus his efforts on trying to derail Kestrel's obvious interest in him. "Well, she is dead now, Kestrel!"

"That was so sad!"

"You know, I got married a few years ago."

"Yeah, she died too. I read about it in the paper recently."

Ephron looked uneasy as she candidly spoke. "You know what I was thinking? Perhaps we could get a cup of coffee and discuss things; it might make you feel better."

"I doubt it. Look, Kestrel, I appreciate your help today, but this is not a good time."

"I understand, this is not the best time."

"Exactly, you understand."

"Perhaps tomorrow would be better?"

Ephron winced as she grinned at him like a hopeful child. He glanced back at Gavin, who was laughing inside his hand.

Chapter 16:

A Knight in Distress

Jonas was walking home, hoping that it wouldn't rain. No one had remembered to pick him up, which was just as well. After the incident with Willet, he was in a bad mood. It was just one more reason to hate school.

He was peering at the approaching clouds, wondering if he would make it back home by curfew. It would be close. Suddenly, he heard the sound of screeching tires behind him. He impulsively darted out of the road as he turned around to face the green Volkswagen that pulled up beside him. The driver rolled down the window and called to him.

"Where have you been, tree boy?"

Jonas caustically responded to Tori. "Avoiding Volkswagens."

"Have you seen Willet?"

I think it's safe to say that I won't be seeing her anytime soon."

"Well, she needs your help!"

"No, she doesn't!"

"What are you talking about?"

"She made it clear she wanted me to stay far away, because I'm a Branson."

"Look, Raven has her sister Adelie!"

Jonas's expression suddenly changed. He thought about his altercation with his sister. "Where did they go?"

"I was hoping you would know."

Jonas grabbed his book bag and quickly hopped inside Tori's car. "Well, I have an idea, but we've got to hurry!"

"Where to?"

"Drive down to Martin Bridge!"

Tori shot off in a blaze, kicking up dirt as they sped down the road. Tori was almost in a panic as she struggled to maintain a normal speed. "So where did they go?"

"Well, Raven likes to bow hunt at the edge of the Greywood."

"What does that have to do with Adelie?"

"Don't ask!"

"Too late, I already did!"

Instead of responding, he nervously barked at Tori. "I need you to drop me off when we get to the bridge, then go find the constable."

"Why?"

"It's getting dark, and the Greywood is not a place to be after dark!"

"Are you sure you can find them?"

"I have pretty good eyes."

"What?"

"Are you sure Willet won't get pissed because you involved me? I mean, she made things pretty clear how she felt."

"You idiot, don't you know anything?"

"What are you talking about?"

"She is like so into you, it's so obvious!"

"What?"

"Why are boys so clueless?"

Just hearing the words (Willet and into you) gave him a queasy, warm feeling in his stomach. The feeling didn't last, as the Volkswagen finally approached the bridge. Almost instantly, they saw Raven's black convertible parked on the other side of the bridge against the edge of the guard rail. Jonas quickly hopped out just as Tori parked the car. The road was like a tree tunnel as gigantic, tall cypresses hovered over the road on both sides. The sun was practically nonexistent here.

As Tori stepped out of her driver's door, she noticed the strange silence immediately. An eerie feeling overcame her. She couldn't explain it exactly, but it seemed to be coming from the trees themselves. A few of the branches swayed, almost beckoning to her.

"This place is so creepy."

Jonas was now standing on the railing, peering below at the dark underbrush. He was about to leap down when Tori called after him. "Wait, what do you think you are doing. You'll fall and break your neck."

Sometimes it was easy to forget that Tori was sleveen and had no idea what he and his family were. Jonas looked down over the bridge. "This is where she took her. It's a quicker way to the cat clearing."

"Cat clearing? What is going on, Jonas?"

Jonas dismissed her question. "There is no time to explain. Just hurry, bring back help."

The urgency on his face caused her to hop back in her car and crank up. She stuck her head out the window and called out to him. "How do we even find you guys again?"

"Come right to this section of the bridge; we should make it back to this very spot."

"Please, be careful, Jonas."

"Thanks. You had better hurry."

Tori veered her bug back toward town. As soon as she was out of sight, Jonas took a deep breath. He allowed his large brown wings to bloom wide as he dove off the bridge into the underbrush below.

Chapter 17:

Ravens Court

Raven led her subjects down a long winding pathway into a clearing. The grass was unusually tall and thick on either side. At one point, she broke from the path and veered into the dense underbrush. The others stared, puzzled, before they all followed her lead. Soon, all four girls were wading into the sea of grass. Adelie held her breath as the blades seemed to creep up around her waist.

Raven had put a distance between them, yet Adelie could see her large bundle strapped to her back. She pulled it out of the trunk of her car when they first arrived at the bridge. Adelie was now curiously staring at the bundle, wanting to ask what it was. Phoebe was rambling about some massive party that she was going to throw. Iris was close behind, giving the necessary hmm's and aaah's.

Of all the girls, Iris was the most relatable to Adelie, probably because they both shared human blood. Because of this, she also wasn't privy to faigal secrets. This was where the similarities ended, though. Iris was, in some respects, just as spoiled as the others. She came from old money and seemed very bored. Adelie tried to strike up a conversation, but it quickly devolved into a series of whatever's and half-hearted wows.

Raven was several feet ahead of the group, inside her own head. She peered about the woods cautiously, as if she were hunting for something. After several minutes of following her deeper and deeper into the ocean of trees and tall grass, Adelie inquired.

"What are we doing, Raven?"

Raven peered back at the young girl with a mischievous grin. "Adelie wants to know what we are doing. What are we doing, Phoebe?"

Phoebe had her arms folded with a deep grin. "Who wants to know?"

Raven teasingly responds. "Adelie does!"

"I don't know, what are we doing, Iris?"

Iris gave a dismissive grunt. "Aren't we walking?"

Raven, unhappy with her response, snapped at her group. "Silence!"

They all complied. Silently, they followed their leader across strange, bizarre weeds that seemed to swallow their legs as they moved through. Adelie repeated her inquiry.

"Where are we going?"

Raven put her dagger-like nail to her own lips. "That would be telling."

Raven's response left her cold and concerned, so much so that Adelie began to think of snakes. The grass was so tall, they could very well run across snakes. Her footfalls immediately became more deliberate and slower. She suddenly voiced her concern.

"What about snakes?"

Raven was dismissive. "What about them?"

"I mean, couldn't snakes be hiding in here, below our feet?"

Raven sneered. "Are you afraid of the woods?"

Phoebe echoed. "I don't like snakes, Raven."

Raven mumbled. "There aren't a lot of snakes here!"

Addie expressed disbelief. "Why not?"

"Because this is not ordinary grass, this is a licweed field. How else do you explain grass growing this tall in all this shade?"

"Licweed?" Adelie was persistent. "You still haven't answered my question. Why aren't snakes in this grass?"

Raven impatiently sighed. "Smell the grass."

Adelie plucked a piece of one of the stalks and put it to her nostrils; almost immediately, she recoiled in disgust.

"It stinks!"

Raven laughed. "Snakes don't like the scent either. It does provide the perfect coverage for hunting."

"Have you been in here before?"

"You're afraid?"

"Well, isn't it supposed to be haunted or something?"

"These are enchanted woods."

"What does that mean?"

"It means the woods themselves are alive."

Raven gently beckoned for Adelie to join her. "This way, young Adelie!"

"I hope I don't ruin my clothes."

"I also love clothes. Especially bold fashions, as does everyone here. That's why you have been selected for this expedition today."

Phoebe smiled. "I love clothes!"

"Shut up, Phoebe, I was talking."

"Sorry, Raven."

"As I was saying, early textiles employed more organic methods of dress. How I do love the old ways."

Adelie looked confused. "I don't understand."

"Well, I am currently designing my own modern take on a fur coat."

"So you're making a fur coat from scratch?"

"I'm almost done, but I seem to be temporarily light on the necessary fabric to complete my creation."

The girls followed Raven, and before long, Adelie noticed that they had reached an open clearing. They were back on the path. This made Adelie overjoyed. She was sure the others felt similar, judging by their expressions.

Raven spread her arms out. "I designed my entire look, which I'm currently wearing."

Iris and Phoebe both began to clap at this proclamation, which Raven quickly responded to.

"Shut up, already!"

Adelie looked at her curiously. "So, you need more animal fur."

"The correct word is animal pelts."

"So, you're hunting animals?"

Raven corrected her. "No, **we** are hunting animals!"

Adelie was suddenly very uneasy. She didn't really want to go out rummaging the forest for fox, deer, or whatever creatures Raven wanted. All she was hoping for was a day at the beach, where Willet wasn't the center of attention, one of those exclusive events where she wasn't someone's little sister. It seemed as if everyone liked to fawn over her; poor little Willet this, poor little Willet that.

Here she was hanging with the coolest, most popular girl in school, yet all she could think about was wanting to be somewhere else. She looked back at Iris, who was standing by a nearby tree with her arms folded. She didn't seem so happy either. It was hard to tell with Phoebe. She seemed to agree with whatever Raven wanted. Addie wondered if sometimes Phoebe really didn't want to but was too afraid to say.

Adelie was about to confess that she just wanted to go home when Raven hollered out in excitement. "Yeah, we are here."

"Where?"

"Our destination, silly."

Adelie looked around her and felt a bit perplexed. All she could see was the remains of a wooden fence in the middle of the clearing. The country-looking structure was old, faded, and partly covered in ivy. The trees of the forest were now surrounding them, save for the narrow path and the patch of space they now stood in.

Raven quickly knelt, removing the bundle from her back and unwrapping a long crossbow. Lifting her weapon high, she stood erect, carefully scanning the various branches.

"My grandfather used this crossbow to shoot a gromnik in these very woods."

"A gromnik? What kind of animal is that?"

"Well, it's large and hairy like a grizzly bear, and it has two great antlers that stick out from the sides of its head. Some ancient cultures use the term wendigo."

"You're not really serious?"

"Stop talking, you're messing up my concentration."

There was a deep swooshing sound as Raven released an arrow into the air. It cut through a section of branches until there was a squeal. Adelie watching in horror, as the arrow returned to earth with what appeared to be a squirrel attached to the end. The arrow had pierced its head and the weight of its limp body, along with gravity ,had brought the arrow out of the tree. Both arrow and prey fell some twenty yards in front of them into the ocean of grass.

Phoebe clapped. "Nice shot!"

Raven glared back at Phoebe. "Silence, idiot, you're going to scare them away."

"You got the squirrel."

"That was just a demonstration for Adelie."

"You didn't have to show me."

"Yes, I did. As our guest, you will have the honor of using the bow first. Father had this especially made for me. It has up to 180 pounds of pressure."

"You want me to shoot a squirrel with that thing?"

Raven pointed proudly ahead at the broken fence railing. Adelie had to squint to see exactly where she was pointing. On top of the railing sat a rather large brown cat.

"That today's target!"

Chapter 18:

Search Party

Constable Fletcher spent several minutes trying to calm down Laraline Swift. He tried to explain to her that a person has to be missing for several hours before they are actually considered missing. However, after her exchange with Lord Branson, she was a bit inconsolable.

"Look, she is still only 15 years old, Constable."

"Ok, where is she usually at during this time?"

"At home, with her family."

Willet hugged her mother, trying to calm her while trying to remain hopeful herself. The last time she saw Adelie, she had gotten into Tori's car that morning. Her teachers had confirmed she was at school. Beyond that, there was not a lot of information.

Laraline exclaimed. "They had exams today, so she was supposed to come right home after the fact."

"Well, I will have my squad car scan the area around the school and your home."

"Great, the two places I know my Addie isn't."

Fletcher snapped his finger, as if he had an idea. "Does she have any friends with whom she may have gone off with? I assume her sister may know."

Willet was on the spot. To be honest, she had been so caught up with her own issues, she never really considered what things were like for Addie, much less anything about her social life.

Constable looked to her directly for answers, but nothing came out but useless denials. "Well, I don't know much about that."

Just as things had trailed off into a kind of dismal standoff. Tori Ingram pushed through the double doors of the station. She was drenched in sweat, out of breath, and shaking. She staggered across the floor and dropped to her knees as she forced out a single word.

"Adelie!"

Laraline ran to Tori, who was on the ground heaving. "You saw her? Where is my Addie?"

Tori was still panting, trying to catch her breath. "Greywood!"

It got painfully quiet as the room processed the location, then Willet and Laraline flipped. Fletcher headed to Tori's defense, as she was being bombarded with questions from Laraline and Willet, still trying to catch her breath.

Fletcher touched the young girl's shoulder. "Ms. Ingram, are you hurt?" All she could do was shake her head.

"You said that Adelie is in the Greywood?" Tori nodded.

"Are you sure she is in the woods?"

"Yes, I'm sure!"

"Did you take her there?"

"No, I tried to stop them, but she got into her car."

"Whose car?"

"Raven Branson!"

The deputy sighed as he looked across at the constable. The constable nervously continued.

"What does Raven have to do with this?" The question lingered unanswered as Tori suddenly became more assertive.

"We don't have much time before it gets dark!"

The constable didn't push her to answer, out of respect for Adelie's family, who were intently listening to every nervous detail.

"Ok, do you know at what part they entered the forest?"

"Yes."

The constable was quick as he pointed to his deputy. Get a couple of firearms and a couple of vests. He turned back to Tori, who was now standing.

"Are you able to show me?" She was much better but still nodded.

"You'd better ride in the back. Mom and sister, I would tell you to wait here, but I know you won't, so you come, but stay out of the way. Travis, you ride shotgun." They all headed out to the parking lot.

Chapter 19:

Without Warning

Raven whispered in her ear gently. "You have it in your sights, Adelie."

The young girl stood trembling as she eyed her prey. The cat had noticed the group staring at her from a distance and was intrigued. It gently purred as it studied them. It had golden yellow eyes that seemed to sparkle in the fading daylight. Suddenly, it leaped off the fence, into their direction. Adelie was frozen as she watched the cat move a bit closer.

"What are you waiting for? Shoot!"

"No!"

"What did you say?"

"I can't shoot a harmless cat."

"Cats are far from harmless, especially the ones here."

"It hasn't done anything to me."

Raven shook her fists in frustration. "I thought you wanted to be one of us! You are truly pathetic!" She quickly snatched the crossbow from Adelie's hands. The young girl fell to her knees, crying.

Phoebe giggled. "I told you she was a baby!"

Adelie snarled back. "Shut up!"

Raven glanced over at Phoebe with her arms folded, grinning. She walked over to where Phoebe stood. With a slight grin, Raven shoved the crossbow into Phoebe's arms.

"You show her how it's done."

Phoebe's grin turned sour. "What?"

"You heard me, shoot the cat."

Phoebe had the same expression as Adelie a few moments earlier. "You want me to shoot it?"

"Did I stutter?"

Adelie lifted her teary eyes and barked at their leader. "Why don't you do it yourself. You're the one who wants it dead."

Raven's eyes flared with rage. "What did you say to me, lek?"

Adelie answered with a bit more confidence. "Did I stutter?"

Before Raven could respond, a voice from the path behind them called out. "What is this, another glorious battle for the kingdom?"

For a moment, Raven seemed uneasy. "Hark, who goes there?"

"You know it's forbidden to kill anything enchanted from the Greywood. I guess you forgot to mention that little detail to your court."

The quartet turned to see Jonas standing before them. He stood a few feet from the clearing. His eyes burned green as he surveyed the scene. His hair was wild and unkempt, and there was an air of danger about him.

"Isn't that right, sis?"

Raven rolled her eyes at him. "You always find a way of interrupting my fun."

Jonas darted his eyes toward Adelie on the ground, wiping her tears. "What do you think you're doing, sis?"

"This is a private party; you weren't invited."

Jonas eyed the rest of the group. "It's not safe here. These are no ordinary cats; they belong to the Greywood. They are the eyes and ears of Greywood. It would bring a curse for us to spill their blood, and she knows this. However, Adelie is a bit different, right sister."

Iris moved closer. "What is your brother talking about?"

Jonas winced uneasily as he recognized Iris Van Warren. He turned back to his sister. "You brought a sleeven here? Do you know how foolish that was?"

Iris folded her arms. "What did he just call me?"

Raven dismissed him. "It's not important. He is just upset because this one's sister broke his poor little heart!"

Raven pointed to Adelie, who looked even more confused.

Jonas tried his best to apologize. "Look, if this is about yesterday, I'm really sorry I attacked you. Don't take it out on Willet or her sister."

"You should have remembered that before you started this game."

"This is between you and me."

"Everything and everyone is fair game, brother."

Adelie looked wounded. "You're using me?"

Raven flung her head around to face Adelie directly. "Do you think I would want to actually hang out with some pathetic lek freshman?"

Jonas moved closer to Raven. "Didn't you inform your court of the risks they would be taking?"

Phoebe murmured under her breath. "What risk?"

"Do they know they are traveling into Greywood to retrieve the cat skins for you? It's the only way she can finish her vest of protection. You didn't think I knew?"

Raven retorted. "Do you realize how crazy you sound?"

Adelie looked back at the cat; however, it wasn't alone. Another three cats had joined it and sat studying the group in front of them. She had to admit there was something bizarre about their behavior. Adelie was completely disillusioned as she turned to Jonas.

"What do you mean? Like... a magic vest?"

"The cats here are enchanted. So logically speaking, if one is wearing clothing made of their skin, it could give the wearer great protection here. Nothing in Greywood can hurt them. Isn't that the plan, sis?"

Iris scoffed. "What's all this about magic? Is your brother on something?"

Raven interjected, trying to downplay the information Jonas was spilling. "Don't listen to him. He climbs trees daily. He's been a bit unbalanced ever since our mother died.

Jonas concluded. "If I'm crazy, just wait till father finds out what you have been up to."

Raven was incensed. "She quickly snatched the crossbow from Phoebe and aimed at the group of cats. "Do you think I give a shit what father says?"

Adelie grabbed a handful of dirt and tossed it in the direction of the felines. "Run, run away!"

They quickly scattered back into the underbrush. Raven screamed at the top of her lungs as she aimed her arrow at empty air. "Noooo!"

Adelie sighed in relief as the cats were all but gone from view. She made the mistake of looking up at an incensed Raven. Out of some primal instinct, Raven quickly aimed her bow down at the young girl. Adelie froze. She was in shock at how things had escalated to this point. Raven's eyes were cold and unflinching.

"You think you're funny, lek!"

Jonas interceded. "Are you insane? You can't just kill her."

Isis called out, confused. "What is going on here? Are all of you guys like, for real? Someone needs to take me home now!"

Jonas tried to talk Raven down. He noticed that her hands were starting to shake slightly. She was in one of her classic meltdowns.

"Calm down, sis."

"Shut up!"

Suddenly, Raven's finger slipped, and the arrow flew forward. Jonas heard it release and quickly anticipated the strike. He dove in front of Adelie. The arrow pierced his right palm as he shielded Adelie from the blow. Immediately, the pain hit his hand and quickly shot up his arm. He leaned back, releasing a rather animal-like howl, as he doubled over on the ground.

Raven gasped at the realization of what she had just done. "It slipped out of my hand, I didn't mean to shoot."

Iris's eyes widened. "Whoa, that was insane, you frickin shot your brother with an arrow."

He rolled over with an uncomfortable grimace.

Phoebe called out. "Jonas is bleeding! This is not good."

Jonas lifted himself, plucking the arrow from his palm. He had tears in his eyes as he held out his bloody hand toward his sister. He tried his best to remain calm under the circumstances. "Raven, could you please lower your weapon?"

Phoebe stood holding herself in fear, as she realized the entire afternoon had devolved into something much darker. Raven had an almost glazed expression, as if she didn't really know what to do next.

Jonas himself didn't really know if Raven would relent. She was deadly behind a crossbow. She very well may decide to take them all. That is, if she could cover her tracks. She was so much like her twin brother Gavin. Neither seemed to deeply care about anyone, save for each other. They had this weird, almost psychic connection that was plain creepy. Regardless, Jonas was blindly counting on her shallow feeling of sibling familiarity to stop this nightmare.

On some level, it seemed to be working. She had lowered her weapon cautiously and appeared somewhat remorseful. However, she was still mulling over her options. You could almost see the gears clicking in her brain. *What was the best option to take*? With Raven, the option of murder was always on the table.

As fate would have it, the strangest thing happened to force her hand. In all the madness, no one had realized that the entire group was being tracked. The scent of blood from Jonas's wound had attracted yet another predator into the game. It hadn't yet made its presence known, as it watched and studied. Stealthily moving ever so closer, until it was in striking distance.

The attack was quick and furious. Iris was violently pulled below the surface of the licweed. Her screams woke Raven from her thoughts, and she staggered backwards beside her wounded brother. Whatever it was, it seemed unholy, human-like with its gangly appearance. A wild, unkempt mane seemed to cover its head. Adelie rose to her feet and began screaming while Phoebe held herself tightly.

Raven finally reacted, quickly aiming and firing. The arrow struck the beastly woman's shoulder. It jerked violently, lifting over the surface of the grass. It was sort of like a woman whose body appeared to be divided into sections, as if it were some insect. In fact, it appeared to have multiple appendages on either side of its long torso. Its strangely wide mouth was covered with fresh blood. It stared directly at Raven as it plucked the arrow from its arm. It then let out the most horrid and inhuman screech, as it angrily considered facing its assailant.

Raven didn't wait to see what it would do, as she fired another shot. This time, the creature anticipated her attack. It dodged as the arrow struck one of the oaks in the distance. It leaped back into the tall grass and started to slither away, as if it were a snake.

Phoebe had her hands over her head, screaming. "What is that thing?"

Jonas looked at Adelie, who was beside herself with fear. He quickly grabbed her shoulder with his good hand and shook her to attention.

"Run! Head into the clearing and keep running. Don't get off the path; it will eventually take you out of the woods.

Don't stop for anything, no matter how tired you get. Now, go!"

She was speechless but complied as she was instructed. Adelie tore past the fencing. Phoebe watched intently as Adelie disappeared down the path. As if some delayed reaction kicked in, she decided she would do the same and ran quickly after Adelie.

Iris was lying somewhere deep below the surface of the tall grass, screaming and writhing in agony. Raven couldn't see her but followed her frantic cries. She headed in the direction of the swaying ocean of grass. With her crossbow pointed in front of her, she occasionally darted her eyes about to see if the bizarre spectral demon was flanking her. Jonas stumbled closely behind, trying to quietly get her attention.

"Raven?"

She said nothing.

He whispered again. "Raven, are you ok?"

However, Raven was possessed with murderous intent. Now she had a worthy opponent. Iris was now silent. Perhaps she had collapsed unconscious or even worse. Jonas reached for Raven.

"We need to get out of here."

"You go!"

"Stop being stupid."

She was silent again.

Jonas felt something wrap tightly around his ankle and pull him backward. There was a clawlike appendage pinching his ankle tightly. Another appendage snaked out and grabbed his calf.

"It's got me!"

Raven spun around to see her brother sliding backward against his will. She hopped through the Licweed after him. Jonas was being dragged toward the fence post. Raven leaped into the air, releasing her wings, so she could see from above what was happening, as the tall grass obscured her view. Just as she reached her brother, he stopped moving. The strange ghoul had vanished. Raven had the bow aimed at her brother's feet, trembling.

"Where did it go?"

"I don't know. It just let go of me."

"Great, it could be anywhere."

As the pair scanned the terrain, it felt as if the grass itself was breathing all around them. Jonas quickly spread his wings and took to the air. He joined Raven, who had already surmised, it was much safer to be in the air than on the ground, in their current situation.

Jonas whispered to Raven. "Is it gone?"

"I don't think so, I can still smell it nearby."

Indeed, there was a foul stench in the air. It almost smelt of rotting soil. Raven squinted at the tall Licweed that surrounded them. Sections of the tall grass did seem to be heaving back and forth randomly, as if something was moving around.

Raven's eyes widened. "It's using the Licweed to hide its scent!"

"That means it's hunting us. Can you sense if Iris is still alive?"

"I dunno."

They both glided over the sea of tall grass in search of Iris. Both expected to see her bloody, mangled body lying within the weeds. However, the grass was empty. Iris was gone. Raven looked at Jonas.

"How is that possible? She was right there!"

Jonas sighed. "Its attack on me must have been a diversion."

"But it couldn't have had enough time to get back here and snatch her away."

"Perhaps, there is more than one."

"We've got to find her before it's too late!"

"I fear it may already be."

Raven shook her head in disbelief. "How is that even possible?"

Jonas glared at Raven. "Iris is not just any sleeven. She is the mayor's daughter. She will be missed."

"I know, I screwed up. Maybe they didn't get that far."

Jonas shrugged. "What if she is already dead?"

"Stop saying that, you will speak it into reality!"

"I'm just saying."

Raven took a deep breath as she rose to the top of a large Weeping Willow. She scanned the field of Licweed. "Only one way to find out."

"Raven, I don't think that is a good idea."

Before he had a chance to say anything else, Raven fluttered into the thicket. Jonas whispered after her. "Raven!"

There was no answer. He quickly flew up to the branches of a rather mature oak to get a better vantage point. Jonas rarely used his wings. At times, they seemed like artificial appendages, and he wasn't really comfortable in his own skin. As he scanned the ground from his vantage point, he could see no sign of his sister.

Raven was headstrong and focused on trying to undo the hole she had gotten them all into. With his injuries, all Jonas could do was pray that Raven would be successful and find Iris Van Warren. Someone important like her couldn't just disappear. Sleeven or faigal, the Van Warrens came from old money. They were also one of the main sleeven families that were tolerant of the Branson and Adler enterprises.

This wouldn't be the first time the twins had brought heat down on the Branson house. Two years earlier, Raven had crept into a neighbor's barn and killed several barn animals with her crossbow. Avis was still trying to make amends to the local farmer. Recently, there had been an incident involving a possible suitor who sailed in to meet with the young Branson heir. Apparently, she broke his arm after he kissed her hand. That had cost the Branson dynasty a possible intercontinental shipping deal.

As for Gavin, he reveled in his bad boy image. Especially when charges like assault, larceny, and vandalism were monthly citations received in the mail. Things came to a head when he allegedly tried to run over one of his classmates with his car. This led to Gavin temporarily having his license suspended, along with a sunrise-to-sunset curfew being instated, and a probation that he had no intention of abiding.

As far as the details of how everything went down, only their family council, Arnold Leech, was familiar with the particulars. Not even Avis knew the sordid details. When it came to Gavin in particular, the father chose to remain ignorant.

His thought suddenly went back to Adelie and Phoebe. They were in the open, tall grass, and easy prey. He looked down at his hand, which was still bleeding. He took a napkin he had in his pocket and wrapped up his wound. As soon as he felt it was secure, he leaped from the tree, extending his wings out. He felt a dull pain in his lower chest. He dismissed it as muscle pain as he was out of practice. He just hoped he wouldn't cramp up in midair. That would be very bad. He soared back in the direction of the clearing. Now that he was flying, it would be easier to find the girls, provided nothing got to them first.

Chapter 20:

Brotherly Love

Ephron listened to Kestrel blather on about fate, how healthy she was, and how she always wanted the opportunity to bear children. He pretended to listen; however, his attention had all but slipped away as their car pulled up to the entrance of his dwelling. He spied a familiar face standing at his front door.

Aunt Aquila was on his front porch and appeared to be pacing. Ephron slid down in his seat before she noticed Kestrel's car. A halo of dread overcame him. He wasn't in the mood for her mind games and flirty innuendos. He deliberately put his hand on Kestrel's shoulder.

"Hey, do you want to get something to eat? We could discuss old times."

Kestrels' eyes all but popped out. "I thought you would never ask?"

"Could you just keep driving?"

"Is something wrong?"

"Please drive, before I change my mind."

Gavin was lying across the backseat somewhere between napping and consciousness, as they drove past Ephron's home. Aquila glanced at the car, but didn't seem to recognize it, as Ephron peered back in the rear-view mirror. He let out a sigh of relief as the house got smaller and smaller in the distance. They had made it down the road a few minutes when Gavin popped his head up and leaned forward. He was covered in sweat and almost seemed near tears.

"Can you let me out?"

Kestrel slowed down in sudden confusion. "What's wrong now?"

It was the only time she had seen the young man look vulnerable, almost fragile. At that moment, he seemed like a seven-year-old boy who had just skinned his knee. He uttered a blanket response.

"I feel sick."

Kestrel slowed the car down to a crawl. Gavin moved close to the door. His hands were shaking, and his complexion was flushed. He did look unwell. Not that she really cared. She finally had Ephron all to herself. This was what she had been dreaming of for almost ten years.

Gavin quickly jumped out of the car and headed into a nearby field. He stumbled a few feet before he dropped to his hands and knees. He was acting most curiously, as he looked about the empty field nervously. Ephron recognized this rare behavior in his brother. He was bothered about something. Sometimes Gavin would nap and have nightmares. Because of this, he suffered from insomnia, though he would never admit this fact. This chronic condition could be mentally debilitating. Ephron climbed out of the car and looked to Kestrel.

"Could you wait here?"

"Sure!"

He quickly ran across the road to join his little brother. Gavin, of all his siblings, was the most aloof. From the outside world, it would appear as if Jonas were. After all,

Jonas was a bit spacey and withdrawn. However, the thing about Jonas was, he was very sensitive because he really did care. Gavin, on the other hand, truly existed in his own moral reality. Psychologists would throw around the terms sociopath and sadistic when describing Gavin's psychosis. Ephron wasn't sure what the deal was with his brother, but he knew that Gavin rarely seemed concerned about anything or anyone. However, at the moment, he seemed as if he were deeply troubled. He had a dream about something that vexed him. In an attempt to clear the air, Ephron brought up the elephant in the room.

"I gather this girl is the one you've been spending your evenings with when you disappear?"

"It's not like that. I just use her to run a few errands."

"Gavin, if you're jealous, please don't be."

Gavin dismissed his words with a wave. "Are you kidding? I'm going to ditch her as soon as I'm driving again."

"Then what's the matter? You look as if you've seen a ghost?"

"My sister is in trouble."

"What do you mean?"

"She's in peril."

"Raven? How do you know?"

"I can feel her crying out even now."

"What kind of trouble is she in?"

"The worst kind, I fear."

Ephron glanced back at Kestrel. She was looking in the mirror, adjusting her face.

"Where is she now?"

"Well, I know she wanted to do some evening hunting in the clearing."

"Hunting, you've got to be kidding. The Greywood is the last place she needs to be during a mandatory curfew. It's not like you two haven't been told!"

"Ok, mommy! This is not the time for a lecture."

"I'm not your damn mother."

"I'm well aware of that. I'm glad you finally can grasp that fact."

"Ever since Aunt Aquila came to town, you two have dismissed any rules or norms."

"Don't blame this on Auntie. It is Father who has played a hand in the current state of our family."

"Are you serious?"

"It was his blasphemous actions that caused Mother's death in the first place."

Ephron felt his growing anger. "Is that what Auntie told you? You know nothing."

Gavin snarled back. "Father is weak. He is not able to do what needs to be done. Auntie has shown me this. If it is anything, it's his inability to be the strong leader that our family needs now."

"Let me get this right. You are really going to try to find a way to blame Father for Raven's impulses?"

"Sometimes I agree with Aquila that he needs to be put out of his misery."

Ephron's reaction was swift, as he punched Gavin in the face, knocking him to the ground. "Get up, you insolent little slug. How dare you!"

Gavin licked the blood from his lips as he struggled to get to his feet. Ephron slammed his fist into his jaw again and stood over him, enraged. "Do you know how much he has given up just for you?"

"That makes him even more of a fool than I thought. When I take over, I will run things differently."

Ephron's eyes focused on Gavin. "As long as I am alive, I will make sure you never become the lord."

"Is that a challenge?"

"It's a promise!"

"You really don't want to get on my bad side, brother. I have no quarrel with you."

"Are you actually threatening me? I can't believe how much you have let that woman poison you!"

Gavin rolled his eyes defiantly. "I expected as much. Look at you. You're just like father."

"He's your father as well."

"I am nothing like him, and when he loses everything, you will rue the day you put your hands on me."

"What is that supposed to mean?"

"Never mind, there are more pressing issues."

Gavin turned his back on Ephron and headed directly into the middle of the field. He looked at the sky, checking the temperature and wind speed.

"Where are you going?"

"I'm going to find my sister."

"Alone?"

"That was the intention."

"If she is in peril, as you say, then let's both go after her, together."

"We don't want or need your help, brother."

Gavin stretched his arms out to the sky, then released his black wingspan with specks of red. They were large and muscular as they violently flapped up dust. Gavin closed his eyes and squatted down on his heels. He took a deep breath, opened his eyes, and thrusted straight into the air.

Ephron shook his head painfully, watching his baby brother heading up into the sky. As Ephron headed back to the car, he glanced over his shoulder, half expecting Gavin to swoop down for a surprise attack. Gavin, like his sister Raven, could be rather vindictive if he allowed himself. The last thing he could see was a faint image of the young faigal headed in the direction of the Greywood.

Ephron winced at the recklessness of his younger brother, possibly exposing himself by taking flight in the open sky. It was getting darker, but anyone who looked hard enough would notice a young man with wings in the air. Before he had a chance to say something, Kestrel exclaimed frantically.

"What in the world does he think he is doing? He could be seen!"

"Get back in the car, we've got to catch him before he endangers himself or someone else."

Chapter 21:

Eyewitness

Phoebe listlessly travelled on by some basic motor instinct, across the grassy field that led up to Martin Rd. It was now dusk, and the wind was quite brisk. The autumn air chilled into the rips and tears in her blouse and dress. She was conscious that she was shivering, but she scarcely recognized the road as she climbed over some bushes that lined the edge. She was now heading back toward town, and everything was blurry. The occasional headlights would sweep over her face, but she was almost oblivious, as she staggered along the long direction of her home. Without warning, an approaching car slowed down in front of her and stopped.

Phoebe pretended not to see, as she didn't have the energy to speak. The door swung open, and Constable Fletcher ran across the road.

"Phoebe, are you ok?"

Laraline hopped out with Willet quick on her heels. Having been informed of the situation and all parties involved, both mother and daughter were ready for a confrontation. Laraline was about a foot away when she saw the condition of the girl and paused for a moment. Willet didn't really care as she almost tackled Phoebe but was restrained by Fletcher.

"What did you do with my sister?"

The deputy had to actually carry Willet back across to the other side of the car. Fletcher eyed her and Laraline cautiously. "Let me do my job."

He turned to Phoebe, who seemed not to notice the mayhem that had just ensued. Laraline, recognizing the look of trauma, helped Fletcher steady the girl.

"Phoebe, can you hear me dear?"

Larraine noticed the cuts and tears on her clothes and skin. "Is she catatonic?"

Fletcher snapped his finger near her face. Her dull expression changed to sudden horror as she broke into a wild scream. "No, I want my mommy!"

At one point, she looked as if she would crawl out of her skin. Laraline assisted the officer in calming her down.

"We'll get you home soon, dear."

When she seemed more lucid, Fletcher carefully probed her. "Hun, can you tell us what happened?"

"It grabbed Iris!"

"What grabbed Iris?"

"This strange woman with wild hair came out of nowhere, and I ran."

Laraline interjected. "Did you see Adelie?"

Phoebe answered without looking up. "Jonas told Adelie to run into the clearing. I followed her, but I lost her in the woods."

Laraline clasped her hands. "Maybe Adelie got away, just as you did." Phoebe turned her head in silence.

Willet cleared her throat. "What was Jonas doing out there?"

Fletcher cut Willet off. "Let me get this straight. You said this strange woman attacked you all. What did she look like?"

"Like nothing I've ever seen. She was naked with really long hair and all these arms like a bug or something."

"You said it got Iris?"

Deputy Hal Dresden interjected. "That must be Iris Van Warren. She was reported missing along with this one about ten minutes ago."

Hal was starting to explain things, just as headlights tore around the corner. As soon as they noticed the flashing lights, there was the sound of tires screeching. A car slowed down beside Fletcher's patrol car. Hal stood erect, seeming suspicious. He moved his focus to the new car. He strolled over to speak to the driver, while the constable continued interrogating Phoebe.

"So, are you telling me that the mayor's daughter is out there in those woods?"

Phoebe quickly nodded, and the constable's demeanor changed to one fueled by anxiety. "Great, that's all we need. This is going to be a media and political circus!"

Phoebe focused on the flashing light as if lost. Fletcher continued his interrogation.

"What about Raven Branson? She seems to be in the center of all of this. Where is she now?"

"She shot at it with an arrow. I don't know what happened to her and Jonas. I just ran.

Phoebe had conveniently left out many key points that would have implicated Raven and her in more dubious activity. The constable probably would have probed her further, but Dresden returned. "Sir, that is Kestrel Faulkner in the car over here."

"Is this pressing?"

"Ephron Branson is in the passenger seat."

"Really, well, I might need to have a word with him. Wait here with her."

"Yes, sir."

Fletcher made his way leisurely over to the passenger side window. Trying to get his words together. The Bransons had a knack for being very prickly and evasive when talking to law enforcement, especially the children. So Fletcher was more than a little taken aback when Ephron stuck his head out the window.

"Constable, I need to talk to you."

"Isn't that ironic, because I need to talk to you. We have about half a dozen missing kids in those woods, including Jonas and Raven Branson."

"Jonas too?"

"So you were aware of your sister's disappearance?"

Ephron, sensing the danger of his loose lips, backpeddled a bit. "Not exactly, but Gavin said he hadn't seen her and was concerned for her."

"Hmm, where is young Gavin hiding?"

"I don't know, he was with us earlier."

"Well, make sure that he stays away from here. He's already in enough trouble. If he breaks his curfew, it's back to court for him."

Ephron suddenly grew irritated at the entire situation. "I'm not my brother's keeper."

Fletcher was surprised by Ephron's vehemence. However, in light of the family Ephron belonged to, he wasn't surprised. He took a deep breath before he continued.

"Could you relay these developments to your father and your aunt? They may be slightly more concerned."

Ephron quickly changed his mood. "Of course, Officer Fletcher. If I was rude earlier, I apologize. This situation is upsetting. I will try to locate them right away."

An image of Aquila on his porch popped into Ephron's head. He knew immediately he had no intention of going back to inform her. As for his father, it seemed that since the arrival of the new weaver, Avis was exclusively indisposed.

Fletcher nodded. "I completely understand."

"It seems as if everything has fallen apart, and it is still early.

"I wanted to ask if you two could do me a favor?"

Laraline didn't know what was being said, but she recognized Ephron from the other night. They made eye contact briefly before she looked back at Phoebe. Fletcher abruptly returned to his car to address his guests.

"They have offered to take Phoebe and the Swifts back home."

Laraline protested. "I'm not going anywhere without my daughter!"

Willet nodded in solidarity. "Neither am I!"

The constable folded his arms as he faced Laraline. "You know I can't let you stay. The situation has changed. This is the very reason the curfew was put in place. Whomever this person is who is killing our citizens, isn't going to stop unless we work together. Besides, there is a very good chance that Adelie may have made it home. According to Phoebe's statement, it seems likely she is home or on her way there as we speak. Especially if Phoebe was following her. You said as much, yourself!"

"I don't know."

"I promise you, if I find out any news, I will have someone fetch you immediately."

"That is what scares me."

Laraline sighed as she clasped her hands together and started to head to the second car that had parked beside them. The remote possibility that her daughter could be at home waiting for her was enough to persuade her to leave. Laraline put her hand on Willet's neck and gently led her in the direction of the car. Willet looked at her in utter disbelief.

"We're not just leaving?"

As Willet, Laraline, and Phoebe piled into the back seat (in that order exactly), Kestrel greeted them politely. With all the hopeful platitudes that came with the current situation.

"I'm sure everything will be ok." Laraline quietly accepted the shallow pleasantries.

Willet, on the other hand, was feeling very bitter and having trouble containing her emotions. Kestrel sent a quick glance towards Willet before making a U-turn. As the car headed back to town, Kestrel tried to engage with Willet, which was a mistake.

"So I understand you go to school with Ephron's other siblings. How are you enjoying school?"

Willet clearly remembered her last interaction with the blonde from the headmistress's waiting room. Kestrel obviously didn't recognize Willet after she insulted her. The thing about an adolescent is that they remember everyone who ever slighted them. Especially so-called adults.

"Not so much since your sister had me suspended today."

"Excuse me?"

"You are related to Headmistress Faulkner?"

"Yes."

"I thought so."

Laraline touched her daughter. "Willet!"

"Mom, I'm just saying, it's not been a great week."

It got uncomfortably quiet as Ephron scrambled for something to say to change the mood in the car. "It's ok, Ms. Swift. No need to apologize."

Ephron looked back at Willet, trying to be sympathetic. "Though we have never met, I can tell you're a very strong young woman."

Laraline smiled. "Thank you."

Willet quickly corrected him. "Oh, we've met before."

Ephron was taken aback by her blunt, matter-of-fact interjection. "We did? I'm sure I would have remembered."

"Let me jog your memory, you and your late wife were driving by in a silver Caddie. You passed me by on foot. You told her not to pick me up, because I was related to the Adlers."

Ephron's face turned red as he tried to backpedal yet again. "Well, I'm not sure it happened like that."

"I don't have a reason to lie. You know, I was really sad to hear about your wife. I only met her one other time; however, she seemed like such a sweet lady."

The mood temporarily lightened. Even Ephron almost had a faint smile until Willet added. "She seemed so lonely, though."

"What do you mean by that?"

"Were you two close?"

"What kind of question is that?"

Laraline cut Willet off, before she had a chance to elaborate, probably to everyone's relief. "So, I understand your father acquired a new weaver; in fact, Willet and I met her today."

"She is not exactly new. For the last five years, Father has secured the services of the Ortega family. They are a very affluent clan in the Sarwat mountains. All Ortega children are raised to be weavers. Because of the high demand in recent years, it is hard to find anyone who will hire out. There are at least half a dozen royal houses that have a full-time weaver!"

"Demand? I didn't realize weavers were so scarce."

"Neither did I, but it makes sense. With each generation, there is less interest in the old ways! You are fortunate to have a live-in one."

"Yes, Mother Hazel is quite a character, but she is getting old. We may have to go the route that your family did!"

"Well, Mother Ortega will serve with us till the end of winter. Shahaf will return afterward. The cycle is something like seven months on and seven off."

"That's quite unusual."

"Life is quite unusual. That's what Gavin said this morning. You know, he said Raven was in some sort of trouble."

Willet scoffed at the idea. "Yeah, right."

"Excuse me?"

Laraline pinched her daughter's knee before she could respond. Willet jerked in her seat as Laraline interjected. "Was he with Adelie and Raven today?"

"No, not all. As a matter of fact, he has spent the better part of the day with me. I was out of town on business. The moment we got close to home, he told me that something was off. He could feel that Raven was in trouble."

Willet thought about what Tori explained about how Raven had taken Adelie out in the woods, armed with a crossbow. An image of the dead cat flashed in her head. That image was replaced with Adelie lying on the ground with an arrow in her head. Willet stood over her body as her little sister looked up, puzzled.

Why didn't you save me, Willie? What happened? She shot me in the head.

While Willet was still inside her own head, Laraline nodded. Ephron proudly beamed about his siblings. She was trying to be sympathetic, even though she partially blamed Raven, in the first place.

"They're twins, right?"

"Yeah, they're the odd ones. I always thought that twins were especially strange. They seem to share a special spiritual link that only they can understand."

Willet moved slightly in her seat against the window. "Sounds creepy."

Phoebe gave Willet a sideways glance as her vegetative state had subsided a bit. The car pulled onto the drive that led to Greywood Estate. Willet noticed several lights on. She guessed word had spread of the eventful evening. A kind of queasiness filled her stomach as they entered the grounds. She could see several cars parked in front of the house. However, something felt off. Adelie wasn't here. She knew the moment they got on Blue Jay Way, after learning that both twins could be out with her sister, she grew tense.

Phoebe announced aloud. "That's my mum's car!"

Willet nudged her mother, "Ma, can I get out? I feel a bit car sick."

Kestrel heard those terrifying words that can cause any designated driver to cringe and quickly put on the brakes. "Willet, please get out and get some air!"

Everyone in the backseat jerked forward when she braked. Phoebe was back to her usual self, as she was the first to remark.

"What's going on? Oh my god, my hair!"

Willet continued. "I just need some air. I can just walk the rest of the way up the driveway."

Laraline's face wilted a bit. "Of course, dear. Just don't take too long."

Willet quickly hopped out with her book bag and slowly headed up the walkway. She let out a deep sigh as she could imagine the drama that would ensue. The car quickly sped up to find a place close to the entrance to park. As Willet looked about the darkening sky, she saw the large shadow of the Greywood to her right.

She paused for a moment and turned to face the forest. Somewhere out there was her sister in trouble. As she studied its dark contour, a feeling of being watched overcame her. It wasn't quite dark, but it would be soon. Then they would call off any search until the morning. She thought of Mother Hazel's warnings and closed her eyes in deep prayer.

As Kestrel parked the car, the front door of the estate exploded open as an assortment of characters poured down the stairwell to greet them. Sirenna and Evelyn were helping Mother Hazel down the entrance steps. Patsy pushed past Ms. Weever until she was within view of the car

"Where is my Phoebe?"

As the motley crew climbed from the car, the crowd from the house gathered. There was a sudden deep hush as Ephron climbed from the passenger seat. Sirenna cleared her throat.

"What is that Branson animal doing here?"

Laraline cut him off before he had a chance to answer. "Look, they were kind to give us a ride home."

Laraline was searching the crowd for Adelie. There was Uncle Merle, Mrs. Weever, one of the Peregrine sisters, Pasty, of course, and Mother Hazel. However, her focus was on Adelie. The last person she saw was Evelyn. She nervously addressed her.

"Did Addie make it home?"

"We thought she would be with you."

Laraline's heart sank in her stomach. She instantly regretted her decision to come home. Evelyn looked at the passengers getting out of the car. Everyone here wanted answers about what exactly was happening.

Evelyn's face appeared confused. "So, where is Willet?

"She got out to walk the driveway. She was feeling car sick."

Ephron leaned discreetly to Laraline. "Hey, I wanted to ask you something. I think I was at your bar the other day."

"I don't own a bar, I just work at one."

"Of course, that's what I meant. Well, I was there, wasn't I?"

"Yes, you were there."

"Did I leave with someone?"

"Excuse me?"

"I need you to tell me what happened to me."

"You're serious?"

"Look, I didn't want to bother you before."

Laraline was irritated. "Is that why you volunteered to take us home. Not because of any empathy. You just need a witness to help you recall your drunken escapades."

"Look, it's not like that. My siblings are out there as well."

Laraline huffed. "Ask your aunt; she came by to retrieve you."

Ephron suddenly grew incensed at the mention of his Aunt Aquila. "She did?"

He quickly hopped back into the passenger seat and slammed the door. He then beeped on the horn to get

Kestrel's attention, who was having a conversation with Uncle Merle. Apparently, the old man thought she was just dandy and was trying to flirt with her over his bourbon and rye.

Ephron called impatiently. "Let's go!"

Kestrel had a puzzled look on her face as she stuck her head in the car. "Where are we going?"

"I thought you wanted to spend some time together."

"What about your brother and sister?"

"Well, I need to contact my father. Besides, I thought you were hungry?"

Her face immediately lit up as she quickly got into the driver's seat. Laraline eyed the curious scene as a few words were spoken between Ephron and the driver. She probably wouldn't have been as irate by Ephron's questions; they were harmless enough. However, her Adelie wasn't home, and she didn't have time to suffer a drunken fool. She watched the car speed off back down the empty driveway.

Evelyn shook her from her thoughts. "Where is Willet? I don't see her, Lynn."

Laraline's stomach dropped. She didn't see Willet either. She looked down the lit driveway and the expansive lawn on either side. She was nowhere to be seen. The only thing in the driveway was Kestrel's car, as it reached the end of the drive and quickly tore down the road.

Laraline suddenly went into a panic. She ran back toward the entrance, and she peered around the large, hulking owls that seemed to be smiling down at her.

"Willet?"

Willet stood at the edge of the tree line, beside a sign that said something about trespassing. Peering into the dark maze of trees that seem to whisper her name. Willet had never really ventured into the Greywood voluntarily, as she was terrified. It felt as if she were constantly being called by the forest itself. The whole situation with Adelie felt almost orchestrated. Like some force was manipulating the situation. Dangling her sister as bait, so she would bite.

Willet felt completely responsible. If she had really been there for her family, Addie wouldn't have been in this situation in the first place. However, she was frozen with fear as she held the fire poker tightly in her trembling hands. Between the strange ghostly woman in white, the night visitors, the black cabin, and now these strange otherworldly beings called griskin, there was no reason why she should even entertain the idea of going inside, especially alone.

"Willet!"

Willet suddenly heard her mother's frantic call from across the field. She jerked slightly at the sound of her mother's voice. She needed to act, or she would never go. Willet took a deep breath and took a step beyond the threshold. Instantly, a cold breeze caressed her face, and a chill went up her spine. Well, she had done it; she had stepped inside.

From the entrance, the forest looked pretty ordinary, as far as forests went. The usual pines, oaks, and elms. The knotted roots and tangled vines were there as well. What was the big deal? Now she was here, she didn't quite know which way to go. According to Tori, they entered at Martin Bridge. This was almost the opposite end. *Now what?*

Then suddenly, out of nowhere, a pathway appeared directly ahead of her. Patches of dead leaves and feathers littered the way. She was sure it wasn't there before. It was beckoning her. However, she didn't really trust the path the woods had offered her.

"No, thank you, I'll take my own way!"

How do I find her in this place? Wait a moment. Willet reached into her pocket and pulled out the arrow tip she found at Branson's earlier. She closed her eyes as she rubbed the artifact gently. Her power was much stronger here, inside the woods.

Suddenly, she was beside Raven. Raven was alone, and she was on foot with her crossbow. *What had she done with Adelie?* She could almost smell Raven, as well as see her in her mind. The wind started to blow around Willet, whipping up her hair and clothes as she focused on Raven's location. Leaves and feathers tossed violently around her in a sort of whirlwind.

"Stop!"

Suddenly, her eyes opened, and the wind ceased. She whispered to Raven aloud.

"I know where you are!"

Willet took a deep breath as she suddenly darted down the pathway before her. As she ran, the trees and foliage seemed to part for her as she approached them. There was an eerie vibe as she could slightly pick up the faint sound of ghostly chanting as she descended deeper into the Greywood. She could hear her own heavy breathing starting to drown out any background noise as she ran faster. Her instincts told her to keep running, not to stop and tarry.

At a certain point, she impulsively veered off the path to the right and deep into the thicket. Trees and vines pelted her face as she jumped and ran across the precarious terrain. She could sense where to go even though she didn't know the way. It was as if she were being drawn like a magnet to her destination. Soon she was breathing hard, but she knew she shouldn't stop. Rage, fear, and adrenaline were starting to take over. She didn't know if he could stop even if she wanted to.

Chapter 22:

Verspa Lynn

The path was littered with leaves and feathers in assorted colors. It was like some colorful menagerie of an earthen floor. Adelie felt as if she were in some storybook. The clearing she had been informed about seemed to morph into another path that led deeper into the Greywood. At one point, the path split into two similar-looking avenues. Whatever path she eventually took led her here.

Earlier, she heard Phoebe calling after her, but she dared not turn around. Her focus was on the path ahead. Phoebe's cries had become background noise. It wasn't until she couldn't hear them anymore that she noticed the tree line seemed to be growing thicker. She kept a steady pace until she came to the realization that she was lost. She stopped walking and plopped down on the ground to catch her breath. She thought out loud to herself.

"Ok, what do I do now?"

This new path was unlike anything she had yet seen. The flooring was so thick with vibrant leaves and feathers that they were almost glowing. Adelie reached down and plucked an orange-yellow feather from the ground beside her. It was almost like snatching a flower from the ground. It even had a thin, wiry root attached to the end.

"What the heck?"

Had it been growing out of the ground? Adelie knelt and rubbed her hand over the spot she had plucked the feather just to make sure. Brown moist dirt mixed with what appeared to be blood covered her fingertips.

"Oh, gross."

She wiped her hands on her pants and stood up. She was thoroughly creeped out. She glanced back the way she had come and was surprised to see just how far she had ventured. The peculiar thing was that she didn't remember walking this far down. She quickly sprinted back until she came to yet another fork. The path diverged in two directions. Both were littered with similar bright leaves and feathers.

"Wait, this is impossible." Adelie was now very confused. She knew she didn't pass a fork like this. She was completely lost. She could feel herself becoming nervous. She closed her eyes and took a deep breath. *You've got to relax and calm down.* When she opened her eyes, she decided to take the right path. *It seems a little brighter.* Of course, with sunset looming, this would be a mute point.

Adelie made her way on the new trail, hoping to see anything slightly familiar. Long gone were the patches of licweed and ordinary clumps of foliage. This part of the forest felt completely alien. Up ahead, she noticed an extremely large oak tree. Its lumbering branches curled out like tortured fingers reaching for something. The tree stood about twenty yards ahead, directly in the middle of the path. She sighed at the prospect of having to pass by this nightmarish bit of nature.

Adelie folded her arms and sighed. It was at that moment she caught the glimmer of light from the corner of her eye. She darted her head to the left. Down the side of the trail, she spied a rather deep ravine. Growing down the side of the edge, the most unusual patch of green and violent flowers were blooming. She was naturally intrigued and carefully decided to detour off the path and down the hill.

It was much steeper than it appeared. In fact, a couple of times she almost tumbled headfirst. However, she eventually made it to the bottom. Red and yellow fuzzy flowers billowed under a strange breeze that drifted throughout the valley below.

Adelie had never seen such vegetation in any forest quite like this. It was as if the very forest was alive. The ravine floor was covered in lush greenish-blue moss. She could tell it was soft. She was considering taking off her shoes when she recognized the sound of running water. About twenty yards in the distance, she noticed a small stream. *This is paradise!*

Her eyes glanced over a patch of tremendously large, colorful mushrooms. They stood a few feet from the stream. Adelie was compelled to take a closer look. She didn't realize they were so huge until she was standing amongst them. They hovered right below her waist, and the circumference was like a car tire lying on its side. She carefully crept up to engage the closest mushroom.

This one was a vibrant red. She noticed that it had gills underneath its dome hood, and they were moving. She was quite startled. It was indeed breathing. It was actually inhaling and exhaling, just as she would. A large fat dragonfly landed on the top of the hood of the mushroom. The strange fungus flinched, as if it were bothered. It was quite a surreal moment. Adelie was about to touch the edge of the fungus with her hand when a very polite voice called out.

"Eve child, I wouldn't recommend you touch that brugaboo tear, they can be a bit temperamental, especially if they don't know you!"

Adelie looked around, startled. Now, a strange, alluring woman stood on the other side of the sparkling stream. The woman was dressed in an elegant black and white robe. Her black hair was long and flowing. Her skin was as pale as a ghost. Her eyes were dark and enticing. She had the aura of someone of importance. The moment Adelie saw her face, she gasped.

"Willet, is that you?"

"Excuse me. What did you call me?"

The woman's expression was odd, as if she were trying to process what was just said.

Adelie, realizing her mistake, quickly recanted. "Sorry, I thought you were someone else."

When the woman finally spoke again, she asked the most peculiar question. "Are you one of the new Eidolons?"

"I don't think so."

"Perhaps you are in disguise?"

"You mean like a costume?"

"What are you doing here, Eve girl?"

Adelie sighed. "Getting lost."

"That doesn't sound very fun."

"You said not to touch the mushroom. What will happen if I do? Will it bite me?"

"It might."

"Oh wow!"

Adelie shrank her hand away as she watched the mushroom inhale again.

"Where are you going, Eve girl?"

"Why do you keep calling me that?"

"Well, I need to call you by something."

"That isn't my name."

"What is your name, Eve girl?"

"Hey, lady, I don't know you."

"Don't tell me, you're not supposed to speak to strangers?"

"Exactly!"

The woman took a step back and cleared her throat. "Of course not. However, that does leave us with a bit of a quandary."

"How so?"

"Isn't that precisely what we have been doing?"

"I guess you have a point."

The strange woman then took a step forward. A long black boot emerged from her gown. The woman did the most elegant bow before Adelie. Her cape flowed like a gentle wave.

"Queen Verspa Lynn at your service."

"You're a queen?"

"Indeed, I am."

"Where is your kingdom?"

"Look about, as far as the eye can see!"

"The Greywood?"

"This is only a part of my kingdom. My Castle is a bit farther from here. We are at least two moons away from the castle wall."

Adelie's eyes widened. "Is this for real?"

"Why not?"

Adelie, suddenly realizing she was in the presence of royalty, bent her knees into an off-kilter curtsey. "Please to meet you, your majesty!"

"This is all academic. By what name would you like me to call you, dear child?"

Before Adelie could respond, the woman snapped her fingers. "Hey, I know a wonderful game. Suppose I make up a name to call you?"

"I don't know?"

"Come on, it will be fun. Don't you like games?"

"Just for a minute, but after that, I really need to be on my way."

Queen Verspa closed her eyes for a moment. When she opened them, she stared intently at the young girl. "How about the name Adelie?"

Adelie's eyes widened. "How did you know that was my name?"

"You look like an Adelie."

"Wow, that was like magic."

"Would you like me to teach you?"

"Could you?"

"What is your surname, child?"

"Swift."

"Swift. I rather like the sound of that. It kind of rolls off one's tongue."

Queen Verspa tilted her head as she recited passages that entered her mind, so she could use the name Swift. "Winter wind came swift, as it chilled the delicate flower. The hammer was swift as it struck the old man across the face. The mother's hand was swift as the blade sliced the child from her belly."

Addie mused to herself. *Those are rather bizarre expressions.*

"Yes. I rather like the name Swift."

"Well. It's getting dark. I need to get going."

"Why don't you join me as my special guest. It's almost suppertime, and my court will be expecting me back before dark. We can discuss magic and other realities on the way."

"A royal court with me as a special guest? You don't even know me."

"Of course I do. Aren't you the one who risked her life to save my cats?"

Just as she said this, a large golden-brown cat carefully emerged. Hopping down from a nearby branch, it stood by the boot of Queen Verspa, purring at its mistress.

"These are your cats?"

"Of course, they are all my lovelies."

"How did you know about me and your cats?"

"They are my eyes and ears, on this side of the fathom black."

"Fathom black? Where is that?"

"It's the most magical place, where anything is possible. It's never boring. Even the sun itself behaves much differently than here."

"Is this where your castle is located?"

"You have so many questions. Why don't you come with me, and you can see for yourself?"

"I don't know."

"If it's not as grand as I say, then I will personally escort you back to where you belong."

"I don't know, my family would worry."

"I wish to bless you, after all, you deserve your just reward."

Adelie heard her mention a reward and started to get excited. The woman extended a black, slender, gloved hand slightly over the water's edge. It was almost as if she didn't want to touch the water itself.

"All you have to do is just reach my hand, and I will pull you across."

Adelie reached out her hand, and as the Queen's fingertip touched her palm, there was a sudden jolt of pain. It was as if she were suddenly shocked. She quickly recoiled her hand.

"Ouch, that hurt!"

She looked at her palm, and there was a deep redness inside. Queen Verspa's eyes were enchanted pools of light as she stared at the young girl. An uneasiness overcame Adelie, and she stepped away. Something wasn't quite right. She could feel it in her bones. The thought of what Jonas had told her about not stopping popped into her mind. She suspiciously grilled her host.

"How did you know I was going to be here?"

"Perhaps the felines told me where to find you hiding."

"Is that how you knew my name?"

"What's wrong, Adelie?"

Adelie suddenly felt scared. "Well, I've got to go!"

"Don't leave so soon, that would be rather impolite."

Verspa twisted her robe open sideways, and Adelie caught a glimpse of her actual torso that was hidden from plain view before. She had an exaggerated form, not unlike a large wasp. In fact, her delicate hourglass-shaped body appeared to be segmented. Her large bum seemed to extend far beyond her thighs into a kind of coned point. Even her outstretched arm seemed to veer into the painfully small joints.

Adelie was horrified. "What are you?"

"Don't be afraid, child. I won't bite."

Verspa's eyes rolled over until they were black pools of emptiness. She had no pupils. Her head arched upward as a long, serpentine tongue slid out.

"But I might sting a bit!"

Adelie didn't wait to see what would happen, as she quickly darted back up the side of the ravine. She dared not stumble this time. From the corner of her eye, she saw Verspa take a running jump across the creek. She was in hot pursuit. Adelie was quickly back on the trail from where she had deviated.

Whatever Verspa was, she would be on right behind her soon enough. Adelie tore off running back down the path. She rounded the bend and began to look for refuge. The crinkle of leaves and feathers under her feet was loud and would give her location away. She frantically looked for a place to hide. To the right of the path, she saw a massive, rotted tree trunk on its side. It was slightly covered in licweed. Perhaps it would cover her scent. She didn't waste any time.

She quickly scurried down the hill to the front of the tree trunk. She realized that it was hollowed out, and she quickly pushed herself deep within its bowels. She removed her shoes as she dug her toes into the trunk's fleshy, decomposing innards.

With all her might, Adelie tossed one of her shoes as far as she could. It landed a mere 20 yards away on the other side of the path. She then held her breath and waited. It was unnaturally silent for several minutes. At one point, she thought she had succeeded in eluding her. Then she heard a gentle humming. At first, she thought it was some landscaping worker with a leaf blower or weed eater. She was about to climb out and start calling for help, until she heard her name whispered in the wind.

"Adelie!"

The humming sound was growing louder. Even the tree trunk began to vibrate, as did the ground about the path. As the sound got louder, she could tell it was from above. She couldn't really see what it was, as she was inside the husk of the trunk. She finally realized the sound was hovering above her; she held her breath and clutched her chest. It was so unusually loud that she began to feel someone was using a chainsaw to cut open her wooden refuge.

Gradually, the sound began to fade away, as if it were moving away. She still couldn't be sure if she was gone. It was still too hard to tell. After a while, it was silent again. She still expected to see the woman's face peer down into the hollow entrance and snatch her out. She was truly afraid. *Why did she look so much like Willet?* Perhaps it was a nightmare forcing her to face her anger at her sister.

The smell of the licweed was starting to become overwhelming. She could almost feel herself getting a headache from the putrid smell. She needed air. After a while longer, Adelie pushed herself forward and peeked her head out of the opening. She took that moment to breathe in fresh air. She had to remain very quiet as she had no idea where Queen Verspa had gone. After she surmised it was safe, she crawled out on her knees. There was a gentle crinkle of leaves as she did this. She winced each time she heard a crunch. Soon she was on her feet, nervously peering around the perimeter. *Where did she go?*

Suddenly, Adelie felt a cold hand wrap over her mouth. She tried to scream, but only a muffled sound came out.

"Shhhhhh, I told you not to stop!"

Adelie suddenly paused, realizing the hand belonged to Jonas. Before she had time to react, she felt his other hand wrap about her waist tightly. He leaned into her ear.

"Don't be afraid, we're going to get you home, ok."

She nodded as if she understood his motivations. She didn't have time to react as she suddenly felt her body rise into the air. His wings carefully lifted them upward into the branches of a large oak directly behind them. They now had a good vantage point to see the area. Adelie looked back down at the ravine and across the small creek. It was empty. There was no one about. Only the memory of what had transpired was strangely intact. She absent-mindedly turned her head sideways.

"Where is she?"

"Last I saw Raven, she was chasing after that damn creature."

"Not her."

"Who are you talking about then?"

Adelie realized that Jonas hadn't seen the strange woman by the creek. Perhaps she had imagined her. Jonas was leaning lazily against the tree, his legs dangling from the branch they were perched atop. Adelie looked at him intently as she changed the subject.

"Thank you for saving me."

"We're not out of the woods yet."

"I meant earlier, with Raven. How did you know where to find us?"

"I didn't exactly; I picked up the scent of Iris."

"Is she dead?"

"I hope she is, for her sake."

"What do you mean?"

"I think it took her body. Raven went after them."

Adelie realized the entire situation was awkward. She was high in a tree with an older boy she didn't know. Jonas had his shirt off, and this made her feel embarrassed. That playground song suddenly popped into her head. *Adelie and Jonas, sitting in a tree...*

She looked away from his face. She glanced down at his hand and noticed it was wrapped up tightly in a bloody t-shirt. She could tell it had stopped bleeding. His wings were at half bloom as he balanced on the thick branch. After a long silence, Adelie asked a question she had been wanting to know for a while.

"What's it like, having wings?"

"Are you serious?"

"Yeah, I don't have any."

"Well, how old are you?"

"Almost sixteen."

"Well, you should find out sooner or later for yourself."

"Can't you tell me what it's like flying?"

"That's like asking someone, what's it like to see?"

"Excuse me?"

"It's almost impossible to describe."

Adelie frowned at his remark before filling the uncomfortable silence with another question. "How does your hand feel?"

"It hurts, but I'll survive."

Adelie looked at his sullen face. He was clammy and looked unwell. She sat up and cleared her throat with a dramatic confirmation. "If we get back alive, I won't tell on your sister."

Jonas had a queer expression. "Really, why wouldn't you?"

"Well, your Willet's friend."

"You are just as unpredictable as your sister."

"You like her, don't you?"

Jonas's expression changed as he changed the subject. "What was that?"

Adelie looked around, paranoid. "What?"

"I thought I heard something."

"What did it sound like?"

"I don't know, probably nothing."

The reality of her current situation had returned. She thought she heard a slight humming in the distance. It quickly dissipated in the wind. Adelie took a deep breath and sighed. Jonas closed his eyes as he mumbled something about taking a nap. That was when Adelie noticed that his stomach and pants were also soaked with blood.

"What happened? Why are you covered in blood?"

"The arrow should have been a clean through shot, but I guess my stomach got in the way."

"My goodness, that's not good. Why didn't you say anything?"

"I thought it was just a cramp. I guess I was greatly mistaken."

"I would certainly say so!"

"Let me just rest for a few minutes, I'm pretty tired."

"That's cause you have a frickin' hole in your stomach and you're bleeding out. We've got to get out of here, like now, or you're going to die."

"Ok."

"You've got to get up."

"Ok."

"I mean, like now!"

"Fine, I'm up!"

Jonas lifted himself and hacked up a bloody loogie. An instant feeling of nausea overcame him. He stumbled forward, trying not to dry heave. The feeling passed, and he lifted his sweaty face.

"See, I'm much better now."

Jonas reached out toward Adelie. The image of the bloody winged faigal startled her.

"What do you think you're doing?"

"Fine, then get behind me and climb on my back."

"You can't carry me in your condition."

"Look, I'll be fine. Besides, I'm the one who has wings."

"Are you sure, you don't look so good?"

Jonas stumbled on his knees, allowing his wings to stretch out. He was breathing hard as he looked at Adelie. "Would you rather walk down there?"

"Are you sure, I'm not too heavy?"

"About how much do you weigh?"

"About 93 pounds."

Jonas had a skeptical gaze as he considered her answer. "Really?"

"Shut up!"

"Never mind, just climb on my back and wrap your arms around my neck, with your fingers locking your palms. We wouldn't want you to fall and break your neck."

Adelie did as she was instructed. She wrapped her arms around his neck as she straddled his back. The feathers tickled her chin, so she had to turn her head sideways. Jonas closed his eyes and took a deep breath. As his wings began to fan the air and create enough wind, he leaped headfirst into the air.

Chapter 23:

Tori's Stand

"What do you mean, you're leaving? It's only been about an hour!"

"It's getting dark, we may need to call it a night. We'll start back at first light. It's almost impossible to find anything out in those woods at night."

Tori clenched her teeth. "You're afraid?"

Fletcher checked his gun in his holster. "With good reason, missy. Someone or something is out snatching people into the middle of nowhere. I have seen a lot of strange things here, in and around those woods, and the one thing I have learned is to have a healthy respect for nature."

"Constable Fletcher, we came to you for help. I gave my word that we would be waiting for them when they returned."

"A promise to a Branson, to retrieve an Adler. Now I've heard of everything!"

"Her name is Swift!"

"I call a spade a spade!"

"What do you have against them?"

"Look, I understand, they're your friends. If it were any of the other families in this town, I might be more sympathetic."

"I don't understand. That's his sister out there as well."

"Doesn't that seem strange?"

"What am I missing?"

"You don't want to get mixed up with Raven: vandalism, aggravated assault, animal cruelty…"

"Jonas isn't like her."

"No, he is a different type of crazy. Rumors about this Jonas haven't escaped my ears. Even if they aren't true, he has issues. That kid has a file as long as my arm, with multiple suicide attempts, dating back to when he was 11 years old. That family is messed up, all around. Then there is your new Adler friend."

"Wait a minute!"

"I know you're friendly with this Willet Swift, but ever since she came to town, there has been mayhem with her flagrant disregard of authority and norms."

Tori jumped to Willet's defense. "Those are headmistress Faulkner's words!"

"Just yesterday, it was I, not Mrs. Faulkner, who found her sneaking around a fresh crime scene, when she should have been in school."

"Is that all, Constable Fletcher?"

"All I am saying is, Tori, you're a good girl. You need to watch the company you keep. One look at her and I can see she is an Adler. The enmity between those two families has caused so much grief in this town. Somehow, I feel like this is just the beginning of something else."

Tori now had her arms folded. She was rolling her eyes at the constable's sudden outburst. He knew it wasn't very unprofessional, as soon as he said it. He tried to walk it back immediately.

"Having said that, I made a promise to serve and protect. I am out here because of a missing child and a distraught mother. That's my job, plain and simple. That is not your job to be out here."

"So what exactly are you getting at, sir!

"Tori, your presence here hampers my ability to do my job. Besides that, if your father learned that you were involved with a police investigation, I don't think he would be none too happy!"

"Please, constable."

"I need to get you home."

"Can we just wait another ten minutes, please?"

Fletcher could see sincerity in her tearful eyes. "I tell you what, we will wait another twenty minutes."

Chapter 24:

Mortal Adversaries

The trees curved inward, creating a sort of woven tunnel that was unseen from above. As Raven descended deeper down the path, the very ground began to change into streams of fine silt and what appeared to be thick webbing. Patches of white silk were starting to become more prominent the further she went. At one point, the entire flooring and walls were completely white and fuzzy. She could still smell that odd scent of the creature that had taken Iris away. It was really strong here. She knelt and touched the ground with her fingertips. As she lifted her fingers, several strands of silt remained attached to them. It was gooey and sticky. She peered around the turn and could see that the tunnel was actually starting to veer down below the surface of the ground. She took a deep breath and lunged forward into the dimly lit cavern below.

The air was instantly putrid with the forgotten odor of decay. As she ventured further, a feeling of peril overcame her. She came across several large white cocoons hanging randomly along the sides of the tunnel. Raven put her hand over her mouth as she struggled to breathe. She held her breath as she used the edge of her longbow to rip open the nearest bundle. The husk of some sort of wild forest boar lay inside. She dug at the top of another wrap, exposing the petrified skull of a person with blond hair inside. Dozens of such cocoons seemed to stretch the length of the tunnel, farther than Raven could see. How could a single griskin accomplish all of this? Perhaps Jonas had a point; maybe there was more than one.

She finally exhaled and sucked in more of the foul atmosphere within the tunnel. Sudden rational thought entered her mind. "*This is a death trap, and I do not want to be here.*" She quickly turned around and sprinted back up the tunnel. Even if Iris were there, she was surely dead at this point. She was doubtful that the creature was inside by the fact that she was able to get back out. As she cleared the branch-wrapped tunnel, breathing became easier. She took several long, healthy breaths of untainted air.

She tore her way into a grove of underbrush that led to a pool. It was actually more like the dead-end of a stream. There was a thick, black, murky, swampy goop, which settled on the surface of the water. Unusually tall greenish stalks grew from the perimeter of the bog. Lumps of uneven rock and tree debris rose from the squishy ground below.

The usual sound of toads and cicadas serenaded their guest with their usual grotesque evening melodies. Raven carefully tiptoed across a muddy log and rock formations that grew from the slime. She spied several large brugaboo tears several yards to her left.

Even from this distance, she could hear the inhuman breathing from the grove of fungus in the distance. As she made her way to the other side of the bog, she let out a sigh of relief. she realized that the lair was on the other side of the bog now.

She turned to glance back at where she had come, when suddenly a clawed hand dug its fingers into her scalp. A second hand snatched the windpipe around the young girl's throat. Her top hat immediately tumbled off her head into the mud. Her crossbow dropped to the ground as well. A slightly familiar voice hissed into her ears.

"What did you do to my sister, you psycho?"

Raven reached behind her and, using her weight, tossed her assailant headfirst into a patch of greenish stalks. Willet didn't stay down, as she quickly rose to her feet. Her large black wings violently bat at the air about her. Raven straightened her posture. She was in complete shock, holding her throat. She struggled to suck the air back into her lungs as she tried to respond.

"Nothing."

Before Raven could finish her response, Willet attacked again.

"Liar!"

This time, Raven was ready, as she countered Willet's attack. Raven leaped up in the air, allowing her own black wings to unfold. The winged girls slammed into one another. Each grappling and wrestling as they ascended midair. They hovered a few feet slightly above the actual bog, as they tumbled against each other's will. Raven grabbed Willet's leg and flung her sideways into a series of branches into a nearby Cyprus tree.

Raven then quickly dove down to retrieve her crossbow. Her hands quickly pulled it from the muck and tried to load it before her adversary could return. However, before Raven could look up, an unusually large Cyprus branch slammed into her chest. Willet held her ground as she watched Raven and the branch tumble backward several feet into the black muck. Willet spied her fire poker lying at the base of a nearby tree. She darted like the wind to retrieve her weapon. She quickly slid across the slimy mud. Unfortunately, a heavy boot stepped on her fingers as she clawed for her weapon.

Willet looked up into the crazed eyes of Gavin Hughes Branson. His white bleached hair clung to his scalp like a helmet. As their eyes met, a twinge of fear overcame her. She recognized that same look from the night he killed Ryn Stowe. He grinned coldly.

"Hello, Willet."

Gavin then averted his attention to the pool where his sister disappeared.

"Raven, are you ok?"

She slowly popped up, looking a bit disheveled and stunned. She nodded instead of vocally responding. The most likely reason was due to the fact that she was still hacking bits of algae and sludge that had made its way into her throat.

Gavin grinned at his sister as she started to crawl back out of the marsh. "So, is this little one giving you a bit of trouble, dear?"

No sooner had he uttered the words than he suddenly felt the heel of Willet's converse slam into the bridge of his nose. Willet was not going to wait to be double-teamed, as she orchestrated a direct upward kick into Gavin's face. He stumbled backward, almost losing his footing, enough to release Willet's fingers from his shoe. Willet snatched her poker and rolled back on her feet. She steadied herself as she quickly moved backward a few feet.

Now, both Branson twins were in her view. Raven to the right end of the bog, and Gavin to her left, rising back to his feet, holding his bloody nose. Willet responded to Gavin with a mock impersonation of his rather pompous way of talking.

"Just a tad bit of trouble, darling!"

Gavin removed his hand from his bruised snout. A stream of blood poured from his nose. He looked absolutely pissed as he faced Willet. Probably realizing the futility of her situation, she added.

"Look, this is between me and her. Though there are several reasons you should go down, right now, Raven and I have unfinished business."

Gavin reached into his coat and unsheathed his crissum. The shiny blade was about the size of a machete, but twice as sharp.

"If your business is with Raven, it's my business now, lek."

Willet cleared her throat as she steadied her fire poker. Raven wiped the remaining goop off her longbow as she loaded an arrow. Her eyes were fiercely glaring at Willet. Willet backed up a few steps as both Bransons started to advance on her.

Willet noticed the blood on Gavin's lips as he got closer. "You may want to wipe that off your face. It's probably going to stain your clothes."

"Keep talking. I'm going to enjoy this."

"Yeah, we both know how you get your kicks."

"What are you talking about?"

"I know what you did to Ryn."

"What did you say, lek?"

Raven looked at her brother. "What is she talking about, Gavin?"

Willet continued to antagonize him.

"Yes, I was there, at the bridge when you and your aunt dumped her down here."

Gavin's eyes widened. "How do you know such things?"

"Because I was at the hotel when Kestrel and you took her, bound, and gagged her. You cut her wing first, that's why she screamed out."

Gavin was a ghost as he looked uneasily at Willet.

"It was you?"

"Yes, I was the one at the door."

Gavin's wings bloomed, and he lunged at her, gliding toward her with his crissum above his head. He came down, but Willet anticipated and blocked his blade with her fire poker. Gavin was stronger, but his angle was compromised by Willet's weapon. The two were in an embrace. She locked his blade with the poker's hook extension.

Gavin considered her weapon. "What is that thing?"

Willet slid the blade from his grip and abruptly popped his wrist. The iron rod thumped his wrist rather loudly. Gavin let out a long, painful bellow as he dropped the crissum.

Willet was quick, as she kicked the blade several feet into the bog. No sooner had she done so than she saw something out of the corner of her eye approaching. She reached out and instantly caught Raven's arrow, a few inches from her face.

Willet tossed the arrow to the ground, and Raven's reaction was to stomp her foot. Willet knew that her intentions were deadly. However, she wasn't prepared to actually fight them both. It was beyond her abilities, and she knew it. The situation, like most situations in her life, was feeling desperate. There was a real fear that they would kill her and leave her body in this bog to rot.

Her survival instincts kicked into overdrive. She had to think of a way to get out of her current predicament. She had to reach higher ground. Maybe she could fight them off long enough for the police to come close. She knew that, on some level, that was completely wishful thinking and unrealistic. She looked around her surroundings in desperation. In the middle of the bog, Willet spied the large, protruding round stone covered in algae and moss.

Willet arched down and dove into the air. A second arrow just missed her as she flew upward. She glanced back. Gavin was mucking around in the mud searching for his blade to undoubtedly try to finish her.

Willet flew in a wide circle around the inside perimeter of the trees, so Raven wouldn't get a clear shot. The tree line completely surrounded the bog, so there was no easy way to fly out. She instead coasted down toward the sloped rock. Her eyes never left Raven and Gavin. She touched down on the rock's surface. Her shoes slightly squished the surface. Willet curiously looked down at the moss-covered stone. Several small, brownish egg-like bubbles covered the edges of the surface like some wacky swamp coral.

Gavin lauded the obvious. "You're just prolonging the inevitable, lek."

Willett's response was quick. "Well, at least I can take one of you Branson pigs down. Then we'll be even."

Gavin mused. "Even?"

Raven snapped. "I told you, I didn't touch your sister!"

Willet barked back. "Then where is she?"

"I don't know and I don't care, besides, it doesn't really matter now."

Gavin eyed a familiar glimmer below the surface of the pool. He knelt carefully as he pulled his sword from the water to face Willet, who was now in a defensive stance. He looked back at Raven, who was visibly upset. Not that she cared what Willet thought. There was something else amiss.

"What's going on, dear, you look troubled?"

"Before she showed up, we were attacked by a creature."

"What creature?"

"I don't know, this crazy looking woman with all these arms came at us. She was hiding in the licweed."

Willett's eyes widened. "The griskin!"

Gavin tried to tune Willet out as he focused on Raven. "What happened?"

"Jonas and I were fighting when it just popped out of nowhere and grabbed Iris and took her away!"

Gavin looked about, confused. "Jonas is here? Where is he now?"

Raven had a sudden, concerned look as if she had something to hide. She was telling the truth; she actually didn't hurt Addie, but only by default. Jonas was collateral damage, and she didn't want to advertise that small detail. She quickly dismissed the question.

"We got separated in the woods."

Willet inserted herself into the conversation. "What were you two fighting about?"

"None of your business, lek!"

Raven darted her attention back to Gavin. "Look, I tracked it to what I believe is a lair, it's right over there, beyond this stream. We just need to take care of this one first."

Willet saw a possible out. "Look, if that thing is indeed what I think it is. You can't defeat it by yourself. There is a good possibility there are more."

Raven barked back. "How would you know, lek?"

"Because I've seen it, up close!"

"You're lying, don't listen, brother!"

Gavin was intrigued. "For an outsider, you know a lot of things. Tell me more."

Willet continued. "It's called a griskin and it's some sort of shapeshifter that pretends to be a faigal."

Raven was enraged as she raised her bow. "Nonsense!"

Willett's reflexes lately were almost uncanny, as she quickly shifted her weight. This allowed the arrow to strike the rock, piercing the spot where Willet was once standing. Before Willet could counter, the most peculiar thing occurred. The rock started to quiver uncontrollably. Willet looked down at the mossy rock and noticed that the brown egg-like bubbles were all changing color. They were turning black. Willet was puzzled until she saw that a couple of the black bubbles were blinking at her.

Chapter 25:

Rendezvous on Martin Bridge.

"Who goes there?" The deputy pointed his gun at the figure climbing over the railing. "Hold your hands up and don't move."

A young woman's voice responded in fear. "Please don't shoot, we need help."

The deputy quickly raised his flashlight, and he eyed a girl covered in sweat and dirt. Her hands were over her head in compliance. Lying on the road directly behind her lay a slightly older young man who was bare-chested, barefoot, and barely conscious.

The deputy tilted his head back and called out down the road. "Constable, over here."

Fletcher, Tori, and a couple of the local sworn-in deputies came running. Fletcher was the first to react. He glanced at Tori. "Sweet mother of pearl, you were right!"

As they gathered around the scene, Fletcher stood directly over the boy. "Jonas, I need to ask you some questions?"

Adelie interrupted. "Can't you see, he's hurt! He needs medical attention!"

Fletcher cast his flashlight at the boy's bloody wound. "Jeez, he's bleeding out. What happened?"

Adelie could feel all eyes on them. This was her chance to change the direction of her circumstances. "Well, we were all attacked by a crazy woman!"

Tori leaned into Adelie. "We were so worried. Did Raven do anything to you?"

With a straight face, Adelie's eyes met hers. "No, she was trying to protect us with her arrow. Could someone get him some medical attention, please?"

Adelie glanced back at Jonas with a wink.

Fletcher quickly pointed at his deputy. "Get Celandine medical on the phone. Tell him we have an emergency."

A second deputy came running in a hurry. "Avis Branson is on his way. He just heard from Ephron about his children."

"Great! Does he know about Jonas?"

"Not yet, but apparently his other son, Gavin, is now missing."

Fletcher sarcastically mused. "But of course, it's not like things aren't complicated enough."

"Also, we have Laraline Swift on the phone."

"Good, at least we can tell her that we found her daughter Adelie, and she is in one piece."

"Well..."

"What man? Spill it!"

"She is actually calling to report her other daughter, Willet, is now missing."

Fletcher hollered out in frustration. "Why can't these people hold on to their children? This is exhausting!"

Chapter 26:

Uneasy Alliance

As the gigantic stone ascended upward to the sky. Willet tumbled off headfirst down into the muck below. She quickly lifted herself in time to see her two adversaries scrambling away from her direction.

She followed suit as she tread frantically toward the other end of the bank. As she climbed out of the water, she glanced back at the large, sloped rock. It was now about 20 feet high. It was a complete sphere now resting on four stilted, jointed legs. It resembled a giant daddy long-leg spider. From its round base, around its mossy thorax, several tentacle-like tongues sprouted from its base. They randomly grabbed at the air around its head. Large, deep creaking moans exploded from its squid-like opening.

Willet held her fire poker tightly as it finally exploded into a stream of fire. The large beast reacted to the flames. Releasing a high-pitched sound. However, it remained still, as if studying her. Suddenly, it was silent. The sound of the cicadas and toads had stopped. The strange insectoid was still. The only sound was Willet's harsh breathing. She carefully walked sideways in the direction of a small opening in the trees. At one point, she thought she would clear the distance, then suddenly the large monster quickly lunged in her direction. It expelled two long tentacles straight for her.

The first one struck the poker, and it quickly recoiled. The second wrapped its tongue around Willet's waist.

Almost immediately, an arrow shot up into the monster's belly. Raven fired another arrow into one of its bubble eyes. It jerked back slightly, dragging Willet along the shoreline. Its grip tightened to the point where she realized she couldn't breathe. As it was lifting her into the air, Willet was struggling against unconsciousness.

Gavin leaped into the air and swung his blade across the tentacle that held Willet. The crissum cut it like butter, and it creaked violently. Willet dropped down to the ground and quickly devoured the air.

The creature turned its attention to Gavin. It flung its ropelike tentacles at him. Snatching him up into the air with his feet. Raven's response was quick as she fired two more shots into its belly. Its long, stalk-like legs galloped in her direction. Its long, spider-like finger clawed at the archer, tearing into a log beside her. Raven leaped to the side to avoid its grab. She did a flip roll, then fired again. This time, she hit one of the tentacles that held her brother suspended. He dropped like a sack of sand directly below the monster.

Willet removed the quivering tentacle that was still tightly wrapped about her waist. She let it drop in the dirt. She still held her fire poker that was now completely ablaze. She glanced up at the spiderlike monster, then began sprinting across the other end of the bank toward Raven. She called out to the archer.

"Duck down, I need the high round."

Raven glanced at her. "You can't make it, it's too high."

"Just trust me!"

"Fine!"

Raven uneasily complied and arched her back down, and braced for Willet's weight. Willet did a running jump as she extended her wingspread. She took a step off Raven's shoulder and did a flip in midair as she dived upward towards the monster. The creature was preoccupied and focused on Gavin, as if it were about to strike again.

It wasn't aware of Willet's counterattack until she landed on its back again. This time, she thrust the fiery stick deep into its meaty flesh. It bellowed a series of obscene creaks and whines, as steamy yellow goo erupted from the fire stick wound.

This attack gave Gavin enough time to catch his breath, as he lifted his crissum for a ground attack. He slashed his blade through the left knuckle of its left foreleg. Almost like a tree, the creature toppled headfirst at the dismemberment of one of its appendages.

Willet hung on to the handle of the fire poker for dear life, as the beast tumbled headfirst down into the mire. For the next few minutes, it quivered, belching in pain, until it finally ceased to move. Willet took a deep breath and pulled the poker from its wound. Steamy hot, putrid white liquid bubbled out as several of the eyes closed. She stepped back from the mound, now out of breath.

"What is this thing?"

Gavin responded. "A maltid."

"A what?"

"Swamp spider. I have only read about them in stories, never seen one up close."

Raven looked at her brother with concern. "Aunt Aquila says they only exist in the Waylands."

Willet was about to inquire about these Waylands when Gavin stepped closer to her.

"Your weapon became fire. How is that possible?"

Willet mused on the fact that it didn't ignite when she was fighting the twins earlier. *Perhaps, it's only sensitive to enchanted danger.* Willet shrugged the fire glow off.

"I don't know, it just does that when danger is near."

Raven suddenly addressed her with less contempt. "Where did you get it?"

Willet quietly responded, still at the ready for a sudden attack. "Here, I found it here in the Greywood."

She saw no need to tell them exactly how she acquired it, but if they knew it wasn't from the Adler dynasty, they might be fixated on her less. Before they could ask more questions, she countered with her own question.

"Seeing as how we may need one another to get out of this place alive. I would like to offer a vertriste."

Gavin looked back at his sister, who had a curious look of surprise on her face. "A vertriste?"

"Yes."

"For a lek, you certainly know a lot about the old ways."

"Apparently, I'm in training."

"So, the rumors are true?"

"What rumors?"

That you're Witch Hazel's new sire.

"Witch Hazel?"

Raven interjected. "Yes. That old bat had Sirenna cast a spell to kill our mother. Didn't she tell you?"

"That's not true. Those are just ugly rumors, as are the ones that Lady Aquila had a hand in your mother's death."

Ravin winced. "I suppose no one will ever really know the truth."

"What's this about my role as a sire?"

Raven balked. "You don't even know that? You are a mere puppet!"

Willet responded. "I suspect you're right. My life doesn't seem to be mine, but no more than either of you."

Gavin was visibly insulted. "You dare compare yourself to me?"

"Really, this from the guy who runs out and murders your own kind for the whims of your aunt."

Raven interjected. "Touché!" Gavin looked bothered but held his tongue. Willet looked at Raven next. However, Raven was quick to answer for herself.

"And I am to remain available for breeding stock and possible marriage, if I don't ruin myself first."

It was a strange moment when the trio realized that the adults in their lives were using them like pieces on a chessboard. It was probably this brief moment of clarity that caused all parties to be receptive to Willet's offer. Gavin was quick to respond.

"So, if we are to entertain this vertriste, what do you offer?"

"The police suspect you already, Gavin, in at least two murders. However, if they come to me, they won't hear it front my lips. That is my offering to you."

Raven leaned into Willet. "What about me? What can you offer me?"

"I know you tried to murder my sister, amongst other things. I will forget that I know what you did."

"That doesn't benefit me."

"Well then, what would you like?"

"I want you to stay away from Jonas." Willet was taken aback. When Raven uttered those words, Willet was angry and devastated at the same time. At that moment, she realized her feelings for Jonas. Willet paused before responding in a cold, detached manner.

"No problem."

Willet turned her head slightly to hide her eyes, which were filling up with water. She must not let them see. She quickly wiped her face just as she heard Raven's whisper back.

"What about us?"

Willet was shocked. *Were they actually considering her offer?*

"Excuse me?"

"What do you ask of us?"

Willet stepped closer. "I thought you would never ask."

Willet pushed her dark curly hair out of her face. "A temporary truce while we are in this town."

Raven mused suspiciously. "Is that all?"

"My sister and friends are off limits."

"Off limits? For how long?"

"For the rest of this school year. It's our first year here, and we have so much to learn. We need to at least be on equal footing if we are to play this game that you two seem so insistent on pursuing."

Gavin laughed out loud to himself. "Just this year"

Willet nodded. "Of course, I wouldn't want to be civil for too long."

Raven corrected. "This doesn't mean Adlers and Bransons are to be friends?"

Willet added. "I hate your guts. Why would I want to be your friend?"

Gavin snickered to himself as he thrust his sword teasingly at Willet's throat. "You're so clever, but how do we know we can trust you?"

Willet was terrified, but put on a facade of calm, cold restraint. She addressed him without flinching. "You can't, just as I can't really know if I can trust you. Isn't that the point of a vertriste?"

Raven was already walking away toward the other side of the bog. "I grow tired of this conversation. If you wish to buy our loyalty, then help us empty the griskin lair, then we will talk, lek!"

"Ok, but let's get one thing clear. I have a name, and it's not lek!"

Raven paused and turned around as if completely irritated. She took a deep breath.

"Well, hurry your ass up, Swift, it's hunting time!"

Chapter 27:

Man Hunt

By nightfall, news hit everywhere in town. Lord Branson's large Cadillac rounded the corner towards Martin Bridge. It had been a very quiet evening when the night man interrupted him in his bedchamber. Ephron had called, explaining what he knew of the situation. Like most parents, he was beside himself with concern. Nashca discreetly put on her nightgown and left his bedchamber. When Avis got in the car, she was waiting for him.

If word had gotten out about his tryst with her, things could get complicated. Although it wasn't unusual for weavers to get involved with their masters, it wasn't recommended. It was frowned on by the Namvula but tolerated as long as there was a fruitful union. As a result, over the years, many of the great houses worked in conjunction with the Namvula to groom acceptable brides. This symbiotic relationship ensured acceptable offspring to carry on the fine faigal lineage.

However, the Branson dynasty had a rather murky history with such unions at best. Lord Augustus Branson, the grandfather of Lord Avis Branson, tried to inject his political sway over the Namvula when he impregnated a young and impressionable weaver. In the months that followed, she shared many of the sisterhood's chants and secret prayers with her new master. One morning, she was found dead under mysterious circumstances. The Namvula denied any involvement, of course. In reality, it was probably a hit orchestrated by the Namvula but carried out by the Swans. The Swans, being a mysterious group of assassins originally trained as mother sisters, but relied heavily on stealth and cunning instead.

Avis himself, since his wife's premature death, had preferred the company of a mistress. In this way, there are no expectations or demands that could be placed on him. The truth be told, he had grown unusually fond of Nashca over the years. All those moments seemed empty now, in the wake of the disappearance of three of his four children. Especially his pride, Gavin. He was the only one Avis had been grooming for his replacement.

Even though Ephron was the oldest, Avis thought that he was too easily persuaded and seemed to lack vision. He was a hard worker, yet had no idea of how to run anything. His middle son, Jonas, was too much of an individual, like his late wife. This would create distrust among the other great houses, even with the more liberal ones still in New Essex.

Raven was the unfortunate one. She was born into a society at odds with itself. A patriarchal and matriarchal power struggle defined the current government. This made her path more difficult. She was smarter and more cunning than all her brothers, and she understood how the world actually worked.

However, she desired to join Covey Elite. Avis was against this decision. In the current climate with warring houses and shifting loyalties, the Covey seemed to be expendable pawns for the whims of the ministry. Yet, the powerful matriarchal Namvula saw her birth as just another commodity to barter and purchase. After all, she was from a royal bloodline, but she had no kali to gain entrance.

The ministry had wrangled some control in recent years, mostly because currently most of the houses involved had more lords than ladies to represent them. This shifting dynamic caused the creation of such positions as patriarchal Eskar to run proceedings. In contrast, the Namvula was almost exclusively female-dominated. There were a few exceptions, but the more powerful weavers tended to be of the female persuasion.

Mayor Van Warren had assembled his sleveen forces to search the depths of the Greywood but was having trouble getting the necessary permission. Avis slowly drove down Martin Road. As his car coasted across the bridge, dozens of red and blue lights danced across his face.

Branson, understandably, had no faith in their ability. This was beyond their depth; they just didn't know it. Which was why Nashca was needed. She could retrieve most scents and even then, pick up most father dust from any faigal within at least a 3-mile radius.

As they passed by the hordes of law enforcement, Fletcher waved them down. The window slid open, and Avis stuck his head out. He could smell sleeven sweat in the air. The smell was pungent. He quickly cuffed his face with a bright blue napkin.

"Lord Branson, we found your son Jonas a little while ago. I tried to reach you, but you had already left. Your son Ephron was supposed to tell you."

"Where is Jonas now?"

"He is in Celandine Hospital."

Avis's solemn expression became more animated. "Hospital, what happened?"

"He was shot with an arrow in the belly."

"An arrow, did you say?"

Branson briefly glanced at Nashca as the officer continued. "We don't really know exactly how that happened at his time."

Branson muttered under his breath. "We shouldn't have gotten her that damn crossbow."

"What was that, sir?"

"How bad is he?"

"He was conscious. However, I'm not a doctor. I know Celandine is your family hospital, so I sent him there."

"Thank you so much for having your people transport him. Any news about Gavin or Raven?"

"Not yet, sir, but we are actively looking."

Avis nodded as he breathed in the filtered air from his cupped hand. Nashca was not as lucky as she had not had the luxury of cohabitating side by side with sleeven. She felt a wave of nausea.

"I think I'm going to be sick."

Fletcher looked puzzled at the scene. Branson explained quickly as he exhaled. "Sorry. We are very sensitive to the aura of death. The air outside is filled with that smell."

"Death? I assure you, we did not find anyone dead!"

"Not yet."

"Excuse me?"

Lord Branson spoke in an almost melancholy tone as he tried to clarify. "Some organisms that don't live as long are slowly decomposing each day. Sometimes I can smell death on them before they even realize that they are dying."

Fletcher sniffed at the air. "What animal are you smelling? I swear I can't smell a thing!"

Avis stared at him intently. "Is there anything else, constable?"

"Yeah, well, the mayor is at the bottom of the hill. I think he hired some wild game hunters to go searching."

"Aren't you in charge of this search?"

"Well, I thought I was, but I guess he is running the show now. I cannot blame him. If it were my daughter out there, I might do the same."

"Is that what all these lights are?"

"Infra-red scanners, heat sensors, and a helicopter, this is costing Meadowlark a pretty penny."

Avis looked at Nashca nervously. "Really, I see!"

"Well, maybe he will have some luck."

Nashca touched his arm in comfort. "Perhaps I should join him while you visit Jonas, my Lord."

"Where did you say Van Warren was, constable?"

"About a half a mile down the bridge. He has a platform glaring with spotlights. You can't miss it. I hope we find the rest of your flock!"

"Thank you for your sincerity!" The car quickly sped off until it was out of Fletcher's sight.

"They have been told to stay away from those woods. Those children are going to be the death of me, and apparently, everyone else in our family."

Nascha turned to Branson, who was trying to hold back visible anger. She began rubbing his back, trying to comfort the old man. "I'm sure what happened to Jonas was an accident."

"Whatever the explanation, I need you to retrieve them right away."

"Yes, my lord."

The driver slowed down to a crawl as soon as they were out of sight. Branson had him cut the lights. The car pulled to a stop, and Nashca climbed out. She was already barefoot as she peeled out of her dress and headed to the edge of the road facing the dark tree line. She held her hands out as she closed her eyes and breathed.

"I can't feel them; I can't sense any father dust though."

Branson opened his door impatiently. "We don't have much time. The last thing I want is some yah-who with a sniper rifle gunning down one of the children out of the air!"

"I'm trying; there is so much activity." Nashca dropped her hands in frustration. "Nothing, I may have to take it on the wind."

"Just be careful. They have a helicopter."

"I promise, I will find your children, my lord."

No sooner had she uttered these words than her long yellow plumage stretched outward. They were magnificent yellow wings with flecks of olive green interspersed. Her slender body extended out as if she were doing gymnastics. She stretched her long, muscular legs forward and took a deep breath. Then she sprinted across the road, before leaping headfirst into the darkness.

Chapter 28:

Secrets

Adelie was reunited with her family, and after a few hours of waiting around for any news about Willet, she went to bed out of complete exhaustion. As she lay there, the entire episode played out in her mind over and over. No one really asked her about the details of her ordeal, as she played shell-shocked. At first, she did this because she didn't really want to explain anything. Over the course of the night, she saw the opportunity. Like a spark, the idea began to form in her head. However, she had to get her story straight.

Everyone, including the police, would be grilling her first thing in the morning. Or that's what she thought, until she opened her eyes and saw Dadu standing above her in the dark. The large owl sat in the rafters of her ceiling. Its eyes blinked intently.

Adelie hopped up. "God, what are you doing?"

Sirenna was like a ghost beside her bed. "You may have everyone else fooled, but I know you're up to something."

"What are you talking about?"

"You went to bed early to construct a lie about what really happened."

Adelie stared blankly at her. She was speechless. The young girl's eyes said no, but her silence instead of denial was deafening.

Sirenna leaned forward. "Want to tell me what really happened?"

Adelie didn't say a word.

"Raven tried to snuff you, did she not?"

"Yes, ma'am."

"Yet, you are trying to find a way to protect her. Which is why you have been acting like the helpless mute all evening. So, you came to bed to get your story in order. Don't worry, I won't say a word. I do warn you, whatever ideas you have formulated, if the seed was planted out there in those cursed woods, it could bring you ruin."

All she could do was watch Sirenna stroll down the hallway. She cleared her throat. *Was she wrong in doing this? She felt so strong about it earlier.* Adelie's eyes drifted to the closed window. She suddenly thought about the strange woman who tried to attack her. She was the only one who saw her, to even know of her existence.

As frightened as she was, there was something that made her keep this to herself. Perhaps it was because it was a secret that only she had. A big secret in this new world full of secrets. Perhaps, she would hold on to this one for a while. She held her hand up in the moonlight that shone into her window. She could still feel a slight tingle from when the woman touched her fingers.

Sirenna walked down the hallway towards Evelyn, on the landing. She was so startled that she almost fumbled over her words. "What are you up to, sister?"

Evelyn eyed her coyly. "Up to? I'm never up to anything, save for the truth."

"Ah, the truth is so overrated these days."

"Even amongst sisters?"

Sirenna paused as she considered what to say, if she should speak at all. Evelyn went straight for the jugular. "You think she's hiding something?"

"It's quite obvious. I recognize that look in her eyes. That is the same glazed expression Oriole had when she first returned from the woods that autumn morning."

Sirenna's eyes seemed watery as if recalling a deep memory that she had all but forgotten. Evelyn touched her shoulder.

"Look, it wasn't your fault; you were protecting the future of this family. What do your tea leaves tell you?"

"It's more than that. I should never have agreed to let Laraline return home."

"You strike me with words as cold as claws."

"I know how much this means to you, but with everything that has transpired since they arrived, it's almost like the final lynchpin has been pulled."

"Are you sure you're not over-dramatizing things?"

"You ask me about the tea leaves. For the last week, when I look at them, I see a cloak of death surrounding this entire town."

Chapter 29:

Lair

It was night when Willet entered the lair, and the scent of old death quickly filled her lungs. She almost strangled as she covered her mouth, the aroma beyond unbearable.

Raven, who was several feet ahead, called back to her. "Put a piece of cloth over your nose, it will cut the smell!

Gavin had unsheathed his blade and was cautiously walking backward behind Willet with his sleeve against his nose. At some point, the cavernous hole started to fill up with cocoons. They seem to have randomly adorned the walls, floor, and ceiling, and in no particular order. Willet noticed that the tunnel was getting dimmer. Raven herself had become a moving shadow. She called from the darkness.

"This was as far as I got."

Willet had all but forgotten Gavin was behind them until he responded. "Yeah, I see why."

This startled her as she blindly grabbed at the walls for some sort of directional orientation. "How can you two see anything?"

"We are faigal, so our eyes adjust quicker to dark than sleeven or lek eyes."

Willet furrowed her brow uncomfortably at the prospect of this. However, she waited patiently as Gavin passed by her. She could see his eyes were slightly glowing. She waited as the ripping sounds from deep within the cavern grew louder. Raven and Gavin both tore open cocoon after cocoon in search of Iris. Willet was staring at the blackness and trying to picture what was happening based on the noises ahead of her. Finally, it was as if someone started to slowly turn the lights back on. She could suddenly see both Branson heirs, tearing the place apart.

"You're right, I can see better now."

Raven looked back at her with a snarky expression. "That's because your poker has turned into a torch again!"

Willet looked down at her hand. She hadn't even noticed that the iron rod was glowing a bright red, as flickers of flames illuminated the dark cavern. Suddenly, Willet's eyes widened as she realized what was happening. She turned around to face the entrance of the tunnel. She arched her back and wrapped her other hand around the handle. Gavin, sensing something was off with Willet, called after her.

"What's wrong?"

She tried to whisper in his direction. "We are not alone."

The twins didn't hesitate. Gavin extended his blade, and Raven arched her bow toward the dark entrance. It remained silent for several moments, as the trio anticipated what it could be. Willet swallowed. Her throat was dry. In that moment, she realized, it had been several hours since she'd had something to drink.

Suddenly, a pair of large yellow eyes appeared. They were about 6 yards away. But it was obvious what they were. Raven fired first. No sooner had she fired than they were gone. Gavin looked concerned. How many more arrows do you have left?

Raven loaded another as she coldly responded. "I'm down to about six shots."

"Well, we need you to be more conservative."

Willet could still sense its presence, but somehow, it had eluded them. "Where did it go?"

Raven joined her chorus. "Yeah, I don't see it anywhere."

No sooner had Raven spoken than Willet could feel a clawed hand from above, grab a handful of her hair. She was suddenly elevated into the air by her roots. Willet let out a vivid scream as she felt herself dangling above the ground.

Raven's eyes enlarged as she screamed aloud the trio's consensus. "Mother Arke, it's crawling on the ceiling!"

Gavin couldn't actually see anything, but began slashing at the ceiling. There was a high-pitched scream as Willet abruptly dropped to the ground. This was followed by a frantic scrambling sound as the griskin darted backwards on the roof toward the entrance. Raven and Gavin followed in hot pursuit.

Willet fell to the side of the woven wall as the fire poker dropped against a nearby cocoon. The dry silk ignited almost instantly, causing a raging fire. She snatched her poker and quickly rose to her feet. The very tunnel quickly became flames. She desperately ran as fast as she could, as fire began to rapidly eat the innards of the lair.

Willet cleared the tunnel; she extended her wings and desperately glided across the bog and out of the black smoke. She looked around the perimeter. There was no sign of anything in the darkness. Over her shoulder, there was a slight flicker from the entrance of the cave. Her lungs were filled with burning smoke. She stood hacking up black phlegm. Raven landed in front of her. She looked over Willet's shoulder as smoke poured from the mouth of the lair.

"What did you do?"

Willet wiped her face as she tried to remain cool. "Nothing."

Before Raven could respond, Gavin landed on an extended tree branch hovering a few feet above them. "Well, we lost it somewhere in the woods. I don't know, perhaps they can fly as well."

Willet nodded. "Geez, I hadn't thought about that."

"Well, we all need to start thinking about that, I mean..."

Suddenly Gavin stopped talking in mid-sentence. "What is all that?"

"What is what?"

"All that smoke, is there a forest fire?"

Raven looked at her brother. "She set the cave on fire."

Willet, not wanting to come across like a bumbling idiot, responded. "Well, that's a good thing, right? I mean, it can't return."

Gavin responded. "Well, it will just return to town. The difference is that now it knows what we all look like. Didn't you say something about it taking the form of someone we know?"

Willet nodded. "It could come at us in the form of a loved one or someone we least expect."

Raven countered. "Well, there is no way to find her now."

Gavin was about to nod in agreement when he took a hard look at Willet's head. "What have we here?"

Willet grew paranoid as he extended his crissum toward her forehead. She pulled her poker out in a defensive stance. "What are you doing?"

Understanding his intentions, Raven grabbed Willet's arm to stop her from attacking. She impatiently responded to Willet. "Relax."

Gavin quickly flicked his blade across the top of her hair, and immediately, Willet felt something drop to the ground. They all peered down to behold three clawed fingers slightly wrapped around a lock of Willet's hair. They were still moving somewhat.

Raven had a deadpan expression as she explained to Willet. "That was tangled in your hair, sunshine!"

Willet stood still, sufficiently creeped out. She responded by digging her fingers through her hair, in case more fingers were hiding in there. Willet was about to protest the entire situation. That is when Gavin excitedly gleamed.

"Well, at least now, we know how to find it."

Willet realized what he was saying. "You're right, whoever the griskin is, someone in town is now missing three fingers from their hand."

The three weary travelers continued on their way silently. After a while, they found that they were near the outskirts of the very field leading to the Greywood estate. Willet uncomfortably turned to her two travelling companions. "Well, we made it out alive."

Gavin sheathed his crissum back into its holster with a humble smile. "Yes, it was quite an adventure."

Willet felt suddenly nervous. She realized that there was no reason either Branson would need to keep their word. They could both kill her, now that they were again the dominant aggressors outside of the woods. Raven picked up on this immediately.

"As we leave these woods, so does our alliance!"

Willet looked back at Raven to gauge her intentions. Raven quickly lifted her arrow and, before Willet could move, fired a shot at Willet's head. It whizzed by her ear and landed with a sudden thud, then a hawking scream erupted.

Willet spun around quickly, startled. She looked down to see a lone harpy that had targeted Willet from behind. Raven's arrow had pierced directly in its forehead. It would have surely killed her if it had reached her moments later. Willet looked back at her adversary in shock as Raven lowered her crossbow. They both stood their ground. Raven finally responded.

"Remember, none of this ever happened, Swift."

Willet was about to thank her properly when a blinding search light flashed across the ground beside her. It was a police helicopter. Willet instinctively dodged the light by hopping into a clump of shadows until the helicopter passed. Willet looked back toward the direction of Gavin and Raven; however, neither one was anywhere to be seen. They had all but vanished into the night.

She thought about Raven's final words that night. As she slowly trudged across the large meadow that led to the Greywood estate in the distance. She had resigned herself to the fact that she could not speak of what had transpired that night. That was part of the vertriste. It had to be a secretly bound agreement. As far as the town was to know, a crazy woman tried to attack some kids who foolishly wandered into the woods. She hoped Adelie would be home and safe. It was clear that Raven had no idea what happened to her.

What about Jonas, was he ok? What did he know about the situation? Those are definitely questions for another day, but not tonight. Willet waited till the light moved across the field before she continued. She had hit a comfortable stride, when she had the most uncomfortable feeling. She glanced back at the woods. She wasn't sure, but she could almost feel eyes on her. Perhaps it was all in her mind.

Chapter 30:

Outside Assistance

Wilson Van Warren stood with a scowl on his face, waiting for someone, anyone, to tell him what had become of his only child. His wife stood beside him, holding his hand as if she were in a trance. Cranston Brittle, one of his associates, climbed up the steps of the manmade platform to brief him on the situation.

Van Warren had his people erect an observation deck that stood some 50 yards high. The platform hovered over the edge of Martin Rd, looking down at the vast expanse of Greywood. From this height, Van Warren had the illusion that he was in complete control of what was happening in the search. He was livid as he stared out of the scene.

"Why is this taking so long?"

"Many of the men are afraid of going down into the woods, sir!"

"Afraid? I have been trying to get those woods excavated for years. The only holdup is those self-righteous Adlers. Sirenna won't sell. She is determined to keep it a wildlife refuge. God only knows what kind of criminals are living in that swamp!"

"Well, this latest misfortune can definitely help your cause."

"Cranston, you do realize that it is my only child who is still missing in those woods?"

"I meant no disrespect to you and your lovely wife, sir."

Prinia Van Warren looked up from her stupor and glared in Cranston's direction. "Why are you even talking to us?" Cranston nodded as he moved away. Prinia continued her tirade. "I blame that Branson fellow for our Iris. His children are horrid, conniving twits."

"Lord Branson has been very sympathetic to us, dear. He is one of our biggest contributors, and may I remind you, his own children are missing as well."

"Why does everyone refer to him as lord?"

"His family is from the old country."

"But you're not, and you fall in line with everyone else."

Cranston cleared his throat. "Mr. Van Warren, one of the hunters you asked for, is here."

Prinia looked horrified. "Hunters! You hired a hunter to find our child?"

"He comes with the highest of recommendations, darling."

A rather odd-looking fellow carefully scaled up the platform. He was a muscular, yet rather slender chap wearing a burly brown fur coat. Real brown feathers adorned his collar. His feet were wrapped in snakeskin boots that shuffled up to his knees, while a brown derby sat atop his balding head. Wilson was very intrigued by this colorful character's approach.

As for his face, it was obscured by a black leather face mask. On the sides of the mask, tiny pinholes peeked out to allow for ample breathing. Even his eyes were invisible, hidden behind rose colored sunglasses. When he reached the top of the landing, he all but dwarfed Van Warren by almost a foot, not that the mayor was short, but this fellow was unusually tall.

Cranston acted as an intermediary as the stranger stopped about a yard away from the Van Warrens. "Mayor Van Warren, this is Dr. Sage Richter."

Warren had a baffled look on his face. "Doctor?"

The stranger just stood still, breathing through his mask, menacingly. Richter was silent as if studying his potential client. To change the awkwardness of the moment, the mayor extended his hand. Dr. Richter's response was cold and detached. He glanced down at Van Warren's hand, then looked away. Cranston looked horrified as he studied Van Warren, who seemed slightly insulted.

Cranston quickly tried to calm his boss. "Oh, Dr. Richter doesn't shake hands, sir."

"He doesn't?"

Ritcher finally answered for himself. "Not at all, sir."

By Richter's diction, it was easy to glean that he was of Irish descent with a slight lisp. He was soft-spoken, but he commanded attention with an almost musical and elegant delivery.

"'Tis nothing personal, sir. Germs and bacteria fill this world with the most troublesome types. There is no telling the kinds of infections I could pick up just from shaking hands!"

Wilson Van Warren didn't seem to understand this type of fear, so he was more put out by the social graces that the stranger seemed to lack. The mayor puffed his chest in an almost aggravated stance.

"Do you even know why you were contacted?"

"What do you mean?"

"I want you to find my daughter!"

"You are the mayor, and you seem to have credible law enforcement here. If it were that simple, you wouldn't have called me here within 12 hours of her disappearance. You want a specialist for this."

"I don't know. Cranston, where did you find this.... person?"

"Sir, he came with the highest recommendations."

"You keep saying that. From whom?"

Richter walked past the couple as if disinterested. He stopped at the edge of the platform and peered down at Greywood below. His nostrils inhaled the fresh air, as if he were acclimating himself to his surroundings. He scanned the forest terrain before he responded to Van Warren's inquiry.

"Your brother recommended I come."

"You work for Harlan. I should have known. How did he even know what's been happening, from up in Melbourne?"

Richter's eye flinched as if agitated. "Perhaps he is no longer there, sir."

Van Warren had a sudden, uncomfortable look on his face. It was the look of fear. "So, he is back in the states. I thought his travelling visa had been revoked?"

"Look, I don't have time for a family intervention. I have other clients waiting."

"Are you some sort of mercenary?"

"That is such a harsh term, sir."

"This is a harsh world."

Richter placed his hands on either side of this collar, with the deepest smile. "I tell you what, call me if you're serious about finding your daughter." Then Richter strolled across the deck and passed by the Van Warrens as he started back down the steps.

Prinia must have been listening to the conversation as she grabbed her husband's arm tightly. "Wilson, please."

Van Warren glanced at his wife, whose eyes were red and puffy. He looked back at the stranger. "Wait, Mr. Richter!"

Richter stood still and, without turning, answered Van Warren. His response was confident and callous. "I'm a doctor, sir."

Wilson sighed as he finished. "Dr. Richter, will you adhere to the terms of the contract?"

Richter turned around, slowly sliding down his mask and removing his glasses for the first time. His appearance was so inhumanly grotesque, both Prinia and Wilson winced as he exposed his face. His eyes focused intently on the couple. His right eye was almost closed, and the pupil was completely bleached out. The left eye was a deep green and surrounded by scars. He slid his mask down to his chin. His nose was somewhat non-existent, consisting of the indication of a bridge and two tiny nostrils underneath.

His mouth was oddly slanted and filled with yellowing, crooked teeth. Chapped and peeling lips were discolored and shiny grey, as if someone had slathered oil all over them. Richter smiled at the couple's obvious repulsion as he regurgitated the terms of the agreement. His soft Irish tone competing with his vile appearance. When he spoke, it seemed as if he had too many teeth for his mouth. He almost seemed to speak with an oddly exaggerated lisp at times.

" But of course, no questions, no witnesses, no advertisement of any sort for the immediate retrieval of such property. One Iris Van Warren, age 16. Such a tender age. Yes, we must save her purity from whatever vile monsters out there who may want to violate her."

Prinia flinched at his words.

"I must remind you that this offer is time sensitive, doctor."

"Aye, you do realize that anything else I find out there in those woods belongs to me."

"As long as you find my daughter, I don't care."

"If she still has a pulse, I'll find her."

Prinia winced again at his nonchalant comment. Catching her expression, he tipped his hat. "Well, let's hope for the best, good lady."

Not wanting to look at his eyes, she lowered her head and nodded. Richter replaced his face mask and started to descend the stairs. Wilson felt a hint of apprehension and followed after. He stopped at the top of the stairs.

"Dr. Richter?"

Richter paused impatiently. "I was under the impression, this was a time-sensitive matter, sir."

"I was just curious. What kind of hunter are you?"

"I'm what you might call something of a specialist when it comes to monsters."

Chapter 31:

Reunion

Willet made her way up the drive and started to realize that her muscles were aching. She saw that most of the cars had dispersed. A few lights were still on inside. She paused for a moment before she decided to climb atop one of the large stone owls that guarded the manor.

As she reached the top. She looked up at the night sky. There were still flickers from the horizon. The lone helicopter was scanning the area around the woods. A grisly reminder that the griskin had most likely claimed another victim. Willet took a deep breath.

"That was quite a long stroll, you took tonight."

Willet was startled at the sound of her mother's voice. She was sitting behind her on a bench by herself. Willet hopped off the great statue to face the music.

"What are you doing out here, Mom?"

"Really, you're going to ask me that?"

Willet sheepishly looked down. "Oh, sorry. Any word from Addie?"

"Yes, she got home about forty minutes after you disappeared."

"What did she say?"

"She didn't say much, just like you aren't really saying much."

Willet tried to change the subject. She realized that her mother's Impala was back in the driveway. "Hey, the car's back."

"Uncle Merle and I just got back from the police parking lot a little while ago. I was too nervous to go to bed, so I decided to sit here, in hopes that my child would find her way back home, and alas..."

"Are you really mad?"

"Ask me that question in the morning. Both my girls are home safe, and I'm too tired to complain."

Willet breathed a sigh of relief. As she sat beside her mother and hugged her. They both embraced for several moments before Laraline continued to speak on the matter. She had tears in her eyes as she emotionally released her fear.

"You two are going to be the death of me."

"Sorry, Mama, I know it was stupid. I just thought I could find her. It's not like the police were doing jack."

"For real!" Laraline wiped her face as she continued to speak. "A Branson boy found my baby girl. Can you believe that?"

"Which one?"

"Don't play coy, you like him, don't you?"

Willet was suddenly embarrassed. "Who told you that?"

Laraline gave her a knowing stare.

Willet rolled her eyes. "Addie is such a little brat!"

Laraline touched her knee. "Calm down, you're ruining my vibe."

"Why do things have to be so complicated?"

Laraline put her arm around her daughter. "I wish I knew." Laraline rubbed her temples, as if trying to decompress. "Your little excursions tonight and the other morning at school, I don't really understand, Willet."

"Mama..."

"Let me finish. When I was your age, I got pregnant, and three years after that, I ran away with a different boy altogether, who, let's just say, was a different breed. We moved to Florida and cut all ties with my family. So, I guess I don't have room to talk about behavior."

Willet suddenly sat up. "You mean pregnant, pregnant?"

"Yes."

"With a baby?"

"Really dear, aren't you about to graduate?"

"Did Daddy know?"

"This was before him, but we never kept secrets."

"So, was it a boy or a girl?"

"It was a little boy."

"What was his name?"

Laraline was almost in tears. "I never got to name him. The adoption was arranged before I had given birth."

"That sucks. Have you tried to find him?"

"Quite a few years ago, but I had to let it go."

"So, I have a half-brother out there somewhere."

Willet could see the conversation was upsetting her mother, so she changed the subject. "So how did you and Dad first meet?"

"That's actually a funny story."

"Really? Tell me. I could use a laugh."

"I met him at my house."

Willet pointed to the Greywood manor. "This one?"

"Yep."

"How is that even possible with the aunts' views on humans?"

"He and his Uncle Silas actually designed Sirenna's aviary."

"I would see him either sanding, hammering, or diligently working on these plans. I was dating someone else at the time, but we occasionally engaged in small talk. By the time the aviary was completed, we were engaged. Since then, Sirenna has never allowed another sleeven in her home."

"What was it about him that made you decide, this is the one?"

"He had the kindest eyes I had ever seen. It was like I was under a spell. Plus, he was charming, brilliant, and extremely sexy."

"Ok, this is getting a bit gross."

"Shut up."

Willet giggled to herself.

Laraline turned to the moon that was high in the sky. "You know, when we returned here, I was afraid that I would remember all the things I hated about this place. What I didn't count on was recalling all these memories of your father, which I had long forgotten. Sometimes memories are secrets we hide from ourselves.

"I guess everybody has secrets."

"Perhaps, but you're still grounded for the next two weeks."

"Ok, I deserve that. Hey, whatever happened to Uncle Sal? Does he even know Father died?"

Laraline was curt. "I'm pretty sure he had some idea."

"How come he never came around afterward?"

"Willet, can I just sit here and enjoy this moment of calm?"

Willet could tell she was tense. "I didn't mean anything. I just missed him."

Laraline reached over and touched her arm. "I'm sorry, I'm having a hard time calming down. It was a difficult week."

"It's been a difficult year!"

The pair chuckled out loud for a moment. Laraline reminded Willet. "You know, it hasn't been easy for Adelie either."

"Is that your way of saying I've been a sucky ass sister?"

"She really misses you."

"I know."

The silence was interrupted briefly by a sound of crickets in the distance. A flurry of fireflies fluttered near a clump of weeds in the field. Willet surmised the search must have concluded for that evening. The natural wildlife was making a late appearance.

Laraline sighed. Maybe we need to get inside; we wouldn't want to encourage our night visitors."

"I wouldn't worry about them, Mama.

Laraline gave her daughter a curious glance. Do you know something that I don't?

Willet held back a devilish grin: as she thought about the harpy struck down by Raven's longbow. I'm sure all this activity should keep them hiding in the shadows.... for tonight."

Laraline closed her eyes and inhaled. "Smell that sea water. Every time I get a whiff, I think about your father on the Lenoir."

"Did you figure out how to get the boat back?"

"Don't remind me. I need to figure something out. My boss will be asking me about it soon. The real joke is that if the boat weren't so far away, we could just fly to the dock and sail it back. I mean, I doubt anyone will be watching the ocean itself."

Willet was staring in the direction of the Greywood when she unstrapped the fire poker from her hip. It was sticky and muddy as she let it drop to the ground. She was contemplating the weapon when suddenly the idea came to her. Willet stood up and faced her mother.

"When do you need the boat, Mama?"

"Don't worry about it tonight, hon."

"Mama, you don't understand. I think I have a solution."

Laraline looked at her curiously. "What are you talking about?"

"Ok, how long would it take for one person to sail from Key West to Meadowlark?"

"You're talking about yourself?"

"Of course."

"Willet, dear, I was just talking. That would take days, at least six or seven, and that's with a steady wind."

"I know that boat."

"Willet, it's been a long night. The idea of my daughter sailing for a week all alone is ridiculous. I'm done with this conversation."

"Please, Mama, just once, please hear me out."

Laraline was silent as her daughter emphatically insisted on her attention. There were almost tears in her eyes as she pleaded to be heard.

"Ok, shoot!"

"What if I told you there may be a way I can get to Dad's sailboat back here to Crecheland dock, without even leaving town!"

"That's impossible."

"Nothing is impossible, just improbable!"

Chapter 32:

Retriever

As Raven touched down, the cool night air caressed her cheeks. She quickly folded her wings inward as she straightened up. She called for her brother, who was 6 yards above her in the air.

"We had better take the rest of the trip on foot. We are getting near civilization." Gavin abruptly landed with a thud. He frantically looked upward at the sky.

"I think we are being followed."

"By whom?"

She removed her bow and arrow, and she steadied her back against a nearby tree. Gavin slowly unsheathed his crissum and held it to his chest as he listened to the night sky. He squinted as he heard faint ruffling sounds of wings from overhead.

Raven rolled from the tree and quickly fired upward into the blackness. A large, winged figure swooped down and wrapped its claws about her neck in a tight grip. She was slightly lifted into the air, then dragged several feet across the terrain.

Gavin gave chase until Raven was tossed headfirst into a briar patch. Her attacker's feet hit the ground, and Gavin watched the screaming girl disappear into the bushes. The intruder's back was now to Gavin. The young man raised his blade and charged headfirst. He would slice the wing, then he would remove the head. His actions were premature, as the other leaned back and extended their foot out. The heel caught the young man in the chest. The force immediately knocked him down to his knees. His hands recoiled into his stomach, causing him to drop his blade in the dark grass. His eyes teared up as he struggled for air that seemed to be eluding him.

Nashca put her heeled boot on his chest, as she snatched his crissum from the ground. She held it to his neck. "Time for all naughty children to return home at once."

"You're not my mother!"

"Yes, thank Arke for small favors. However, your father is worried sick and sent me to retrieve you and your sister."

From the briar bush, a loud, venomous scream erupted. "Help, I'm stuck, you bitch!"

Nashca turned her attention toward the bush as she pulled the crissum away from Gavin's neck. He exhaled as he rolled over on his stomach to throw up."

Raven was livid as she blasted at the older woman. "Why did you do that?"

"Because you were trying to kill me and would have succeeded, had I not sent you tumbling across the ground."

"Just get me out of here."

"Just keep talking, so I can find where to free you from."

"What do you mean?"

"Suddenly, Nashca began to strategically attack the bush. Whacking a bit here and there until she could see the back of Raven's head. "Hold on, love, you may feel a bit of pain."

"Hey, wait, what are you going to do?"

Nashca reached down with her free hand and grabbed Raven's tangled scalp and quickly plucked her from the bush. She screamed in horror as several briar thorns clung on in resistance. She collapsed on the ground beside her brother. Clumps of her hair remained attached to the bushes.

Nashca winced. "My, that's got to hurt."

"You horrible woman, wait till my father finds out what you have done to me, you have probably disfigured me for life."

Nashca ignored her. "What are you two doing out here?"

"Heading home."

"This is the opposite direction of Branson Estate."

Raven snapped back at her. "We were looking for our brother; he got lost in the woods, you evil witch."

"You mean the brother you shot with your crossbow, that brother dear."

Suddenly, Raven's disposition became a bit calmer as she looked up at Mother Ortega.

"He told you?"

"No, he didn't. We deduced from his wounds, and seeing how you just handled yourself with your crossbow."

"Did you tell father?"

"I didn't have to. He knows you all too well."

Raven gritted her teeth. "Crap"

Gavin temporarily turned his rage on his sister. "You shot Jonas?"

"It was an accident. I didn't mean to; besides, I just shot his hand. It can't be that serious."

Nashca corrected her. "Actually, the arrow went through his hand and into his stomach. But I suppose you were too preoccupied to realize that."

Gavin rose to his feet, wiping off the vomit debris from his lips. "Where is he?"

"He is in the Celandine hospital."

Gavin's eyes glared back at Raven, who was still. Her face had several tiny scratches across her cheeks and lips. A line of blood ran down her face from her scalp, where there was a bald scab. He was about to rip into her until he saw her condition. Gavin immediately began to laugh out loud.

Raven looked paranoid. "What?"

"Where is your hat, dear sister?"

"I lost it in the woods."

"Well, you might need it until your hair grows back."

Raven touched her scalp and started to pout at the condition of her head. "Oh no."

"Classic."

"Don't forget I have a key to your room, brother, and I know when you sleep."

Nashca glared at the pair. "Silence, you two! I'm growing tired of this bickering."

Gavin finally responded to her. "Where's my father, weaver?"

Nashca quickly whipped the blade back against his throat. Gavin didn't flinch, but he was still. "You wouldn't dare!"

"Don't try me, boy."

"I much prefer the company of your predecessor."

"I bet you do."

"What do you mean by that?"

"It means I know your secrets, and if you don't want them exposed, then from here on, you will address me as Mother Ortega. Do you understand?"

Gavin begrudgingly responded. "Yes."

"What?"

Gavin breathed out his nostrils, which were flared with contained contempt. "Yes, Mother Ortega."

"Your father is at the hospital with Jonas. Come with me, you two, let me take you to them."

Chapter 33:

Meditation on the Greywood

Evelyn stood at the river's edge looking into the shallow pool. At the age of seventeen, her hair was almost down to her knees. Sirenna was late returning and a growing sense of dread overcame her. Perhaps she had been captured. A gentle breeze ran though her red hair as she touched the water with the tip of her toe.

Suddenly a soft voice spoke from across the river. "Don't move, there is no escape."

Oriole had landed without incident. Her Large majestic white wings extended almost seven feet at either side of her torso. Her flowing black hair obscuring any sign of remorse as she carefully addressed Evelyn.

"Where is my child?"

"Please, don't do this."

"I will ask once more."

"So, you would strike down your own sister?"

"Don't tempt me, Evie."

"She doesn't belong to you."

Oriole hopped across the river with a single bound. Her hands outstretched ready to lunge at her younger sister. "I beg to differ."

Suddenly, Oriole's claws were about her sister's throat. Her grip tightened as Evelyn dropped to her knees. She realized she was being strangled. Tears in her eyes, she gargled a single word to Oriole.

"Please."

Evelyn hopped up screaming from her nap. It was midmorning and she had fallen asleep in the car on her way to town.

Sirenna looked at her crossly. "There is nothing more pathetic than watching an old biddy having a nightmare."

"How do you know it was nightmare?"

"You were yelling out, please, please! Though I suppose you could have been having some naughty sex dream."

Evelyn blushed. "Sirenna, please."

Sirenna turned her attention to the driver. "Merle, are you sauced up already? Why are you driving so slowly?"

He cryptically answered. "You're going to miss me when I'm dead."

"Well, you're not dead yet, so hurry up!"

Evelyn was visibly upset. "Merle, please don't talk like that. It makes me nervous, with all that drama last night and the weekly disappearances. Violet Peregrine believes that Arke is punishing us for not being diligent with faith and allowing sleeven to infest our home!"

Sirena quickly retorted. "Please don't talk to me about Violet. That cow had the nerve to allow that Branson woman into my gallery!"

"Sirenna that was several months ago, she didn't know. You know I heard that she and her sister will be having another of their interventions this Sunday."

"They are so pathetic. They should really go out and make some friends."

"Sirenna!"

"Well, who is the lucky victim this month?"

"Kestrel Faulkner, of all people."

"Who?"

"She was at the house last night. She was the one who drove Laraline home."

"I can't seem to grasp the fact that my niece actually lives in the same house as I do."

"Sirenna, are you listening."

"Wait, are you talking about the spinster who works at the library?"

"Spinster! She is Ephron's age."

"Oh yeah, she brought that Branson heathen to our doorstep last night as well, don't remind me."

"Do you think they're an item?"

"I don't know. There have been a lot of rumors about Branson's youngest and her keeping close company with him, if you catch my drift."

"I've heard the rumors. You know I was talking to her briefly last night and really feel sorry for her. She seemed so sad."

Sienna slid her sunglasses on and peered back out the window. "Perhaps she has gas."

As the car drove into the parking lot of the municipal building, a weariness overcame Evelyn. The Majid, as it was called, was one of the oldest buildings in town. Once, these ancient masques were the spiritual nucleus of early faigal society. Now they were centers of prayer and functioned as places to discuss local government issues.

As both sisters got out, Sirenna gave a stern look in Merle's direction. "Keep the car running. I don't have any intention of staying more than fifteen minutes."

Evelyn corrected. "That's what you always say."

"Make it twenty minutes."

He nodded indifferently. "Yes, ma'am."

Sirenna snapped back. "Don't be coy."

The board meeting itself was a who's who of Meadowlark. The mayor was surprisingly there with his five o'clock shadow. The result of spending several hours searching for his missing daughter. Cranston Brittle was beside him. Lord Branson sat across the room with his son Ephron to his left side. On his right, sat his new weaver, Nashca Ortega.

Beside Mother Ortega sat Lillian Finch. Deloris Peregrine was beside her, with a somber look on her face. Two seats down from her sat headmistress Rhea Faulkner. Two seats over sat Koko Tuludge, the renown madam of old Crecheland.

In the last few years, Tuludge had bought a sizable amount of real estate and acquired a voice on the council. In fact, she had become a force to reckon with, much to the chagrin of the Peregrines, the Cranes, and Rhea Faulkner. To them her very presence was a stain of contention.

Right beside her sat professor Ezio Dyveke, who always seemed as if he were half sleep when he had a mind to show up. Sirenna and Evelyn were to the right of the professor.

Finally presiding over the session stood Patsy and her obedient husband, Nester Crane.

As soon as the twins sat down, Patsy slammed down the gavel. There was a delayed hush as the group halfheartedly turned to face her.

"I call this meeting to order, in accordance with the laws and rituals of the guidebook. I would like to recognize the esteemed mayor, Wilson Van Warren. Despite the distressing situation his family is facing at this moment, he is present. Which ironically segways into the very topic this afternoon, the issue of Greywood Forest."

Sirenna mumbled aloud, so the council could get an earful. "Why am I not surprised?"

Van Warren addressed Sirenna directly. "Something has to be done with that swampland."

"You mean my forest. I have a permit that you signed and renewed, not just two years ago."

The Greywood is not safe. It has become a hazard!"

"So, you're actually going to try and force me to get rid of the land that has been in my family for over 700 years. One little girl gets missing, and it's Sirenna Adler's fault. I might remind you, they were trespassing on private property."

"You wretched woman, have you no compassion."

"When it comes to this topic, none."

"I believe undesirables are using that forest as a hunting ground and have taken my daughter, along with several other residents, over the last several months. It's time to take drastic measures."

Sirenna mumbled to herself. "Here we go again."

Van Warren responded. "What was that comment?"

"Have you seen these undesirables?"

"Really, Lady Adler."

Sirenna was just getting started as she went into a tirade. "What are their names? What do they look like? Do these undesirables read? Perhaps, if they have taken your Iris, she can teach them to read the signs that are stretched all around the perimeter. Especially the ones that say No Trespassing."

Van Warren snapped back. "I find your behavior is rude and insulting."

Sirenna had a puzzled look. "You do realize that rude and insulting means practically the same thing. Why are you even the mayor again?

Koko finally spoke from her lonely corner. "Insulting, wasn't it your little Iris who disappeared for two whole days last year because, as you put it, she was kidnapped by undesirables in Crecheland."

Cranston Brittle tried to calm her down. "Lady Tuludge, please wait your turn."

"Quiet flunky, I have the floor now."

Lady Tuludge's eyes were directly on the mayor. "You came into our community, roused up the locals, and you had your storm troopers tear Crecheland apart, searching for her."

Sirenna gladly interjected. "Come to find out, that dear Iris had ran away to Vegas with another boy she met at one of your own religious retreats!"

Van Warren turned back to Sirenna. "Are you insinuating something about my daughter?"

Sirenna was about to stand up and explode the gossip about Iris, until she saw Evelyn frowning at her attack on the missing girl. Instead, she folded her fingers in her hands and took a deep breath. "No, I'm done."

Koko interjected. "Well, I'm not. I might add, you still have yet to repair the Crecheland Renton dance hall, mayor."

Evelyn uncharacteristically interjected. "You seem to overlook mayor, that my niece and Lord Branson's own children were along with your daughter. His middle child is still in the hospital. Yet, you have made no mention of this."

Branson glanced in Evelyn's direction, yet remained silent. After being ganged up on for a few minutes, Van Warren sat stewing impatiently. He had expected more sympathy from his peers. He thought of Dr Richter, wondering if he could hunt down some of his council members. A dark fantasy of Richter shooting the Adlers put a slight smile on his face.

Most of the faigal on the council understood the spiritual importance of the Greywood presence, Branson included. No one would voice their true feelings since the inclusion of sleeven representation on the board. There were still secret meetings, where only the faigal board members actively convened. Those meetings tended to be more productive. The concerns of sleeven were usually of no consequence for the faigal community at large.

The griskin attacks weren't the first time a few feathers were ruffled. The last secret meeting was the day that Sirenna first took her great nieces to town. She pretty much dumped them off on the street with a wad of money.

That meeting had been a contentious one as well. Lord Branson and Ephron going toe to toe with Sirenna on docking rights. As the Adler's had acquired more land than any other family in Meadowlark. The Bransons had acquired more legal fishing permits and dock ports. It was almost impossible to dock anywhere in Meadowlark without a few nickels going into the pocket of the Branson family trust. Financially speaking, they were becoming more powerful. Today's meeting was a more civil consideration between the old foes, but only by default.

Koko continued her attacks. "It also seems to me; the constable isn't doing his job either. I reported to him about a child disappearance similar to this situation almost six months ago. You know what he told me?" The entire room was silent in anticipation of her words. "He said they have missing files going back several years. A loud hush fell over the group." Koko added. "You don't seem to care unless someone important goes missing."

Sirenna had lit the fuse, as Koko venomously attacked the mayor and the local law enforcement for the current state of affairs. From there the entire meeting turned into a series of finger pointing and name calling. Sirenna and Evelyn sat back silently and just watched, as the subject of the possible Greywood renovation was temporarily curtailed.

Chapter 34:

Burning Bridges

Kestrel sat behind the front desk in the most pleasant mood. In fact, she couldn't remember feeling so content for quite a while. She hummed to herself as she changed out the news periodicals. She thumbed through many of the headlines. Most of them were not really news anymore. In fact, most of the gossip-based bating wasn't really news anyway.

Most mornings the library was fairly empty. This gave her the flexibility to get more personal tasks done. Professor Dyveke would sometimes frequent the days the new science periodicals came out. He was regular as clockwork as he eagerly waited for Kestrel to resubmit the new periodicals so he could hurry back to class.

A most unexpected voice addressed her from across the room. "You seem chipper today."

Kestrel heart jumped a beat, as Aquila slowly sauntered toward her front desk. She reminded kestrel of some dangerous cat of prey. "Arke, I didn't hear you creeping around Lady Branson."

"Because you weren't intended to hear."

Kestrel's eye widened, as if suddenly put on guard. "What brings you here?"

"Relax, Gavin says he hasn't been able to reach you. I have another task for him and he needs a chauffeur for this evening."

"Well, perhaps you can chauffer him around, for a change."

Aquila's one good eye widened in utter shock. "What did you say?"

"I didn't stutter, I'm done with you and Gavin."

"Don't be foolish, you know too much."

"Are you threatening me?"

"What would happen to your reputation, if everyone found out the exact nature of your relationship with Gavin?"

"Are you serious, you are trying to blackmail me, because I refuse to hang around with your underage nephew?"

"Blackmail is such an ugly word. Let's call it a friendly reminder to help you put things in perspective."

"Wow, Ephron was right. You really are sick."

"Ah, now the clouds are beginning to clear. This is not about moral duty. This is about Ephron. You're still pining for him. After all these years?"

"Good things come to those who wait."

"That is true, however your timing is a bit off."

"What are you talking about?"

"It seems Ephron has place himself in a bit of a quandary. On one of his many drunken binges, he has gotten entangled with another woman."

"Your lying!"

"Am I, in fact he was with her the other night, at some seedy hotel outside of town."

Kestrel heart sank as she thought about picking him up at the Moonlight Inn. It was a rather strange situation, but she hadn't questioned it. Her lips quivered. "Who?"

"Do you really want to know the explicit details? I will try to spare you."

"Don't do me any favors."

"I understood you and Gavin picked him up. I cannot express my gratitude, which is why I have come by. I wanted to thank you personally."

"I know Ephron, more than anyone."

"Did you know that this woman called our offices today. She has documents showing she is now with child. Now, we have a possible paternity lawsuit."

"That's not possible."

"Not probable, but definitely possible. So now, he has a responsibly to the unwed mother and this unborn child."

"Who told you this lie?"

"Let's just say, I have a have a reliable source."

Kestrel eyes were filled with water as she studied Aquila's aloof expression.

"Ephron is supposed to be picking me up tonight. We have a date."

"Poor dear. If you wish, I can call him and cancel it for you. You can then pick Gavin up on main street outside Linnet's."

"No!"

Aquila was taken back by Kestrel's defiance. "What do you mean, no?"

"Don't you Bransons understand the word no. Everyone can't be bought and sold, just because you desire something."

"My patience is growing thin."

"Then leave."

"Watch your tongue."

"You stopped us before. I was supposed to be married. That was supposed to be my life. All I ever wanted was Ephron, and you took him from me."

"To be fair, Meena was the perfect companion. She has the right bloodline."

"You and your brother conspired to end our union. I know it was the Bransons that destroyed my father."

"Poor Ira Faulkner. He was a hard worker, but your family would have contaminated our royal blood line. there was never a chance for you, dear!"

"You accepted my dowry, then you spent it, then took everything from my family. My sister had to grovel on her knees to Sirenna just get that dead-end teaching position, just to feed us!"

Aquila mockingly sighed. "The way you describe it, it sounds so tragic. You should write a book. Perhaps it will bring in some additional finance to furnish a more current wardrobe."

"Why are you so heartless? Did you have come here today just to stomp on my happiness? Well, perhaps I will do my own stomping for a change."

Aquila eyes widened. "Excuse me?"

"Yes, you heard me. Perhaps the mayor, or the constable, or mother sisters back in Essex will find it interesting the things I could tell them about you, Lady Branson. What would they think of your blood rituals and sacrifices of our own kind? What do you think?"

Aquila's eye was burning with an inner fire. Her teeth gritted. "I think I'm looking at one more dead faigal."

Kestrel's reaction was impulsive. Her clawed hand struck Aquila across the face. The slap seemed to startle both parties. The older woman touched her face in shock as a light graze mark remained. Aquila carefully looked around at the library. A few patrons were now staring at the scene. Her eyes darted around furiously trying not to react. There were too many witnesses. Before she had time to properly respond, Kestrel snarled at her.

"Get out!"

Aquila relented, as there were many people watching. She had to revisit the situation. Things had gotten volatile. She would have loved to rip Kestrel into pieces, but this wasn't the time. She placed a pair of sunglasses over her eyes and hissed.

"You will wish you hadn't done that deary." Aquila then turned around and headed out the door.

Professor Dyveke clasped his hands together along with a few others. There were even a few cheers, as Aquila stomped to the parking lot and got into her car. The tires of her caddy squealed as she drove away.

"Man, I never thought I would see anyone handle Lady Branson like that. It was worth the price of admission. She was scared."

Kestrel quickly corrected him. "No she wasn't, she just didn't want an audience to witness the monster she really is inside."

Chapter 35:

Raven's Alibi

Jonas was half asleep. After he was discharged from the hospital, he spent the rest of the afternoon in bed resting. He would occasionally peer out his window at the Robins in the tree just outside. They had built a nest, and he rather enjoyed the purity of their existence.

The thick bandage around his stomach started to itch as he moved to his side. This caused him to scratch carefully around the edges of his bruises. When Raven popped her head inside the door, he was startled. She pretty much avoided him at the hospital. Even in his own house, the events in the Greywood seemed to have lost its importance, in spite of Iris Van Warren's disappearance.

Raven looked every bit as worn down as he felt. She wore a knitted cap over her mangled hair. Several stitches decorated her chin and right eye. Most of the other scratches were superficial. Jonas tried to appear civil as he quickly acknowledged her.

"I thought you would be out practicing."

"Father took away my crossbows as punishment for you."

"For how long?"

"He doesn't think it's a very ladylike sport to attract an acceptable suitor. I don't want a mate, and I definitely don't want a brood of brats. Sometimes, I really loathe him."

Jonas was rather surprised at her admission. He knew that there was a disconnect with Avis and her sometimes. However, it never seemed overtly antagonistic or volatile to warrant such animosity.

"Did you tell him how you feel?"

"He doesn't care. As long as he can have me betrothed by the time I graduate."

"What happened to the last suiter?"

"I broke his arm, so his family would return my dowry."

"Not to your liking?"

"Let father marry him. I have no need for a husband. I envy you, Jonas."

"Me?"

"You're already a loser, so he doesn't have any expectations of you."

"Gee thanks."

It suddenly got uncomfortably silent as Raven walked to his bedroom window and looked out without so much as a sound. "Why didn't you snitch on me?"

"Which transgression are you referring to?"

"About me trying to snuff Adelie."

"Well, that was her idea."

Raven turned around with a queer look. "Really?"

"What? I thought you would be happy."

Raven was instantly pensive as she paced back and forth in front of the window. "That means she also has an agenda. These Swifts are more devious than I expected."

"What are you talking about?"

"Never mind, you wouldn't understand the female mind."

Jonas thought briefly about the situation with Willet. "I guess not."

Raven backed across the room toward the door. She opened the door and paused for a moment. "Hey, I never apologized for shooting you."

Jonas glanced curiously at his sister in the doorway. Raven was the type of person who never apologized. Though she didn't actually apologize, it was the closest she ever came to entertaining the idea. He felt a twinge of peace. It would be one of the very few brother and sister moments he would ever share with Raven. He absorbed her acknowledgment of the incident with a deep sigh just as she vanished.

Raven made her way downstairs; she could sense a strange presence. She scanned the foyer with much suspicion. Finally, her eyes settled at the front door. Within a few moments, the doorbell rang. Raven tensed, as she reached for the handle. The door swung open and she was greeted by the unlikely presence of Adelie Swift. The young girl stood at the door with her hands in her pockets. She had a serious expression on her face. Raven reacted accordingly.

"Why am I not surprised?"

Adelie ignored her. "We need to talk."

"Do we?"

"We don't have much time."

"Well, I don't know if I can welcome an Adler on my land."

"Well, its lucky, I'm a Swift."

"Same difference."

"You'll want to hear what I have to say. It's in your best interest."

"Are you trying to blackmail me?"

"Look, I want you to help me get on the fencing team."

"Ok, this conversation is so random, I'm completely lost."

"I need to get on fencing team."

"Well, perhaps you should talk to Gavin, since that's his deal."

"Well, I don't know Gavin."

"Like I care."

"Can you help me?"

"How about, not."

"You'll change your mind."

"You obviously don't know me."

"Of course I do, you're my good buddy Raven, who took us out for a joy ride to the forest. Suddenly she just snapped, and she started to pick us off with her bow and arrow. The first one she shot was Iris."

"You lying little pip!"

Adelie's eyes focused intently on her. She had a kind of smile hidden under the surface.

"She shot her own brother next."

"Do you honestly think you can get away with this?"

"I am, or you would have attacked me by now."

"So, this is why you didn't tell what I did to the police. What if killed you now, then this scheme would just fade."

"Of course, I may have a diary somewhere, where I have recalled the day in great detail."

"You're lying, you have no such diary. Why would you change your story to the police?"

"Actually, I have yet to give a statement."

"What do you mean?"

"I have been in shock, but my memory is starting to come back. I think by tonight, I will be fully recovered. When the police come back to my house to pick up the written statement that was given, that is folded in my diary, the one that I don't ever write in daily."

Raven had a cross expression on her face. "Clever."

"You should thank me, Raven. You're getting off easy, considering what you tried to do to me."

Raven gritted her teeth as Adelie stood with a smug expression, in any other circumstances she would tear her apart, right in the driveway for even suggesting a threat. However, she had already agreed to a vertriste with Willet. Besides that, any entanglement with the police would probably make things difficult. It wasn't as if she was afraid about any legal consequences. The cloud of perception would make the rest of her popular school life more difficult. Raven sighed and her nostrils flared.

"What exactly do you need me to do?" Even saying those words almost made Raven gag. If word got out that she was pulling favors for not only a lek, but an underclassman she could be socially ruined.

"Talk to your brother. Rumor is, he has a lot of pull on the fencing team. I am sure that if he puts in a good word for me, I'm a shoe in!"

"Do you even know how to fence?"

"Not really!"

"Do you even like the art?"

I couldn't care less."

"Then why? This makes no sense, of all the things to request. What is the point?"

"All you need to do is get me an audition; I will take care of the rest!"

The two were in a heated discussion when Fletcher's squad car pulled up into the driveway. Both girls stood frozen at the approaching flashing lights. The police car came to a stop as Adelie and Raven looked at one another. Raven gasped.

"What is he doing here?"

Adelie discreetly whispered. "Last chance."

"Ok, you have deal."

Fletcher got out of the car and folded his arms. "Wow, this is a peculiar site. You're both here together. Why aren't you in school Adelie?"

"Exam day. I will be going soon. I was just coming over here to see if Raven could take me to school today."

Fletcher glanced to Raven, who had a painfully morose look on her face. "Is this true Raven?"

"Yes, she left a book in my car; so I said; Hey, let me take you to school in the middle of the day, in broad daylight, where everyone can see us!"

"I guess this is my lucky day. I can talk to both of you about what happened in the woods."

Adelie quickly interrupted the conversation. "It's quite simple. We were exploring the woods officer, when this strange woman grabbed Iris. Raven tried to shoot it with an arrow but missed. The woman took the arrow with her right arm and stabbed Jonas in the stomach. He tried to block it, but it went in his hand."

"She stabbed Jonas with an arrow?"

"Yeah! I know it sounds crazy, but that's the truth."

"So, you seem to remember what happened now?"

"I'm still foggy on certain points but I basically started remembering everything."

"Well, I still need to talk to you both separately."

"Why? Don't you believe us?"

In that moment, Adelie had clued Raven in on what their basic narrative to the police would be. This way they wouldn't contradict one another. By insisting that certain points were vague could give Raven the chance to elaborate for herself or just give bland explanations to a certain point. The stories would be similar enough.

Fletcher looked up at the house. "Is your brother up? I would like to talk to him also."

Raven's response was quick. "He was in a little pain, so he just took some medicine and laid down. I could have father wake him up."

"Never mind. Don't disturb him. I can come by later."

Raven released an internal sigh. Fletcher moved closer to the pair with his paper and pen pad. He removed his sunglasses and addressed the two.

"Well, which one of you is first?"

Chapter 36:

A Curious Gathering

Mother Hazel sat impatiently beside Laraline in the study, the sacred den of planning. The old woman kept tapping her cane impatiently. Sirenna and Evelyn entered the room with equal parts curiosity and trepidation.

Mother Hazel gripped her walking stick and stood up abruptly. "Ok, what is this about?"

Sirenna raised her eyebrows. "What do you mean, I came as soon as I got your note?"

"My note?"

Evelyn added. "The note about an emergency meeting."

Sirenna pulled a piece of paper from the side of her bosom. The old woman snatched the paper and began to read. Sirenna frowned.

"You must be getting old, dear!"

"Stop talking foolishness. This is my napping time, you know that. Why would I arrange a meeting now?"

Sirenna was dismissive. "Well, Evelyn and I have been in a meeting in town all day and the last thing I want, is to have another one of these meetings. I just want to go to my aviary and have a drink!"

Laraline mumbled under her breath. "Or two"

Mother Hazel snapped. "This is not even my handwriting."

Evelyn looked about the room. Her eyes caught Laraline. "Well, who wrote this note?"

The other woman looked in Laraline's direction. By process of elimination, she was the only one left. Laraline quickly shrugged.

"Hate to disappoint you all, but I got a note myself." Laraline held up a similar piece of paper. Just as things began to unravel in communication, Willet entered the room.

"I called this meeting." All four women looked at her, astounded.

Sirenna was beside herself. "Are you insane, we don't have time for romper room."

"I have decided to comply and continue my formal training as a weaver."

Sirenna winced. "Well, that news could have been announced over supper! Can we go now?"

Mother Hazel looked cautiously at the young girl. "She has assembled us here to offer a vertriste."

There was a sudden hush amongst the room. Evelyn looked at Willet curiously. "Is that true?"

Willet removed her fire stick from her side and sat it on Sirenna's desk. "It's a possibility."

Sirenna glared at the fire poker laying on her shiny mahogany table. "Please, remove that filthy thing!"

Mother Hazel held her hand out to shush Sirenna. "Quiet. What do you seek child?"

"First, let me ask you a question."

"Ask."

"Is it possible for me to drift outside of Meadowlark?"

"You already know the answer or we wouldn't be here. What do you desire from us?"

"I wish to retrieve an item far away and bring it back here."

Laraline quickly interrupted. "Willet, what madness are you talking about?"

"I have done it before, Mama. That's how I acquired this fire poker."

Laraline was about to dismiss her words until Mother Hazel cut her off. "The child speaks truth to you. You must listen, with your heart and mind, to what she says."

The old woman turned back to Willet. "What do you wish to retrieve?"

"The Lenoir, my father's boat."

"How do you intend to bring it back?"

"I wish to sail it back."

"That port is almost 233 miles from here. You would have to be in a meditative state for over six days. That is provided you have a good wind. That is far beyond your abilities."

Sirenna broke into the discussion. "I've heard of enough of this foolishness. This is my study and I will not entertain this child anymore."

Willet darted around the desk to face Mother Hazel. "What if I broke the trip up? I could sail to a port halfway. Take a break for a day then continue. Is that possible?"

"It's possible, but not very probable."

"But it is possible?"

Mother Hazel looked around the room at the shocked group. "It is."

Sirenna looked at the old woman. "Are you going to seriously consider this?"

"This is her destiny alone, not yours, Sirenna. Though it may be risky."

Willet continued. "Then I wish for you to help guide me, through this odyssey. In return, I will immediately continue with my training in any manor you see fit."

Laraline finally interjected. "Willet, if this is true, I don't want you to do this. It doesn't sound very safe."

"What do you seek at the end of this odyssey, if you happen to succeed?"

"Answers."

"What kind of answers?"

"About my father's death."

"Any answers he may have are the answers for the dead, not the living."

"This is what I want."

Mother Hazel looked at her intently. "Are you sure you know what you're asking. You are committing to opening a doorway to unknown things. It's not for a mere ten minutes, or an hour, but for several days. Remember there are always consequences to one's actions."

Sirenna and Evelyn looked soberly at one another. Evelyn quickly interjected. "Is this necessary?"

Willet glanced at the twins. It was the first time she saw fear on their faces. Willet soberly nodded. "I will accept the consequences."

Mother Hazel sighed to herself. "Then I agree to your vertriste."

Laraline stepped up to the desk. "As your mother, I forbid you to do this. I evoke matriarchal parental law."

Mother Hazel grimly looked at Laraline. "It is too late. She has entered a fully consensual vertriste, where both parties have agreed. You have borne witness to this exchange. If you had reservations, you should have spoken up before the vertriste was agreed upon."

Laraline nodded in disbelief. "She is still my daughter!"

Sirenna coldly responded. "This is the one area of faigal law where you have no say over her life, even as a mother. It's her choice and her choice alone." Sirenna's eyes drifted to Willet, who had an empowering sense of accomplishment on her face. "Foolish child, you really have no idea what awaits you."

Sirenna abruptly left the large study. No one said a word, as the matriarch hurried down into the dark hallway. Sirenna quickly disappeared behind the doors of the aviary. Her fingers scrambled at the latch, so no one could disturb her. Her wings bloomed wide as she went into a blind rage and began to rip at the flowers and plants about her. Her wings ferociously flapped, creating a violent wind within the glasslike dome. She rose into the air; her hands stretched upward to the ceiling. Tears dripped from the corners of her eyes as she closed them and wept uncontrollably.

Chapter 37:

Changing of the Guard

Jae had just finished her science quiz, when she spied Tori in the courtyard. It was one of the few times she got to hang out with her at school. Willet was scheduled to return to school, but rumors were going around that something had happened to her, and since Adelie's disappearance, word was she would not be returning for the rest of the semester.

Tori didn't seem to know what exactly was happening either. The whole situation was strange. All she knew was that their mother informed them that Adelie would be staying with them for a few days. The entire situation had invigorated the friendship between Deryn and Adelie for the better. They had never had an issue with one another. Jae was reminded of this, as she noticed both girls sitting together on a bench laughing a few days earlier.

This predicament caused Jae to reflect on her own treatment of Willet. She had not really talked to her since they fell out earlier that year. All she knew is that even around Tori, things were awkward. On the surface, Willet's life represented everything she hated about the rich and privileged.

The Adlers and Bransons had a monopoly on everything in town. Her father once owned a newspaper. He printed several unflattering stories about the two families. Things came to a head when a story about the mysterious death of Lord Branson's wife hit the front page. The article threw shade at, not only the Bransons, but the Adlers as well. Two weeks later his printing shop caught on fire and was burnt to the ground. The authorities never could find out who or what caused the fire. The why was definite. He had ruffled too many feathers. As a result, he died a slow death over the course of ten years.

The final death blows came when because of economic hardships, Branson Real Estates bought his property, as well as other foreclosed properties. Dean Weever had to move his family to the mayor's economy home community, Crecheland Estates. Crecheland was far from an estate. It was more like a weigh station for those who were out of economic options. Jae was 3 when they moved in and by the time she was ten, most of the other families she had known, either left town or ended up in Crecheland with her family.

To add insult to injury, her mother Derora had to take a job working for the Adler's as a common maid, even though she was 6 months pregnant. While some of her peers like Tori Ingram, had managed to keep from moving to Crecheland. Most families were about two paychecks away from the Crecheland slums.

When Willet arrived, her natural and well-deserved distrust extended to Willet and her family. Willet was an easy target to strike back at them. Even though she did like Willet and missed talking to her, it was hard to forget her lineage. However, there was greater part of her that was ashamed. They may not be friends anymore, but she couldn't forget the day they met, how Willet had put herself out and tried to protect her from the wrath of Phoebe Crane.

As a result, Willet herself was targeted and bullied. Jae didn't really want to understand the extent of what Willet dealt with, until she realized what her absence meant. The range of victims from the more popular kids and administration had extended. Many of Jae's Crecheland classmates were now fresh meat.

Strangely, this new treatment was largely absent on her and her little sister Deryn. She made her way across the teenage wasteland, to the main sitting area. She noticed that Raven's car had pulled up to the popular area. The passenger door opened and who should walk out, but Adelie herself. Raven didn't bother to get out, in fact, her car promptly took off after a couple moments. Phoebe came out of nowhere and approached Adelie. They exchanged a few words and then she quickly left. The entire thing had a very surreal feeling.

Tori looked up and addressed her curiously. "Jae, everything ok?"

"Phoebe hasn't said a word to me all day."

"Well, that's a good thing."

"I guess so."

Jae looked back in Adelie's direction. A couple more girls had gathered around Adelie, including Deryn who sat beside her. Jae looked in amazement. "Is Adelie becoming popular?"

Tori shook her head. "I tell you one thing; she doesn't behave like someone who witnessed one of her classmates brutally attacked."

"Has Iris been listed as officially dead?"

"I think the family is still holding out hope, but everyone else has pretty much accepted the worst."

"You working today?"

"No, I'm off today. Business kind of fell off after that deal in the Greywood."

"Yeah, I bet."

"Do you need a ride? I'm supposed to take Adelie home today to pack some things?"

"That would be great!"

Tori looked over in Adelie's direction. Her and Derryn were whispering to one another. "I guess they really missed each other."

Jae gave a half smile as if she didn't know how to respond. It was one of those uncomfortable moments, as Jae looked across the courtyard. She hoped the moment would pass. She nodded at Tori before responding.

"Thank you, for the ride."

A nervousness overcame her as she rose from her seat and headed down the steps to her next class. She was crossing the open hallway into the garden, when saw Headmistress Faulkner stomping in her direction.

Her nervousness turned into anxiety. For some reason, Jae quickly ducked down a nearby stairwell and waited for her to pass. Faulkner was very much an elitist. One day she all but informed Jae that she was lucky to be accepted into Talomore.

The headmistress was busy talking to another woman who was wearing dark shades and a brown sunhat. From what she knew about her town's residents, it appeared to be the librarian. It wasn't common knowledge that these two were siblings, as they were almost never together in public. Unlike today, where they seemed to be having a heated conversation. The headmistress in a hushed voiced fussed at the other.

"I just don't think that is a good idea."

"You know, for months you preached to me about doing the right thing. Now that I am, you are suddenly changing your tune. What gives?"

"All I'm saying is you don't want to make Aquila an enemy."

"Well, it's a little late for that. Besides, I'm not afraid of her. Maybe you are, or perhaps you're afraid of anything that might come out about me."

"Listen to yourself."

"That would embarrass you to no end, wouldn't it sis? It's always, somehow, about you."

"Kestrel please."

"Why do I even bother?"

Jae perked her head up just in time to see the librarian start to walk off with a desperate headmistress calling after her. "What are you going to do?"

"I guess you'll just have to wait and see."

Jae wasn't sure what she had witnessed, but it felt serious.

Chapter 38:

Sister Time

Even though Willet received the go ahead on her little experiment, a lot of things had to be put into place before then. For one thing she had to get permission to miss the entire following week of school. This normally would be very dicey, especially since her suspension from school would technically end the following evening.

Thankfully, being implicated in the Iris Van Warren affair by association, gave her some leeway. It was seen as extra time to deal with the trauma of the situation. Evelyn had visited Talomore and pleaded the case for her great niece.

The response she got was a stack of school assignments, so Willet would not get behind. Only Mother Hazel, Sirenna, Evelyn and Laraline knew exactly what was happening. Adelie, Mrs. Weever, and Tori were told that the family was dealing with some family trauma. Because of the situation, Adelie would stay at Mrs. Weever's for the week. Laraline even took off work siting a vague doctor referral about family trauma. Greenbaum wasn't happy, as Laraline had become quite popular among his regulars. However, this gave her time to avoid the request for offshore deliveries.

If the plan was going to work, everyone who wasn't involved had to be completely in the dark. That was the basic mechanics of a vertriste. A secret agreement or arrangement, which all parties involved, agree to take the truth to their graves.

She elected to spend the evening before her spiritual exodus, hanging out with Adelie. Adelie in recent days had become a bit distant from her older sister, however she still did enjoy being in Willet's room. As the two sat playing some variation of snakes and ladders, Adelie started their conversation by asking the most unusual question.

"Do you think you will get married?"

"I don't really know, I guess if I met someone."

"I want to get married."

"Really, anyone in particular?"

"Perhaps some enchanted prince living here in Meadowlark under a curse, originally from a faraway land."

"Sounds intriguing, anyone I know?"

Adelie coyly responded. "I don't know, perhaps."

"What about this far away land?"

"Perhaps you could be a princess. Princess Willet Swift from the Greywood."

A scowl quickly overcame Willet's face. "Not funny."

"I'm not joking."

"Maybe a distant land beyond the Greywood, where I can be a queen."

Willet picked up her fire poker and started to use a pompous royal accent. "My dear subjects, stand to attention. There is a new decree. From this day forth, no one is allowed in my kingdom without a bald head."

Adelie burst out into a deep laugh. Willet soon joined her. Soon the laugher died and Willet smiled. "I miss this."

Adelie's eyes widened. "You do?"

"It seems we never get along anymore, you always want to be around Aunt Sirenna."

Adelie coldly responded. "Are you jealous?"

"Kind of."

"Really?"

"I miss my little sister."

Adelie was defiant. "Well, I'm not little anymore."

"Sorry, I guess you learned how to handle yourself out there in the woods."

"So, you really came after me?"

"Of course, were family."

Suddenly, Addie asked the most curious question. 'So, you won't just leave us, like daddy left?"

Willet was taken aback by the question. Adelie was definitely aware that something serious was going on. Instead of answering, Willet did the one thing that adults did, that she herself hated. When they didn't want to truthfully answer a difficult question, they pivoted. She changed the subject.

"So, what's all this jazz about princesses and things?"

Suddenly Adelie's face became animated. She looked around cautiously to make sure no one was listening. When she spoke again, it was in a deep whisper. "Can you keep a secret?"

"Of course!"

Adelie leaned in , excited to share her secret. "That day I got lost in the woods, I met a queen."

Willet sat waiting for the punchline until she realized Adelie was serious. "What do you mean, you met a queen? Where?"

"By a stream, near the most incredible looking mushrooms. She called them booga tears. Isn't that the most curious name you ever heard?"

"You say you met this woman and she talked to you?"

"No, I met a queen."

"Says who?"

"She did. She called herself the Queen of the Greywood Kingdom."

Willet was suddenly concerned. "Did she try to hurt you?"

Adelie was silent for a moment, before changing the subject. "She invited me to tea."

"Tea?"

"Now, promise me you won't tell anyone else."

"You met a strange woman calling herself the queen of the forest, and you want me to keep quiet?"

"You promised Willie."

"Ok fine, I won't tell your secret, under one condition."

"What?"

"I don't want you going into those woods anymore."

"Come on."

"Promise me."

"Ok, I promise."

"So, what did this queen look like. Did she have a name?"

"She had a funny sort of name. I don't remember her name. For some reason the entire situation has become cloudy. I do remember what she looked like though, because that was the strangest thing."

"How so?"

"She looked a lot like you."

"What do you mean, she looked like me?"

"I'm serious! At first, I thought she was you. Maybe an older version of you."

"You mean I have a doppelganger in the woods?"

"You don't believe me?"

"I didn't say that."

"You didn't have to, it's the way your behaving."

"Really, I meant nothing..."

Suddenly Adelie blurted. "Verspa!"

"What?"

"I remember her name. Queen Verspa Lynn."

At that moment, the sound of several wild cats howling filled the air. Willet looked towards her window. Both girls looked out through the blinds across the field. Neither could see a thing but the Greywood in the distance. The sound of howling continued for another few moments before it ceased. Willet raised her eyebrows to Adelie.

"That was weird."

Chapter 39:

Secret Treaties

It was dark when Patsy arrived. The observation tower was usually well lit; however, it was dim this evening. As she carefully ascended the steps, she could pick up a slight hint of movement from above. She was suddenly enraged. Gavin sat in the crow's nest perched beside Aquila. His eyes moved toward the steps at he heard Patsy's footfalls as she approached the top. He unsheathed his weapon as he addressed Aquila.

"Auntie, your snitch has arrived."

Aquila was still, but her voice was impatient. "You're late, I'm not in the habit of waiting."

"I'm not used to climbing such heights. I thought we would meet in some bar or restaurant."

"If your sister, Sirenna, saw you in plain sight with me, what do you think would happen to you?" Patsy had no response.

Raven calmly responded from the other side of the wall. "Perhaps you should have used your wings, if you were so concerned with heights." Raven glanced at Patsy's' hands. She noticed that she was wearing gloves.

"You're wearing gloves?"

Gavin followed her lead. "Remove your gloves!"

"Excuse me!"

"You heard my brother, let's see if you have all your fingers!"

Both twins moved closer in a threatening manner. Patsy quickly complied. She slid off her white silk gloves showing her long delicate fingers. After she had done so, they nodded at one another before stepping away, granting Patsy her access to Aquila.

By now Patsy was quite offended. "Can I put my gloves back on, sprite?"

Both twins nodded in unison. "You're safe."

Patsy slipped her gloves on as she huffed at Aquila. "I didn't know there would be an audience up here."

"How do you mean?"

"I thought this was a private meeting. Why are these children even here? I have no time for games!"

"Gavin often assists me on the more nocturnal outings. Raven is a surrogate for one of Gavin's previous acquaintances. However, I assure you that my niece and nephew are cut from the same cloth as I."

Gavin interjected in Patsy's direction. His eyes were almost crazed as he stared her down. "What my aunt is saying, is that me and my sister are loyal."

"My dear Patsy, I wouldn't advise insulting them."

"Me insulting them?"

"They aren't as forgiving as most."

Gavin whispered. "An Adler in the crow's nest surrounded by three Bransons, I like those odds."

Raven whispered back. "So do I, brother."

Patsy was almost groveling, as she felt a veiled threat from the twins. "Ok, can we start over, I meant no disrespect. I have always thought of them both as lovely children."

Raven was wearing a black knit cap as she moved closer. Her face was obscured by large wide sunglasses that obviously hid several bruises. She was intently staring at Patsy, as if trying to make her nervous. Patsy noticed that Raven wore a vest made exclusively of animal fur. At closer inspection, she realized what kind of pelts she was wearing. She looked at the young girl partly disgusted, yet trying to make polite small talk.

"Why cats?"

Aquila's voice responded from the shadows as if she were flanking her. "Cats can intuitively sense our true nature. In our lore, sleeven would often use cats to oust a suspected faigal. In the 10th century, a powerful religious order known as einin, used cats to hunt and kill our species by the hundreds. We had to go into hiding. Our culture, religion and society had to go underground. This threat of exposure has over time caused a deep seeded dislike and distrust for these creatures. If you think about it, as a whole, most faigal instinctually don't like them. I for one, can't blame her!"

Suddenly Raven held up a large crossbow toward Patsy's head. Patsy was so startled she nearly jumped backward. Aquila rose and approached them both. Her one good eye glowing yellow.

Patsy nervously turned to Aquila. "Could you tell her not to aim that thing at me?"

Aquila motioned to Raven. "What's wrong dear niece? You seem bothered."

"All I see is an Adler pitkin, I wish to shoot between the eyes."

"Relax dear niece. Patsy is on our side. She didn't mean to insult you. She has been a dear friend to the Branson house for many years."

"Yes, I'm a friend."

"You must excuse poor Raven; she has had an awful week. She has not been herself. I don't have to tell you; your daughter dealt with some trauma herself."

Patsy tried to show hollow empathy. "Yes of course, and if I insulted you both, I am truly sorry!"

Aquila seemed bored with the entire situation and quickly changed the subject, which probably helped to ease Patsy a bit. "So, what do you have to tell me this week?"

"You're right, they are making some sort of move. Laraline called out of work for a week. Willet will be taking an extended leave from school, and everything is hush hush!"

"What else?"

"Evelyn says they are dealing with family trauma."

"Is that all you have?"

Patsy dug into her purse and removed a piece of paper. "I removed these from the glove compartment of Laraline's car." She promptly handed the papers to Aquila.

"What is this?"

"It's a past due bill from Sun Crest Boat Marina. That's the street address on top."

"This is very interesting."

"Do you actually think they will break the sanctuary?"

"They want this boat so bad, at some point they will have to risk leaving town. The thing to do is actually catch them in the act."

"How are you going to do that, they will most certainly be expecting to see one of you waiting?"

"That's why sometimes, it's necessary to employ outside sources."

Chapter 40:

Forbidden Fruit

Jonas sat in his favorite tree. The bandage around his waist was starting to itch again, but he didn't feel quite as weak. The current moonlight bathed the front yard with a glow of soft white light. From this vantage point, he could see tiny field mice scurry around the patchwork of green grass that made up the large yard. He was close to drifting into listlessness, when he heard her voice from across the yard.

"Hey, tree boy!"

Jonas looked around startled. Willet stood at the edge of the driveway. He thought she was absolutely gorgeous. Her long, dark, curly hair gleamed in the moonlight. Her sparkling eyes with a hint of shyness gazed up at him. She wore a loose knit sweater and jeans as she slowly strolled across the yard barefoot. He was suddenly nervous.

"Wait!"

"What?"

Jonas leaped from the tree, his wings extended to break his fall. He landed a mere foot from her, grabbing her bare foot with his hand a few inches in midair. Willet's eyes caught his and there was an awkward moment. His warm fingers slightly tickled her foot, and he instantly let go.

"Sorry, there still might be traps in the yard."

Willet turned away looking around paranoid. She was flustered and her heart was beating erraticly. After a few moments, she felt as if things were ok.

"It's cool."

"Why are you here?"

"Gee, thanks!"

"I mean, you're the last person I expected to see."

"I deserved that."

"I mean, is it safe for you to be here?"

"Can you let me speak, before I regret coming here at all?"

"Ok, I can do that."

Willet was visibly nervous, as she took a deep breath and carefully tried to explain her presence. "I owe you an apology for the other day. There are a lot of things going on lately that I'm still trying to get a grip on, but I shouldn't have taken it out on you. You have been nothing but good, sweet, and decent, despite what our two families' reputations may imply. You saved my sister and I won't ever be able to thank you enough."

Jonas was civil and nodded. "You're welcome!"

There was an uncomfortable gap of silence as Willet continued. "I heard what happened to you, and I was a little worried."

"Just a little?"

Willet put her fingers together. "Just a tad."

"It's not as bad as it looks."

"Really?"

"I'm lying, it's worse."

They both broke into nervous laughter, before it got silent again. Willet turned her head slightly to avoid his gaze.

"I still can't imagine, considering how the whole thing went down?"

Instead of elaborating Jonas intuitively changed the subject. "Ok Swift, what do you want to know?"

Willet was slightly embarrassed. "Damn it, am I that obvious?"

"Transparent."

"I really did come to see you too."

"Spill it!"

"Ok, I know this may sound redundant, in light of what you guys went through..."

"Come on Swift."

"When you were out there with Addie, did she mention anything really strange to you?"

"Strange, strange how?"

"I don't know, did she say anything kind of loopy?"

"Not really, I was pretty loopy."

"Well, being shot by your sister can do that. Sorry, I didn't mean to say that."

"What else did Adelie tell you?"

"That's the thing, Addie didn't say much about that particular situation."

Jonas folded his arms. "Nothing? What's going on?"

"Well, she mentioned experiencing some unusual things that I'm not at liberty to discuss."

"Wait, she got lost at one point. When I found her again, she did mention that someone was after her. I assumed she was talking about that crazy lady that took Iris. But the way she said it, I got the impression that it had nothing to do with that at all. She seemed kind of spooked. I didn't press the issue. After all, there are a lot of dark things in those woods."

Willet looked down. "That's what worries me."

"She did just go through this huge ordeal."

"I know. I keep telling myself it's nothing, but something about her seems different."

"Like how?"

"I can't explain it. Perhaps it's nothing."

"Look, we can finish this conversation when you return to school."

Willet had tears in her eyes as she spoke. "No, we can't."

"Why not?"

"I'm going to be leaving."

Jonas's heart sank. "Leaving where?"

"Nowhere, I don't know!"

"What's going on, Willet?"

"I can't tell you and I'm very afraid. I may be doing something dangerous. But I can't tell anyone. But I just wanted to see you once more."

"What are you talking about, I'm getting nervous?"

Willet caught herself. "I got to go, you take care."

Willet turned away feeling mortified. *That went really bad!* Without a word, Willet headed out into the street. Jonas sped after her. He reached out and grabbed her shoulder. Her response was almost immediate, as she slapped him across the face.

Jonas grabbed at the sting of his cheek. "Hey, what gives?"

Willet's eyes were dark as she responded. "I shouldn't have come."

"I'm confused, I thought we were friends."

"You thought wrong. I can't be your friend."

Jonas held his head down, obviously wounded. "I don't understand!"

Willet turned around to face him with her eyes glaring. Tears ran down her face as the urge inside mounted. She grabbed his shirt collar and shoved him back against an ancient willow tree. Before he had time to react, Willet was atop of him. She pressed her lips against his fiercely. The warm touch of his face against hers made her feel weak. He suddenly grabbed her waist and pulled her closer. His hand grabbed the back of her hair. He tasted her lips as if he were trying to devour her. She couldn't breathe.

She turned her head slightly to catch her breath, and he gently nibbled her neck. Willet could feel his breath; it sent tingles down her spine. Suddenly she caught herself and pushed him away. She had an embarrassed look on her face, as she wiped her lips. Her legs were trembling.

"Do you understand now?"

Before he had time to respond, Willet quickly extended her wings and ran down the drive, without looking back, she took to the sky. Jonas had an urge to follow after her, but he was almost frozen with shock at what had just happened. He watched her disappear into the night sky.

Chapter 41:

Feather

By the time Willet had returned home, she had calmed down a bit. Her tears had dried onto her cheeks, and the scent of Jonas had finally left her nostrils. As she landed on her toes, she took a deep breath. She now had a sense of closure, as she headed toward the steps of the large wooden door. It might have been selfish, but she at least wanted to kiss him, before she adhered to Raven's vertriste.

Out of the corner of her eye, she sensed movement. She spun around uneasily. The Greywood stood erect in the distance. Did she imagine seeing something? She quickly moved across the field to the edge of one of the owl statues and scanned the landscape.

That was when she saw the feather, a few feet from where she stood. She carefully walked over to where the large white feather lay. She looked down at the strange artifact. There was something familiar about this particular feather. It was not unlike the feathers that the strange woman in Willet's dream had.

Willet plucked the feather from the ground and held it up in the moonlight. It was real. Ten months earlier, she would have dismissed her dreams as strange and weird. Here in Meadowlark, it seemed almost ordinary, even common place.

A flash of light bathed her as the front door opened wide. Mother Hazel was calling her. It was almost time for bed. She had to get a lot of rest tonight. Tomorrow would be the biggest day of her life.

Chapter 42:

So, It Begins

Laraline drove Adelie to school that morning with a suitcase filled with clothes. While Evelyn helped Mother Hazel set up Willet's bedroom properly. A large mirror was placed directly above her bed. As several herbs and incents were lit or left burning to create an easier transitional path, as mother would say.

Willet sat on the head of one of the great owl statues. She held the white feather in her palm, considering if it was wise to pick it up. She almost felt like she had a death wish. Why else would she go to Jonas and make out with him despite the possible fallout. She looked out across the field at the Greywood as she slowly breathed in the fresh morning air. She wanted to get as much fresh air as possible.

After a bit, she climbed off and headed back inside. When she returned to her room, it was finished. The air was slightly foggy with burning sage, as she made her way across the floor. Almost immediately, she started to cough and wheeze.

"Does it have to be this much? I can hardly breathe."

Mother Hazel, who was near the window hanging herbs, responded. "You will get used to it in time."

Willet furrowed her brow as she made her way to her bed. She sat watching the old woman reciting a series of chants and prayers. It was so outside the realm of what she had experienced with the old woman, Willet almost began to laugh at the bizarre spectacle before her. Finally, Mother Hazel stopped and looked at Willet.

"Whenever you're ready."

Willet's door opened and Laraline discreetly crept inside. As much as she was at odds with her mother, she was overjoyed that she arrived. She coughed slightly as Laraline made her way to the bed.

"Good, I didn't miss anything."

Willet took a deep breath. "You're just in time."

"For the record, I don't fully understand, but I support you."

Laraline had a concerned expression as she reached into her pocket. She pulled out a large chain necklace with a key attached. Willet recognized it immediately. A stream of tears poured down Willet's face as her mother placed the necklace over Willet's head and around her neck. Willet gently cupped her father's boat key in her palm.

"Be careful!"

Willet responded by grabbing her mother's hand and squeezing it tightly. "I will, Mama!"

Evelyn looked about the room, trying to fight off her own tears. "Where is Sirenna?"

Laraline had a dire look. "She said she didn't want to come up."

"Well, it's not easy for her."

Laraline snapped back. "Stop making excuses for that woman."

Mother Hazel cut them both off. "Quiet, the aura must remain pure in this room."

Willet kicked her shoes off and stretched out on her back. She was facing the mirror on the ceiling. Her reflection looked peculiar today. Perhaps, it was because she was so aware of what she was about to attempt.

"Any words of advice for me?"

Mother Hazel peered over her the rim of her glasses. she took a deep breath as if trying to summon knowledge. "Watch out for dead debris."

"What do you mean by dead debris?"

"You are becoming very comfortable with drifting. Make sure you don't employ anything that was once alive to help you drift."

"That was a bit random, but alright."

It was quiet for several moments as Mother Hazel sat in her rocking chair beside Willet with her eyes closed. She began to rock very slowly. After a few moments she had created a steady rhythm. She then instructed Willet to focus on the mirror and to start a focused breathing.

Willet did as she was instructed and after a while she became calm, even tired. As she considered the mirror, she could feel her toes tingle as she continued to breathe. She closed her eyes, as she tried to focus on all the new sounds that were starting to emerge around her.

Chapter 43:

Stealth

Willet opened her eyes and thought she had finally awoken from a terrible nightmare. She looked about, only to realize she was in her old childhood bed again. She recognized the wood paneling on the walls and cracked plaster on the ceiling. She sat up and studied the familiar surroundings. She was no longer in Meadowlark. She was back in her old house in Key West. She was home.

Willet felt excited as she stood up and ran out to find her family. She was about to call for her father when she saw the bizarre stranger in the now empty and decrepit living room. He was sitting in her Father's old wicker chair that was now falling apart.

He wore sunglasses and a black face mask. At the top of his head sat a fuzzy brown derby. His entire body was wrapped in a brown fur coat, with long faigal feathers sown into the collar. Long lanky legs sprouted from beneath the coat, exposing paramilitary style boots made of some sort of reptile skin. Willet shuddered at the idea of a strange man in their home. Of course it was no longer her home, and most importantly she wasn't there, so he couldn't actually see her.

However, he could possibly still sense her, if she gave him any reason. In fact, as soon as she stormed into the room, he turned in her direction slightly. It was as if he could sense someone behind his chair in the hallway. She stood absolutely still, like some wandering ghost, waiting for him to turn his attention away. Finally, he did.

He started to fumble about with some sort of rifle that lay in his lap. He clicked a button and a green light beam flashed on the top. It was the type of gun that had a scope on top. He lifted the gun and spun it around toward the window. The window was dirty and caked with dust. Several tiny window moths fluttered about the light from his gun. He ignored them, took a deep breath and focused his attention across the street.

Who was this guy, and what was he hunting? Willet carefully crept closer, keeping her breathing in check. At this point she didn't know what to expect. She was almost behind his chair, as she squinted down at him.

He wore black latex gloves on his hands, the kind you might find in a medical office. As Willet was observing, he daintily took one hand off his gun and reached toward the window. He snatched a moth that had settled on one of the few clear spots on the window.

He pulled his mask down and with a quick flick, tossed the tiny insect into his mouth and began to chew. Willet caught a glimpse of his teeth and they were completely inhuman. They were large yellowish and double layered incisors. In fact, all of his teeth looked like incisors.

As bizarre as his actions were, his concentration at the window remained steadfast. Willet soon directed her gaze to whatever was outside. Looking out the window, she peered across the street. All she could see was the marina, where her father kept his boat. Willet suddenly felt a sinking realization. *He is here waiting for me to show up!*

At one point, he pulled up his sleeve to look at his watch. On the inside of his wrist, she noticed a peculiar looking tattoo. She had seen it somewhere before. Although she couldn't recall where. The familiar circle with three lines inside, in a row, itched at her memory.

Willet turned her head in the direction of the front door. It was an aqua green wooden door with a wooden latch pulled down over the front. All she had to do was go out the front door and cross the street down to the marina. Unfortunately, the door was a mere 2 feet from the creep in the chair. If she opened the door, he would hear.

She had to do something to distract him. She looked about the empty room. There was nothing left, just him, his gun, and the old wicker chair. Her eyes surveyed the room for anything. She looked down at the floor and near his foot lay an empty bullet cartridge. She quickly snatched it up and tossed it down the dark dim hallway. There was faint knocking sound of the cartridge hitting against the edge of her bedroom door.

The stranger twirled his gun around and instinctively let off a quick round at the bedroom door. The sound of glass breaking was unsettling to Willet. She watched him quickly rise from his chair and dash down the hallway. She didn't have time to wait. She moved to the door and lifted the latch. The door slowly swung wide open with an annoying creak. She dashed out the front door across the yard and onto the sidewalk.

She looked back to see the stranger now standing at the door. He was looking out the front door, scanning about with his rifle. There was a thin green beam that flickered about from its sights. The hunter spoke from behind his mask.

"I know you're out there!"

He took a step forward, as he removed his hat and waved sweat from his brow. He was completely bald with a series of similar tattoos on his head in the shape of a natural hairline. He abruptly returned his hat and panned the laser scope across the perimeter of the yard. Willet was terrified. She quickly ducked down so the light wouldn't touch her. *Was he bluffing? Could he actually sense her?*

She squatted in the middle of the pavement, waiting. On the other side of the street, she could see the docks. She was almost there. She had an impulse to make a run to the docks, when her eyes caught a serious of unexpected obstacles. Right in front of her path, she beheld four rather large black harpies perched on the fence posts that led down to the docks.

The hulking beasts could almost be mistaken for vultures, save for the curious humanlike infant heads that sat on their narrow shoulders. Their surreal expression gave the illusion that they were sweet and innocent. Even their eyes had an endearing malevolence about them. It was only when they opened their mouths and exposed tiny dagger like fangs, that their viciousness was real.

They didn't see her...yet, but they would definitely recognize her scent any moment. The thin green light from the rifle scope washed by her shoe. How could she ever get away. Even if she did escape, the minute she cranked the boat, they would hear. She had already failed her mission. She was almost in tears as she saw the hunter advance in her direction. Even though he couldn't see her, he could somehow still sense her.

Willet had to think quickly, as he was getting closer. She needed a distraction. Willet looked about the road. She saw a slab of concrete lying on the edge of the curb. Her fingers grasped it as silently as she could. She looked ahead at one of the harpies sniffing the air. With a steady aim, she pelted the slab into the air. It struck the harpy at the end of the post. It screeched in shock, as it was knocked to the ground. Willet had knocked it on its ass, and it was pissed. It sniffed the air, aggravated. It swooped down in Willet's direction. However, it didn't get very far as it was suddenly riddled with bullets.

Willet looked back at the hunter, who was now standing at the edge of the sidewalk. Reloading his rifle. The other three harpies looked up at him. Their eyes were burning with rage.

"You killed our sister!"

"That's what you get, you were told to stay away from the house!"

"And we have done what mother asked of us, it is you who have broken the vertriste, with the murder of our sister!"

Willet suddenly had an idea. She deepened her voice and blurted out a low insult. "That's cause I didn't like her smell."

The other three harpies gasped. "What did you say?"

The strange hunter looked confused. "I said nothing."

Willet interjected again. "He is a dirty lying sleeven, sisters!"

The hunter looked down toward the road. "Who was that?"

One of the other harpies proclaimed. "I should have said that!"

The hunter scanned the road with his green light. "Wait, someone else is out here with us."

One of the harpies snapped back. "There is no one here with us!"

Willet slid to the side to avoid the beams detection; she mumbled under her breath. "Shut your mouth, or I'm going to shoot you next fatso!"

The hunter looked directly in Willet's direction. "Did you hear that; it's coming from the ground?"

Two of the other harpies hopped off the fence enraged. Their angry baby lips quivering, as they swooped down on the sidewalk. "So, you think you can shoot us all?"

Realizing the chaos ensuing, the hunter turned back to the two large beasts slowly approaching him. "I didn't say anything, someone else is here. Someone is trying to pit us against one another."

The last harpy on the fence leapt down and joined her sisters who were now in the front yard. "That's what you say, but you are the one with the gun. You are the one who shot her dead!"

The hunter slowly backed up a few feet, making sure they were all in his sites in case things popped off. "Shut up and listen."

"We are now in your precious yard, sleeven. What are you going to do now?"

The hunter positioned his gun back toward the closest harpy. "I'm warning you, you step any closer, I'll blow your greasy carcass away!"

Willet screeched in a high voice. "I'd like to see you try!"

The hunter turned the gun and fired in Willet's direction. The bullet whizzed by her cheek. He cocked the gun and yelled frantically. "Who is that speaking, did you hear that voice?"

The remaining three were not listening, instead they were focused on Richter, as they slowly began flanking the sleeven hunter. They were still cautious, but they were at the edge of attack. Things were at a standstill. Willet carefully picked herself off the pavement and quietly tipped across the street.

She kept glancing back, as she quietly made her way out to the entrance of the pier. She passed several schooners and boats as she began to run frantically, expecting not to see the boat. Suddenly she saw a familiar image.

The Lenoir was docked two spots down from where it was usually docked. A strip of yellow police tape still blocked the entrance to the deck. She quickly climbed underneath the tape and made her way onto the deck. She rushed to the anchor and began to release it from the watery depths. The turquoise stern rocked slightly as she pulled in the anchor.

Suddenly, she heard several gunshots in the distance. She looked back toward the entrance of the pier. She couldn't see anything. But she didn't have to, as she already knew what was going on. She moved back to the pier and scrambled to remove the dock line. It was one of those chores that was always cumbersome. The thick knots were showing early signs of decay and neglect as they were overgrown with coral. As a result, the lines scratched her wrists as she worked the knots. After much discussion from the stubborn line, she was able to remove the rope. Almost instantly the Lenoir started to drift away from the pier. Willet leapt back aboard. Still, there was no sign any pursuit.

She kept looking back, half expecting to see the stranger with his gun. As soon as she was about a good ten yards from the pier, she saw a figure moving. It was a man, running past the pier and down the street. Her heart jumped a beat until she realized it was someone out for a morning jog.

She reached into her blouse and pulled at the key they was on the chain. She closed her eyes and removed the chain from her neck. She took a deep breath and stood in front of the helm. She put the key in and turned it. Almost instantly, she heard a low purr as the engine clicked on.

There was a tingle in her stomach, an excitement that she hadn't felt in almost two years. That's how long it had been since she had actually sailed the Lenoir. She looked at the compass and steered northeast. Willet knew what direction roughly to head and wouldn't need to look at the map for at least another hour. Paranoia overcame her and she would periodically look back at the pier. Still, she saw nothing.

She continued to look back until the pier vanished into the horizon.

Chapter 44:

Secrets Exposed

Laraline sat beside her daughter, watching her still body. Every now and then, Willet would twitch uncontrollably. As much as she wished to wake her from what appeared to be nightmares, she was warned against this by Mother Hazel. According to the old woman, drift transference was unstable at best, and it could cause several mental scars, if the link was not naturally dissolved.

Evelyn entered the bedroom with two cups of hot tea. She handed Laraline a cup and found herself a seat at the foot of the bed. "How is she doing?"

"How am I supposed to know?"

"Well, her levels may be slightly elevated, especially her temperature. That's expected, even under normal circumstances. If it fluctuates in either direction, about 20 degrees, then we have a problem."

"Mother Hazel says it's dangerous to wake her, yet I can see my daughter suffering. Look at her, she is in pain."

Mother Hazel was suddenly behind her at the door. "I understand, but this is no ordinary slumber, she is practicing the art of Drifting. Even as we speak, part of her is travelling abroad."

"How do you know all this stuff?"

The old woman snapped back. "It's my job to know!"

Evelyn leaned close to Laraline. "Oriole developed this particular kala early. Neither me nor Sirenna were ever able to accomplish what she did. She was always drifting into altered states. Believe me, we got plenty scared for her."

"Really?"

"Was she in one of these states when she walked into the Greywood and disappeared? All my life I heard she just walked into the Greywood without provocation. You said she was almost possessed."

"I see where you're going, but this situation is much different."

"How?"

"Because we are all working together and have a complete understanding of what she is trying to accomplish. We are all here, watching over her."

In spite of the voiced concern, things were pretty calm. Then Laraline asked a simple question that resulted in the most unusual domino effect of consequences. It was silent for a few minutes when Laraline looked at Evelyn.

"Was my mother a good person?"

Evelyn's expression was that of uncomfortable queerness. "Laraline, why would you ask such a question?"

"I never hear a single word spoken about anything kind or noble she has done or said. All I ever hear is how smart or pretty, or talented she was."

"What is wrong with any of those attributes?"

"I notice you have yet to answer my question."

Evelyn dismissed the question. "You're being ridiculous. Of course, she was a good person!"

Laraline's eyes were hard. "Really, then why aren't there any images of her in this house. No photos or paintings anywhere. If one didn't know any better, one would think she didn't even exist."

"Nonsense."

"Really, that's your response. A thirty-five-room home adorned with hundreds of photos and paintings, yet not one single image of your sister anywhere to be found. Don't you find that peculiar?"

"I'm sure we have a few things in the attic. I'll have Mrs. Weever retrieve something this afternoon."

"Why pack your beloved sisters memories away, hidden in storage, unless she's not as beloved as you say?"

"Lynn, calm down."

"You're lying. I can hear your heartbeat."

Mother Hazel finally looked up at Evelyn soberly. "Tell her."

Both women looked up at the old woman. Mother Hazel removed her dark spectacles. "Evelyn, tell Laraline the truth about her mother."

Just to hear those words uttered filled Laraline with a creeping dread. All her life, she felt as if something was off, but she couldn't put it into words. Perhaps Evelyn had knowledge that would explain why. Laraline's lips quivered.

"Tell me what?"

Mother Hazel hummed. "Evelyn?"

Evelyn snapped back. "Sirenna is right, you are a wicked old woman."

"Am I? There is but one party who was not complicit in the original vertriste, and it seems to me, this is the party most effected."

Laraline stood up agitated. "What is she talking about, auntie?"

Mother Hazel touched Evelyn's shoulder. "Go find Sirenna, take Laraline with you. End this charade today. The Adler affairs must be put back in order for this house to begin to thrive again. This is what has been revealed to me about this situation."

"What if all becomes broken again?"

"Can't you see, it's already broken, woman."

Evelyn nodded in compliance, as she turned and headed out the door. Laraline looked hard at Mother Hazel. The old woman sat back down in her chair.

"Follow Evelyn, there you will find the truth you seek."

"Why can't you tell me?"

"It's not my truth to tell."

Laraline felt a pit in her stomach as the old woman closed her eyes and started to rock in her chair. Laraline slowly turned toward the door and followed Evelyn down the hallway. Laraline could hear her footfalls, as they descended the stairwell. The aviary was quiet that morning. The sound of birds was almost absent as they approached the large glass door.

Evelyn wrapped on the glass wall with her knuckles. There was a slight echo, as she listened for a response. Evelyn put her ear to the wall and listened. "I don't hear anything."

Laraline pointed at the handle. "Look, it's not locked, the door is cracked."

She quickly snatched the handle and turned the latch and the door slowly swung open. Laraline stuck her head inside. Without warning, a flock of lovebirds poured past her head. She jumped back clutching her chest. She was almost laughing at herself, as she sighed in relief.

"Just birds."

She really had no idea what she was expecting, however she didn't have time to reflect on the absurdity of the moment, as a voice from within called out. "Shut the door, you are letting all the warm air out."

Evelyn responded. "Sirenna, are you ok, dear?"

As both women made their way inside, they could see several plants and bushes were ripped up and uprooted. There were claw marks in the ground and in several trees. At first, Laraline couldn't see Sirenna, until she looked up. In a tree branch near the roof, a slim woman in a traditional silk nightgown perched. Her long blonde hair hung down her back wild and unkempt. She was peering down at them, as if they were tiny ants. She smiled down.

"Never better."

Evelyn mumbled to Laraline. "Something is wrong with her."

Laraline leaned in whispering. "Do you think she is dangerous?"

Sirenna called down. "You do know, I can hear both of you discussing me?"

Evelyn called up with her hands cupped around her mouth. "Sirenna, come down, we need to talk."

"Isn't that what we are doing at this moment?"

Laraline called after her. "I want the truth about my mother."

Sirenna sprang down from her branch to confront Evelyn. "Old boring conversation, is this your doing?"

Evelyn was tongue-tied as Sirenna was face to face with her sister. "What did you say to her?"

Laraline hopped in front of Sirenna to block her direct access to Evelyn. "Nothing, she didn't expose your little secret."

"My secret? You have no idea!"

"I put the innuendos together, and double talk together. You did something to my mother. I want the truth."

"You can't handle the truth."

"I want to know, now."

"Whose idea was this?"

Evelyn timidly spoke up. "Mother Hazel said it was revealed to her."

"What are you blathering on about?"

"She says it's time to undo the vertriste."

Sirenna looked at Evelyn harshly. "And you're ok with this?"

Evelyn was almost in tears as she nodded. "It doesn't matter anymore."

Sirenna cleared her throat, as her gaze shifted to her niece. "Well, what do you want to know sprite?"

Laraline was suddenly afraid to ask. She stood in the intimidating silence. Sirenna continued. "You want to know if I had something to do with Oriole's death?"

"Did you?"

"Of course I did."

Laraline wasn't expecting such brutal honesty. "What did you do?"

"I murdered her."

Laraline's eyes widened in complete shock. "What?"

"I buried an axe in her head and watched her die."

Laraline's response was sudden, as she grabbed her aunt by the throat. Her wings expanded and they began to violently flap. Laraline then began to repeatedly strike the older woman across the face. Sirenna lay limp as if unfazed. A hint of madness overcame Sirenna as she began to laugh.

"I saw this day coming."

Laraline extended her claws and began to slash at Sirenna's face and neck. Finally, Evelyn grabbed Laraline's clawed hand as she tried to restrain the younger woman.

"Let go of me, she killed my mother!"

"But she didn't tell you everything."

"I've heard enough!"

"She didn't kill your mother; she killed your aunt."

Laraline paused and turned to face Evelyn. "What are you talking about?"

"Oriole didn't give birth to you!"

Evelyn cupped her mouth as if she had spoken some profanity. Laraline turned her attention away from Sirenna who lay scarred and tattered on the ground.

"What did you say?"

Evelyn's lip was quivering, as she continued. "Oriole was barren. She couldn't have any children. She acquired you as part of our vertriste. She promised me that you would become the rightful heir of the Adler dynasty. That is the only reason I agreed to her terms."

"Oh my god, you're not saying what I think your saying?"

Evelyn broke into tears. "I only wanted to protect you, I was forbidden to tell anyone."

"This can't be true."

Sirenna lay on her back. She clapped her hands together. "How sweet, a mother and daughter reunion, perhaps we should preserve the moment in pictures."

Chapter 45:

The Open Sea

Things had settled a bit, and a feeling of nostalgia overcame her. Willet was on her father's boat again. She had so many memories on this deck. A sweet smile overcame her. It was like rediscovering a part of herself she had completely forgotten.

She spent several minutes investigating the Lenoir. She climbed below to take a look at the sleeping cabin. She dashed down the steps and flicked on the lights. The room came alive amid several decorated streams of cobwebs that had begun to infest the interior. The sleeping cot, daybed couch, table and cabinets were draped in thick translucent white webbing.

Willet quickly opened the utility closet and retrieved a dust broom. She then spent the next half hour cleaning webs and dust from the mahogany interior. As her eyes scanned the room, she spotted a familiar object lying crumbled on the edge on the daybed.

"Mr. Claude, it's been such long time!"

Memories came trickling back as she lifted the shabby brown teddy bear in the air. Mr. Claude was her first and only toy that she had formed any attachment to. Willet was seven when she acquired the teddy bear. Adelie was always into the latest dolls and gadgets, but for Willet, Mr. Claude was the only thing she truly loved from her childhood.

In the excitement of discovery, she had almost forgotten her journey, until she felt the sway of the water from above splash against the side. Willet quickly tore herself back on deck. The night sky was illuminated by the moon, and only the tiny light on the Lenoir kept Willet company. She would occasionally hear the sound of whales calling. The gentle sound of the ocean rocked the boat softly, as it steadily headed up the coast.

She looked across the water, wondering what her friends and family were doing back home. It was strange to consider the fact that Meadowlark had become a second home for her. It was even more bizarre to know that members of her family were watching over her body at this very moment. She looked into the sky.

"Are you still there, guys?"

Willet gazed back over the ocean. She noticed that the breeze was steady but fairly mild. At this rate it would take her almost two weeks. She needed a lot more wind for her trip to be a success.

Perhaps, I could create a wind, similar to what I did at the school several months ago. The problem was, she did not actually know how she achieved that result.

Willet didn't know exactly what to do, but she found herself walking out in the middle of the deck. She sat down with her legs crossed evenly. She closed her eyes and began to visualize the wind. She had no idea what it actually looked like, but soon, color blotches of clouds formed in her mind. She carefully began to inhale and exhale in the same manner that she used on her flight. She then found herself whispering loudly into the darkness.

"Wind. Wind. Wind."

Willet repeated this mantra for several minutes to no avail. She looked up in frustration. "Come on, give me a frickin' break!"

Then she started to yell out random words. "Bam! Shazam! Supersonic! Zap!"

She broke into frustrated laughter at the ridiculousness of her situation. Soon she just sat in the moonlight staring into the sky. The rhythm of the water slapping against the side of the hull was almost mesmerizing.

Willet unconsciously started to focus on her heartbeat, trying to match her heart rhythm to that of the water around her. She closed her eyes and started to breathe deep. Suddenly, she felt a soft tickle in her chest. It was as if she were an empty tunnel and air was running though. She again started to visualize the image of wind. The color blotches popped back into her mind. This time she could visualize the blotchy clouds inside of her chest. It was as if the wind were actually travelling though her body.

Suddenly, she felt a shift in the air around her. She focused harder on the inside, trying not to get distracted and open her eyes. But she was consciously aware of a breeze starting to pick up. Her internal breathing sped up and intensified as she could feel the boat start to rock uncomfortably from side to side.

The first few drops of rain were expected, but soon it was a downpour. Willet finally opened her eyes slightly as she felt water pouring freely across her face. She quickly closed them back, not wanting to stop the deluge she had opened.

However, the wind became too much as Willet rolled across the deck against the side. She opened her eyes and there was no moon, it was just darkness, howling wind and water splashing across the boat. She needed to get to the bow to complete her shamma, or the Lenoir would surely capsize.

Willet clawed her way across the deck on her hands and knees. The wood panels were so slick with water that she could hardly stand. She squinted to find her location. She could see the railing ahead was close.

Willet took a deep breath and stood up against the storm. She carefully tipped forward until she was at the edge of the bow, overlooking the deep darkness below. She extended her arms out over the water. Her eyes focused on the direction of the horizon. She started to chant again.

"Wind! Wind!"

The rain stopped. The howling wind, suddenly muffled. It was still howling but the volume was turned low. Willet opened her eyes and beheld the most peculiar site. The boat was now sailing fairly steady and calm. Yet, the Lenoir was surrounded by a consistent spiraling wall of water. Willet's eyes looked around her and finally upward, she gasped in utter disbelief. She was literally sailing inside the eye of a hurricane!

There was a moment of empowerment as she felt the Lenoir glide across the ocean. She had created this by herself. She stood on the edge of the bow and marveled at the swirling water above and below. She exhaled triumphantly as she could feel the Lenoir ripping across the ocean at three times her original speed.

The sudden thought entered her mind, that she didn't know how to stop the storm. She quickly dismissed this thought, as she wanted to savor this moment. Despite the disrupting thought, Willet giggled aloud.

I actually created a fucking storm! How cool is that. At this rate, I should be back in three or four days, tops. Willet glanced up at the dark sky through the swirling funnel. The clouds overhead were zipping by.

"Wow, I wonder how fast I'm travelling?"

She glanced over the railing at the choppy dark water below. From her perch, Willet marveled at this strange and beautiful anomaly. A kind of peace overcame her as her ship slipped rapidly across the pull of the ocean.

This peace was disrupted when Willet noticed movement to the right side of the hull. Her body tensed as she beheld dark green eyes staring up at her. From just below the surface of the water, a woman's face had appeared.

Chapter 46:

Bishop to Queen: Check

Aquila silently made her way into the large dimly lit parlor. Avis was behind the desk with his head in his hands. He sighed deeply as Nashca stood behind him, caressing his broad shoulders. The nubs of his wings jerked away out of reflex and Nashca leaned closer.

"You need to relax, my lord."

He touched her wrist gently. "I grow tired of this complicated existence."

Aquila coyly responded from the shadows. "Perhaps, I should have brought a noose from the trunk of my car."

Nashca frowned. "I didn't hear you slither in, Lady Branson."

Aquila's eyes were on them both. "That's quite obvious. Aren't we getting a bit too friendly with the help, Lord Branson?"

Nashca abruptly removed her hands from Branson's back. Avis looked up sullenly, as he greeted her. "Good afternoon, Aquila. I have been waiting all morning, what took you so long?"

"The weather outside."

"What are you talking about, it's a lovely sunny day."

"I was referring to the storm brewing about town. Ever since that sleeven child disappeared in the woods, one can't go anywhere without being accosted in the street."

"There is a lot of fear amongst the faigal community. There are rumors of a significant griskin activity here in Meadowlark."

Nashca interjected. "I fear these are not mere rumors, my lord."

"How is that even possible?"

By now, Aquila had poured herself a drink and was nursing her glass. "This mayor is not doing a very good job protecting his citizens. You need to find another sleeven figurehead."

"I'm afraid you may be right. Wilson is not very effective at containing the growing panic. All he has been focused on is bulldozing the Greywood."

"That is hallowed ground. It must not, cannot, be allowed to happen!"

"Don't worry. He found Sirenna Adler quite the formidable foe on the subject."

Aquila took another sip. "As detestable as Harlan was, at least he commanded respect during his tenure. From what I gather, even the law enforcement view Wilson with a certain disdain."

"Who told you this bit of gossip, Nevermore?"

Nashca chimed in. "I thought the idea of a personal specter was for communication and personal protection, not for community spying."

"Nevermore protects my self-interests."

Nashca looked away. There was no need to respond. In the scheme of things, she was sure Aquila wasn't the only who took advantage of this rule. The room was uncomfortably silent, until Avis spoke again. His voice was coarse, yet sincere as he glanced over at Aquila.

"Why is it that we have never gotten along?"

"It's because I loathe you."

"We are still siblings."

Aquila sat in a recliner, close to his desk and crossed her legs, her long curvy thigh exposed. Even at her age, she kept herself in extremely good shape. She mused aloud.

"I remember when father first brought you into our home. How I detested you even then. I was tempted to smoother you with a pillow in your sleep."

Avis tried to change the subject. "Look, we could be sharing the load."

Aquila had a raw tone in her voice. "Sharing the load? I'm the eldest, not you. All of this should be my birthright, not yours, and you stole it from me. How dare you toss scraps to me."

"Aquila, I didn't mean any disrespect."

"I was once betrothed to Lord Daulus! I was to be the queen of the West Provence of Essex. The Branson Manor was to be my summer kingdom. That was my destiny and you stole it from me."

Avis struggled to look her in the eye as he responded. "I was a spoiled, petulant child. There is not a day that goes by that I don't wish I hadn't picked up that cross bow."

She was visibly upset as she continued. "When you took my eye, you destroyed my future. Lord Daulus called me a one-eyed freak when he returned my dowry. I was mortified in front of my friends, family and everyone else. Don't you understand, this wasn't supposed to be my life!"

"I ask your forgiveness, as an old man beside himself for the pain I have inflicted on your life. I'm very sorry for what I did to you. Is there any way I can make amends?"

"Now you wish to make Amends?"

"We should be working together, not trying to pull each other apart. Arke knows we have enough enemies."

"Do you know what it's like to have your own father refer to you as a cyclops. Do you know what it's like to glance into the reflection of a pool of water, or a passing window, and not recognize yourself. I don't even own a mirror! Can you amend that? Unless you can undo this, your words are useless."

"Please, forgive me. I am humbled by the prospect of losing my family. I do not want to spend the rest of my living days fighting my own sister."

Aquila held her hand up and began to clap out loud. "Bravo, great performance."

Nashca glared at her. "You are a detestable creature. He's offering you an olive branch and you're literally chewing it up and spitting it back in his face. This is your family."

"As you have pointed out, this is my family, which means this is none of your concern."

Avis's mood shifted to anger. "You will not talk to her in that tone concerning family, especially in light of certain incriminating allegations that have come to my attention."

Aquila stood up with a bemused expression on her face. "Now we have the real reason you have summoned me here."

Branson looked at her harshly. "It was worth a try, but I can see you far from reproach. Now, you will reap my whirlwind."

Aquila turned toward the door and headed away from Branson. "I grow tired of your empty threats, half-brother."

Branson then uttered a single word. "Jasmine."

Aquila paused and turned slightly. "Excuse me?"

"You wear Blue Jasmine."

"Yes, it's a proper fragrance."

"It's pretty rare."

"That's because it's exclusive. I'm the only one in this backwards town that can afford the price tag."

"Your absolutely correct. Even Shahaf rants about how alluring your scent can be."

Aquila furrowed her brow, as she tried to understand where the conversation was going. "What are you getting at now?"

"You know, a most curious thing, Shahaf discovered that scent one other place. That very scent was found on the body of Meena Corbett. He thought it was most unusual and so did I, so he worked with the coroner. They suggested that she may not have died from natural causes."

Aquila was visibly agitated by the conversation. "What is this nonsense?"

"You see, Shahaf had some questions and concerns about the sudden death of Meena, before he left. He did some investigating. To my understanding, he inscribed several detailed notes highlighting certain suspicious activities. Naturally, these notes were entrusted to his successor, Mother Ortega."

"Are you insinuating that I did something to my niece, based off the silly scribblings from a former employee's diary? This is ridiculous. Meena herself loved perfumes."

Nashca moved away from behind the desk to face Aquila directly. "That may be true, but unfortunately, in her condition, she was advised against wearing such fragrances, as it would irritate her skin."

Nashca had the older woman's attention and she teasingly elaborated. "In a related side note, I have discovered that in the hotel room that Ephron was mysteriously left in last week had the undeniable scent of Blue Jasmine on the sheets!"

"Maybe Meena rose from the grave."

"Or maybe, you took him there for some twisted alterative motive."

Avis weighed in. "Please don't tell me you would seduce my own son."

"You have no proof of these baseless suggestions against my character."

Avis folded his arms and leaned forward in a cold response. "I don't need proof, I have suspicion, and I intend to share this suspicion. Suspicion can be a powerful ally, as you once told me yourself. Remember, the seed of an idea could be more powerful than the idea itself. It's not up to me to prove these allegations, it's up to you to disprove them."

Nashca folded her arms as well as she leaned in close to Aquila and whispered. "Bishop to queen, check."

Aquila gritted her teeth in a controlled rage. She hissed at Branson who now sat watching her like a lion ready to eat its prey. Instead of a confrontation, she turned away and stormed down the hallway. She opened the door and paused briefly.

"I really should have smothered you with that pillow." The door slammed behind her and Branson took a deep breath. Sweat covered his brow as he looked up in Nascha's direction.

"That was difficult!"

"It had to be done. I'm telling you she is going to make a move on you soon."

"How can you be so sure?"

Mother Ortega ignored his question as she continued. "You need to call all your investors immediately and tell them Aquila is under investigation by the police. They will do an inquiry."

Branson sighed. "Aquila is right. They won't bite on something as trivial as a notebook."

"That is why, before she arrived today, I already sent an anonymous note to the police. I told them she may have information about the missing girl. When they get there, they will find bloody hair particles in the trunk of Aquila's car."

"What?"

"Relax, they belong to your daughter Raven. When she slipped into the briar patch the other night, she lost some hair. I saved a few strands. The investors will assume it's about the murder of Meena. Aquila will not want to discuss things publicly, which will fuel speculation. By the time she is cleared, the investors will have lost faith in her. They will demand that you replace her."

Branson grinned. "My, you are a scary creature, but you better be careful. Aquila is not one to take lightly. She will be like an old wolf caught in a trap. If she must chew off her own leg, she will come after you for a replacement!"

Chapter 47:

The Forgotten Vertriste

Laraline shut the door to Willet's room. It was now nighttime and she lay on her side peacefully. Mother Hazel was in the rocking chair beside the bed nodding off. As soon as Laraline was in the hall, she cornered the two aunts outside the door.

Laraline glared in Evelyn's direction. "So, all this time, you allowed me to believe a lie. My own mother has been a part of my life all this time. I don't even know what to call you now!"

Evelyn protested. "I've always thought of you as my child, even in the beginning."

"I feel like such a fool. What else have you been lying about?"

"I was forbidden to speak of the arrangement."

"Stop, please stop! I am so tired of this vertriste excuse. I've heard this my whole life, whenever secrets should have been exposed."

Mother Hazel abruptly cracked open the door. "Breaking a vertriste is nothing to laugh at. Entire kingdoms have fallen because of the betrayal of secrecy."

Laraline spun around to see the old woman's intense stare. Laraline reacted. "I thought you were asleep!"

"Well, the noise out in the hall is a bit disruptive."

Evelyn's voice wavered. "She is right, I owe her an explanation of her true lineage."

The hallway was silent. No one spoke, as the enormity of the situation filled the space. Finally, Laraline took a deep breath.

"Well, I'm waiting."

Sirenna began to speak instead of Evelyn. "In those days, Oriole was a surrogate mother to Evelyn and me, and we adored her. She was always so beautiful and strong. She made me feel safe and loved."

Sirenna paused as if gathering her strength. "She had inherited three of the seven Kala of the weaver craft. Because of this, she was going to the Namvula to learn the craft properly and take over the duties as the new eidolon. Oriole was to enter as a new sister mother, and this ensured her place as our new house weaver. Her future was right before her, then one day everything changed."

All eyes were on her as she continued. "Oriole was fearless. She would often trek through the Greywood on many hikes. Quite by accident, she discovered a tiny dwelling in the woods. She described it to us all as a quaint little shack, but when she took us out to see it, it was nowhere to be found. She tried several times to show her shack, but to no avail. She and only she alone, had beheld its existence."

Sirenna's continued, in spite of the sorrowful expression sliding across her face. "For a while, we thought her mad. She would draw pictures of this place. She began referring to it as the black cottage. It became her secret place. It allowed her to visit several times over the course of a year. She would disappear for hours at a time, sometimes not returning till the morning. This continued for a while. Then she began to change. Before we realized what had happened, Oriole had become bewitched. Life began to unravel outside of herself as well. There was a brutal civil war between our family and the Bransons. Our father, being who he was, used Oriole as a pawn to smooth things over."

Laraline interrupted. "I don't understand."

"Oriole always wanted to be sired at the Namvula, but she had duties to her house and position that had become more pressing. Her dreams of attending the Namvula had all but come to an end. According to our father, her duty was to the House of Adler. I truly feel this moment vexed her beyond repair."

"She agreed to an arranged marriage between the two great houses. A bloodborne offspring would end a war. However, she soon discovered that she was in fact, barren and could not conceive a child. The union was in danger of becoming forfeited unless they could produce a royal offspring."

"She had sacrificed all to please the family, and this cosmic joke was laid at her feet. However, an idea was soon formed. Perhaps, originally it was seen as an innocent solution, but it grew into a dark solution that almost destroyed this house under its oppressive weight."

"It would require unconditional love and a sacrifice for the promise of a greater good. I personally believe the idea germinated from the cottage itself. Oriole and her husband to be went to her two younger sisters, asking for a favor like no other."

Laraline's face looked gaunt, as she listened in anticipation to the disturbing tale. "What about Patsy?"

"Patsy was a mere child at the time."

Evelyn's eyes were watery as she interjected. "So were we Sirenna. I didn't even know how to use cosmetics yet."

"Since we shared the same noble blood, we were both asked to lie down with Oriole's betrothed and each bear a child. One of us refused this offer emphatically and immediately was treated as a pariah amongst all of the family."

Evelyn glanced at Sirenna who had stopped talking. She seemed to be trying to contain herself, so Evelyn finally continued.

"Having to bear witness to what my twin sister had to endure, I halfheartedly agreed to the desperate couples' terms. So, one April morning, Oriole's fiancé secretly came to my bed chamber. As fate would have it, the inception took root quickly and legal plans were officially drawn up. A child that would never know me as mother. The birth of this child would stop the feud. This was the plan. However, sometimes plans don't go as expected."

Mother Hazel took over the rather long explanation. "By now, Oriole was bewitched and her mind was now poisoned by the promises of the black cottage. Oriole was convinced that the black cottage was the key to immortality and the keys to the seven Kalas that she so desired to possess. Even if she attended the Namvula for a lifetime, there was no guarantee of obtaining all seven. It was as if her dream was now within reach. However, to gain these treasures, she had to pay a price."

"About a month before the birth of the child, Oriole made a second vertriste. This one was even more secret. Only Oriole and her new masters beyond the black cottage were the participants. Not even her betrothed was aware of these plans. All she had to do was offer a gift to her new master."

Laraline looked troubled. "You're talking about the child?"

"Not just any child, a special child. A child born of two warring tribes with an innate knowledge of the weaving ways."

Laraline impatiently pressed. "So, what happened?"

"Within two days after the birth, Oriole had her marriage annulled. Oriole claimed infidelity arose between her sister and her betrothed. Needless to say, this caused a distance between the Adler house and all the other houses. This was Oriole's plan. She no longer needed a husband or a family. All she needed was the infant child."

"Most of the royal covey knights were loyal to Oriole, even with her growing madness. When she called for the execution of both her twin sisters, it wasn't questioned. Sirenna was gifted enough with her own shammas to discover Oriole's true intentions prior, so the sisters fled their home."

"Where did they go?"

"The only place we could, the Greywood. We lived in the forest for weeks."

"What about your father?"

"He mysteriously grew sick and died in his sleep. I suspect it was Oriole's doing. She never forgave him for taking away her freedom. There was a private ceremony, but we dared not show our faces."

"You two were fugitives?"

"Those were dark times."

"How did you resume your positions?"

Evelyn took a deep breath as she concluded. "Well, even back then, the Greywood had a reputation. Most of the covey knights were too afraid to venture in. Only the captain of guards, Orsclick would follow Oriole into the woods. Eventually, she found us, but I had you hidden in the trunk of an oak. She confronted me and demanded I give you to her, so she could offer you as a sacrifice to the black cottage. I refused, so she proceeded to strangle me."

Laraline had a broken expression on her face.

"And damn near succeeded. If Sirenna hadn't arrived with Orsclick's hand axe..."

"What happened to him?"

Evelyn touched Sirenna's hand. Sirenna was visibly upset, as she candidly responded. "I did what I had to do. However, there is not a day that goes by, that I don't replay those events over in my mind. It almost seemed as if everything was a dream that day."

Evelyn added. "More like a nightmare. It was the day we lost our Oriole forever. When we returned to the forest, Oriole's body was gone. We searched for her everywhere, but we couldn't find her anywhere. We assumed the forest swallowed her up, as it seemed to desire her so. We never saw her again."

Laraline had a somber expression. "That's the real reason you're both afraid of those woods."

Evelyn wiped mascara from her eyes. "Over the years, we have seen and heard things out there that one should not."

Laraline nervously whispered. "Ghosts?"

Sirenna abruptly left the hallway and entered Willet's bedroom. Evelyn tried her best to change the subject by tying up any loose ends to the story. "Any paperwork of a marriage was destroyed from public record. Since the vertriste was a secret, the child's conception and birth were never revealed. A narrative was constructed to explain the child. Oriole had wed a covey soldier who died in battle. She had given birth and it drove her mad. Because of this, Sirenna and I were awarded guardianship of our niece."

There was a visible exuberance, as she gave a recount of how things came to be. Perhaps a weight had been lifted, and Evelyn felt more emboldened to speak.

"According to popular opinion, the twins of power, as we were dubbed, had systematically planned, and orchestrated a hostile takeover, removing the lord and the true heir of the kingdom, Oriole Ambrosia Adler. This situation only added to our ruthless mystique over the years."

Laraline interjected. "So only those involved with the original vertriste know the full truth."

"Well, Mother Hazel was brought in out of necessity, as we needed someone to clean up the mess we made, after all we were still kids."

Suddenly Sirenna was at the door. "Come quickly, something is wrong with Willet."

Both women dashed across the hall, back into the bedroom. As Laraline reached the bed. Mother Hazel had

Willet's head in her lap. She purposely had her face sideways, as she was hacking and wheezing, as if trying to breathe.

"What's wrong with her?"

"She's coming out of her current state. We need to allow her to release whatever she may have had to experience and let it dissolve naturally. Remember she has not physically experienced whatever she is dealing with. This is a manifestation of what is in her mind."

No sooner had Mother Hazel uttered these words than a stream of liquid poured from Willet's mouth. Mother Hazel tilted her over, so she was facing down. This allowed Willet to vomit freely. Dark water and strange vegetation poured from her, as she emptied a pool on the hardwood floor beside her bed.

Laraline exclaimed. "Manifestation my ass, that's sea water!"

Laraline quickly began to rub on her daughter's back. Evelyn held herself back as the scene unfolded. Within a few moments, Willet sat up and opened her eyes. They were blood red and puffy. She immediately began to shiver uncontrollably. Laraline looked into her eyes.

"Are you ok, honey?"

Willet's lips quivered as she tried to form words. "Cold."

Mother Hazel snapped at Evelyn who was frozen. "Hurry, get a quilt!"

This command shook the older woman from her state, and she quickly responded. Evelyn pulled a quilt off Willet's dresser and wrapped it around her shoulders. Laraline pulled it firmly, making sure she manually rubbed her daughters arms and shoulders. Mother hazel allowed for the things to settle before pushing Willet with the obvious questions.

"What happened, any success?"

Willet nodded. "The Lenoir was off sailing through Miami when I left."

Evelyn clapped her hands. "My god, it actually worked."

Mother Hazel looked concerned. "So, you were able to take it without being seen?"

"Actually, when I first arrived, there was a man at our old house waiting for me."

Laraline furrowed her brow nervously. "What man?"

"I have no idea. I never saw him before."

"He wasn't a Branson?"

"No, he was definitely human, but he was not alone. He seemed to be working in concert with a flock of harpies."

"That's impossible. A sleeven and night visitors, that doesn't make sense."

Sirenna snarled. "This has Aquila written all over it."

"They ended up fighting amongst themselves when I set sail. But they didn't see me, I made sure."

Laraline was agitated as she took over the conversation. "Never mind that, what happened? It was almost as if you were drowning when you woke up."

Willet thought hard before she answered. It wasn't necessary to divulge everything. Besides, she wasn't sure how much of what she had experienced was reality.

"I got lost in the storm."

"What storm? According to the weather forecast, this was the perfect weekend to sail."

Willet looked down, trying not to make eye contact. "Well, I kinda had to create extra wind to make up time."

The room was uncomfortably silent. Sirenna calmly cleared her throat. "So, you actually created a tropical storm by yourself?"

"I wasn't trying to create a storm."

Sirenna looked at Mother Hazel. Her expression of gleeful triumph was obvious. Laraline leaned closer to her daughter.

"Look, I cannot begin to understand the powers you have at your disposal, but you need to be careful, a tropical storm is serious. You could be endangering thousands of innocent people."

"I tried to aim it off the coast."

"Even so, you could have lost control. You almost drowned! You haven't had enough experience."

Willet thought of the water nymph, however she nervously agreed. "Yes, mama."

"How did you know you could do such a thing?"

"I didn't know, I just felt it inside."

Mother Hazel interjected. "That is the weaving way."

"Plus, I've done it before, accidently."

Mother Hazel looked concerned. "Yes, you're talking about the fish storm?"

"What? Oh, I don't know about that incident."

Laraline had to clarify. "Mother Hazel thinks you caused the fish storm this past summer."

"I was unconscious, I don't even remember."

Sirenna interjected. "Willet is talking about the storm that struck Talomore a few weeks later."

Willet glanced at her. "Yeah, how did you know?"

"A little birdy told me."

Willet looked around the room for any sign of Dadu. "It figures."

Mother Hazel looked confused. "When did this happen? I have no recollection of this."

Willet glanced back at the old woman sheepishly. "It was during your last trip to new Essex."

Evelyn hopped up nervously. "Perhaps, I should try to find some news about the weather conditions in Florida."

Laraline caught her eye. "Good idea, let me help you."

The two women had temporarily forgotten their issues, as they headed out to locate some news. Sirenna herself headed up the hallway. Perhaps she was heading to her bedroom. She didn't really say much.

Willet looked about the room. There was an uneasy energy about the place. "What happened? Why is everyone acting so weird?"

Mother Hazel looked at her soberly. "They are slightly afraid of you, though no one would admit to it."

"Afraid?"

"You are a young emotional woman with enough power to destroy a town. You are also happening to be going through puberty."

"Great, they think I'm a freak at school and now my family thinks so too."

"Willet, you must understand, there are consequences to weaving. I don't think you fully realize just how powerful and dangerous your Kala may become. You must be slow to give yourself over. You mustn't be impulsive or allow emotional reactions. The Namvula can properly train you when you're ready. They can help calm the emotions that will grow over time."

"You know, it was so easy to build a storm, I must admit, it's a bit scary knowing I can do that."

"It's a gift. There are seven sacred Kalas that can be bestowed. This means there are seven major classes of weavers; Healers, Sages, Avatars, Changelings, Pyroteks, Drifters, and Tempests."

"Why are you telling me this?"

"Because I'm trying to tell you what you are. You can control and manipulate the natural physical world. You can create storms or earthquakes, and change the weather, among other things."

"So what Kala is that?"

"These are the traits of a Tempest."

"A Tempest?"

"It is the rarest of all the Kala. Within the entire lore on record of the Namvula, there have only been nine other Tempests in existence. Because this Kala is rare, it's also the most coveted and misunderstood."

"Wait, is that what I'm doing when I travel out of my body, is that a Tempest thing?"

"No, that's called Drifting. I think we have covered that one."

"I don't understand?"

"It's like basic skills. You may be good at gymnastics, but also good at running. Things can kind of overlap. Kalas work the same way, especially with a Tempest."

"So, you're saying that I may have more of these Kalas."

"You definitely have at least two."

"Do I have any others?"

"How in Arke should I know. Stop acting so simple, child."

"Well, how am I supposed to figure this out?"

"Finish your training at the Namvula. They can help you figure out who you are."

"Why are you trying so hard to push me to go to this place?"

Laraline returned to the door. Something was bothering her.

"What's wrong mama?"

"Two hours ago, a tropical storm suddenly popped out of nowhere around the tip of southern Florida. It has been upgraded to a hurricane. They're calling it Hurricane Edgar. It is a category five and it's moving quickly and steadily up the east coast, with no signs of stopping."

Willet's eyes were somber. "Where is it now?"

"About 50 miles from Hilton head."

Mother Hazel's eyes widened. "You really did want to make up time."

Willet looked ashamed as she addressed Mother Hazel and her mother. "I guess I need to go back and try to remove the storm."

Laraline looked at Mother Hazel, concerned. "Perhaps she should just let the storm run its course."

Mother Hazel snapped her cane. "Absolutely not! I know you are worried about your daughter, but she needs to undo what she has created, and you know that."

Laraline was silent. Willet hopped on her bed and quickly settled in her place.

Laraline moved to her side. "Just be careful dear."

Mother Hazel touched her forehead. "Just relax or you will never be able to drift properly."

As Willet closed her eyes, she thought about her father. She really wanted his advice about now. She was stepping into a situation where she really didn't know what to expect.

Chapter 48:

Not Myself

Adelie looked out the window at the illuminated nightlife. That night she shared a small bedroom with Deryn. Jae had converted the master bedroom into her own, while their mother resided on the family room couch. Mrs. Weever had pretty much adopted this area for the last four years after Jae had requested her own privacy. The quaintness of the Weavers' home reminded Adelie of her old home in Florida. It was like the simple family home she had spent her formative years in, growing up. Unlike the monstrous mazelike feel of the Greywood Manor, the Weavers' home was warm and inviting.

How ever similar the home was, the neighborhood was unlike anything Adelie had ever experienced. It was as if it was a completely different town. Most of the homes were old and kind of rundown. However, there were candles and lanterns flickering in almost every dwelling.

Whereas, the rest of Meadowlark was quiet and dead, especially in the wake of the recent curfew, here it was the opposite. Crecheland itself almost felt alive. It was like a neighborhood with a pulse. Cars cruised up and down the main drag, as loud music blared. Adelie counted not one, not two, but five bonfires in random parking lots, usually in front of the few dwellings that seemed empty of light. The closest bonfire housed a handful of street performers.

A guy with an acoustic guitar, an older woman with a fiddle, and a squalid short fellow playing a pair of congas, performed traditional faigal folksongs. The guy playing guitar was singing in some odd language that Adelie wasn't familiar with. However, there were moments when she could recognize certain words. She figured it was some variation of faigal speak, the language that her great aunts had started to push on them. Adelie thought it sounded a lot like pig Latin, with a series of strange vocal clicks.

Adelie turned to Deryn, who was thumbing through some old fashion magazine of some sort. With a giddy smile she shook her friend. "Hey, is it always like this?"

Deryn looked at her, passively bored, near the edge of sleep. "Pretty much!"

"Wow, there is so much activity here. Over at Aunt Sirenna's house, it's pretty much dullsville."

Deryn was suddenly alert, her two pigtails bobbing about her neck. "Yeah, but you have so much stuff. I mean I could be over there a whole year and not get bored."

"Stuff? What stuff?"

"Well, I've been dying to play that giant chess board: The one with the bird pieces. Once Miss Evelyn let Jae walk right across the board."

Adelie frowned at the thought. "Aunt Sienna's new dogs dug up a couple of the squares last week. She's been a bit paranoid about people using it, but if you come visit me when this is all over, I can let you use it."

"Really!"

"Sure."

"Hey, why are you sleeping over here anyway?"

"Something is going on with Willet. I think she is sick or something."

"There are a lot of rumors going around school."

"What rumors?"

"They say she got arrested or something. She's been seen hanging around with Jonas, and perhaps they are both involved with all the murders!"

Adelie felt a moment of rage and blurted out. "That's a lie!"

"Ok, I didn't mean anything." It got very uncomfortable and silent as each girl tried to think of a way to change the subject.

Adelie turned back toward the window. "I would love to live here. All the people are much more interesting on this side of town. It's not easy living with a bunch of boring old people."

"I find that hard to believe, with all that you have around you."

Adelie looked at her with a curious look. "Well, I did meet someone the other day who was far from boring."

"Who?"

"Can you keep a secret?"

"Of course!"

"No, I mean you can't tell anyone!"

Deryn looked solemnly at her friend as she quickly nodded.

"Well, I met an enchanted queen."

"What are you talking about, like in a fairy tale?"

"Exactly!"

"You're serious?"

"As serious as a knife across my forehead."

"Where did you meet this queen?"

"That evening, when I got lost in the woods. She was standing by a stream."

"You were pretty tightlipped about what happened to you. I thought Raven had threatened you or something."

"No. We're cool, we have an understanding."

"So I've noticed."

"Don't worry, you're my real friend."

Deryn didn't quite understand but changed the subject. "So, what was this queen like?"

"You know, I can't quite describe her. She is like no one I have even met. Besides, things are getting a little cloudy."

Deryn waved her hand. "You're lying!"

Adelie's eyes turned dark with rage. "No, I am not!"

There was a menacing darkness about Adelie. Her eyes sparkled in the dimly lit room. They were almost glowing, as she responded in a deep gruff voice. The rumbling in her throat hummed like a low running engine.

"You are issuing a clear invitation to the dance, sleeven."

Deryn shrank back against the wall. It was as if she didn't even recognize her friend.

Almost immediately, Adelie jerked back as if waking from a trance. "What happened?"

"Don't you remember, I thought you wanted to hurt me."

Adelie looked confused. "I don't feel so good. Is it hot in here to you?"

"I don't know but, your acting really weird. What happened to you out there in the woods?"

"What do you mean?"

"You're not the same."

Adelie leaned her face against the window. The cool windowpane gave her some comfort as she slowly breathed. "Can we go outside and get some air?"

Deryn's eyes widened. "Now?"

"Yeah, now."

"It's getting late."

"Just for a few minutes, please."

Deryn looked down the hallway and contemplated the situation. "Just a few minutes and then we have to go inside."

The two girls made their way onto the front porch. By this time, Adelie was drenched in sweat. Her red hair was soaked and pressed against the side of her face. A wave of sensations overcame Adelie. She quickly cupped her hands over her temples, so she could take it all in slowly. It felt as if the world was changing right before her eyes. As she slid her fingers down over her face she yelled out.

"Ouch!"

Deryn jerked. "What's wrong now?"

"I think I scratched my face with my fingernails."

"What? Let me take a look."

Deryn arched her friends head up so she could see Adelie's face in the porch light. "Oh my god, you drew blood."

"No way!"

Adelie looked at her own reflection in the front door sidelight. She could see a couple of red marks on her face. She feverishly looked down at her hands. Before she had time to react, Deryn commented.

"Wow, you really need to cut your fingernails. They almost look like claws!"

Chapter 49:

Visitations

When Willet opened her eyes, it was morning. She had survived the onslaught of the storm so far. Upon her return she had found the Lenoir almost capsized. It lay sideways, within the storm's eye. As easy as she found it to create a storm, she found it was far more challenging to undo one.

When one sets something in motion, it then has purpose and intention and can never be fully dissolved. She closed her eyes, trying to allow the wind to funnel itself back into her chest. She recalled disrupting the eye of the storm earlier. However, that hadn't caused her to fall off the deck in the first place. It was the strange woman under the sea who had something to do with her almost drowning.

When she returned to consciousness, Willet didn't mention the woman, and now she was glad she didn't. *Where was she now?* Perhaps she had imagined her after all. This time Willet made sure to wrap a thick rope around her waist. She tied herself to the mast and took a deep breath. Willet sat, tied to the mast, and focused on the rhythm of the wind. She visualized the storm clouds in her chest fading away. It was like tiny blotches of infection. With each blotch, she imagined herself swallowing it back. The images were vivid, as violent dark waves crashed over the deck, at times submerging her under walls of water. At one point she blacked out in her mind.

It was like she was in limbo, not in her body, and not in her father's boat. All she knew was the complete silence. She couldn't see, hear or feel. Perhaps she was dead. She was aware of being conscious. It was almost like floating. Perhaps she had drowned after all. At some point she became aware of the sound of seagulls. The sound was distant, but it was there.

Soon she could hear her own pulse within her head. This was followed by labored breathing. As she listened, she began to realize the water was calm. The storm had passed. As she opened her eyes, she became aware that her eyebrows felt itchy. The sunlight rushed in, blinding her. She twitched away but couldn't move very well as she was still tied to the mast. The Lenoir was completely upright now and rocking to the gentle waves. Willet was groggy and very weak. The ordeal had zapped her energy. She lay against the mast, trying to force herself awake.

Through her blurry vision, she noticed the mysterious being standing a few feet from the edge of the bow. This wasn't a dream or hallucination. The strange woman stood about seven feet tall with iron scaled heels. Her naked body was wrapped in constant writhing snakelike tentacles that covered her unmentionables. Her face was pale and grey with smooth skin. Two ram-like horns sprouted from either side of her scalp. They projected from beneath thick threads of oily black hair that poured down her back into a single thick braid. Her hair was the same color as her cold dark eyes. Her black lips pursed into a smile as she glanced in Willet's direction. Willet was still out of it, as she called out to the strange visitor.

"Have we met before?"

The towering maiden barely acknowledged Willet and then yawned as if bored. Have we? I have no recollection."

Willet recognized her immediately. "Of course, you're the one who tried to drown me!"

"Perhaps I'm a figment of your imagination."

This was the strange being that had lured Willet off the deck and into the water below. Now she remembered what happened. Something about her eyes were so alluring, Willet was compelled to dive headfirst into the hurricane. She almost drowned but fortunately she awoke. Willet elected not to share this detail with her family. Until this moment, she wasn't even sure it had happened. Willet turned her head away from the siren's direct gaze as she spoke.

"Why did you try to drown me?"

"You can't blame a girl for trying."

"Excuse me?"

"You're a tourist loitering around in places you don't belong, mortal."

"Who the hell are you?"

"We are Pandora Prime."

"What?"

"You're a long way from home, Tempest. I suggest you return from whence you came."

Willet's eyes widened, even as the strange being seemed to slither back over the edge of the rail. The serpentine woman disappeared just as quickly as she had arrived. Willet sat up in silence, anticipating another disruption. She was now alert. She just sat and stared at the railing where the strange woman had stood.

Was she even a woman What had she just witnessed? Was that actually real?

Willet's eyes began to drift about the boat again as she realized the woman was not coming back. At the helm, she saw another blurry figure steering the boat. The pings of reality entered her consciousness, and she started to freak out. She needed to get her bearings on what was happening around her. She tried to get up once again, but the rope around her waist held her down. Willet's fingers scrambled to untie the rope, as she intently stared at the new visitor. Their back was to her, steering the boat. Her adrenaline spiked. *What is going on?*

Willet found herself speaking out loud to herself. "How did anyone else get on aboard in all of this? It's impossible! Perhaps I'm dreaming, or worse yet hallucinating. Oh my god, maybe I died."

She was still weak, but she had to do something. She couldn't let all these apparitions completely invade the ship. She had to take a stand. As soon as she was loose, she rose to her feet and cleared her throat.

"Excuse me, may I help you?"

Willet waited as the stranger stood motionless. It was if she hadn't spoken a word. A chill went up her spine at the lack of response. The helmsmen wore a long black rain slicker and brown boots. The hood of the slicker was down, and the stranger wore a black knit skull cap. *It wasn't the murderous woman from the sea, so who was this visitor?* This was something new altogether. *What game was this new visitor playing?*

Willet noticed strong rubber gloved fingers grasp the wheel, as she tipped closer. Perhaps her visitor was a ghost. Oddly enough, she wasn't afraid anymore. She didn't know why. Well, since she wasn't even physically here, she could just wake up.

However, there was something else. Willet walked in a wide perimeter around the side of the helm to get a look at the possible saboteur, stowaway or whatever he was. She continued to speak to the stranger in a cautious tone.

"Why are you here on my boat?"

Suddenly an eerily familiar voice responded. "Because you invited me here, Willet."

"How do you know my name?"

Willet froze in her tracks as a sudden realization struck. The world had just gone sideways and surreal that morning. It was as if things had come full circle.

"Daddy, are you really here, or are you just in my mind?"

"What do you think princess?"

Langston Swift stood upright with a soft smile. His dreadlocks hung down from under his skull cap, framing his almond brown skin. Willet almost ran to embrace him, then she stopped herself.

"Wait, I'm not really here and neither are you."

"Why wouldn't I be here?"

"Because your dead, you must be a part of my memories."

"Just because I don't belong to this realm, doesn't make me any less real. She extended her arms and she tried to embrace him. It was like hugging mist. She could see him, and smell him, but he wasn't tangible.

Willet quickly moved back. "You said I invited you here, why?"

"Your desire to see me brought me here before you."

"Is that why you were sailing the boat?"

"Well, it was my boat."

"Are you haunting the Lenoir?"

Langsten responded with a dry smile. "We don't have much time, princess."

"What do you mean?"

"I can already feel myself starting to slip way, you don't contain enough father dust for me to remain here."

"Daddy, were you murdered?"

"My death was a cruel example of disobedience."

"An example? I don't understand."

"It's up to you to protect your mother and sister now. Will you promise me this?"

"Daddy, what are you talking about?"

"They are still after the Einin Blade. You can't let them get their hands on it, Willet."

"Who are you talking about?"

"It was so nice seeing you again."

"Don't go away!"

A gentle wind started to invade the deck and like fine dust, he started to dissolve before her eyes. Within moments he was completely blown away with the sea wind. Willet sat on the deck staring at the spot where he dissipated. She could feel her eyes welling up with tears. The rest of the morning, things were a bit somber, as Willet mourned her father's passing again.

The Lenoir sailed past Wilmington, NC. Willet started to become hungry as it was lunch time. She decided to stop in a few hours for the day, after all she had significantly made up some time.

Chapter 50:

Birthright

Lord Branson sat at his regular table overlooking the view of the ocean. With his hot herbal tea warming his face, Avis quietly sipped out of his glass mug. His penthouse suite located in The Dampton Inns, was one of the most exclusive properties in Celandine. The events of the week had put a damper on his mood, and so he decided to seek solace from his daily grind.

Avis was reclusive by nature. He would rather remain behind the scenes than milk his public persona. Even though his position had offered him many advantages. His anonymity was the one sacrifice that was hard for him to reconcile at times.

The day had started like any other, until he had an early afternoon visit from both Evelyn and Laraline. Nashca led both women to his room patio. Avis had just finished his tea when he heard a barely audible voice call to him.

"Lord Branson, could I speak with you a moment?"

Avis looked up and beheld Laraline Swift. Her expression seemed a bit troubled. He was immediately concerned, especially after their last conversation.

"Please have a seat. Is there a problem?"

"Well, this is sort of awkward."

"Have my children been causing you any trouble? They can be a bit rambunctious."

"First, I want to extend my gratitude to your Jonas for saving my Addie."

"Thank you, I don't get many opportunities to hear praise about any of my children."

Laraline nodded. "He has been very accommodating to both my daughters."

"He is a lot like his mother. He's the sensitive one."

"You know, it's ironic you brought up this conversation of children, because that's kind of what I wish to discuss."

"Yes?"

Against Evelyn's advice, Laraline didn't waste time with subtle hinting. "I know about the vertriste with Oriole and about my birth."

Avis glanced at Evelyn uneasily. The older woman grimaced to herself as the air was sucked out of the room. Laraline leaned over the table, staring him directly in the eyes.

"Don't worry, she didn't tell me about your identity. I just put two and two together. I just want to hear it from your lips."

Avis stood up from his table and walked over to the edge of the balcony. He seemed lost in thought. "You know, there is not a day that goes by, that I wonder what might have been. Do you hate me even more now?"

"I don't know how I feel. This definitely explains why auntie wanted to talk to you about the sanctuary first." Avis just nodded.

Laraline looked wounded. "You knew Langston and spoke to him. Did he ever find out who you are?"

"I never told him anything. I didn't think it was my place. Where does that leave us?"

"What do you mean?"

"You and I."

"Look, this is a lot to take in, even if I can move on, and that's a big if. I need some time. l have to let you know."

"That's fair enough."

"Can I ask you a question? It's been bothering me since I found out."

"Shoot."

"Why did you even agree to this arrangement. I thought you loved Oriole."

"It's because I loved her, that I agreed. Anyone who knew Oriole, will agree, that it was hard to say no to her. She could be very persuasive."

Laraline mumbled. "Well supposedly, one of her Kalas was an avatar."

Evelyn interjected. "As barbaric and troublesome as the arrangement seemed, in hindsight, Avis tried to be a gentleman, as much as he could, under the dubious circumstances. It could have been a lot worse for me."

Laraline nodded, but her eyes never left Lord Branson. "Was there ever anything between you and Evelyn? I mean beyond this arrangement."

Evelyn was somber. "There was something between us, it was you. Perhaps there wasn't a covenant union created to bond the two families, but you birth was enough to create a mutual friendship that has informed a stalemate all these years."

He directed a warm smile in Evelyn's direction as he clasped his hands. "Well, it appears that the original vertriste is now dead. There is no point on continuing this charade."

Avis placed his hand over the necklace around his neck. His fingers grasped the chain, and he pulled it over his head. He dangled the chain in the sunlight before tossing it toward Laraline, she snatched it out of reflex.

Evelyn gasped. "Avis, what are you doing?"

Laraline looked puzzled. "What is this?"

"It's your birthright."

Laraline looked at the emerald pendant at the end of the silver chain. "I can't accept this."

"I haven't been there in the past, please allow me to rectify this for you and my granddaughters' future!"

Just hearing him say granddaughters brought a kind of realization to her mind. As her eyes moved along the surface of the strange necklace, she noticed a hidden compartment.

"It has a latch."

"Open it up!"

Laraline did as she was instructed. She popped open the locket and a light airy mist drifted forth. Laraline beheld the stream of green dust like escaping steam. She quickly snapped the lid closed, thus stopping the flow of escaping Father dust.

"It's full."

"It contains 400 eons worth of Feather dust."

As she looked closer at the locket, she noticed an inscription. To my beloved daughter, LVB

"Are these letters my initials?"

He leaned close as he pointed to each letter. "Yes, that's Laraline Victoria Branson. My grandmother was named Victoria."

"What does this mean?"

Avis whispered proudly. "It means, you are the original first heir of the Branson dynasty."

Evelyn stood beside her and rested her hand on her daughter's shoulder. "And you are now effectively the heir of the Adler dynasty as well."

Laraline stood in shock. "This quite a homecoming."

Avis added. "This is unofficial of course. I will have the necessary paperwork drawn up, but that is a formality."

"Wait, there is a lot happening here, can I have a day or so to process all of this?"

"Sleep on it, if you wish. But let me inform you. if you do decide take on this responsibility, there would no longer be any need for sanctuary."

Laraline cupped her mouth. "Oh my."

"Yes, you and your daughters would be free from running. Just something to think about. However, tell no one until it's all official."

Laraline looked intently, half expecting him to start laughing in her face. But his expression was sincere. For some reason, his eyes did not seem as cruel as she remembered. Now, they seemed weary and sad.

Chapter 51:

Old Adversaries

It was late afternoon, almost dusk, when Willet opened her eyes again. She sat up in bed, excited to share her latest adventure with everyone. Mother Hazel was nodding in her rocker. Laraline and Evelyn had made their way back into her bedroom and were having a somewhat intense conversation. Before anyone had time to address her current state, Willet blurted out what had happened.

"I saw dad!"

Laraline had been in deep thought after the discovery of her own birth parents and the offer from Branson. Even after she returned to Willet's bedside; she found herself slipping into hopes of reconciliation. All of that changed when Willet related her current adventure.

"What do you mean, you saw your father?"

"He was aboard the Lenoir. I think he was a ghost."

"Well, I know how you've missed him. It's just natural, you would dream of him."

"I didn't dream of him. He was there."

Mother Hazel touched her forehead concerned. "Are you certain? There are many renegade phantoms and echoes roaming the steams of consciousness looking for a weary drifter to possess."

Laraline shook her head. "Willet, that's just not possible."

"I'm not lying. He even talked to me. He warned me of the ones who murdered him."

Laraline was shocked. "He spoke of his murderers, is this true?"

Willet was now irritated. "Of course, it's true." At that moment was glad she didn't mention the bizarre woman with horns. *She would really think I was off my rocker.*

Laraline was almost condescending as she grilled her. "What did he say exactly?"

"He said his death was an example."

"That makes no sense."

Mother Hazel shifted her gaze to Sirenna. "Did he say why?"

"It had something to do with some weapon. He called it an Einin blade, and that I was not to let them get their hands on it?"

Mother Hazel shifted uncomfortably. "What did you just say?"

"What?"

Laraline looked suspiciously at the old woman. "Do you know what she is talking about?"

Evelyn huffed. "The Einin blade is a myth! It doesn't exist."

Willet's eyes never left Mother Hazel. "What is this Einin blade?"

Mother Hazel quickly dismissed the conversation. "There are more pressing things at foot. You say he specifically mentioned the word, Einin?"

Willet nodded. "Yeah. What does it mean?"

"The Einin are a sleeven religious order. They are aware of our existence and intent on our eradication."

"Why?"

"What causes any conflict? It's the fear of the unknown."

Laraline cupped her mouth. "That doesn't make sense. Langston was just a fisherman."

Mother Hazel folded her hands. "What about his association with Silas minor?"

Evelyn's eyes widened. "Don't mention that name in this house."

Willet was now curious as she glanced over at Evelyn. "What's the deal with Uncle Sal?"

Laraline touched Willet's hand. "There is lot about Uncle Sal you don't know."

"Did he kill father?"

"Of course not!"

"Where is he?"

Laraline changed the subject. "I still don't know why the Einen would be after him."

Willet reiterated her concern. "Look, my father said they were after this blade. The next thing you'll be telling me is I didn't make a storm."

Laraline was almost in tears. "Willet, please."

A hush fell over the room, as if she had just brought up a taboo subject. Willet looked around confused. Something else was wrong. She felt it the moment she got back. "What did I say?"

No one spoke until Laraline cleared her throat and changed the subject. "So where is the boat at now?"

Willet paused as she had to recall her last location. "Off the coast of Jacksonville, I think if I keep steady, I could make it to Norfolk by morning."

"That is unnaturally fast sailing."

"Well, I had lot of help from the storm."

Laraline soberly responded. "Willet, we need to talk about your storm."

"Something's wrong! I knew the minute I drifted back here."

Mother Hazel interrupted. "Willet, every time you exercise your Kala, you are wielding a great responsibility. One that can come with consciences. Remember I told you that earlier?"

Willet was suddenly nervous. "What is she talking about mama?"

Laraline seemed on the verge of tears. "Willet, according to the news, people died in that storm."

Willet was silent. She felt completely numb all over. At that moment, she never wanted to close her eyes and disappear so badly.

"Do you hear me, Willet?"

Willet was unnaturally calm. "How many?"

"I don't know, so far there are 11 confirmed dead and another 12 missing."

One moment everything was great and she was a hero; the next moment she was a murderer. Panic had taken over. Willet suddenly felt as if she couldn't breathe. She hopped to her feet and ran out of the room. She faintly heard her mother call after her as she left. Willet descended the stairs, rushed out the front door and into the yard.

She had to get outside. She was beginning to hyperventilate. She pushed open the door and took in the fresh air by the mouthfuls, but it all tasted artificial. The actual sunlight was low in the sky. There were faint hints of sun disappearing over the horizon. After several moments of controlled calm, she felt herself trying to hold back tears. Willet finally dropped to her knees and began to sob.

"What have I done?"

Her palms were soaked with her tears as she violently shook the chills that had invaded her body. She used her sleeve to wipe snot that had dripped down onto her lip. She would have still been crying, but she saw a movement from the edge of the Greywood. The ghostly woman was standing with her arms folded watching her. Willet hopped up. She looked straight ahead into the shadowy tree line of the Greywood, both of them now facing one another.

Willet stepped forward in defiance. "What do you want with me?" The other was like a statue. "Can't you speak?" The silence continued. Willet roared impatiently. "Whatever you are, leave me alone!"

The other said nothing, but instead she stepped back into the shadows of the tree line. She had disappeared again. Willet took a deep breath as her eyes searched the vacant space where the specter had just been standing.

She was about to let it go when she heard the sound of a car door slam. Willet glanced back in the direction of the garage. The garage housed at least five vehicles, most of them antiques. The doors were open wide, as they usually were. Between the aunts many town excursions, and her mother's third shift job, shutting them seemed a futile exercise.

However, the open garage wasn't the source of Willet's concern, it was the shadowy figure digging around in her mother's car. Willet's frantic sadness and fear, turned to anger as she approached the vehicle. She suddenly felt violated.

"What are you doing in our car?"

A startled Phoebe looked up. She pulled herself out of the car seat and faced Willet. "Nothing, I was rolling up the window, it looks like it might rain."

Willet folded her arms as she moved closer. "I doubt it will rain inside the garage."

Phoebe struggled to search for an answer, as a voice from behind them both called out. "Did you find a rat in our garage, Willet?"

Both Willet and Phoebe looked back at Sirenna. who was standing at the entrance of the garage with her arms folded. "I told your mother I would come check on you. I'm glad I did. We seem to have a saboteur in our midst."

Phoebe blew off their suspicions. "As if, you should keep your windows up. I'm trying to do your mother a favor. We are in for some nasty weather."

Willet cleared her throat. "You don't know the half of it sister."

Phoebe started to walk past but was blocked by the menacing Sirenna. "Where do you think you're going?"

"I'm going home!"

Suddenly Dadu flew at Phoebe's head, causing her to stumble backward onto the ground. The large white owl seemed emboldened, as it dove back at her before landing on the hood of the dodge beside Willet.

Phoebe rose to her feet, wiping her clothes. She glared at the giant bird hissing at her. "What's wrong with your dumb specter?"

Sirenna responded. "Not so fast, did your mother send you here to snoop?"

"I don't know what you're talking about, Auntie."

"I'm sure you don't, but I'm also sure you do know you're trespassing."

Phoebe was defiant. "You can't do anything to me, so you might as well get out of my way."

"Well, you're right and wrong. I won't trounce you because I am your godmother and aunt. However, I can hold you accountable for your prior obligations."

Phoebe looked confused. "What are you talking about?"

"As I recall, you and Willet have unfinished business, something to do with an outstanding grievance."

"I do not know what you are talking about."

"Sure, you do. Willet tossed you into my lawn chairs last summer and your mother demanded justice. Since you have returned here by yourself, on your own volition and asserted yet another antagonistic violation on your adversary. I would say that you have made your desire clear. You wish to engage her.

Phoebe huffed. "I don't have time for this."

Willet still had her arms crossed as she responded. "Are you afraid I'll give you another bloody nose?"

Phoebe responded by slashing her claw toward Willet's face. She caught wind, as her adversary was quick and ducked. Phoebe kept on swinging with her long talonlike fingers. Finally, she scratched the side of Willet's forehead creating a deep wound. With her high heel, she kicked Willet in her abdomen. Willet doubled over as Phoebe snickered to herself.

"Oops, my bad!"

Phoebe then leapt triumphantly into the air, as her long bright red wings bloomed. They aggressively flapped her upward. She extended her arms gracefully to the clouds, as if she were dancing.

Willet touched her forehead and felt blood trickling down. Enraged, she looked up at phoebe who was now in midair. Willet was about to leap after her, then thought against this. Instead, she took a deep breath and held out her right palm in Phoebe's direction. Almost immediately, Willet felt a tiny tickle from inside, as she focused her attention on the flying faigal.

The wind was gentle at first, then it got more pronounced. Willet could feel the wind starting to rage inside her chest. Even at forty yards out, Phoebe was starting to feel the effects from Willet. Her wings began to violently jerk about in the air, as if being hammered by wind gusts. Phoebe began screaming frantically, as she lost control of her wings and her bearings. She appeared as if she were a rag doll, twisting and twirling, uncontrollably in the sky.

Without warning, Willet put her arm down and the wind ceased. Phoebe tumbled downward in a violent tailspin. She slammed back to the ground with a deep thud. Phoebe was stunned as she slowly crawled across the lawn using her claws to dig into the dirt.

Willet sprinted toward Phoebe, reached down and quickly dug her fingers into her cousin's long blonde hair.

Phoebe felt her head being lifted by the roots of her hair. She let out a violent scream, as Willet proceeded to drag her across the gravel driveway.

Phoebe screamed at Willet. "Stop! That really hurts!"

Phoebe tried to kick at her attacker until Willet grabbed two fistfuls of her hair. Willet suddenly started to swing her around by her roots. There was a steady squealing as the young faigal felt herself twirling just above the ground. After the fourth rotation, Willet released her tight grip, allowing her baggage to fly several yards across the loose gravel.

Phoebe stood up, dazed and bruised. The world was spinning as she struggled to find her bearings. She stumbled in Willet's direction, just in time to feel a fist strike her in the mouth. The pain jolted Phoebe to attention. Willet reacted immediately and pulled her bloody fist away in pain. A large tooth was now imbedded into the knuckle of her ring finger.

Phoebe, in the meantime, was crying profusely. Her hands cupped over her mouth, trying to stop the flow of blood. With a pronounced lisp, she began to whine. "You knocked out my tooth, you evil troll!"

Just as the situation threatened to become more volatile, a familiar voice boomed from the entrance of the door. "Willet, are you out here?"

Laraline was on the front steps, Evelyn was slightly behind her. They were now looking for Willet. Phoebe's eyes widened as the yard began to get crowded. She looked up to see Sirenna motion to her. "If I were you, I would make haste."

Phoebe didn't have to be told twice, as she sprinted frantically down across the lawn and into the road. By the time Willet had removed the tooth from her hand, Phoebe was already midair, fleeing the scene.

Willet turned her frustration to Sirenna. A small wind surrounded the young girl. "Why did you let her get away? I wasn't finished with her."

Sirenna placed her hand firmly on Willet's shoulder, trying to restrain her from giving chase. "You've proved your point. It's not about destroying one's enemy, it's about letting them know you can destroy them. I doubt you will have any more trouble with your cousin."

Laraline caught a glimpse of her daughter's bloody forehead from a distance. "My god, Willet, what happened? You're covered in blood!"

"I caught Cousin Phoebe digging around in our car."

"She attacked you?"

"What do you expect, Mama? We hate each other."

Laraline turned her attention to Sirenna. "What were you doing while this was going on?"

"Watching them fight, of course."

Laraline rolled her eyes. "Well, I need to talk to Patsy."

Sirenna looked into the sky, but the young girl was no longer in sight. "Patsy put her up to this, no doubt!"

"Why was she in my car?"

"How should I know?"

"This is not healthy, we're leaving Meadowlark. We were better off in Florida!"

Willet was standing up and squinting, as blood dripped into her eyes from the gash in her forehead. "We can't, not now Mama. All I need is a couple more days and I can get the boat here safely."

"At what cost? Look what this is doing to you. Look at us. We can't live like this."

Evelyn looked concerned. "If you leave, the sanctuary would be broken. You and your daughters would be hunted, even outside of Meadowlark. You could spend your life running!"

Laraline sighed deeply at Evelyn. "Unless I took Lord Branson up on his offer."

Evelyn had a hopeful look on her face. "Well, everything happens for a reason."

Willet used her shirt sleeve to wipe off her blood-soaked face. Trying to appear as if she were ok. She cleared her throat. "What offer? What did I miss while I was gone?"

Chapter 52:

Aquila's Move

She tried to ignore the knocking at her studio flat; however, she recognized the urgent voice calling to her on the other side of the front door. Aquila adjusted her evening gown, as she went to answer.

An hysterical Patsy stood, with an equally upset Phoebe. "Lady Branson, they're here!"

"Do you know what time it is?"

"Excuse me?"

"It is evening and I happen to be entertaining guests."

"I'm sorry, its urgent, do you mind if I come in a moment? I won't stay long as we are on our way to the hospital."

"Yes, I do mind. Tell me the urgency now, while you're camped out on my doorstep."

"My Phoebe was attacked!"

"Attacked, by whom?"

"That horrible Swift girl again."

"Willet?"

"This time she knocked her tooth out!"

Phoebe stood slightly behind her mother, whimpering the entire time. Her blouse, around her neck, was covered in blood. It was only when her mother mentioned what happened that she grinned so Aquila could see the evidence of the assault. The bloody gaping hole between her almost perfect smile, seemed cartoonish to Aquila.

"Wait! Willet just attacked Phoebe, I thought you said they were gone?"

"That's what I have been trying to tell you. She and her mother are still here in town!"

"Where did this happen?"

"Phoebe was in the Greywood Manor driveway when it happened."

"Why was she at their home?"

"She was just returning some paperwork to Laraline's car, when she was trounced without warning. She said Sirenna just watched as it happened."

"Sirenna witnessed this."

Patsy nodded. "Yes."

"You simple idiot, I suggest you find you and your daughter a solicitor immediately."

"A Solicitor! What are you talking about?"

"She was trespassing on private property."

"I was only getting information, as you asked."

"There are several ways to retrieve information. Not once did I tell you to break into your niece's car. That sounds a bit criminal to me."

Aquila started to shut the door, as Patsy protested. "But, I came to warn you!"

"Well, you have, so thank you and goodnight."

Aquila then slammed the door and locked it back. She headed back out on the patio, where Monsignor Dowd waited patiently. Aquila put on her plastic smile as she pulled the patio door shut to obscure any more knocking from Patsy.

"Sorry for the disturbance, your excellency. I know you have come a long way and I appreciate you seeing me on such short notice."

Dowd's eyes were looking back in the direction of the entrance. "If you have some other business to attend to, we can discuss this later."

"Nonsense, that was just a member from the local prayer group."

"I didn't know you were involved in the local ministry."

"Yes, I do love a little mission work at times."

"Is that how you acquired all of these artifacts?"

Dowd was studying a small black bookcase against the patio wall in the corner. The doors were open, exposing several odd cups, elixirs and other items. They were placed carefully on each shelf. Something in particular had caught the old man's eye. The monsignor squinted at what seemed to be some sort of fetish doll.

"What exactly is this?"

"I believe that is a carved statue of the Guluimla. It was an ancient deity of the Polisuan folk."

"Hmmm, it looks like something I might have seen at Namvula."

"Well, I wouldn't know. I haven't stepped into that world for a long time."

He eyed the choker around her neck. "Yes, I see. Do you ever miss the arts?"

Aquila smiled uncomfortably. "Could we get back to what you were talking about before we were interrupted, Monsignor."

Dowd cleared his throat and put on his business face. "Well, as I was saying Lady Branson, this is highly unusual. The Ortega house is well respected and to make a claim such as this, would cause a scandal not only within their house, but in your house as well."

"Would you care for some herbal tea, Your Excellency?"

"No. I have a long trip back in the morning. I don't want to be up half the night."

"I demand a formal investigation of this creature immediately."

"That's not protocol. There must be an informal investigation first."

"Then I want to file one now!"

"These are serious allegations."

"That woman is a clear and present danger to our family and way of life. I know this."

"Lady Branson, you do realize, that if you file this, it could very well leave the Branson house without a weaver in place for a few months. This could also cause a possible security risk for your family. They could be vulnerable to outside threats. Aren't the Adler twins part of this very Province?"

"Don't remind me."

"I don't know if that's a good idea."

"Look, I will take full responsibility for my family's safety in her absence."

"Perhaps I should contact your brother so he can start to make plans."

Aquila's heart jumped at the mention of this. "Don't worry, I won't hesitate to tell him tomorrow morning. Things have been difficult for him, with his children."

"Yes, I heard. It's most distressing."

Lady Branson knew that if Avis ever got wind of what she was up to, he would have her head. "I will inform him first thing in the morning."

"This is most unfortunate."

"Yes, I wish your visit was under more pleasant circumstances."

Monsignor Dowd rose to his feet. "Well, when I get back to the Ministry, I will make sure that Eskar Laruth contacts Lord Corbett and your cousin for possible travel plans."

Aquila's eyes darted uneasy. "Is that necessary?"

"Necessary?"

"Well, we wouldn't want to bother them, Monsignor."

"Aren't they Meena's next of kin. If she died of unnatural causes, they would be the first ones who would want to know. After all, they are your family as well."

"Of course, how silly of me."

Aquila knew the blind accusation against Nashca wouldn't stick. It would just give her enough time to ensure Avis was vulnerable. Unfortunately, she hadn't counted on the possibility of the Corbett clan returning to town. This could be a problem in itself.

The truth be told, Aquila didn't much like her family. Montague Corbett was a senior member of the ministry and a self-proclaimed grifter. He was a penny pitcher and was always looking for the perfect angle. He had, over the years, slid into several influential pockets with hints of blackmail and larceny as incentives.

Because of this position, he was able to garner a lot of favors among the elite. He even gained an emergency hearing for his only child ZuZu Fatale, who was serving a life sentence in Darkmore prison, after she killed a former lover in a murderous rage.

This, in itself, would not have been enough to incarcerate her. However, her intended victims were burned alive in their bed, along with all the other tenants in the hotel. There was a total of 28 victims. Her actions were framed as a terrorist attack because of her affiliation with the Smile, a secret Swan faction that had infiltrated the elite. Because of the political fallout, the ministry was less sympathetic to her plight.

However, quite recently, Aquila had received a very curious request from poor little Zuzu. Apparently, she was asked to give a glowing character review about how her forlorn cousin had all but recanted her association with the swans and became a model citizen. Naturally, Aquila was quite surprised at the news that her letter, in particular, was instrumental in ZuZu being granted an audience with the Eskar himself, to discuss her case.

Ironically, her other cousin, Melania, had funded at least a half dozen extreme causes, for the benefit of the Swans over the years. As of late, she had invested into the research of guru metaphysicist, Aryden Ibis to obtain priceless ancient religious artifacts called ikons. If there was a possibility for more wealth, Melania was usually involved. The idea of any of these halfwits returning to Meadowlark, filled her with a sinking dread.

Chapter 53:

The Frenchman

Kestrel walked down the dim corridor with a handful of books in her hand. It was almost time to close-up and plan her potluck dish for the next day. The event had almost slipped her mind until she received a handwritten mailer from the Peregrine sisters. It was discreetly dropped in her mail slot, so she wouldn't forget.

The week had been quiet so far, especially considering that Aquila had made such a stink at her job. It was getting dark outside and she was a bit uneasy. As she made her way to the front desk, she was met by a rather tall lanky young man in a long black leather coat. She jumped when she saw him standing in the dimly lit room.

"Arke, sake, you startled me!"

"Sorry, we wouldn't want to do that, luv."

His hair was slicked back and he wore sunglasses. A thin mustache and a tightly cropped goatee wrapped around his mouth. He almost reminded Kestrel of a possible variation of what Gavin may grow up to be.

"What are you doing here anyway? We're closed."

"Well, the door was certainly open, how else do you explain the fact that I could be standing before you, Kestrel?"

"Hey, how do you know my name?"

"Your name tag on your desk. It's a dead giveaway, my love."

"Look, I was just going to close up, it's time."

"How sad, I came all this way to find some reading materials."

Kestrel looked oddly at the young man. His demeanor was peculiar, yet polite. She didn't know if he was dangerous. However, she didn't want to cross him.

"You got two minutes."

"Lovely."

"What are you looking for?"

"Do you have the novel, Parish Boy's Progress, dear?"

"Is that the one by Dickens?"

"The very one."

Kestrel turned around and disappeared down one of the aisles. Her voice boomed back at the desk. "So, you fancy sleeven authors, do you?"

"No so much, how can you tell I'm faigal? You a weaver or something?"

Kestrel returned with a small thick hardback book. "I smell your wet feathers; you must have been out in the rain earlier."

"I'm impressed."

"Don't be, we tend to pay more attention to strangers in town."

"That obvious, so I don't blend in with the natives?"

"Not so much. Here you go; one copy of Oliver Twist."

Nashca handed him the book, as he quickly inspected it eagerly. "That's the very one."

"Anything else Mr... what is your name sir?"

"You can call me Mr. Bragg."

"Mr. Bragg, what a peculiar name."

"These are peculiar times."

"Well, I can't argue with that, will this do, Mr. Bragg?"

"Do you have the Catcher in the Rye?"

"Wow, another sleeven author. You must be a connoisseur of that culture."

"Perhaps I just like a good story, Kestrel."

Kestrel made a grunt, as she quickly thumbed through her card catalogue. "Sorry, that one's checked out."

"Ah well, one out of two ain't bad."

"Do you have a library card and a current ID."

"I have a passport."

"I'm sorry, I can't help you."

Bragg removed his shades and looked intently into her eyes. "Come on, be a lovely."

Like some odd impulse itching in her mind, Kestrel decided to let him slide. She didn't really know why. It wasn't like her. She took her job very seriously. For some reason though, she accepted his passport.

"Wow, you're from Paris?"

"I grew up there, but I was actually born in this very town."

"You were born in Meadowlark? Are you related to anyone?"

He evaded the question. "I thought you had to leave, lovely."

"Damn it, what time is now?"

Mr. Bragg coyly answered. "It's getting late."

Chapter 54:

Alouette

Tori was locking the front door to the diner when she noticed the black muscle car across the dimly lit street. It was suspiciously parked near the municipal building. She remembered seeing it driving by earlier that afternoon. Work had been so haphazard, she almost didn't realize.

Now it was late and the driver was just inside waiting. It was facing the opposite direction of the diner with the lights off. Her eyes never left the strange car and as she clicked the lock in place. She made her way down the sidewalk to her Volkswagen, parked a block down the side of the street. Tori glanced back several times, as if she were expecting the driver to suddenly make a U-turn on the road and chase her down.

She absentmindedly reached into her purse to retrieve her keys and instantly pulled back wincing in pain. She forgot she still had gauze wrapped around her right hand. This would be the second injury she received at Linnet's in less than two weeks. Perhaps she should hit Lady Adler up for workman's comp.

She was about to reach into her purse for her keys again, when she heard a voice beside her. "Have you seen Willet?"

Tori quickly lashed out, almost striking Jonas in the face. "My god, what are you doing creeping around? You scared the crap out of me!"

"Creeping around?"

"I told you I haven't heard from her."

"Geez, sorry I asked."

Tori glanced back at the strange car. Someone inside had lit a cigarette. She quickly grabbed Jonas's shirt as he was about to leave. "Wait, you can make it up to me, now!"

"How?"

"Walk me to my car and I can give you a ride home."

"Well, I'm supposed to be waiting for Gavin to join me."

"How is it, you belong to one of the richest families in town, and yet you never have a way to get home?"

"Gavin had his license suspended for six months."

Tori huffed impatiently as she glanced suspiciously at the vehicle. "Look, I can give him a ride, if he shows up."

Jonas directed his eyes to the car. "Are you afraid of that car?"

"So, what of it. Do you know who it is?"

"I've seen it before."

"Where?"

Jonas was about to answer, when Tori shoved him. "Don't stare!"

"Hey!"

"Keep your voice down. There is someone inside."

"Who?"

"I don't know."

"Why are we whispering?"

"Ok, where?"

"Where what?"

Tori struck him with her purse. "Are you completely brain dead?"

"Ouch. What gives?"

"Where have you seen the car before?"

"I'm sure I saw it parked outside the Crecheland Inn a few times."

"You're lying!"

"Hey guys, what are you doing?"

Tori almost jumped off the sidewalk. She turned around and Gavin was right in front of her. "Geez, do all you Bransons move around like ghosts?"

Gavin furrowed his brow. "What's wrong with her?" Gavin was dressed in along flowy black jacket. His white hair fluttered in the evening wind.

"I'm walking her to her car, because she's creeped out by that red car."

Tori threw her arms up emphatically as Jonas pointed behind them. "Does anyone understand the art of discretion?"-

Gavin glanced back and shrugged his shoulders. "I think the car belongs to Lucien Bragg."

"Who?"

"He's Koko's new driver!"

Tori paused a moment as she recalled meeting him. "Wait a minute, I think I remember him in the diner the other day. He was dressed in leather like some biker or something, very odd."

Jonas was curious. "What was he doing?"

Tori exclaimed in a low whisper. "As far as I can tell, he was reading a book while he sipped a coffee; extra cream and extra sugar."

Jonas snarked. "That's so deep."

Gavin added. "I think he's foreign, from oversees or something."

Tori looked at Jonas in shock. "I guess you were right, you did see it parked at the Crecheland Inn."

Suddenly, from across the street, a tall young woman with a long overcoat and sunglasses ran down the sidewalk to the side of the car. Other than the clacking of extremely tall high heels, she moved like a silent gazelle. The front passenger door popped open and she quickly hopped inside. As she pulled the door shut behind her, she glanced back. Her gaze met Tori's and there was a painful hint of recognition, even from behind her sunglasses. She paused a moment as if she didn't know what to do next. Suddenly she pulled the door shut and the car took off. Tori stood frozen, as she watched the car disappear around the corner.

Jonas looked at Tori. "Who was that girl? She looks familiar."

Tori was almost in shock as she confirmed what they had witnessed. "That was Alouette Heron!"

Jonas bemused. "The homecoming queen?"

Tori eyed him. "Does that matter?"

"I suppose not."

"Why is she even with that creep?"

Gavin shrugged his shoulders. "Her scholarship didn't come through, and her family needed the money."

Tori's face contorted out of empathy. "My god. She worked so hard."

Gavin grinned. "Well, she is still working hard?"

"You pig."

"Hey, a girls got to eat, right!"

Jonas quietly interjected. "Do you think her mother knows?"

Gavin exclaimed. "Knows, she probably had her sign the contract with Lady Koko!"

Tori shivered. "That's horrible!"

Gavin put his hands in his pockets. "Horrible, from what I've heard Alouette is the hottest pip Koko has had in years. She supposed to really be something, **cloaqa** speaking, if you know what I mean!"

Tori gave Gavin a dirty look. "You are a misogynistic pig! You're what's wrong with the world!"

"Look, a year from now, she'll probably be a courtesan for some high-ranking cabinet member in the ministry. I would gladly lay on my backside and submit to get those opportunities that easily."

Jonas snickered. "I bet you would, regardless."

Gavin's eyes glared. "Raven may have missed your vital organs, but I wouldn't."

Tori put her purse on her other shoulder and tried to reason with the young man. "Look, Gavin, you have a sister. How would you feel if Raven were in Alouette's position?"

Gavin's face turned despondent. "Who says she isn't already. As a matter of fact, who says we aren't all just a step away."

"You are truly a dark, strange little man."

"Hey, what's that?"

"What?"

Gavin was staring at Tori, cupping her fingers. Gauze was slightly wrapped about the edges. Gavin shifted his gaze to her fumbling fingers. "What's wrong with your fingers?"

"I hurt them!"

"Did you lose any?"

"What kind of question is that?"

Gavin's mood became threatening and confrontational. "Are you hiding amputated digits from me?"

Jonas stepped in front of Tori, shielding her from the darkness he sensed bubbling up in Gavin. "Calm down. What gives bro?"

Tori extended her hand to show the red welt on her index finger and thumb. "No, you weirdo, I burned them on the fryer."

Gavin's mood softened just as quickly. "Sorry, I was just being cautious."

Jonas remained protective of Tori. "What is this obsession with you and Raven about missing fingers lately?"

Gavin snapped. "Look, I said I was sorry. You can't be too sure."

Tori was taken back by Gavin's sudden mood shift. It was like a switch turned on and off. In that moment, she wouldn't have been surprised if Gavin had tried to kill her. She rolled her eyes and tried to play it off.

"Whatever that means."

She was lost in thought when Jonas interrupted. "Hey, you still giving us a ride?"

Something in Tori snapped. "You know, I'm not!"

"What's wrong?"

"I'm done with you both. Happy walking boys!"

Gavin looked confused. "What ride?"

Tori got in her car and slammed the door shut. She took a deep breath to calm down. She revved up the Volkswagen and quickly drove past both Branson boys, pretending not to see either. It wasn't just Gavin's strange scary behavior, it was the idea that someone as sweet and innocent as Alouette would have this whole other life.

She thought of Willet, how she suddenly vanished, yet presumably, still somewhere in town. It was as if everything she thought was real was a lie. The stones of life were being overturned and beneath there was this slimy ugly underbelly that she had never observed before.

Chapter 55:

Second Visitation

By morning things had calmed down in terms of Laraline and her feelings towards reconciliation. She still hadn't told Willet about the dynamic changes going on. As recommended by Mother Hazel, it was crucial that Willet stay focused on the task at hand.

That was one bit of advice she completely agreed with. However, she wasn't sure if it was because she didn't want to deal with explaining and reliving the disappointment and betrayal that she was still struggling with.

By 5 a.m., Willet was relaxed enough to drift back again. As exciting as it was, there was a part of Laraline that wasn't sure anything was really happening. She had to take Willet's word that she was actually sailing the boat back.

What if it turns out that the boat was still docked: a decomposing derelict at the pier where they had left it docked almost a year ago. After all, she claimed she spoke with her dead father. Laraline's own faith had been shaken to the extent that she wasn't sure of who or what to believe. She would play along with the charade for the time being, on the off chance she was proven wrong. If this wasn't the case, at least Willet would be innocent of the storm.

Willet allowed her mother to clean the scar from the fight the previous afternoon. It had healed quite a bit since. There was now a thin scare on her left temple. Willet was really growing into her faigal metabolism. After a while, she calmly announced to the room in a determined voice.

"Ok, I'm ready!"

Mother Hazel gently began to speak the words of meditation to help her relax. This may be the last session before she could prove that she wasn't lying. Willet knew that the only one who partly believed her was Mother Hazel.

Everyone's body language and mannerisms in her presence gave them away. They all believed she had created the storm, yet somehow the boat was another matter. They were much more willing to believe the worse. Her mother was supportive, but the way she acted when Willet mentioned her father was very telling.

As she drifted off, the feeling of floating permeated her consciousness. She was starting to feel at ease; even comforted in her new surroundings. It was even better than the real thing. If only it were possible to live in some alternate existence. Soon, the smell of seawater filled her lungs as she opened her eyes again. She was surrounded by a cold mist.

The Lenoir was travelling steadily though a fog bank. She quickly made her way across the deck, her arms reaching and feeling about trying to get her bearings. Her wrist slapped against the large wooden mast. She darted her head about trying to find the helm, where a familiar figure stood adjusting the wheel.

"Daddy, your back!"

"I never left; you did."

"I don't understand."

"You know, transcendence is nothing to be afraid of Willet. Even death is a necessary stage of life."

"Why are you telling me this?"

"Would you tell Adelie and your mother how much I love them?"

Willet was almost in tears. "Mama doesn't believe I saw you!"

"She does, she just doesn't know it yet."

"You said something about an Einin blade."

"I must have been rambling again, time moves so differently here, it's all jumbled up in the most confusing manner."

"What are you talking about, Daddy?"

"I wasn't aware that you had already acquired the blade."

"I don't have anything."

"Maybe you just don't recognize it yet, precious."

"Could you tell me, what does it look like, Daddy?"

"I couldn't tell you because it's for your eyes only."

No sooner had he spoken, than his image started to fade into the misty fog. Willet ran to where he had stood, but he was gone.

"No wait, please come back." Frantically, she called after him. "Daaa-ddyyy!"

By sunrise the fog had lifted, and it was possible to see where she was heading. It was going to be a long hot day. By her calculations, she was somewhere outside of Norfolk. By that evening, she hoped to dock in New Haven. Hopefully, if everything goes as planned, she could reach the Crecheland Heights Dock by the following afternoon.

Chapter 56:

The Trouble with Cats

It was early Sunday morning. The crickets were chirping up a chorus, as Adelie and Deryn strolled down Harris Avenue. Harris eventually changed into East Sabine. In reality, Crecheland wasn't actually that far from Talomore Academy. It was almost a straight shot up Harris, then about a half a mile down East Sabine.

In fact, it seemed almost unreasonable to walk around Harris, turn on Blue Jay Way, and then straight up West Sabine. This added an extra mile and half to the journey. The only reason for this diversion was the comfort of the upper crust residents who lived on Harris Avenue. Many of its homeowners felt uneasy watching Crecheland children walking up and down the sidewalks inhabited by the likes of Mayor Van Warren and Constable Fletcher.

A service road was constructed to run parallel with Harris, but further away from the sight of tourists sightseeing the early historical rustic homes sprinkling Harris. Adelie questioned Deryn about the practicality of taking the short cut to school. Her reply was a caviler shrug.

It didn't matter today because it wasn't a school day and they were going scavenger hunting. Several patches of bramble bushes scattered the main field that connected the Greywood Estate from the Greywood themselves. Jae was, of course, supposed to be babysitting the pair that morning.

However, morning for a 17 year old teen can sometimes start after the wee hours of 11 o'clock a.m.

By the time Adelie and Deryn reached the field, they were exhausted from walking. It didn't help the fact that none of the bushes seemed to be thriving at this time of the season. Desperately trying to find an alternative to their plans, Deryn spied Greywood Estate in the distance.

"Hey, you said we could play on the chess pieces outside, can we still?"

Adelie begrudgingly rolled her eyes, as she half-heartedly agreed. "Fine, I guess so."

Deryn clapped her hands. "Oh goody."

For the next several minutes the pair slowly trudged up the field toward the house. Adelie had a thought. *What would happen when she showed up home? Would she get in trouble? Technically they weren't supposed to be there. It's been almost a week since she had been home.* She was about to mention her predicament to Deryn, when they heard a faint crying in the distance.

Deryn's head darted about. "Was that a baby?"

Adelie looked about the field nervously. "I don't hear anything."

Then the sound returned. Deryn perked up. "It sounds like a cat."

Derryn was excited and tore back down the field aimlessly searching through the tall grass. Adelie walked after her, listlessly for a few yards then stopped. Her feet were tired of motion. After a while Deryn started to go near the entrance of the Greywood.

At this close proximity, Adelie felt uneasy. "Hey Deryn, let's get going. I thought you wanted to play yard chess!"

Deryn was about to give up chase, when a brown cat popped out of nowhere. It was medium sized and it sat some 5 feet from the entrance of the woods, cleaning itself. Deryn knelt down close to eye level.

"Hello cutie pie!"

The feline seemed to be studying her. Deryn extended her arm out to the cat. It seemed unafraid as it just watched. Adelie was uneasy, as she recognized it as the same feline from the woods. It even seemed to nod at Adelie. She interrupted Derryn.

"Hey, don't touch!"

"Do you think she belongs to someone?"

"It's a feral cat. You don't want to mess with that thing!"

The cat let out a patient squeal. Deryn had moved within touching distance. When she heard another cat trill from her left side. Another cat started to move in her direction, seemingly from out of nowhere. Soon it was followed by another, and then yet another. Within a few minutes, Deryn was completely surrounded by dozens of feral cats. Deryn looked about in utter excitement.

"Wow, it's a whole family."

Adelie cautiously stood still watching the scene from afar. One of the cats seemed to glance in her direction with a wink. Almost instantly, every single feline leaped atop Deryn. The meows and purrs soon turned to growls. Claws and teeth started to scratch and bite into her.

Her natural response was to scream and run away. The major problem was that Deryn was completely covered in cats and couldn't really see where to run. One cat in particular was stretched across her face. Its claws were dug into the back of her head. After stumbling about, Deryn slipped and fell over, bumping her head.

She stretched her arm out toward Adelie. "Help me!"

Adelie rushed closer. As she reached out to touch Deryn's fingers, she suddenly noticed her own. Her hand was long and fleshy. Long strands of hair were protruding from her knuckles. Her fingers had all but turned into paws. Adelie instinctively shrank her hand away in horror, just as Deryn was about to grab her outstretched fingers.

Without warning, Deryn started to drift backward across the ground. Adelie did not know what was happening. However, at closer inspection she noticed the group of cats were physically dragging her into the threshold of the forest. Adelie got over her initial shock from the condition of her hand and ran toward the entrance of the Greywood. By now, the feral cats had successfully pulled Deryn inside. Adelie looked about frantically and picked up a stick with her paw hand. She then began to swing it furiously at the mountain of cats that seemed to have tripled in multitude.

Before she could get close, about five felines broke from the pile and confronted Adelie. They formed a lined barrier directly in front of her. They all began to hiss in unison. Their golden-brown fur frizzled up on their backs as if they were about to attack. Adelie paused cautiously at the apparent standoff. She watched helplessly as Deryn disappeared further beyond the tree line.

The five cats remained still but insisted that she was not welcomed any further. Adelie dropped the stick from her malformed hand. Almost at once, they dispersed back into the tall grass. Adelie didn't hesitate, as she ran to the edge of the woods and peered inside. However, she dared not venture any further.

She almost felt as if the woods themselves were trying to entice her back. Perhaps this was really a trap for her instead and Deryn was just bait. Adelie stepped back a few steps away from the entrance of the trees. The path ahead was dark and windy, as the branches gently beckoned. She could almost hear whispering from the trees and the shifting shadows beyond.

Chapter 57:

Strange Bedfellows

Aquila stood in the observation tower, as she peered at the town below. From this vantage point, she almost felt as if she were a god. Everything under her seemed so insignificant. She took a deep breath as she considered her meeting with the monsignor.

She tried her best to stay away from the ministry. However, she would need the Eskar to become involved. It was the only way the council would consider bringing criminal charges against Nashca Ortega. Avis, with his open threat to expose her, didn't really force her hand, but it sped up her timetable.

"Why up here?" Mr. Richter made himself known from the shadows that obscured the spiral staircase.

Aquila grinned. "Discretion. This vantage point is very private. It wouldn't be in my best interest to be seen with the likes of you, sleeven."

Sage Richter pulled his thick fur coat tighter as he climbed up on the landing. "Same here. From what I hear, you're the Bloody Mary among your kind."

Aquila finally faced him. She had a bemused look on her face. "Are you here to kill me?"

"Well, the thought had crossed my mind. Why shouldn't I, especially after the double cross you pulled."

"Excuse me?"

Richter reached under his coat and dropped an object on the floor. The head of a harpy rolled at her feet. "What do you call this thing?"

Aquila was curt. 'Population control."

"What?"

"I thought there were three others."

"Well, it's a long drive from Florida, and I got a wee bit hungry."

"Is that why there is only a head left?"

"Useless small talk."

"So, where did you dock?"

"What are you talking about?"

"The boat."

"That's what I'm talking about, there is no boat."

Aquila looked visibly troubled. "What do you mean, I paid you handsomely to bring back that boat, after you killed any occupants."

"When I first got there, it was docked alright. However, after my little dance with your friends. I went back out to check and imagine my surprise when it was gone. The way I see it, you had someone else steal the boat, while your flying freaks tried to kill me, and have me framed for the theft."

"That's ridiculous nonsense."

"How is that so ridiculous? Makes sense to me."

"Because they weren't supposed to kill you until after you had brought my boat back here."

"Hell, that's honest."

"How do you know you weren't looking at the wrong boat?"

"I don't make mistakes; besides, I've been on that boat before. I know exactly what it looks like."

"What do you mean, you've been on that boat before?"

"Let's just say, the group I work for were very interested, in the previous owners knowledge about certain stolen items."

"So, you're the one responsible for this whole situation in the first place."

"What situation?"

"Never mind. Well, if you don't have my boat, who does?"

"If I had to guess, probably the rightful owner. I think the original mark had a wife and kids. Perhaps they came and stole it back."

"That's impossible, they're still here in town. They never left."

"I know for a fact, someone else was there. I could feel their presence."

Aquila, in a fit of rage, stomped the harpy head with her boot until it was pummeled into the floor. All that remained was a gooey stain. She looked up in a frenzied rage.

"I bet it was my brother. He is the only one who would have crossed me, but how did he find out about my plans?"

Richter held his gun at his side. "Well, I guess we both got played."

Aquila suddenly turned to Richter. "I know you were expecting some sort of payment. Would you like to be paid in live currency?"

"What did you have in mind?"

Chapter 58:

Search Party

Constable Fletcher and his men spread out about the perimeter of the field. Adelie was silent as the officers dug around the tall grass for clues. She knew their attempts to locate Deryn would be futile. No one would find any sign that she was even there.

She wasn't sure how, but she knew Verspa Lynn had something to do with Deryn's abduction, just as she had something to do with her funky hand. She looked down at both her hands. They were now covered with long black gloves, so she wouldn't attract attention. Sooner or later, she would have to tell someone, but what could she say?

As far as anyone knew, Deryn saw a cat in the field and chased after. Adelie followed her but lost her in the tall grass. The entrance of the Greywood stood a mere 50 yards from them. It was like the elephant in the room. No one mentioned the fact that she may have wandered into Greywood. Adelie herself didn't even reference the possibility once.

Finally, Fetcher looked at Mrs. Weever, shaking his head. "Perhaps she ventured into the forest."

She shook her head vehemently. "She wouldn't go there; she is a smart girl."

Laraline interjected. "Both girls are terrified of the Greywood, especially after what happened last week!"

"Well, she is definitely not anywhere in this field!"

The group got silent, as if the truth couldn't be denied. Fletcher turned to his deputy. "Go to the car and get a flashlight and a couple of rifles."

"Sir. It's the Greywood!"

"What am I supposed to do?"

"Well?"

"This is yet another child. It has to stop!"

Fletcher knelt down, as the other officer went to retrieve the items from the patrol car. Fletcher's gaze met Adelie's. He was trying to read her honesty and sincerity.

"Is there anything else you want to tell me, Adelie?" .

She quickly nodded.

"I mean, this is your best friend. I need for you to try hard so we can get her back home safely."

Adelie internally responded. *It's too late for that!* She had her game face on, as she looked down at her gloved hands. She could feel the long nails digging at the corners of the leather gloves from inside. She took a deep breath and quickly responded.

"No, I told you all I know. We were walking up the hill when she saw the cat and she started to chase it. When I got up here, I didn't see her anywhere. I went to the edge of the woods and called after her, then I got scared."

Adelie felt herself well up with tears. Her mother quickly embraced her. "Constable, she has told you everything she knows. She's been through a lot this month!"

"Fair enough, Mrs. Swift." He rose to his feet as the other deputy returned with a long-range rifle.

"Private property or no private property, this place is now under criminal investigation. You make your Aunt Sirenna aware, that at this moment, I have full jurisdiction of this field and those woods!"

"You tell her yourself. We're going home!"

Laraline was worn out as she led Adelie back across the field. As they made their way back to the house. Uncle Merle and Evelyn were on the front steps with blank expressions, as if they already knew what the outcome would be. Adelie hung her head down and began to cry to herself.

Chapter 59:

Errands

.

Nashca strolled into the study where Lord Avis was signing some documents. The study was a formal place, very traditional. Even the writing pens were long puffy quills dipped in ink.

Raven was standing over him impatiently. She glanced up in Nashca's direction and quickly rolled her eyes. She looked back down at her father's hands carefully signing his signature. "Please father, do hurry!"

He responded. "I hope this is the last discipline referral I receive from your instructors."

"Yes, Father!"

After a few moments, he lifted the paper and handed it to the impatient girl. She rushed by Nashca without even acknowledging her. Nashca folded her arms as she moved close.

"Are you ok, my lord?"

"I don't know what to do with her lately."

"You look concerned."

"Aquila has me on edge. She is up to something."

"She is always up to something."

"I believe she has involved my children; I noticed Raven didn't even bother to speak to you. I was hoping that having another female in the house would soften her."

"Ever since this past summer, Raven and I have been at odds with one another, but I'm a bit surprised about Gavin."

"What are you talking about, you weren't even here this summer."

Nashca corrected herself. "Of Course, my cousin's letters are so vivid, sometimes I feel like I'm experiencing what he has."

Avis's attention suddenly turned to an envelope that he quickly opened. "Speaking of cousins, it appears that one of Meena's cousins is requesting a visit. This is most unusual."

"I didn't know she had family still alive."

"Well, ever since my wife's death, they have pretty much distanced themselves from us. Meena was a sweetheart though. It's hard to believe that she was spawned from that family."

"I always thought the Corbett line was the preferred breeding line for the Branson dynasty."

"Well, our lineages are so close, it just makes things convenient. For years, our ancestors tried to bond with the Adler blood line, but after a few obvious mishaps, we began to consider alternatives. Eventually, I picked Meadow Corbett as my queen.

"Is that why Aquila retains the name Corbett as well?"

"Only when it suits her. My father married Aquila's mother, Queen Nina Corbett. So, we are not blood related. Which is why we have never been close, I suppose!"

"How many of her family are still alive?"

"Well, she has an Uncle Montague in the ministry, her cousins, ZuZu, Melania, Prince Erik and then of course,

Aquila. That is pretty much, the extent of her surviving family."

"Really, with such an influential family name, I expected many more offspring."

"Well, diastasis runs rampant in the Corbett blood line. Those that were spared, pretty much killed one another off over the last few years!"

"What do you mean they killed each other off?"

"They are a rather vicious clan."

Lord Branson turned his attention to the letter, which he quickly peeled open with a golden letter opener. He silently studied the contents before deciphering its meaning to Nashca.

"Speaking of vicious, this letter of announcement is a legal document titled, In Care of ZuZu Fatale."

"In care of, what does that mean?"

"It's an official letter about her parole hearing."

"Parole, is she incarcerated?"

"Sweet little ZuZu has been a guest of Darkmore Keep for nearly three years now."

"Darkmore! Whatever did she do?"

Branson slid the letter back in its envelope and tossed it aside. "Her crimes are too numerous to mention."

"Then why is she being considered for release?"

"Because her Uncle Montague is on the ministry. Never mind that, we have a busy day ahead of us."

"We do?"

"I have an errand for you my dear."

Avis pulled a thick envelope from his drawer. "I need you to give these to my lawyer, Arnold Leech."

"Where is he, I haven't seen him of late?"

"He was called away to Monticello on important business."

Nashca looked curiously at the thick envelope she held in her hands.

Avis quipped. "Be careful with those papers, they are very important."

"Are these what I think they are?"

"Stop looking at me like that!"

"This is crazy, do you know what you're doing, my lord?"

"I'm preparing for the future: nothing more, nothing less."

Chapter 60:

Specters, Echoes and Other Sightings

Ever since Langston's second visitation, Willet realized just how alone she felt. She had pretty much felt this way all her life, but actually being inside her own mind for so long was like torture. She looked across the isolated deck of the Lenoir and inhaled the fresh sea air. It was at that moment she came to a realization. She was very much like her father.

Langston Swift was also a very private person. Especially at the end. He kept himself at a distance, not allowing others to get too close. Not even his own family.

The hull remained still except for a slight breeze overhead. Flapping sails answered with their own ambient rhythm. It was unusually quiet, in the dull overcast sky. Willet scanned the grey horizon. She first noticed a single red buoy to her right. It gently rocked back and forth in the water. *Where did that come from?*

At closer inspection, there seemed to be something slightly obscured directly behind the buoy. It was as if someone was hiding from her. That's impossible, they would have to be standing on the water. Willet slowly walked down the side of the railing to get a better look from another angle. The more her eyes revealed the nature of the being, the more her heart began to race. The veiled threat of the horned nymph entered her thoughts. Perhaps she had come back to finish her.

Indeed, she wasn't mistaken. Some sort of person dressed in a yellow raincoat was actually standing on the water. However, this was yet something different. They had a large red umbrella draped over their head and shoulders.

Willet's eyes bulged with disbelief. "Is this real?"

As if anticipating her stare, the strange figure began to slide across the top of the water to the other side of the buoy so she couldn't get a good look. It was definitely hiding from her. This unnerved Willet even more. As the Lenoir trudged silently by, it almost seemed as if the phantom was not only deliberately moving from her sight, but further away from the buoy itself. When the Lenoir finally passed the red buoy, Willet could see the figure clearly moving quite urgently toward the horizon. She could barely see it now from this distance.

She had an impulse to change course and follow the bizarre phantom. However, that desire quickly faded, as she thought of the bizarre horned nymph under the water. Willet was afraid to discover anything more about this new apparition.

Willet stood on the deck staring blankly into the horizon. Apart from the occasional seagull, it was vast emptiness. Perhaps it was her mind playing tricks on her. Willet decided to go below deck and get a change of scenery. The trip was starting to take a toll on her psyche. She had to keep reminding herself that she wasn't actually on the boat. Her current existence was that of a waking dream.

She climbed below deck and looked around the dim cabin. In the light, the interior looked less menacing. She kept thinking about what her father had told her. *For your eyes only!*

Perhaps it was something she was supposed to see aboard the boat. She looked through the various shelves and cabinets. However, there were so many nooks and crannies something could be hiding. To properly look, it could take hours, even days.

She sat on the edge of the small day bed under the window beside Mr. Claude. She folded her arms and took a deep breath. Willet was sufficiently tired of looking. Whatever she was supposed to find, she hadn't a clue.

She caught the glimpse of a cobweb in the corner above the bed. A fat nasty spider lay stretched out, frozen in suspended animation within her threads. It was like a wind up zombie waiting in anticipation for its webs to be disturbed.

An image of the strange woman with the multiple limbs popped in her mind. Back in her real life, she was still out there hunting the people in her city. The griskin, as Mother Hazel had called her, reminded Willet of the spider.

Willet found her way back on deck and spent a few hours trying to relax and mediate. After a while she opened her eyes and considered the day. If she were a tempest, what could she actually do? I know I could start storms, but could I do anything else? What does that actually mean? She extended her arm out to the sky. She flicked her wrist about in the sky trying to get some sort of reaction.

Intention, you must have intention to succeed in anything in life. What is my intention? What is motivation?

Willet yelled out loud. "I don't know what my intention is. To be honest, I don't know if I even have one."

Willet leaned over the edge of the railing and looked down at the waves crashing gently against the sides. The water was so blue, it was almost artificial looking.

For the first time since her odyssey began, she had a momentary thought of Jonas. The image of grabbing him and kissing him played over in her mind. She cringed at the embarrassment of what she had done. *How could she face him after she returned? Why was I so impulsive?* But when she thought about the actual reality of it, it seemed ridiculous, even cartoonish.

She began to laugh as she tried to cover her eyes, as if others were there to expose her embarrassment. "Mr. Claude, if only you could see what a fool I have made of myself."

Suddenly, a light bulb went off, and Willet hopped to her feet. "See! See!"

She ran across the deck and down into the cabin. She looked about frantically until she spied the teddy bear.

I was always afraid you would fall overboard and drown, so I would never have taken you aboard the Lenoir. I'm also sure you were not on the boat before Daddy's death or the police would have returned you. Which means, someone placed you here after the fact. Only I would know that you don't belong.

Willet grabbed the teddy off the daybed and began to study it carefully. "Could you be placed here for my eyes only?" She shook Mr. Claude suspiciously. *But by whom?*

Willet closed her eyes and took a deep breath. *I don't know, it sounds a bit too easy. Well, one thing's for certain, it's going to be difficult to inspect you, if I'm not physically here!*

Willet tossed the stuffed animal back on the mattress. She looked carefully around the cabin. It was almost as if she could feel her father's eyes watching.

Chapter 61:

Bubble Bath

Adelie sat in the bathtub slowly unfolding the events of the last two weeks. Her mother had run her a bath after the nasty incident with Deryn. In light of the current situation, it was understood that Adelie should just remain back at Greywood estate, especially since Willet's little experiment was close to ending. Adelie was overjoyed. Strangely enough, she really missed seeing Willet.

In light of certain events, she felt Willet was the one person who might understand. However, she was informed that she would have to wait at least another day or so. Everything was so hush, hush about Willet.

Adelie lifted her hand from the soapy water and beheld the strange anomaly. *What was happening to her?* Her other hand was, for the moment, normal. However, it had already started to itch in the same way the first hand did. She was trying to calm down when she glanced back at her hand which resembled a paw. Adelie let out a deep sigh of frustration.

She stretched her legs out in the tub and placed her toes on the edge of the tub, when she noticed that both her feet were starting to resemble paws too. They were catlike in nature. She squealed in horror only to have her mother tap on the door concerned.

"Addie, are you ok in there, dear?"

Adelie quickly put her feet back down and submerged her bad hand below the surface of the water. The door swung open wide as Laraline popped her head inside the door.

"Do you need to talk?"

"No, not right now Mama!"

"Please don't shut me out, Addie."

Adelie sighed. "Fine."

Laraline slipped into the bathroom. Seeing a way to change the subject, Adelie looked in her mother's direction. "How is Willet doing?"

"She's ok."

Laraline's mood shifted away from her subtle prying into her daughter's thoughts to a less confrontational exchange. Her mother held two large mugs in Adelie's' direction.

"I brought some hot chocolate."

"Really!"

Adelie was about to reach for the mug but caught herself about to use her claw hand. She quickly dismissed her previous statement. "Thank you, mom. Can you just put it on the counter, I'll get some later!"

Adelie was hoping that her sudden dismissal of a sugary bribe would dissuade her mother from staying. Instead, Laraline pulled up a wooden bench and sat beside the tub. She then reached across Adelie and slid the bathtub tray down across the front, until it was a few inches from her daughter's chest.

"Excuse me, Mama, what are you doing?"

Almost immediately without speaking, Laraline took the brush off the tray and started to comb through her daughter's hair. It was a typical ritual that they had engaged in several times and normally, Adelie would relish the attention. However, she was in a panic that her mother would discover her strange changes.

"Ow!"

"Sorry, it's been a while since I've done your hair."

"You don't have to do this, Mom."

"I want to, dear."

"Ok."

"I feel like sometimes, you get completely forgotten, because you're the younger sister."

Adelie remained silent. She didn't really have a response. Instead, she focused on keeping her limbs in the water until her mother decided to leave. It was uncomfortably silent until Laraline started to hum to herself.

"My, your hair has gotten so long and beautiful. You always had beautiful hair."

"Do you think I'm pretty, Mama?"

"Are you serious, your drop dead gorgeous!"

"Mama!"

"You will have a hard time fighting off the boys, so don't be in a hurry."

"What are you talking about?"

"Your almost sixteen and you look like your twenty-two."

"Did you do Willet's hair, when she was younger?"

"Are you serious? That girl wouldn't dare let me near her hair."

"Really?"

"You were always my little princess."

"What was Willet then?"

"She was always our little rebel. She didn't like dresses, or dolls, or fancy perms or even makeup."

"She wears it now. In fact, I've seen her spend almost 25 minutes doing her face."

"Well, she had to grow into her looks."

"She's not ugly at all!"

"No, I didn't say she was. She is very beautiful. However, for a while, she never really thought she was in that way."

"Really?"

"She didn't have it as easy as you. When she decides on a life mate, I have no doubt they will be just as adventurous and challenging."

"Is that why she is so mean sometimes?"

"Don't fool yourself kiddo, you're not a day in the park either."

Adelie was silent before continuing. "Mama, is Willet dying?"

"Of course not, why would you ask such a question?"

"Remember, Daddy disappeared before he was found dead!"

"You think too much."

Laraline was about to correct Adelie, however she had to admit she had a point. Even though Willet's physical body was just down the hall, her mind and spirit were gone at the moment. She quickly changed the subject to Adelie's hair.

"How's that look?"

"What?"

Laraline picked up the small hand mirror from the tray and held it in front of her daughter's face. "Your hair, silly!"

"Oh yeah, thank you Mama."

Both looked at the reflection in the mirror. The moment had somehow calmed Adelie down a bit. Unfortunately, this wouldn't last.

Laraline finally mused. "Look at your eyes. They have this exotic quality to them I never noticed before! "

Adelie was suddenly uneasy. "What do you mean?"

Laraline held the mirror up so Adelie could see herself. "They remind me of some wild jungle cat!"

Adelie was defiant. "No, they don't!"

"Calm down. I didn't mean anything!"

Adelie realized her behavior was extreme and quickly backpedaled. "I'm sorry, Mama. I guess I'm tired."

"Well, it's perfectly understandable. Think of everything you've been through these last few days."

She kissed her daughter on her forehead and quickly rose to her feet. A silent sigh of relief poured out of Adelie's lips, as her mother walked to the door.

"Don't forget about the hot chocolate, it's going to get cold!"

"Ok, thank you."

"Do you want the light on, dear?"

"Yes, please."

"Ok, enjoy your bath."

"Wait!"

"What's wrong?"

"You don't think Deryn would try to come back, do you?"

Laraline leaned against the side of the door, taken back. "What an odd question?" Adelie didn't respond, as she waited for Laraline to continue.

"Adelie, she's only been missing a few hours. Heck, you and your sister were gone several hours between the both of you. Deryn has been living in this town all her life. I bet there is a good chance she will be found alive."

Adelie sunk her head down. "Oh, ok."

"I swear Adelie, she's your best friend and you act as if you don't want her to return." Adelie held her tongue, as her mother shut the door behind her. She heard Laraline's footfalls disappear down the hallway and a wisp of fear overcame her.

Chapter 62:

Monticello

The streets of Monticello were damp and cold, as Nashca made her way to the private offices on Floral Street. In front of the building there was a lot of activity. Recently, there had been some unrest, and several flocks of covey knights were present. She squeezed her way through the agitated crowd and pushed her way inside the entrance of a three-story yellow brick building. With her black suitcase and her long walking stick she cautiously tipped past through the main lobby. The offices were on the third floor, so she elected to take the back stairwell to be more discreet.

Nashca passed many doors on either side of the hallway. At the end of the long corridor, she made her way into a dimly lit office at the end. Inside the room sat a long desk, a couch, and a single large file cabinet. Long gone were the large sculptures, water coolers, plush plants and a smiling receptionist. Such pleasantries were the victims of the current state of economic unrest in town. All that remained was a quaint picture. On the back wall hung a niche painting of the Elysium on its maiden voyage.

Nashca studied the work of art. It had a festive aura that contrasted with what was happening today in the city. She recognized the dock from the painting; it was same one she had just arrived on. Though now it was more contemporary looking.

A voice from the corner addressed her. "They say it took almost 5 years to complete that ship, yet it took the artist less than five hours to complete that painting."

She looked about the relatively empty room and caught a glimpse of a well-dressed fellow nervously peering out of the window. His hands were in his pockets, and he seemed troubled by the activity outside. Nashca glanced back at the painting, touching the edge of the frame with her fingers.

"Where did you acquire it?"

"I bought that painting about ten years ago from a peddler on these very streets."

Nashca took a step forward, this time directly addressing the troubled little man. "Excuse me, Mr. Arnold Leech. Lord Branson sent me. He wanted to make sure you received these. He wants them processed right away. They are of the utmost importance."

Nashca sat her suitcase on his desk and popped open the contents. She removed a thick manilla envelope and extended it toward Leech.

Without looking up, he took the packet and cleared his throat. "Please lock the door, we don't want and unwanted visitors." Leech started to peel though the papers. An occasional grunt or snort erupted from his lips. Suddenly he glanced over and responded with an odd question.

"Are you still you?"

"Excuse me?"

"Never mind. I assume this is Lord Branson's revised will? I will be sure to catalogue the other affects contained in the envelope as well."

"How long will this take?"

"Not long, a day or two. If you wish I will waive the processing fee."

"We can't accept that. We can more than pay you for your trouble."

"Avis has always been good to me. This one is on me. Call it a parting gift."

There was an uncomfortable silence. She understood at that moment that whatever was going to happen, he had accepted his fate. It was doubtful that he would ever return to Meadowlark. He carefully changed the subject.

"So, you are the new weaver for Branson? We haven't properly met. I fear this will be the only time we actually do!"

"What's going on!"

"All these extremist groups are causing a bit of trouble. Even here in Monticello, they have gotten stronger."

"Is that what all the chaos is outside?"

"This has practically devolved into a police state. I'm surprised you were even allowed inside."

Nashca walked to the window and peered out curiously. "You know it's funny, we haven't met in all this time. Leech, that name is familiar all the same."

"That's because I brokered the original arrangement with the Ortega family."

There was uneasiness in Nashca's face as he revealed this detail. "So, you know about the arrangement?"

Leech, sensing her fear, gently smiled. "Don't worry, I will carry any details about your condition to my grave."

Nashca exhaled relief. "Thank you, Mr. Leech. Avis is right, you are a decent man. In another life, perhaps faigal and sleeven could truly find a way to coexist."

The quiet moment was broken, as there was a loud explosion from the street below. Both Nashca and Leech ducked away from the window. She turned to Leech.

"What has caused this madness?"

"They found the remains of a former cabinet member of the ministry this morning. The body had been eviscerated. This is the fourth body found in this condition in the last month. Two others were located in a similar fashion in new Essex."

"Is it Einin?"

"Possible. It could also be Swans. They aren't fans of the ministry either. Because of the ease with which they were taken, the ministry itself is on a witch hunt within their own ranks. They feel the Smile have infiltrated. Avis's name has come up several times within secret meetings."

"They couldn't think anything like that about Lord Branson. He hates the Swans."

"Even so, he is being labeled a sleeven sympathizer. Namely because he hired me. I have been ordered to stay here in Monticello. I suspect I will be arrested within the week."

"You can't leave?"

"I wish I could. It's too late for that. They have all entrances and exits guarded."

"I saw no one."

"They are the covey knights; you weren't meant to see them."

"I didn't know things had gotten so dire."

"That's not the half of it. Word is, a delegation is on its way to Meadowlark today so they can informally investigate criminal charges concerning Meena Corbett's death."

"Yes, I have evidence that suggests Aquila was involved with her death. Still, that is a rather quick turnaround."

"What are you talking about, Aquila is the accuser."

Nashca's eye widened in horror. "Aquila?"

"Of course, that is classified. So, you didn't hear that from me!"

"I must return at once to Meadowlark."

"What about the paperwork, if I'm arrested. You may not have another way of attaining these documents, especially if they are as important as you say."

"Aquila is planning to have her own brother arrested so she can take over his estate. I must try to warn him."

"That's ridiculous. There is no evidence."

"I suspect she will use it as a platform to expose him in other ways."

"How?"

Nashca was suddenly embarrassed about the nature of her relationship with Lord Branson. "Never mind that, can you leave the papers in your desk?"

"In light of certain circumstances, perhaps I should hide them."

"Where?"

"I don't know, off hand. If things start to go sour; I will hide them someplace, where only you will know where to find them."

Chapter 63:

Mr. Claude

It was dark when Willet opened her eyes. She was back in her bedroom. Her mother lay on the foot of her bed asleep. She carefully slid out of the covers and made her way to the bedroom. She reached for the faucet and quickly began to splash water on her face. She was drying her face when she heard a soft nondescript whisper coming from behind. She spun around to the dark bathtub behind her.

The voice was undecipherable. However, it seemed to be coming from the depths of the bathtub. A mumbled sound as if someone was gargling erupted from the direction of the tub.

Willet looked horrified. *It's just in my mind. It isn't real!* Willet took her right foot and stretched it out. Her goal was to slam the bottom of the tub to stop the strange ghostly hallucination she had been having about her bathroom lately.

Willet took her bare foot and slammed it down inside the tub, except her foot didn't slam on the bottom, it splashed deep, almost pulling her down inside of the tub. As far as she could tell, the water extended well beyond the bottom surface of the tub. A greenish light emanated from below the surface as Willet frantically pulled herself back out of the tub.

She quickly turned on the bathroom light and spun around. The tub was normal, save for a small puddle of greenish water that poured back down into the drain hole. There was no deep pool as she had thought. Just a slightly singed white tub. She used her hand to slam the now solid bottom. It banged with a faint metallic echo.

"Willet, is that you?"

Her mother was calling from the other room. The bathroom chaos had awakened her. Willet walked to the door with a troubled expression. Though the pool seemed like a dream, her leg and foot were still damp. In fact, her foot was glistening with wetness, as she made her way back into the bedroom to meet her mother's gaze.

"Is everything ok? You look frazzled, dear."

"Just nightmares."

"How can you tell the difference?" The question was such a loaded question, that Willet didn't really know how to answer.

Instead, she pulled something out from under her covers. "Hey, look what I found on the Lenoir the other day." She held up the dingy teddy bear.

Laraline's response was immediately fearful. "How did you get that thing?"

"I told you; I found it in the cabin on Daddy's boat."

"That's just not possible. Unless it's all real, the things you are able to do!"

Willet was disturbed. "So, now you believe me. All this time, what did you think I was doing, just taking supervised catnaps?"

"I had hope you were right, but I wasn't sure. Sometimes one becomes accustomed to not having much faith in even the little things around us. I'm so sorry I doubted you."

"Well, why do you suddenly believe me now?"

"I believed you believed, and that was enough, until you conjured this thing back into existence."

Willet winced. "What do you mean, back into existence? It was just lying on the daybed below deck."

"Mr. Claude shouldn't be here at all. I destroyed him, or at least I thought I had."

"You what? Why? That makes no sense!"

"I didn't understand it either, but it was your father's dying request."

"Dying request?"

"I know it sounds weird, but this lawyer drew up a letter that your daddy had drafted weeks prior. A few hours after he was pronounced dead, they delivered it to me."

Willet felt a chill up her spine. "It sounds like he knew what was going to happen to him?"

Laraline was silent, but her expression let Willet know she had obviously thought the same.

"Who was this lawyer?"

"I never met him before."

"Do you have that letter now, mama?"

"Willet, that's kind of personal."

"Mama, it's important. I have spoken to my dead father twice in the last week, and from what I gather he intended for me to find Mr. Claude. If he requested you to destroy him, I need to know why?"

Laraline reluctantly nodded. "Wait here."

Willet watched her mother silently disappear into the dark hallway. An antsy feeling started to permeate As she waited for her mother to return, Willet looked down at the grungy little teddy bear.

"So, what is your story, little fellow?"

Before she could glean any reply, she heard Adelie calling. "Willie, you're here!"

Adelie stood at Willet's bedroom door. She had a toothbrush crooked on the side of her mouth. She was fully dressed in long fuzzy pajama pants and a long sleeve shirt. She wore pink fuzzy mittens over her hands with matching booties on her feet.

As soon as they made eye contact, Adelie ran inside the room and embraced her sister. "I missed you so much!"

Willet was taken back by her unusual display of affection. "I missed you too!"

"Where have you been, Willie?"

"Well, it's complicated. I went on a trip across the ocean."

"Where, anyplace I've heard of?"

"Several places. I'm actually not done. But I will be finish travelling sometime tomorrow afternoon if I'm lucky!"

Adelie looked perturbed. "That makes no sense, you're standing right in front of me."

"It's a bit complicated. I'll explain tomorrow at dinner, I promise."

Laraline was at the door with a brown envelope. She looked up with a delicate smile as she witnessed her two daughters together. "You're both here."

Adelie yawned. "Hi Mama."

Laraline moved across the floor and draped her hand affectionately on the back of Adelie's head. "This one has been bugging me about when you were returning!"

Willet cut her mother off. "I can't stay long, Ma!"

Laraline pursed her mouth, as she finally had accepted the reality of what Willet was doing. "I know."

Adelie was defiant. "Well, I don't! What's the deal?"

Willet changed the subject. "Speaking of deal, why aren't you over at Ms. Weever's house, I thought Deryn was your best friend."

The room got silent. Adelie put her head down, as did her Laraline.

Willet suddenly felt awkward. "Did I say something wrong?"

Adelie answered. "Deryn's gone?"

Laraline tried to correct her. "We don't know just yet, the police are still looking!"

"Please Mama, everyone knows. No one wants to be the first say it out loud!"

"Jeez, what happened? Did that creepy woman get her, too?"

"We don't know exactly."

Laraline was about to elaborate when she noticed her daughter's hands. "Adelie, why are you so insistent on wearing those ridiculous gloves. It's almost bedtime!"

"They make me feel safe."

Willet shot Adelie an uncomfortable glance and then her eyes shifted to Adelie's gloved hands. Willet instinctively sensed that the subject should be changed.

"What happened to Deryn, Mama?"

"Apparently, your sister and her were playing in that large field to the right of the driveway."

Willet pointed to the right of the window. "Out there?"

"Yeah. Anyway, Deryn saw a cat and went after it. She followed her into the tall grass and got lost. Adelie didn't see what happened to her, and no one has seen her since."

No one said anything, but there was an unspoken understanding that the Greywood must have played a role in her disappearance. Willet sat on the edge of her bed, as if the wind had been knocked out of her.

"This quiet town of Meadowlark Downs can be deafening."

Adelie winced at the wordy commentary. "What?"

Willet quickly glanced back at Adelie. "So, you were playing with her, and you didn't see anything?"

Her response was typical, as she turned away from direct eye contact. "No, I didn't!"

She is hiding something. Willet knew her sister well enough to know when she was lying. *She knows more about the situation than what she has told anyone.* This would not be much different from the Greywood incident that just happened. However, this was not the time to confront her. She couldn't get distracted with yet another crisis.

Instead, Willet offered an olive branch. She held up the ragged teddy bear in front of Adelie's face. "Look Adelie."

Adelie's mood shifted to bubbly excitement. "Mr. Claude, where did you find him? "

"I found him on my trip, which I need to be returning."

"Can I go with you, Willie?"

Laraline snapped. "Addie!"

"Please, I won't be any trouble. I am sure we would have lots to talk about."

Willet gave her a knowing glance. "I'm sure we would, but, it's just not possible. I can only travel alone."

"Why?"

"It's a bit complicated."

Willet glanced at her mother who had temporarily forgotten her concern with Adelie's gloves.

"Do you have that letter mama?"

Laraline extended the folded paper in Willet's direction. "Here it is, please be careful."

Adelie looked suspiciously between the two. She seemed confused, as if she was trying to process what was being said. "Hey, what's happening?"

"I told you before, I have to go."

"Where are you going?"

"Hopefully, I will see you tomorrow afternoon and we can talk then."

"Wait, if your leaving, why do you look like you are dressed for bed?"

Laraline's voice finally boomed from across the room in complete impatience. "Adelie, stop bothering your sister and go to bed!"

Adelie quickly hurried to the door, as she passed Willet, she touched her sister's shoulder. "I promise we will talk later!" She felt guilty, but Adelie wasn't part of the vertriste.

Laraline yelled down the hall. "I will come kiss you in about twenty minutes."

As soon as things had settled a bit, Willet turned to her mother. "May I open the letter?"

Her mother sat on the bed and nodded. Willet stood in front of her mother as her bum was a bit sore from spending so much time in the bed. She carefully unfolded the yellow sheet and began to read out loud.

To my beloved wife,

If you are reading this letter, then I am no longer with you. It is up to you to carry on with our family and all the challenges that may come in the years ahead.

As you know, it's been many years since I gave up my practice, however I would ask that you grant me one last request. This may seem a bit of an odd request; however, it is imperative that it is done as soon as possible.

The teddy bear that Willet has grown fond of, must be taken away from her discreetly. Place the toy with my remains, so it can be cremated along with me. There will come a day, when she will come to you with questions and concerns. On this day, she will be tasked to complete my final rites.

Please allow her to complete this task without judgment, as only she will be able to see and know the nature of where and when this should happen.

Please don't lose faith, no matter how difficult things may appear, my dear Laraline.

This life has been a wonderful adventure, and I will cherish the moments we have had together.

Always your loving husband,

Lance

Willet was speechless as she read over the letter again. This time she picked apart several words and phrases, grilling her mother about the meaning.

"He didn't really say a lot to me Willet."

"He was your husband."

"He was a very private person, as I have discovered. It's ironic, I ran away from my family because of all the deep secrets and ended up marrying a fellow with just as many secrets. What's important is he truly loved his family. I guess in the end, that's what really matters."

Laraline held her head up to the ceiling as tears began to flow from the corners of her eyes. Willet suddenly realized her mother was troubled by something else, other than the current discussion.

"Mama, what's wrong?"

"While you were gone, I learned a fair bit of news here, as well." Willet stood patiently as her mother continued to speak. "I learned a lot about who my mother was and what happened to her. You know grandma Oriole wasn't really your grandmother."

"She wasn't?"

"She never was my mother."

Willet almost forgot her own issues as her own expression changed. "Then who is?"

"Evelyn is actually my birth mother."

"Aunt Evie?"

"Yes."

"Who is Oriole?"

"That's a bit complicated. One explanation is she was my aunt. Another explanation is she was a dangerous sociopath who tried to destroy her family."

"I don't understand?"

"I don't understand it all completely myself. I do know that if it weren't for your Aunt Sirenna, I wouldn't be standing here today."

Laraline really didn't want to explain the gory details of how Sirenna had to save Evelyn and her newborn from certain death. Willet could feel the hurt in her mother's voice as Willet rubbed her back.

"I'm sorry Mama."

"They have known all this time and kept it from me."

"Wow, that's pretty messed up."

"That's not the punchline."

"What are you talking about?"

"Guess who my father is?"

"Uncle Merle?"

"Now that's gross."

"Well, who?"

"Lord Avis Branson himself."

Willet stood silent as her mother continued. She suddenly felt ill as she thought about the fact that she could be related to that family. This also meant that she was related to Jonas and she kissed him.

"Whoa."

"I was led to believe, all this time, that he had something to do with my mother's death. I was taught to hate everything about him and his family name. It was all a big fat political lie!"

"Does that mean that you're a Branson?"

"I don't know what it means, dear. When I went over there to confront him, I was so determined to tell him off."

"So, what happened? Was there a huge throw down between you guys?"

"I envisioned this huge scenario, where I took him to task."

"Yeah!"

"He opened his mouth and started to speak, and I quickly realized that he and my mother and my aunt, were children, just as you are now. They were being forced to make adult decisions about things they were not equipped to handle. They did this without any guidance or knowledge of the consequences of their actions."

Laraline turned her head to the window and continued to speak. "I didn't see hatred or greed or apathy. What I saw was regret. I don't want to have any regrets, and I don't want you to have any either."

Willet's toes began to itch, as she watched her mother look directly into her eyes.

"Willet, I have always tried to shield you from having to make such difficult and unfair decisions. However, you are not me and your journey is yours alone. I will respect and accept whatever you feel you need to do."

Willet sat down beside her mother and they hugged. "Thank you, Mama." Willet sighed slightly. "What now? I mean, that changes everything if it's in fact, true."

"I knew it was true, the moment she told me."

"What are you going to do, Mama?"

It was silent for several moments as they both just sat contemplating. Laraline, half serious and half joking, finally spoke. "Willet, can you ever forgive me for burning up your teddy bear?"

Willet burst out laughing at the absurdity of the question. She had tears in her eyes that she tried to wipe as she continued to laugh. She looked at her mother who was also crying and laughing at the same time. Willet cleared her throat.

"No comment, woman."

"I deserve that."

"What's this practice that Daddy said he gave up? Was he a doctor or lawyer or something?

"Well, your father would perform shammas, mostly charms and minor protections for his clients."

Willet's eyes widened at the prospect of what her mother was telling her. "You mean to tell me my daddy was a weaver?"

Laraline gave a hush sound, as she looked at the open door. The dark empty hallway seemed as foreboding as ever. "Not so loud!"

"Wow. Was he any good?"

Laraline was now whispering. "I'd rather not discuss this too much!"

"Could you at least tell me what shammas he invoked?"

"Most of what he did was medicinal, because of the fear of his family being exposed by any ambitious doctor. He kind of took that roll."

"He did shammas on me and Addie, didn't he?"

"Only when necessary, other than that, you two had bumps and scrapes, just like any other kid."

"Please tell me when."

"The only time I remember is when you were seven. You got extremely ill. We had to take you out of school because you were prematurely going through the change. Langston was finally able to evoke something that stopped it from progressing."

"What did he do?"

Laraline became defensive. "He saved you, that's what he did, young lady."

"Then why did you make him stop?"

"Look, I've answered you questions Willet. As to the specifics of mine and your father's relationship, that's none of your business."

Chapter 64:

Dinner Is Served

The evening wore on as Kestrel was subjected to dozens of pamphlets and leaflets filled with religious testimonies and diatribes. Most of them were about living horrid shameful lives in which Arke was not a meaningful part of modern faigal existence. Throughout the evening there were several food trays laid out before the timid librarian. The Peregrine sisters were notorious for their love of cooking. Both were involved in several bakeoffs. They saw these dinners as the prefect testing ground for their culinary creations.

Violet sat with her tightly wound casque and clean white linen gloves. Her voice rattling in a wavery voice singing traditional hymns. She almost looked like a thin vulture, slightly hunched over. Deloris turned in Kestrel's direction and grinned.

"Would you like more tea, dear?"

Kestrel looked at the half-filled cup she was holding. She was not really in the mood, seeing how they had filled it twice before. "No thank you, mum."

"Suit yourself."

"It has a very unusual flavor."

Violet glanced over at her sister. "We grow our own flowers."

Kestrel looked at the wall clock. "So, is anyone else coming tonight?"

"It's all about you tonight dear."

"This is so much food for just the three of us. Aren't you going to eat more, mum?"

"Well, a lot of this food is quite rich for our dietary needs. We prefer a plain protein diet."

Kestrel gave a sideways glance. "You really didn't have to go to so much trouble, I'm a light eater."

"Nonsense, eating should be more than a function. It should be savored."

Violet paused from her current song to interject. "You know, we need to have your sister for dinner as well."

Deloris nodded. "I agree, I haven't seen her nearly enough lately."

Kestrel took a sip of her tea and responded. "Well, she is quite busy."

"I image so, being a headmistress is a difficult profession."

Kestrel turned her attention to Deloris. "That's right, you were the headmistress before Rhea."

"Yes, in those days, you could just snatch up a child for misbehavior."

"Well, is that why you retired from teaching?"

"No dear, it was just time."

Kestrel chimed in to try and sound relevant to the conversation. "There is a time for everything, I suppose."

"Why didn't you follow in your sister's footsteps?"

"Well, my family wanted us both to become teachers, but I guess it wasn't my calling."

Deloris leaned over with her fan. "What exactly is your calling, sleeping with underage boys, pipping yourself and loose ways?"

Kestrel was so taken aback that she gasped. "Excuse me, what did you say?"

Deloris responded with the most polite grin.

The tension was broken by her sister Violet interjecting. "From what I heard, it's a lot harder to be in education these days. What are your thoughts on all this integration within the school?"

Kestrel's focus was still on the rude comment that Deloris tossed at her so candidly. "Sorry, I didn't catch that?"

"Now, from what I understand, sleeven children can mingle along with faigal children. Even Talomore is not immune to this infestation. That doesn't seem right."

Deloris clasped her hands together. "I agree sister. I find it shameful that they have to be huddled up together. Sleeven children, as a whole, are morally corrupt!

Kestrel, still bothered, countered. "Well, I don't know."

Deloris reached and pulled a piece of lint from Kestrel's hair. "Perhaps we should have invited your sister, I would love to pick her brain."

Violet sighed. "So, would I."

Both sisters giggled to themselves. Kestrel sat uncomfortably, still reflecting on the inappropriate dig she had received a few moments earlier. Deloris finally continued. "All it leads to is species mixing, and that is the most unconscionable evil."

Kestrel nodded. "Yes, it's important to keep the integrity of both species I suppose."

"Integrity! There is no integrity in sleeven blood. When it taints faigal blood, it becomes something completely alien and unholy! Look at the trouble over at the Adler estate. Poor Sirenna, I love her to death, but the shame she must feel having that loose niece of hers flaunting those lek half breeds about town."

"I understand you met one of them; the older one."

Kestrel, not realizing they were talking to her, shook herself alert. "Well, I drove her and her mother home."

"Yes, I was there. I was trying to give moral support to Patsy. Her daughter was lost in the Greywood as well."

Kestrel corrected them. "So were the other children."

"Yes, but sleeven breed like rabbits. It's not as serious if a few of them perish. I want to know about the elder lek child. The one called Willet. What was she like?"

Violet answered her sister. "She is dangerous, that one. You can see it in her eyes. See how she manipulated those poor Branson offspring into wickedness."

The tone of the conversation was exactly why Kestrel didn't want to come to dinner in the first place. Kestrel raised her voice slightly in response. "Those poor Branson children, as you call them, were monsters even before that girl arrived!"

Both women looked at one another as if they had a secret they didn't wish to tell. Kestrel felt very irritated. "Look, it's getting pretty late and I am obviously beyond saving, so let me just thank you for the evening and get back home."

Kestrel eyed Deloris intently before continuing. "For the record, I never did anything with Gavin Branson. In fact, he doesn't even like girls in that way!"

Kestrel rose to her feet and felt a strange dizziness. She staggered forward toward the door. The room was suddenly spinning as Kestrel bumped against the wall. Both sisters sat still, watching her quietly.

"What's happening to me?"

Neither sister responded, they just sat patiently.

"What's wrong with you, why don't you answer?'

Kestrel fell to her knees as both sisters slowly rose to their feet in unison. They slowly followed behind, allowing space for her to fumble about on the floor. Soon she was on her back gasping.

"I don't feel well."

Deloris finally cleared her throat. "I promise, it won't last long!"

Kestrel grabbed at the old woman's shoe but was unsuccessful at doing much of anything in her dizzy haze. Deloris responded by shoving her back down with the tip of her toe, as she antagonized the young woman.

"Dear, did you honestly think we invited you to try to save you?"

"What did you do to me?"

Violet, who had been quiet, politely answered. "It's just a simple poison in your tea that causes paralysis for the better part of half an hour."

Deloris added calmly. "This way you won't scream and make a lot of noise."

Kestrel's eyes widened at the implications. "You won't get away with it, whatever your planning!"

"Don't worry, we don't need much time."

Both women stood over Kestrel as she finally began to freeze up. Violet removed her gloves and immediately Kestrel saw that her right hand was missing the first two digits: her pointer finger and almost her entire middle finger. The ends were wrapped in blood stained gauze. Violet caught Kestrel's gaze. Wicked little children, all of them! Look at what they did to my hand. This is the result of mixing with other species!"

Deloris stroked her sister's shoulder. "You see, Gavin maimed my sister. It will take weeks to heal. If he hadn't been consorting with that lek, this wouldn't have happened."

Violet nodded. "Not at all."

"Look, I don't know anything about this. I wasn't with him; I told him I don't want to be around him anymore. I swear we never did anything, it was just for show!"

"As was this lovely dinner."

Kestrel noticed that both sisters' appearances had changed a bit. Their eyes were now large black glassy pools, deep and sunken in their strange heads. Their mouths were quite wide and filled with sharp yellow teeth. She gasped as she tried to drag herself away.

"What are you?"

Violet shook her head impatiently. "That's a rather long conversation dear."

Deloris placed her hands on her hips and glanced around the quaint little parlor. "Where did I put those plastic sheets for the floor. We need to get started?"

Violet pointed with her good hand. "They are under the sink, dear."

Kestrel's neck was tensing up and she struggled to speak. "If you didn't want to save me, why did you invite me to dinner?"

"Silly, we told you before, we wanted to have you... for dinner!"

Chapter 65:

Parting Words

"Where are you, Father?"

Willet stomped about the deck in search of the familiar specter that seemed to be haunting the Lenoir. She had called him when she first returned, and there was no response. Since she had read the letter, she had more questions than answers. She stood silently steering until the cusp of sunlight started to peek over the horizon.

"Come on, I know you're here. I can feel you." Willet strolled down the deck facing the starboard, when a gentle voice whispered in the wind behind her.

"So, you found Mr. Claude?"

She spun around just to see a fuzzy translucent apparition. It was less defined than before. The ghostly figure flickering, as if it was a weak transmission. His mannerisms were still familiar to Willet as she addressed the phantom.

"Is that you, Father?"

"It's getting harder to remain relevant in this consciousness. If you have questions, you had better hurry before I return to the ether."

"Ether? Where are you now?"

"Is that really what you needed to ask?"

His question was pointed and reminded Willet to refocus her emotions. "No, it isn't. Mama said you asked Mr. Claude to be cremated with you, yet this week I found him aboard the Lenoir. What kind of shamma were you performing?"

"Shamma, that's a word I haven't heard in quite a while."

"So, you were a weaver. Why didn't you tell me?"

"You know, you were always very fond of that bear, and with good reason. Mr. Claude is not just a teddy bear. He acts as a kind of elixir."

"An elixir, that's like medicine."

"Well, a long time ago you were very ill. Mr. Claude was originally created to heal you. Do you remember when I first gave him to you? You were lying in your bedroom."

Willet had a glimpse of her old bedroom with the ugly green lime door. She smiled as he continued to explain in a wavery voice.

"You were in so much pain; we had just pulled you out of school. So, you were sad. I remember how your eyes lit up when you first saw Mr. Claude. Within a few days, he started to heal you."

"Heal me from what?"

"A spiritual parasite was trying to invade you."

"What is that?"

"Well, the faigal call it a parasite, the einin call it a possession."

"Possession, you mean like exorcisms and priests?"

"That's a bit over simplifying things."

"Am I ok now?"

"Of course you are. Whatever was wrong, Mr. Claude healed your infection, and you got better."

"How is that possible, he is just a stuffed animal."

"Because as I said earlier, Mr. Claude is special. His innards are filled with a substance called father dust."

"That still doesn't answer my question. Why burn Mr. Claude now, after all these years?"

"The spirit had to be made flesh, so they couldn't reach you from the other side."

"The other side? I don't understand. Who Daddy?"

With a flicker of light, the mirage of the figure was gone. It was almost as if he never was.

"Daddy, where did you go? Daddy, please come back."

Soon, the only sound Willet could hear was the gentle waves crashing against the hull of the boat. A low flock of seagulls passed by from overhead. Willet eyed them suspiciously until they disappeared. It would morning soon, and hopefully she would return home tomorrow with the Lenoir.

Chapter 66:

It's Me Again

It was still dark when Adelie made her way down the long stairwell. Everyone was still asleep. Even Willet's door was closed. She didn't know exactly what to do, but things were starting to get serious. Her other hand had started to show signs of changing as well.

The decision to wear both gloves was now a necessity. As she made her way out into the courtyard, a feeling of frustration overcame her. She didn't have much time. She could feel her body changing even now. Soon, she wouldn't be able to hide it from anyone. Adelie walked around the grounds aimlessly, as she was lost in her head. There had to be some solution. She soon found herself on the chess field. The pawns were roughly her height. While other pieces such as the rook and knights were slightly taller.

The king and queen seemed to tower over her omnipotently. She tipped silently about the various pieces, as if she half expected one of them to come alive and snatch her. She was about to sit on the stone bench at the edge of the outer corner square when she heard her own name being called from afar.

"Adelie!"

A chill went up her spine as she looked out into the field. She peered into the dark nothingness. Beyond the large owl statues, someone was out there, waiting for her. Adelie squinted her eyes. As if turning on a light switch, Adelie suddenly could see a small silhouette standing about two yards from the nearest owl sculpture. Her long wild black hair hung over her face, obscuring her identity.

However, Adelie knew exactly who it was. She had been expecting her visitor to come calling for a while. It startled her to see it was happening now, but it was expected.

The shadowy figure inched closer. "You knew I would be here."

Adelie uneasily nodded. "I suspected."

Adelie moved closer toward the great owl's perimeter. The stranger stood on the other side of the owl, motionless, as if waiting.

Finally, Adelie impatiently asked. "What do you want Deryn?"

"I have a message from mother."

"What are you talking about?"

"Hey, is that the chessboard you're standing on, I do wish we could play just once."

"Well, I'm here."

"Could you move a bit closer Adelie?"

Adelie suddenly realized that for whatever reason, Deryn could not cross over into the yard. The owls that encircled the manor, acted like a sort of barrier. Upon this realization, Adelie became more embolden.

"No, thank you."

"Please come with me."

"You must be insane, you're dead."

"It's so much fun beyond the Waylands. It's even better than this world!"

Adelie shifted the conversation. "Don't you miss your mother or your sister Jae? They miss you so much."

"I have a new mother now and so do you, if you accept her."

"Why didn't she come herself?"

"You know she can't do that."

Adelie held up her gloved hand. "She did this to me, didn't she?"

"It's a great honor to be selected for her royal court. You should be honored dear sister."

"I already have a family."

"Don't be like that, just take my hand. As soon as we get back to Castle Aldan, you will feel brand new again."

"Castle Aldan, is that where you live now?"

"It's the most wonderful place. It's a large castle made of glass, with toys everywhere."

Adelie suspiciously frowned. "Is that really how you feel?"

Deryn suddenly fell on her knees and started to cry. "Please help me! She won't let me go, Adelie!"

Adelie moved closer until she was right beside a large owl. She stopped just short of crossing the barrier. "Well grab my hand. Let me help you!"

"Are you sure?"

"Please!"

"Why did you let them take me away?"

Adelie was overcome with guilt. "I'm so sorry, I didn't know. Everything was happening so fast!"

"Adelie, please help me, I'm too weak to get up."

"Is it safe out there?"

"Hurry, before they come!"

"Who?"

"We don't have much time!"

Adelie took a step back as if threatened suddenly. "Just a few moments ago you wanted to play chess."

There was uncomfortable silence, as Adelie suddenly realized what was happening. She folded her arms and glared at her guest. "You're not Deryn."

The stranger rose to her feet and began to wipe off her clothes. Within moments her appearance changed to its natural form. Adelie recognized the strange exotic woman from the forest. Verspa Lynn approached the barrier and stopped a few feet away from where Adelie stood.

"What gave me away?"

"What did you do with Deryn?"

"That would be telling."

"You're crazy!"

"I'm much more than that, Eve girl. I can be whatever mother you wish me to be for you. All you need to do is walk out beyond the perimeter, take my hand and let me lead you into the woods and down the golden path."

"What if I refuse?"

"Meow."

Adelie was enraged and terrified at the same time. "Leave me alone! I will never be your daughter."

"Either you become my daughter or you become my pet, the choice is yours. Don't take long to decide."

No sooner had she uttered these words than a light flicked on from the back patio. Adelie turned around, startled. The door to the guesthouse quickly swung open. Uncle Merle staggered out onto the patio.

"What's all that racket?"

Adelie turned back to face Verspa, but alas she was gone. It was almost as if she hadn't been there at all. Adelie looked around the yard and scanned the sky. There was no sign of her. However, she could almost make out a strange buzzing sound in the distance. The hairs on the back of her neck were standing up.

Uncle Merle wiped his face. "Who were you talking to out there, girlie?"

"I was talking to myself, sir."

Uncle Merle looked at her suspiciously for a moment. Then he growled at her. "It's too early to be up. You should be in bed child."

Adelie nodded. "Yes sir, right away."

Chapter 67:

Guilty By Exposure

It was almost 10 a.m. when Nashca returned to the Branson manor that morning. The trip had been stressful and she was tired. All she felt like doing was going to sleep. However, she had to warn her master of what she had learned from Arnold Leech.

If she had had foresight, she would never have returned to Meadowlark that day. When she made her way into the living room, they were all waiting for her. The ministry had sent at least a half dozen covey in full dress gear. They all wore their sheathed crissum on their sides. Lord Branson sat with Ephron, between two covey guards to the right, and to the left sat members of the Corbett clan. Montague, Melania, and Aquila wore cold somber expressions. Down the middle of the room were a dozen members from the ministry. Monsignor Claymore and a few medical doctors, were the only ones she actually knew. Most of the faces, Nashca didn't recognize.

A rather tall, lanky fellow with long stringy hair and wearing high heels approached Nashca. "We have all been awaiting your arrival, Mother Ortega."

Nascha was in shock as she greeted him. "Lord Snee, you're here?"

Nicodemus Alexander Snee was the most notorious barrister for the ministry, and he was here in the flesh. His

418

reputation was infamous among his faigal brethren as a ruthless prosecutor. Recently he hired out as a legal contractor.

"Yes, I was contacted by the ministry late yesterday to oversee the following proceeding."

"Proceeding? I'm the house weaver, why was I not informed? What exactly is going on?"

"This is just an informal hearing. However, if the accusations have merit there will be an arrest."

"Hearing about what?"

"The untimely death of Meena Branson Corbett, of course. We very well couldn't begin, until you arrived."

"Of course, I wasn't expecting things to move so fast. I have notes on the activities of Lady Branson. If you allow me to go to my room. I will prove that she was poisoned."

"That will not be necessary, if you have any evidence to help your case, that can be brought up later, if a formal hearing is necessary."

"My case? What are you talking about, Lord Snee?"

"You are the accused in this matter."

"Accused? That's madness. I reported this matter to the ministry myself."

Lord Branson protested. "Lord Snee, this is ridiculous. Charging a weaver under my employ, who was carefully vetted and screened under Namvula bylaws, is unnecessary."

"The ministry is its own separate entity, and we will take into account any recommendations by the mother sister assigned to Mother Ortega's case."

Nashca glanced at Aquila briefly. "If I'm being accused, I demand to face my accuser."

"That information is irrelevant at the moment."

"Irrelevant, what kind of political farce is this?"

"I may remind you; this is a public hearing."

"I wasn't even here when the murder took place."

"Are you sure, I would beg to differ."

"Excuse me?"

"Perhaps we should request that your cousin Shahaf come to speak on your behalf."

Nashca remained painfully silent as he continued. "I thought so. I wish to bring this document to the panel's awareness."

Snee extended a folder held in his claw-like fingers. "This is the full recorded autopsy of Meena Branson. It was obtained from Celandine Hospital, the very night she succumbed to her mortal coil."

"Though your claims that Meena was being poisoned, are valid. Her initial death was not caused by poison, as you claim. There were bruise marks on her neck that were discovered during her autopsy. Meena was choked to death. A very strong fellow had to have done this."

There was an uncomfortable hush across the room. Ephron seemed as if he was jarred awake. His eyes locked on the barrister intently. Snee gave him a knowing wink.

Nascha looked puzzled at the new revelation. "How is that even possible?"

Lord Branson stood up on Nascha's behalf. "If that is the case, why is she being accused. It makes no sense in accordance to this timeline."

"I am getting to that, Lord Branson."

Snee then turned his attention to Ephron. "How does that make you feel, good sir?"

"Excuse me?"

"I should think her husband would be enraged and hungry for answers, as to why his lovely wife was murdered while seeking medical treatment."

Monsignor Babbet looked confused. "Could you explain your last statement council."

"The victim was murdered at the hospital." There was deep hush amongst the crowd.

Snee leaned in toward Ephron. "Yet, you're strangely quiet. Don't you want to find out who murdered your wife?"

Ephron sat uncomfortably in his seat, as he kept his head down. He made sure he didn't make eye contact with anyone. "Of course, I'm just in utter shock!"

Avis countered. "Leave him alone, he has been through enough this year!"

"Of course he has; what a poor suffering lamb he is."

Lord Snee held up a thick bundle of papers in his hand and turned his attention to Lord Branson. "I have here private medical records of the accused. While researching, I came across a startling discovery. Your weaver that stands before you, has a rare medical condition, that has not been made public."

Nascha suddenly felt nervous and glanced at the crowd before she put her head down. "Please can we do this in private, Lord Barrister?"

"Are you admitting your guilt?"

"I didn't kill anyone, I swore to protect this family!"

"The Ortega clan along with the Namvula has guarded your little secret for years, haven't they?"

"Please don't!"

Snee let the revelation roll of his tongue with glee. "The accused is a diamorph!"

A great rumble overcame the crowd. Lord Branson had a look of disbelief on his face. He looked toward Nashca who was now in tears.

"You lied to me... all these years?"

Lord Snee walked over to Nashca, who was crying in her hands. He looked at Mother Ortega as if disgusted. "He lied to us all."

The truth was out, and now they would pick her apart. Snee stuck out his chest and proceeded to grill Nashca. "What is your cycle, diamorph?"

"Seven months."

"So, when does your next cycle start?"

"About five months."

"Do you have total recall of the events of last year?"

"No, I don't."

"So how do you know that Shahaf didn't murder Meena?"

"Shahaf isn't a murderer."

"How do you know? It's not like you were there, or were you in spirit?"

"It's not like that, I have glimpses and memories, but that's all."

"Like false memories?"

"No, I keep a daily journal, so I can keep track of what has happened when I'm the other."

Lord Snee addressed the crowd while speaking to Nashca. "Ahh, so what you're telling us is that your cousin Shahaf and you are in fact, the same being. Is this true?"

"Yes."

"You each share the same body, which as I understand, shifts it's form, involuntarily, from male to female every seven months."

Nashca paused, before answering. She could feel Avis's glare as she responded. "Yes."

"Do you share the same memories?"

"No, but sometimes memories overlap, it depends."

"So, we have two distinct personalities existing in one vessel at different times?"

Nashca nodded silently.

"So, it is possible that Shahaf could have done this to Meena and you wouldn't have any knowledge?"

"No, that is not possible!"

"How would you know? You weren't even here, as you so elegantly pointed out earlier, unless you are lying about your memories."

Nashca remained silent, as did the room. The uncomfortable quiet didn't last long as Lord Snee made his decree.

"Since certain facts have come to light, I request that the accused be taken back to New Essex, to be held there until such time as a formal investigation is conducted."

There was an uproar among the crowd. Nashca's peers were about to seal her fate, and poor Shahaf had no way of defending himself. He should have known better than to suggest such things about a royal.

Snee extended his hand in a courtly fashion as he finished his speech. "Alas, I humbly leave this decision in the hands of this committee. All those in disagreement of further proceedings say nay, all those who are in favor of a formal investigation say I."

"All those who say nay?"

The room was painfully silent. Nashca looked across the crowd of faces, some of them she knew personally. Even those faces were now hard and unforgiving. She was now a vagria, an outcast among her kind. Even if she was found innocent, her career as a weaver was officially over.

Snee continued. "All those who say I?"

There was a unanimous chorus from the entire room. She wouldn't let them see her upset, no matter what happened. Snee clasped his hands together.

"Until further notice, Aquila Branson has offered her services as acting house weaver until this matter is resolved."

Nashca glanced in the direction of Aquila who had a triumphant expression on her face. She had planned it all along. As their eyes met, there was recognition. Snee tried to appear civil as he politely addressed Nashca.

"Is there something you would like to say, before you are escorted off the property?"

Nashca response was quick and deliberate, as she stood and clapped loudly in front of the entire crowd. "Well played Aquila, I underestimated you!"

Aquila's expression shifted to one of confusion. Whatever are you talking about? Are you still in denial about your actions, freak?"

The ministries elite covey escorted Nashca past the silent crowd. Aquila made sure Nashca was close enough to see her face.

"We will surely miss your presence around here, dear!"

Nashca hissed at her. "You won't get away with this."

Aquila's response was quick. "Queen to bishop, checkmate."

As the covey escorted Nashca away, Ephron glanced over at the solicitor carefully packing up his belongings. "What now?"

Snee glanced at the young man with a weary, almost detached stare. "I have done my job. Now it's time for me to return to New Essex with the prisoner."

Ephron fumbled over his words. "So, so, so will she be prosecuted for what she did to my Meena?"

Snee snapped his case closed. "We need to have a formal investigation first."

"What's the difference?"

"At the moment, these are just allegations. We won't really know until mirror dansers are employed."

Ephron suddenly felt uneasy at the mention of the term. "Mirror dansers! Is that really necessary?"

"I was under the impression that you wanted your wife's murderer exposed. Great Arke man, the only way to discover what actually happened is to use mirror dansers. They have a way of uncovering every motive, every emotion and every secret. If this diamorph is indeed guilty, they will find out."

Ephron nervously protested. "They can make mistakes. I mean, they're not infallible!"

"True, however they are extremely efficient."

"What if they decide that she didn't do it?"

"Well, then she is innocent of that crime and will be released immediately. But have no fear, once the mirror dansers are released, they always find their prey!"

Ephron's mouth was now dry. "Great!"

Chapter 68:

A Spoon Full of Sugar

Evelyn and Laraline sat in the sunroom patiently waiting for Willet to rise. There was great anticipation around the estate regarding Willet's return. They drank their morning tea in silence. Evelyn coughed uncomfortably as she glanced at Laraline.

"So, have you thought about Branson's offer?"

"It's tempting. If I did, my daughters would want for nothing, and we wouldn't be physical prisoners. However, the responsibly of taking over that estate could turn into another kind of prison. As stressful as Sirenna can be, I could only image having to deal with Aquila! I'm still not sure."

Uncle Merle passed by looking more disheveled than usual. He was grumbling under his breath, deep in thought.

Evelyn noticed his grumbling. "Uncle Merle, what's wrong?"

"These children and their wild ways."

"What are you talking about, you old buzzard?"

"That child was up talking to someone half the night on the patio, the noise kept me up."

Laraline cleared her throat. "That's impossible, Willet hasn't moved from her room since about 11 p.m. last night."

"I'm talking about the other one."

"Oh my, you mean Adelie."

"That's the one."

"I completely forgot she was back home. Sorry Uncle Merle. I'll talk to her."

Mother Hazel popped her head into the sunroom entrance. "What's all this commotion?"

Laraline looked up at the old woman curiously. "Apparently, Addie was out on the patio talking to some friends late last night, according to Uncle Merle."

Mother Hazel responded. "That's queer."

Evelyn turned to Merle. "Who was she talking to Merle?"

"Excuse me!"

"You said she was talking to someone. As far as I know, she doesn't have many friends."

"I couldn't swear to anything, but to me it sounded like Ms. Weever's little girl, the one that went missing."

Laraline suddenly frowned. "That is queer."

Evelyn looked back at Laraline. "How is that so?"

"Something Addie asked me yesterday. I was combing her hair during her bath when she asked me if I thought Deryn would return?"

Evelyn shrugged her shoulders. "Sounds perfectly ok to me."

"That's not the weird part. She was asking me as if she were afraid that she would. She seemed genuinely scared."

Mother Hazel looked at Uncle Merle. "Did you see who she was talking to?"

"No, I can't say that I did. When I looked outside, she was alone. She said she was talking to herself, but I know I heard another voice."

Laraline, in an almost condescending tone asked him. "Are you sure you weren't into your drinks Uncle Merle?"

Uncle Merle curled his lips, as if trying to contain his irritation. "Today is Monday. I don't drink on Mondays."

Then he stormed out of the room. Laraline immediately felt ashamed after she realized how she had just treated him.

Evelyn turned to Laraline. "Well, that's true, he never drinks on Mondays."

Mother Hazel nodded in agreement. "That's right."

Laraline was defensive. "How do you know that?"

"Because Sirenna buys him just enough booze for a week. He always finishes the last bottle on Sunday evening. Sirenna won't buy him more until this afternoon."

"So, Auntie Sirenna is his enabler!"

Evelyn shrugged. "It's the only way she can get him to take his medicine."

Laraline nodded. "So, Sirenna hides it in his drink, so he won't know?"

Evelyn gave Laraline a harsh look. "I would stop with the judgments while your ahead, dear."

Laraline humbly closed her mouth and rose to her feet. "Do you think I hurt his feelings?"

Mother Hazel concurred. "Probably, he seemed kind of pissed off to me."

"Perhaps I should apologize to him."

Evelyn nodded. "That would probably be a good idea, especially since the docking license is in his name!"

As Laraline rose from her seat to find Uncle Merle, Mother Hazel addressed her sincerely. "If you wish, I can check on Adelie on my way back to Willet's room."

"Could you please?"

"Let me just collect a few ointments and tonics from my room first."

"Tonics, is something wrong?"

"The best weaver is a prepared weaver."

Laraline found Uncle Merle sitting in his caddy, the music was on and the engine was running. His eyes were closed; however, she was sure that he wasn't asleep. She stood beside the driver's window waiting for him to notice her presence. Either he was lost in thought or he was ignoring her.

Finally, she rapped on the window impatiently. His eyes remained closed as he responded. "I heard you, what do you want?"

"I owe you an apology Uncle Merle. That was rude of me before. You were simply telling me something important about my child and it made me feel threatened."

His eyes opened, but he remained silent.

"I really don't know how to raise two children by myself, much less two girls. Thank you for telling me about Adelie."

He was silent, and Laraline stood up. "Well, I'll leave you alone."

Merle finally spoke. "I know Sirenna puts medicine in my drink. She needs to feel like she is making a difference, even though I'm dying."

"You're not dying, sir."

"Don't tell me my business. You are looking at a walking corpse. I can feel the life draining a little more every day."

"Yes sir."

"Please don't tell Sirenna I know."

Laraline nodded in agreement. "It will be our little secret."

She hopped up from the car and made her way to the entrance of the open garage. She paused and glanced back at him. "Well, at least you're an elegant corpse."

Merle pulled at the collar of his red and gold smoking jacket. "Well, if you got to go, go in style, I always say."

Chapter 69:

Confessions

Mother Hazel stood directly over Adelie as she lay still in her bed. Sirenna stood by the door, making sure their business with Adelie was discreet. The old woman carefully scanned the young girl suspiciously. At one point she even sniffed the air around the bed. Mother Hazel then glanced at Sirenna.

Sirenna nodded and quietly shut and locked the door. She then joined Mother Hazel. She leaned over the foot of the bed and stared directly at Adelie. "Sit up, we know you're wide awake."

Adelie huffed. "How?"

"We are faigal."

Adelie sat up, making sure the covers were tightly wrapped over her feet. She had wisely slipped her gloves on earlier. She watched the old woman place a large knit bag on the foot of her bed. She then rummaged through the bag until she pulled out a small pin light.

"What are you doing?"

Sirenna yawned. "She is treating you."

"Treating me for what?"

Mother Hazel finally spoke. "For whatever shamma has been placed on you. It must be a strong one to make you hide your hands."

"How did you know?"

"I can smell the infection!"

"Does it stink?"

"Well, apart from the usual sleeven stink, that we won't go into, there is a sweet saccharine odor about your body, like burnt honey."

Adelie looked dumbfounded, as if she was just told the world was really flat.

"Ok, please remove your gloves, and let's have a look."

Adelie was nervous. She looked about the empty room and at the door. Then she looked back at Mother Hazel, speechless. Mother Hazel responded to her silence. "The door is locked and I won't say a word."

"Please don't tell Mama."

Sirenna sighed from the edge of the bed. "We don't have all day."

Adelie thought hard, she had to do something. The situation was beyond what she could handle. She took a deep breath and removed both gloves. It had been a couple days since she had allowed herself to look at them in daylight, much less anyone else.

Mother Hazel's reaction was pointed. "Oh my, this is a nasty one."

"Is it bad?"

"That depends, do you want to change into a cat, child?"

Adelie shook her head defiantly. "No way!"

"Then it's pretty bad."

"How do your feet look?"

Adelie cleared her throat. "Their pretty bad."

She flung off the covers, exposing her paw like feet. Mother Hazel moved to the bottom of the bed and lightly tapped the penlight on each toe. Adelie flinched.

Sirenna scoffed at the young girl. "Did you really think you could hide something like this? Sooner or later, we would have noticed the changes."

"I didn't really think, I just..."

Mother Hazel finished her sentence. "You just instinctually wanted to hide your condition, as if you were a cat."

Adelie looked down. "Exactly."

Mother Hazel glanced grimly at Sirenna, before she continued her interrogation. "Is there any pain, when you walk?"

"No, it just feels weird when I wear shoes."

"That's good, at least we know the shamma was constructed pretty sound."

Adelie crinkled her face at the odd term. "Shamma, is that the same thing as a spell?"

Mother Hazel nodded. "Spells of this sort can be spotty, if the weaver isn't a proficient alchemist."

"I have no idea what you are saying?"

"Your definitely not Willet."

"Thank god!"

Sirena quipped. "Don't thank your maker just yet!"

Mother Hazel gave Sirenna a stern look. "Please, I'm trying to concentrate."

Mother Hazel moved back to the top of the bed and began to flash the light in Adelie's eyes and check her ears and mouth. "What are you doing?"

"Morphing shammas start infecting the extremities first, fingers, toes, ears, feet, and sometimes teeth. We need to see how quickly it is progressing. I notice that both your pupils are starting to dilate. That could be a sign that it's actively attacking your nervous system."

"That's bad, huh?"

"Well, it's not good."

"Will there be any permanent damage?"

"That depends when the shamma was cast."

"Can you cure me?"

"Hard to say at this point, without more information!"

"Like what?"

"Do you have any knowledge of who may have done this?"

"Yes!"

"Are you positive, usually this is one of the main issues with trying to cure someone."

"Of course, I remember when she touched my hand!"

Sirenna hopped up, almost confronting her. "You said she, was it perhaps Aquila Branson?"

"No, it definitely wasn't."

"Are you sure it wasn't her in disguise? Rumor has it, that Lady Branson is supposed to be a skilled changeling."

"Changeling?"

"One who can take on the form of anyone or anything living."

Adelie eyes widened as if paranoid. "Anyone?"

"But of course."

"Sirenna, you're scaring the child. Besides, this shamma affecting Adelie is beyond even Aquila's capabilities."

Sirenna stepped back impatiently as the old woman continued. "One of the issues in trying to undo a shamma, is discovering the origin of first contact. Do you remember the exact moment this happened Adelie?"

"First contact? You make it sound like a virus!"

"Well, that's what a shamma is really. In order for it to work, the weaver must introduce something alien into another's mind or body."

"I never thought of it like that."

"Some shammas are milder than others and they usually run their course, while others can be life threatening. In fact, that is how the disease, diastasis, was created. It started as a morphing shamma to turn one's enemies into fungus or mushrooms, or some such nonsense."

"Is that something like diabetes?"

"Well, it's a faigal sickness. I guess cancer would be the closest sleeven counterpart."

"Wow, I always thought that magic and spells were so..."

"So, what?"

"I don't know, different."

Sirenna scoffed. "Sleeven romanticism about fairy god mothers and such foolishness is not rooted in reality."

Mother Hazel huffed. "Sirenna, please stop interrupting."

"Sorry, mum."

Mother Hazel cleared her throat. "You said earlier that you were touched. I need all the details: when, where and who?"

Adelie put her head back, as if she were trying to pick answers off the ceiling. "Wow, you know there are times when everything gets foggy."

"It's because you're trying to retain your natural memories. The cat thoughts are starting to infest your mind. Just take your time. The more stressed you are, the more your mind will speed up the infection. The most important thing in undoing any shamma, is keeping the victim calm."

Mother Hazel glanced to Sirenna. "Do you understand?"

Sirenna stood silent with her arms crossed as if she had just been scolded.

"I need you to tell me exactly what happened on the day you were affected."

Adelie looked at Mother Hazel intently. Then she sighed and continued the story. "That was the day I went with Raven and her friends into the Greywood. Raven took us there to hunt cats, but we didn't know."

"How were you to hunt these cats?"

"She had this bow and arrow."

Sirenna snickered. "It's called a crossbow. So, I suppose you were to be initiated into her little click by shooting one of the watchers."

"Well, I didn't do it, in fact, I stopped her from shooting one."

Mother Hazel rolled her eyes at Sirenna before looking to Adelie. "The events of how things played out are immaterial at this point. Please continue. You said you stopped her."

"Well, she got mad and tried to shoot me, but her brother shielded me."

Sirenna mumbled to herself. "That must be how that Branson boy got shot."

Adelie was visibly upset, as she continued. Both women listened intently, as she told of the strange woman from the weeds and how Iris was taken. It was at this point where her recollection of the events became a bit more sparse.

"I saw a woman in the woods. She reached out and touched me. When she touched me, it felt like I was being stung by a wasp or something."

"Did this woman have a name?"

"You know, I can't remember."

"Could you have been talking to her this morning on the patio."

"Perhaps, I can't recall."

Sirenna had a puzzled stare. "You can't recall who you talked to a few hours ago?"

Mother Hazel interjected. "Never mind that. This woman from the woods, do you remember what she looked like?"

"Sure... well, I can almost see her face, but its blurry. I know there was something familiar about her. You know, I don't remember."

"This is a very sophisticated shamma. It appears to have been constructed with emotional memory blocks."

"What does that mean?"

"You have been enchanted."

"Can you heal me?"

Mother Hazel looked to Sirenna. "Could you find the grey flask out of my bag. It's somewhere near the side. It's by those small bags of Licweed."

"You collect Licweed?"

"What do you know of Licweed, child?"

"We walked through fields of that stuff when we were with Raven."

Both women looked at one another in amazement. Mother Hazel commented. "Well, we may have to take a field trip into the Greywood soon Sirenna. That stuff isn't cheap domestically!"

Sirenna had dug around inside the bag and removed a rather dull looking copper bottle. It had a corked top with strange symbols on the side. "Is this it?"

The old woman's eyes brightened up, as if some forgotten treasure was found. As soon as she received it, Mother Hazel gave it a couple of quick shakes.

"Well, we can try this."

"What is it?"

"It's an elixir, it can act as an antibiotic, however it is only a local."

Adelie didn't really understand but was hesitant to ask another question. "Ok"

"That means it's like pain medicine, it will remove the symptoms and maybe break down the shamma's resistance, provided it isn't too strong. Drink this every four hours over the course of the next 24 hours and your hands and feet should appear normal in the morning."

"Really!"

"I warn you. You must keep an eye out for the next few weeks. If any of these symptoms start to return, you must let me know immediately."

"It could come back?"

"I told you; it depends on how strong this shamma is we're dealing with."

Chapter 70:

Home

The Lenoir passed the small series of island coves around 2 o'clock. Willet looked curiously at the small lumps of land in the distance. She remembered seeing them several months earlier. She was on the beach then. In fact, it was the first beach she had seen since leaving Florida. Willet would be passing them on the starboard side soon.

She was about half a mile from the closest one. Suddenly, the thought entered her mind. *I wonder if these are the same islands that Mama was talking about us visiting.* She would be within view of the Crecheland Docks soon. She knew she was getting close. She recognized the smell. Meadowlark had a very distinct scent.

Willet had butterflies in her stomach. The prospect of what she had truly accomplished finally struck her. The gentle wind caressed her face as she stuck out her chest proudly. The islands became distant dots again as she neared the shoreline. She saw a depressed looking pier half a mile away. That was her destination.

She patiently waited until the boat started to drift beside the pier. She began to tie up the line. The Lenoir came to a stop with a glorious thump against the side of the dock. She had done the impossible.

Willet looked at the clouds, closed her eyes, and took a deep breath. *Just let me enjoy this moment, this one moment* of success. Mother Hazel was sitting beside the bed when Willet finally opened her eyes and looked around. She was back in her room and somehow it felt glorious yet alien at the same time.

Willet sat still, taking in the real world for a change. The room seemed unusually tiny and dull. She could feel the actual silk bedding on her skin. It's cool sheets were slightly damp from several sweaty nights. The tingling sensation from her toes relaxed her. The familiar aroma of sage filled the stuffy air.

Laraline rushed beside the bed in anticipation. Willet acknowledged them both with a faint smile. Laraline touched her daughter's head. "Are you ok?"

"I think so."

"So... where are you now?"

Willet calmly held back a smile as she proudly answered. "It is done!"

"The Lenoir is here?"

"It's safely docked at lot number 4."

"Which docks?"

"The southernmost ones."

"That's means it's parked in Crecheland."

Mother Hazel looked at Laraline. "She actually did it, by herself. That is unbelievable. I have never known of anyone to drift so long, so far. How are you feeling?"

"I feel a little numb and a bit tired."

"The effects should wear off in a few hours."

Laraline hugged Willet tightly and kissed her forehead. "I'm so proud of you. I think this calls for a breakfast celebration. What do want to eat?"

"I'm fine."

"Aren't you hungry?"

"Not so much."

"Nonsense, you have hardly eaten in several days. I will have Ms. Brooks fix something for you immediately."

"Ms. Brooks?"

"Mrs. Weever took a leave of absence."

"Oh yeah, her daughter disappeared. Any news?"

"Not so far, they are still listing her as missing, as well as Iris Van Warren."

Evelyn popped her head in the doorway cryptically. "Well, you can add Kestrel Faulkner to that growing list!"

Laraline turned her head to Evelyn with a horrified expression. "What happened?"

"Apparently, she never showed up to open the library this morning. Her sister went to her house. Her car was there, but there was no sign she was ever home."

Mother Hazel looked at her with a curious expression. "It's happening again!"

Evelyn addressed her. "What's happening?"

"Roach infestation."

"What are you talking about?"

"Nothing."

Willet glanced at the old woman. She knew exactly what the old woman meant. Before she had time to contemplate the matter. Laraline caressed her daughter's hair.

"How about some oatmeal and fruit?"

"I guess so. Thank you, Mama."

"I love you, Willet."

"Aren't you going to check the dock, Mama?"

Laraline smiled. "I trust your word, dear."

Willet cocked her head. "You do?"

"You look exhausted, we need to let you rest. Perhaps we can both go down to the dock after you rest."

Evelyn and Laraline both abruptly strolled out of the bedroom. Laraline called Mother Hazel, who was still standing at the foot of Willet's bed.

"Out of her room and let her sleep!"

"I need to at least check her quickly, to make sure there is no residual damage."

Laraline frowned as she left the room. "Please make it quick."

Mother Hazel removed her pin light from her bag. She then extended an arm toward Willet's face. "Is your mother always like this?"

"Worse."

"Mercy!"

The old woman shined a pin light in Willet's eyes. She didn't speak, but her coarse breathing was just as loud. Willet folded her arms and looked up.

"Ok, what's on your mind?"

"Nothing, I'm just old."

"Right."

"I do want to mention that we had a vertriste and I have honored my part of the agreement."

"So that's why you stayed behind? Look, I made a promise to learn the art of weaving, and I will honor that as your new sire. You have my word mother."

The old woman paused, as if in shock. "Why the change of heart?"

"I don't know, maybe I want to have a little more control so I can take care of myself wherever I travel."

"What happened out there?"

Willet took a deep breath. "What I tell you, must never leave this room."

"That's why I'm here."

"The first time I returned during my drift, when I almost drowned, I lost control because I was attacked."

"Attacked."

"A strange woman with horns from under the surface of the water tried to drown me."

"What did she do?"

"It's hard to explain. Something about her eyes convinced me to leap off the Lenoir. I think she wanted me to drown."

"Sounds like you were under the spell of an Avatar. I suppose that's why you were hacking up sea water when you came back to full consciousness."

"Yes, I didn't want to tell anyone because I was afraid you would make me stop the drift."

"You are extremely foolhardy. Well, tell me more about this water nymph."

"She said I was trespassing, and she introduced herself as Pandora Prime."

"Pandora Prime?"

"Who is she?"

Mother Hazel furrowed her brow. "There is but one true Prime and that is our beloved Mother Prime, who is the creator of all things. I suspect this Pandora is one of the many lost entities who have disconnected from her eons ago."

Willets eyes were tired, but she was intrigued as she leaned closer. "You're speaking of dark primes. Is she one of them?"

"Not one of consequence. Regardless, do not utter that name out loud ever again, or you may invite her into your conscious thoughts."

"Will she come after me?"

"She and her brethren cannot exist in this realm of ours. This is your saving grace."

"And I thought it would be safe to drift across waters I've known."

"You must realize that when you allow yourself to enter that state, you are actually passing through another type of realm, one that is not dictated by the laws of the physical world."

"Gee, is it safe for me to sleep?"

"You have completed your task, do you have a desire to further explore the previous trek you have already taken?"

"Not really."

"Then you should sleep well. If it makes you feel safer, I could leave the sage burning in here tonight."

Willet nodded emphatically. "Yes please."

Mother Hazel nodded. "Well, get some rest, sister mother."

"What did you just call me?"

"In the Namvula, all students are referred to as sister mothers, during formative training."

"Yes, Mother Hazel."

Mother Hazel hobbled to the door and glanced back just in time to notice that Willet was already lying on her side. Her eyes were closed and she was breathing steady. She was exhausted. Over the course of the last several days of trance states, this was probably the first actual real sleep she had experienced. With her cane, the old woman pulled the door shut behind her.

Chapter 71:

The Lenoir

Aquila stood on the landing outside of the broken-down pier. She personally came to touch base with Arlis Greenbaum. Being the owner of Kuzz, he had grown weary of Ephron Branson and his drunken antics at his bar. The very presence of the young man had caused a steady decline in patronage. This caused loose talk about bringing a lawsuit upon the powerful house.

Seeing as things had grown precarious around the Branson Estate, the possibility of any further legal entanglements needed to be eased for the moment. Lady Branson was sent down to the dock to meet Arlis personally. She approached him, dangling a blank check between her fingertips.

Arlis may not have been cultured but he wasn't ignorant. His first response was candid. "What is this, a bribe?"

Her demur attitude was that of a naïve innocent. "Of course not, we understand there have been certain difficulties, and we thought you could decide what amount would be suitable."

"Ephron is a belligerent drunk who has scared off most of my regulars."

"As I was saying, we hope you can write in whatever amount you think will fix this."

"You have some nerve. You Bransons and Adlers think you can just buy off anyone, if the price is right."

"Is the price, right?"

Arlis rolled his eyes and turned away.

"Touchy."

Aquila didn't really care if he accepted the offer. After all, the more trouble it caused for Avis the better. In fact, there was a part of her that kind of relished the idea of relaying Greenbaum's sentiments. She couldn't wait to see the expression on her brother's face. It would be a nice appetizer to give him, before she revealed her master plan in full.

She was about to head back down the walkway, when she spied the unusual boat docked at the pier. As long as she had been in Meadowlark, she had never known for Greenbaum to own a boat of this sort.

Covering basic ship upkeep and docking insurance was too costly for a small enterprise such as Kuzz. It was easier to hire out to more experienced fisherman for his catered deliveries. Aquila surmised he must have had a change of heart after he lost the services his last semi-permanent fisherman.

"So, you have finally purchased a boat?"

Arlis stopped in his tracks. "What are you talking about woman?"

"I was admiring your new boat."

"Save your empty praises, that's not my boat."

"Well, it's parked at your broken-down dock."

"It's a public dock, unlike the ones in Celandine Springs."

"We have to make a living, same as you Greenbaum."

"Make a living; that's what you call it? Others would call it price gauging."

"Save me the bleeding-heart violins, if it's not your vessel, why is it here?"

"It belongs to my new bartender, Laraline Swift."

Aquila's eyes bulged in shock. "That's her vessel?"

Arlis stuffed his hands into his pockets. "I have to say, The Lenoir looks almost the same, as when her husband was at the helm."

Aquila was enraged. "If this is the Lenoir, how did it get here?"

"Well, I assume it was sailed here. That's what one does with boats."

"I meant, by whom?"

Arlis was grinning. "What do I care. All I know is the fishing season is here, and we already have five deliveries starting next week."

Aquila's eyes were burning with disgust. As far as she could tell, no one left town with enough time to bring it back. Yet someone had stolen the boat from right underneath Richter and her night visitors' noses. She folded her hands together as Arlis walked off. She stood stewing about how the Adlers had accomplished such an incredible feat.

She finally hissed under her breath. "There are dark shammas at work here."

Epilogue

Silas made his way through the thick underbrush that grew wildly about the stream. The stream snaked down the middle of the forest, creating a cool rush of wind on his face. However, the wind carried the scent of death into his nostrils. As he crept along the bank, he saw the first body. It was a rather large lump of a man, lying face down in the pool of running water.

He seemed to be dressed in some sort of armor at first glance. Lying against him lay what appeared to be a very long broadsword gently swaying against the waves. Silas felt an instant twinge in his stomach as he quickly hurried up on the bank, away from the corpse.

He had travelled another twenty yards before he saw the second body. This one was a bit different from the first. It was lying curled up on its right side, dressed in similar armor and a helmet. Instead of half-submerged in the stream, it lay on the dry bank some 8 yards away from the water.

From its back stretched out two of the most unusual things. Wings, the body had wings, large full feathered wings. It definitely wasn't human, even though at first glance it appeared to be. The body was also much smaller than the one downstream. In fact, it appeared to be a woman.

Silas silently moved closer to get a better look. That was when he noticed the small hand axe imbedded in the side of her helmet. Dried blood and flies matted her face. Regardless of this, she was still unusually striking. There was something quite exotic about her.

He moved closer until he was about three feet from her. Her eyes opened wide. Silas froze as they stared at one another. It was as if they were in some strange standoff. The young man then knelt down very slowly and spoke.

"Can I help you in any way? Are you in pain?"

She just blinked, as if listening intently. Silas moved closer still, as she began to slowly mouth words. "Aqua."

"You want water?"

She repeated the phrase again. "Aqua!"

Silas quickly tore back down to the edge of the water. He pulled a handkerchief from his pocket and quickly dipped the cloth below the surface of the water. As he scrambled back up the bank, the young female was somewhat alert. Her wings were now gone and her legs extended out. The young man knelt down beside her and held the dripping cloth over her head. Instinctively she opened her mouth wide.

Silas squeezed the cloth tightly as water poured heavily down her throat. It reminded him of one of those images of a mother sparrow feeding her young. After a few gulps she gave a violent gargle and she slowly sat up. The axe didn't flinch as it remained stuck into her helmet. Silas couldn't keep his eyes from the surreal projectile.

"Do you want more water?"

"No, enough."

It was the first time he actually heard her voice in full. Silas sat down beside her and moved his hand close to her face with the wet cloth.

She instinctively snatched his wrist. "What are you doing sleeven?"

"Here, you have blood in our face. I was just trying to help."

Her eyes were cold and unflinching as she suspiciously stared into his eyes. Finally, she let go of his arm, as if she decided that she needed to save her strength.

He slowly wiped the blood from the side of her face. He was careful not to rub too tenderly as she was definitely a warrior. If she thought his intentions were improper she would cut him down. Even in her current condition, she was like a wolf in a trap.

"Is that your friend lying in the creek downstream over their?"

"Aye, Orsclick was a loyal warrior."

"What happened to your wings?"

She glared at him. "You ask a lot of questions."

"Sorry!"

"Why are you doing this?"

"Excuse me?"

"You are sleeven, what is your angle?"

"Sleeven?"

"We are different and yet you give me aqua."

"You are hurt!"

"I need no pity!"

"I just wanted to help, this forest is no place to die alone."

"You don't want anything from me?"

"If you can just tell me your name, so I know what to call you."

"That is all you require?"

"I have low expectations."

"Lady Oriole Patricia Adler, what is your name, boy?"

"My name is Silas Swift my lady."

"Swift, I like the sound of that. Death comes swift as the night."

"Something like that."

"Well, Mr. Swift, if you wish to assist me, I want to get back home. It's not too much further in that direction."

"A thousand pardons, if I insulted your forest, my lady. I didn't know you lived here. I was sure you lived in the Adler mansion on the hill outside."

"A lifetime ago, I once inhabited that world. However, that is not my home. There is a small cottage beyond the clearing. If you can, just help me there. I will make it worth your while."

"Do you need any help standing up?"

Oriole extended her arm out and Silas quickly clasped her gloved hand. He pulled hard as she slowly and carefully rose to her feet. The axe shifted slightly and a stream of blood ran down the side of her face. She stumbled as if the movement had suddenly made her dizzy.

"Perhaps we need to get a doctor. That wound on your head looks serious."

"It's much too late for that now. I just want to die in peace."

The words struck the young boy somewhat dismal. However, he obliged the wounded woman. He pulled her arm around his shoulder, so she could lean most of her weight on him. she was definitely weak and trembling. Her body was in a kind of shock from her wound as they methodically made their way across the forest terrain in silence.

As many times as he had ventured into the woods, he had never once laid his eyes on a cabin that Oriole had described. He didn't want to question her sanity as she seemed so fragile. However, in a moment when that very cabin seemed to materialize out of thin air, it was as if it were waiting for them to grow near. Silas's eyes widened.

"I had no idea such a place existed here!"

They were about a hundred yards from the dwelling when Oriole fell to her knees.

"I'm so tired and I can't feel my legs."

"Look, were almost there!"

Silas quickly reached down and wrapped his arms around her waist. He began to drag her backwards toward the tiny shack. At one point, he looked over his shoulder to see the door of the cabin slowly swing open. She was expected.

He glanced at his dying companion. "Do you have family inside?"

Oriole was silent.

"Oriole, wake up please! Stay awake, were almost there!"

As soon as they got to the entrance, he placed her against the edge of the door frame. He stuck his head inside and looked around uncomfortably. The room was empty save for a small wood-burning stove and rocking chair in the corner and a small straw cot in the other corner.

Silas immediately began to pat her face. She jerked slowly as she frowned. "I'm so tired, I just want to sleep till we get there."

"Were here, at your cabin. What next?"

She groggily responded. "Thank you, Silas. I'm good."

"No one is home. It's empty. I was sure the door opened up just for you."

Oriole's eyes were at half-mast. "Don't worry."

"I can't leave you alone."

"If you can, just help me onto the bed, I can rest until they come for me."

"Who?"

"Please, just help me inside."

Silas did as he was told and carefully dragged her into the threshold, so sooner had he stepped onto the wood floor when a stream of hot humid air flowed across his face. The force of the wind abruptly shut the door behind him. It was almost like being directly breathed on.

"What was that?"

As he placed Oriole on the cot, her eyes opened wide as she responded. "You are the first sleeven to ever step inside. It's not familiar with your taste."

"My taste? I don't understand."

The incident had slightly freaked him out, especially having a door open and shut by itself.

"Well, I guess I'd better get going."

"Wait, I have something for you. Around my neck I have a necklace." She fumbled with her fingers about her collar until she pulled a strange seed looking capsule from the chain necklace.

"I can't take that!"

"We had a vertriste, you get me here and I make it worth your while."

Silas reached down and took the odd-looking seed from her cold fingertips. He held it in the light to get a better look. It was round, smooth and slightly larger than a walnut.

"What is this?"

"It's called father dust."

"What's it for?"

"It contains the most magical memories inside."

"If that is the case, perhaps you need to keep it, miss."

"Where I'm going, it will have more use here on this side."

"I don't understand."

"Because of your kindness, perhaps I can leave some little part for myself for you to let me bless you and your future generations. A tiny little echo, so I won't be forgotten."

"Don't worry, you won't be forgotten."

Silas started to rise, just as Oriole grabbed his hand. "Thank you."

Silas almost immediately knelt down beside her and squeezed her hand back. For the first time she had faint smile. In that brief moment, he realized just how beautiful she actually was. All he could do was smile back. They sat there in silence, until Silas became curious.

"Who are we waiting for?"

"Excuse me?"

"Who is coming to get you?"

Oriole's expression changed. There was a coldness behind her eyes as she answered. "Friends, very old friends."

"Could I meet your friends?"

She chuckled to herself, before letting out a series of coughs. When she finally stopped, she seemed even more tired. Her reply cut off any further questions.

"Do you think you can get me some aqua, my mouth is pretty dry?"

"Are you going to be ok while I'm gone?"

"Just go."

"I'll be right back."

Silas rose to his feet. Almost immediately, the cabin door creaked open. He spun around to see the world outside, inviting him back.

Without looking back, he hurried outside into the fresh air. As he ran beyond the threshold, the world outside was bright and lush green. He could hear the faint sound of the stream in the distance. He quickly darted in the direction of the water. It made no sense, but for a moment it was as if he had left the woods and went somewhere else completely.

The air outside felt gentle and crisp. Silas took a deep breath and exhaled. He looked back at the cabin to make sure Oriole was still awake. However, much to his surprise, the cabin and the place it once stood were no more. In its place stood a rather large clump of trees. He stumbled back in horror as he looked all around in search of the cabin. *Did I dream the entire afternoon. Perhaps Oriole wasn't even real.* Silas suddenly opened his palm. He still had the strange looking seed.

With his fingers, he touched the smooth surface. Almost instantly, it began to glow. A slight tingling overcame him as he silently headed west out of the Greywood forest. Within a few hours, he hoped he would reach the ocean.

The end.